Pattern Recognition

Pattern Recognition

William Gibson

This large print edition published in 2003 by
RB Large Print
A division of
Recorded Books
A Haights Cross Communications Company
270 Skipjack Road
Prince Frederick, MD 20678

First published in hardcover by
G.P. Putnam's Sons, 2003

Publisher's Cataloging In Publication Data
(Prepared by Donohue Group, Inc.)

Gibson, William, 1948-
  Pattern recognition / William Gibson, 1948-

    p. ; cm.

    ISBN: 1-402-55690-X

1. Women private investigators—England—London—Fiction. 2.
Business intelligence—Fiction. 3. Large type books. 4. London
(England)—Fiction. 5. Mystery fiction. I. Title

PS3557.I2264 P38 2003
813/.54

Typeset by Palimpsest Book Production Limited,
Polmont, Stirlingshire, Scotland
Printed in the United States of America
By Bang Printing
3323 Oak Street
Brainerd, Minnesota 56401

To Jack

CHAPTER 1

THE WEBSITE OF DREADFUL NIGHT

F ive hours' New York jet lag and Cayce Pollard wakes in Camden Town to the dire and ever-circling wolves of disrupted circadian rhythm.

It is that flat and spectral non-hour, awash in limbic tides, brainstem stirring fitfully, flashing inappropriate reptilian demands for sex, food, sedation, all of the above, and none really an option now.

Not even food, as Damien's new kitchen is as devoid of edible content as its designers' display windows in Camden High Street. Very handsome, the upper cabinets faced in canary-yellow laminate, the lower with lacquered, unstained apple-ply. Very clean and almost entirely empty, save for a carton containing two dry pucks of Weetabix and some loose packets of herbal tea. Nothing at all in the German fridge, so new that its interior smells only of cold and long-chain monomers.

She knows, now, absolutely, hearing the white

noise that is London, that Damien's theory of jet lag is correct: that her mortal soul is leagues behind her, being reeled in on some ghostly umbilical down the vanished wake of the plane that brought her here, hundreds of thousands of feet above the Atlantic. Souls can't move that quickly, and are left behind, and must be awaited, upon arrival, like lost luggage.

She wonders if this gets gradually worse with age: the nameless hour deeper, more null, its affect at once stranger and less interesting?

Numb here in the semi-dark, in Damien's bedroom, beneath a silvery thing the color of oven mitts, probably never intended by its makers to actually be slept under. She'd been too tired to find a blanket. The sheets between her skin and the weight of this industrial coverlet are silky, some luxurious thread count, and they smell faintly of, she guesses, Damien. Not badly, though. Actually it's not unpleasant; any physical linkage to a fellow mammal seems a plus at this point.

Damien is a friend.

Their boy-girl Lego doesn't click, he would say.

Damien is thirty, Cayce two years older, but there is some carefully insulated module of immaturity in him, some shy and stubborn thing that frightened the money people. Both have been very good at what they've done, neither seeming to have the least idea of why.

Google Damien and you will find a director of music videos and commercials. Google Cayce and

2

you will find "coolhunter," and if you look closely you may see it suggested that she is a "sensitive" of some kind, a dowser in the world of global marketing.

Though the truth, Damien would say, is closer to allergy, a morbid and sometimes violent reactivity to the semiotics of the marketplace.

Damien's in Russia now, avoiding renovation and claiming to be shooting a documentary. Whatever faintly lived-in feel the place now has, Cayce knows, is the work of a production assistant.

She rolls over, abandoning this pointless parody of sleep. Gropes for her clothes. A small boy's black Fruit Of The Loom T-shirt, thoroughly shrunken, a thin gray V-necked pullover purchased by the half-dozen from a supplier to New England prep schools, and a new and oversized pair of black 501's, every trademark carefully removed. Even the buttons on these have been ground flat, featureless, by a puzzled Korean lock-smith, in the Village, a week ago.

The switch on Damien's Italian floor lamp feels alien: a different click, designed to hold back a different voltage, foreign British electricity.

Standing now, stepping into her jeans, she straightens, shivering.

Mirror-world. The plugs on appliances are huge, triple-pronged, for a species of current that only powers electric chairs, in America. Cars are reversed, left to right, inside; telephone handsets have a different weight, a different balance; the

3

covers of paperbacks look like Australian money.

Pupils contracted painfully against sun-bright halogen, she squints into an actual mirror, canted against a gray wall, awaiting hanging, wherein she sees a black-legged, disjointed puppet, sleep-hair poking up like a toilet brush. She grimaces at it, thinking for some reason of a boyfriend who'd insisted on comparing her to Helmut Newton's nude portrait of Jane Birkin.

In the kitchen she runs tap water through a German filter, into an Italian electric kettle. Fiddles with switches, one on the kettle, one on the plug, one on the socket. Blankly surveys the canary expanse of laminated cabinetry while it boils. Bag of some imported California tea substitute in a large white mug. Pouring boiling water.

In the flat's main room, she finds that Damien's faithful Cube is on, but sleeping, the night-light glow of its static switches pulsing gently. Damien's ambivalence toward design showing here: He won't allow decorators through the door unless they basically agree to not do that which they do, yet he holds on to this Mac for the way you can turn it upside down and remove its innards with a magic little aluminum handle. Like the sex of one of the robot girls in his video, now that she thinks of it.

She seats herself in his high-backed workstation chair and clicks the transparent mouse. Stutter of infrared on the pale wood of the long trestle table.

The browser comes up. She types Fetish:Footage:Forum, which Damien, determined to avoid contamination, will never bookmark.

The front page opens, familiar as a friend's living room. A frame-grab from #48 serves as backdrop, dim and almost monochrome, no characters in view. This is one of the sequences that generate comparisons with Tarkovsky. She only knows Tarkovsky from stills, really, though she did once fall asleep during a screening of *The Stalker*, going under on an endless pan, the camera aimed straight down, in close-up, at a puddle on a ruined mosaic floor. But she is not one of those who think that much will be gained by analysis of the maker's imagined influences. The cult of the footage is rife with subcults, claiming every possible influence. Truffaut, Peckinpah . . . The Peckinpah people, among the least likely, are still waiting for the guns to be drawn.

She enters the forum itself now, automatically scanning titles of the posts and names of posters in the newer threads, looking for friends, enemies, news. One thing is clear, though; no new footage has surfaced. Nothing since that beach pan, and she does not subscribe to the theory that it is Cannes in winter. French footageheads have been unable to match it, in spite of countless hours recording pans across approximately similar scenery.

She also sees that her friend Parkaboy is back in Chicago, home from an Amtrak vacation,

California, but when she opens his post she sees that he's only saying hello, literally.

She clicks Respond, declares herself CayceP.

Hi Parkaboy. nt

When she returns to the forum page, her post is there.

It is a way now, approximately, of being at home. The forum has become one of the most consistent places in her life, like a familiar café that exists somehow outside of geography and beyond time zones.

There are perhaps twenty regular posters on F:F:F, and some much larger and uncounted number of lurkers. And right now there are three people in Chat, but there's no way of knowing exactly who until you are in there, and the chat room she finds not so comforting. It's strange even with friends, like sitting in a pitch-dark cellar conversing with people at a distance of about fifteen feet. The hectic speed, and the brevity of the lines in the thread, plus the feeling that everyone is talking at once, at counter-purposes, deter her.

The Cube sighs softly and makes subliminal sounds with its drive, like a vintage sports car downshifting on a distant freeway. She tries a sip of tea substitute, but it's still too hot. A gray and indeterminate light is starting to suffuse the room in which she sits, revealing such Damieniana as has survived the recent remake.

Partially disassembled robots are propped against one wall, two of them, torsos and heads, like elfin, decidedly female crash-test dummies. These are effects units from one of Damien's videos, and she wonders, given her mood, why she finds them so comforting. Probably because they are genuinely beautiful, she decides. Optimistic expressions of the feminine. No sci-fi kitsch for Damien. Dreamlike things in the dawn half-light, their small breasts gleaming, white plastic shining faint as old marble. Personally fetishistic, though; she knows he'd had them molded from a body cast of his last girlfriend, minus two.

Hotmail downloads four messages, none of which she feels like opening. Her mother, three spam. The penis enlarger is still after her, twice, and Increase Your Breast Size Dramatically.

Deletes spam. Sips the tea substitute. Watches the gray light becoming more like day.

Eventually she goes into Damien's newly renovated bathroom. Feels she could shower down in it prior to visiting a sterile NASA probe, or step out of some Chernobyl scenario to have her lead suit removed by rubber-gowned Soviet technicians, who'd then scrub her with longhandled brushes. The fixtures in the shower can be adjusted with elbows, preserving the sterility of scrubbed hands.

She pulls off her sweater and T-shirt and, using hands, not elbows, starts the shower and adjusts the temperature.

$\star$ $\star$ $\star$

7

Four hours later she's on a reformer in a Pilates studio in an upscale alley called Neal's Yard, the car and driver from Blue Ant waiting out on whatever street it is. The reformer is a very long, very low, vaguely ominous and Weimar-looking piece of spring-loaded furniture. On which she now reclines, doing v-position against the foot rail at the end. The padded platform she rests on wheels back and forth along tracks of angle-iron within the frame, springs twanging softly. Ten of these, ten toes, ten from the heels . . . In New York she does this at a fitness center frequented by dance professionals, but here in Neal's Yard, this morning, she seems to be the sole client. The place is only recently opened, apparently, and perhaps this sort of thing is not yet so popular here. There is that mirror-world ingestion of archaic substances, she thinks: People smoke, and drink as though it were good for you, and seem to still be in some sort of honeymoon phase with cocaine. Heroin, she's read, is cheaper here than it's ever been, the market still glutted by the initial dumping of Afghani opium supplies.

Done with her toes, she changes to heels, craning her neck to be certain her feet are correctly aligned. She likes Pilates because it isn't, in the way she thinks of yoga, meditative. You have to keep your eyes open, here, and pay attention.

That concentration counters the anxiety she feels now, the pre-job jitters she hasn't experienced in a while.

She's here on Blue Ant's ticket. Relatively tiny in terms of permanent staff, globally distributed, more post-geographic than multinational, the agency has from the beginning billed itself as a high-speed, low-drag life-form in an advertising ecology of lumbering herbivores. Or perhaps as some non-carbon-based life-form, entirely sprung from the smooth and ironic brow of its founder, Hubertus Bigend, a nominal Belgian who looks like Tom Cruise on a diet of virgins' blood and truffled chocolates.

The only thing Cayce enjoys about Bigend is that he seems to have no sense at all that his name might seem ridiculous to anyone, ever. Otherwise, she would find him even more unbearable than she already does.

It's entirely personal, though at one remove.

Still doing heels, she checks her watch, a Korean clone of an old-school Casio G-Shock, its plastic case sanded free of logos with a scrap of Japanese micro-abrasive. She is due in Blue Ant's Soho offices in fifty minutes.

She drapes a pair of limp green foam pads over the foot rail, carefully positions her feet, lifts them on invisible stiletto heels, and begins her ten prehensile.

CHAPTER 2

BITCH

CPUs for the meeting, reflected in the window of a Soho specialist in mod paraphernalia, are a fresh Fruit T-shirt, her black Buzz Rickson's MA-1, anonymous black skirt from a Tulsa thrift, the black leggings she'd worn for Pilates, black Harajuku schoolgirl shoes. Her purse-analog is an envelope of black East German laminate, purchased on eBay—if not actual Stasi-issue then well in the ballpark.

She sees her own gray eyes, pale in the glass, and beyond them Ben Sherman shirts and fishtail parkas, cufflinks in the form of the RAF roundel that marked the wings of Spitfires.

CPUs. Cayce Pollard Units. That's what Damien calls the clothing she wears. CPUs are either black, white, or gray, and ideally seem to have come into this world without human intervention.

What people take for relentless minimalism is a side effect of too much exposure to the reactor-cores of fashion. This has resulted in a remorseless paring-down of what she can and will wear. She is, literally, allergic to fashion. She can only tolerate things that could have been worn, to a general lack of comment, during any year between 1945 and 2000. She's a design-free zone, a one-woman school of anti whose very austerity periodically threatens to spawn its own cult.

Around her the bustle of Soho, a Friday morning building toward boozy lunches and careful chatter in all these restaurants. To one of which, Charlie Don't Surf, she will be going for an obligatory post-meeting meal. But she feels herself tipping back down into a miles-long trough of jet lag, and knows that that is what she must surf now: her lack of serotonin, the delayed arrival of her soul.

She checks her watch and heads down the street, toward Blue Ant, whose premises until recently were those of an older, more linear sort of agency.

The sky is a bright gray bowl, crossed with raveled contrails, and as she presses the button to announce herself at Blue Ant, she wishes she'd brought her sunglasses.

Seated now, opposite Bernard Stonestreet, familiar from Blue Ant's New York operation, she finds him pale and freckled as ever, with carroty hair upswept in a weird Aubrey Beardsley flame motif that might be the result of his having slept on it that way, but is more likely the work of some exclusive barber. He is wearing what Cayce takes to be a Paul Smith suit, more specifically the 118 jacket and the 11T trouser, cut from something black. In London his look seems to be about wearing many thousand pounds' worth of garments that appear to have never been worn before having been slept in, the night before. In New York he prefers to look as though he's just been detailed by a tight scrum of specialists. Different cultural parameters.

On his left sits Dorotea Benedetti, her hair scraped back from her forehead with a haute nerd intensity that Cayce suspects means business and trouble both. Dorotea, whom Cayce knows glancingly from previous and minor business in New York, is something fairly high up in the graphics design partnership of Heinzi & Pfaff. She has flown in, this morning, from Frankfurt, to present H&P's initial shot at a new logo for one of the world's two largest manufacturers of athletic footwear. Bigend has defined a need for this maker to re-identify, in some profound but so far unspecified way. Sales of athletic shoes, "trainers" in the mirrorworld, are tanking bigtime, and the skate shoes that had already started to push them under aren't doing too well either. Cayce herself has been tracking the street-level emergence of what she thinks of as "urban survival" footwear, and though this is so far at the level of consumer repurposing, she has no doubt that commodification will soon follow identification.

The new logo will be this firm's pivot into the new century, and Cayce, with her marketable allergy, has been brought over to do in person the thing that she does best. That seems odd to her, or if not odd, archaic. Why not teleconference? There may be so much at stake, she supposes, that security is an issue, but it's been a while now since business has required her to leave New York.

Whatever, Dorotea's looking serious about it. Serious as cancer. On the table in front of her, perhaps a millimeter too carefully aligned, is an elegant gray cardboard envelope, fifteen inches on a side, bearing the austere yet whimsical logo of Heinzi & Pfaff. It is closed with one of those expensively archaic fasteners consisting of a length of cord and two small brown cardboard buttons.

Cayce looks away from Dorotea and the envelope, noting that a great many Nineties pounds had once been lavished on this third-floor meeting room, with its convexly curving walls of wood suggesting the first-class lounge of a transatlantic zeppelin. She notices threaded anchors exposed on the pale veneer of the convex wall, where once had been displayed the logo of whichever agency previously occupied the place, and early warning signs of Blue Ant renovation are visible as well: scaffolding erected in a hallway, where someone has been examining ductwork, and rolls of new carpeting stacked like plastic-wrapped logs from a polyester forest.

Dorotea may have attempted to out-minimalize her this morning, Cayce decides. If so, it hasn't worked. Dorotea's black dress, for all its apparent simplicity, is still trying to say several things at once, probably in at least three languages. Cayce has hung her Buzz Rickson's over the back of her chair, and now she catches Dorotea looking at it.

The Rickson's is a fanatical museum-grade replica of a U.S. MA-1 flying jacket, as purely functional and iconic a garment as the previous century produced. Dorotea's slow burn is being accelerated, Cayce suspects, by her perception that Cayce's MA-1 trumps any attempt at minimalism, the Rickson's having been created by Japanese obsessives driven by passions having nothing at all to do with anything remotely like fashion.

Cayce knows, for instance, that the characteristically wrinkled seams down either arm were originally the result of sewing with pre-war industrial machines that rebelled against the slippery new material, nylon. The makers of the Rickson's have exaggerated this, but only very slightly, and done a hundred other things, tiny things, as well, so that their product has become, in some very Japanese way, the result of an act of worship. It is an imitation more real somehow than that which it emulates. It is easily the most expensive garment Cayce owns, and would be virtually impossible to replace.

"You don't mind?" Stonestreet producing a pack of cigarettes called Silk Cut, which Cayce, never a smoker, thinks of as somehow being the British equivalent of the Japanese Mild Seven. Two default brands of creatives.

"No," says Cayce. "Please do."

There is actually an ashtray on the table, a small

14

one, round and perfectly white. As archaic a fixture in America, in the context of a business meeting, as would be one of those flat and filigreed absinthe trowels. (But in London, she knew, you might encounter those as well, though she'd not yet seen one at a meeting.) "Dorotea?" Offering the pack, but not to Cayce. Dorotea declining. Stonestreet puts a filter tip between his tidily mobile lips and takes out a box of matches that Cayce assumes were acquired in some restaurant the night before. The matchbox looks very nearly as expensive as Dorotea's gray envelope. He lights up. "Sorry we had to haul you over for this, Cayce," he says. The spent match makes a tiny ceramic sound when he drops it into the ashtray.

"It's what I do, Bernard," Cayce says.

"You look tired," says Dorotea.

"Four hours difference." Smiling with only the corners of her mouth.

"Have you tried those pills from New Zealand?" Stonestreet asks. Cayce remembers that his American wife, once the ingénue in a short-lived X-Files clone, is the creator of an apparently successful line of vaguely homeopathic beauty products.

"Jacques Cousteau said that jet lag was his favorite drug."

"Well?" Dorotea looks pointedly at the H&P envelope.

Stonestreet blows a stream of smoke. "Well yes, I suppose we should."

They both look at Cayce. Cayce looks Dorotea in the eye. "Ready when you are."

Dorotea unwinds the cord from beneath the cardboard button nearest Cayce. Lifts the flap. Reaches in with thumb and forefinger.

There is a silence.

"Well then," Stonestreet says, and stubs out his Silk Cut.

Dorotea removes an eleven-inch square of art board from the envelope. Holding it at the upper corners, between the tips of perfectly manicured forefingers, she displays it to Cayce.

There is a drawing there, a sort of scribble in thick black Japanese brush, a medium she knows to be the in-house hallmark of Herr Heinzi himself. To Cayce, it most resembles a syncopated sperm, as rendered by the American underground cartoonist Rick Griffin, circa 1967. She knows immediately that it does not, by the opaque standards of her inner radar, work. She has no way of knowing how she knows.

Briefly, though, she imagines the countless Asian workers who might, should she say yes, spend years of their lives applying versions of this symbol to an endless and unyielding flood of footwear. What would it mean to them, this bouncing sperm? Would it work its way into their dreams, eventually? Would their children chalk it in doorways before they knew its meaning as a trademark?

"No," she says.

Stonestreet sighs. Not a deep sigh. Dorotea

returns the drawing to its envelope but doesn't bother to reseal it.

Cayce's contract for a consultation of this sort specifies that she absolutely not be asked to critique anything, or provide creative input of any sort. She is only there to serve as a very specialized piece of human litmus paper.

Dorotea takes one of Stonestreet's cigarettes and lights it, dropping the wooden match on the table beside the ashtray. "How was the winter, then, in New York?"

"Cold," Cayce says.

"And sad? It is still sad?"

Cayce says nothing.

"You are available to stay here," Dorotea asks, "while we go back to the drawing board?"

Cayce wonders if Dorotea knows the cliché. "I'm here for two weeks," she says. "Flat-sitting for a friend."

"A vacation, then."

"Not if I'm working on this."

Dorotea says nothing.

"It must be difficult," Stonestreet says, between steepled, freckled fingers, his red thatch rising above them like flames from a burning cathedral, "when you don't like something. Emotionally, I mean."

Cayce watches Dorotea rise and, carrying her Silk Cut, cross to a sideboard, where she pours Perrier into a tumbler.

"It isn't about liking anything, Bernard," Cayce

says, turning back to Stonestreet, "it's like that roll of carpet, there; it's either blue or it's not. Whether or not it's blue isn't something I have an emotional investment in."

She feels bad energy brush past her as Dorotea returns to her seat.

Dorotea puts her water down beside the H&P envelope and does a rather inexpert job of stubbing out her cigarette. "I will speak with Heinzi this afternoon. I would call him now but I know that he is in Stockholm, meeting with Volvo."

The air seems very thick with smoke now and Cayce feels like coughing.

"There's no rush, Dorotea," Stonestreet says, and Cayce hopes that this means that there really, really is.

Charlie Don't Surf is full, the food California-inflected Vietnamese fusion with more than the usual leavening of colonial Frenchness. The white walls are decorated with enormous prints of close-up black-and-white photographs of 'Nam-era Zippo lighters, engraved with crudely drawn American military symbols, still cruder sexual motifs, and stenciled slogans. These remind Cayce of photographs of tombstones in Confederate graveyards, except for the graphic content and the nature of the slogans, and the 'Nam theme suggests to her that the place has been here for a while.

IF I HAD A FARM IN HELL AND A HOUSE IN VIETNAM I'D SELL THEM BOTH

18

The lighters in the photographs are so worn, so dented and sweat-corroded, that Cayce may well be the first diner to ever have deciphered these actual texts.

BURY ME FACE DOWN SO THE WORLD CAN KISS MY ASS

"His surname actually is 'Heinzi,' you know," Stonestreet is saying, pouring a second glass of the Californian cabernet that Cayce, though she knows better, is drinking. "It only sounds like a nickname. Any given names, though, have long since gone south."

"Ibiza," Cayce suggests.

"Er?"

"Sorry, Bernard, I'm tired."

"Those pills. From New Zealand."

THERE IS NO GRAVITY THE WORLD SUCKS

"I'll be fine." A sip of wine.

"She's a piece of work, isn't she?"

"Dorotea?"

Stonestreet rolls his eyes, which are a peculiar brown, inflected as with Mercurochrome; something iridescent, greenly copper-tinged.

173 AIRBORNE

She asks after the American wife. Stonestreet dutifully recounts the launch of a cucumber-based mask, the thin end of a fresh wedge of product, touching on the politics involved in retail placement. Lunch arrives. Cayce concentrates on tiny fried spring rolls, setting herself for auto-nod and periodically but sympathetically raised eyebrows, grateful that he's carrying the conversational ball. She's way down deep in that trough now, with the half-glass of cabernet starting to exert its own lateral influence, and she knows that her best course here is to make nice, get some food in her stomach, and be gone.

But the Zippo tombstones, with their existential elegies, tug at her.

PHU CAT

Restaurant art that diners actually notice is a dubious idea, particularly to one with Cayce's peculiar, visceral, but still somewhat undefined sensitivities.

"So when it looked as though Harvey Knickers weren't going to come aboard . . ."

Nod, raise eyebrows, chew spring roll. This is working. She covers her glass when he starts to pour her more wine.

And so she makes it easily enough through lunch with Bernard Stonestreet, blipped occasionally by these emblematic place-names from the Zippo graveyard (CU CHI, QUI NHON) lining the walls, and at last he has paid and they are standing up to leave.

Reaching for her Rickson's, where she'd hung it on the back of her chair, she sees a round, freshly made hole, left shoulder, rear, the size of the lit tip of a cigarette. Its edges are minutely beaded, brown, with melted nylon. Through this is visible a gray interlining, no doubt to some particular Cold War mil-spec pored over by the jacket's otaku makers.

"Is something wrong?"

"No," Cayce says, "nothing." Putting on her ruined Rickson's.

Near the door, on their way out, she numbly registers a shallow Lucite cabinet displaying an array of those actual Vietnam Zippos, perhaps a dozen of them, and automatically leans closer.

SHIT ON MY DICK OR BLOOD ON MY BLADE

Which is very much her attitude toward Dorotea, right now, though she doubts she'll be able to do anything about it, and will only turn the anger against herself.

CHAPTER 3

THE ATTACHMENT

She's gone to Harvey Nichols and gotten sick.

Should have known better.

How she responds to labels.

Down into menswear, unrealistically hoping that if anyone might have a Buzz Rickson's it would be Harvey Nichols, their ornate Victorian pile rising like a coral reef opposite Knightsbridge station. Somewhere on the ground floor, in cosmetics, they even have Helena Stonestreet's cucumber mask, Bernard having explained to her how he'd demonstrated his considerable powers of suasion on the HN buyers.

But down here, next to a display of Tommy Hilfiger, it's all started to go sideways on her, the trademark thing. Less warning aura than usual. Some people ingest a single peanut and their head swells like a basketball. When it happens to Cayce, it's her psyche.

Tommy Hilfiger does it every time, though she'd thought she was safe now. They'd said he'd peaked, in New York. Like Benetton, the name would be around, but the real poison, for her, would have been drawn. It's something to do with context, here, with not expecting it in London. When it starts, it's pure reaction, like biting down hard on a piece of foil.

A glance to the right and the avalanche lets go. A mountainside of Tommy coming down in her head.

My God, don't they know? This stuff is simulacra of simulacra of simulacra. A diluted tincture of Ralph Lauren, who had himself diluted the glory days of Brooks Brothers, who themselves had stepped on the product of Jermyn Street and Savile Row, flavoring their ready-to-wear with liberal lashings of polo knit and regimental stripes. But Tommy surely is the null point, the black hole. There must be some Tommy Hilfiger event horizon, beyond which it is impossible to be more derivative, more removed from the source, more devoid of soul. Or so she hopes, and doesn't know, but suspects in her heart that this in fact is what accounts for his long ubiquity.

She needs out of this logo-maze, desperately. But the escalator to the street exit will dump her back into Knightsbridge, seeming somehow now more of the same, and she remembers that the street runs down, and always her energy with it, to Sloane Square, another nexus of whatever she suffers these reactions to. Laura Ashley, down there, and that can get ugly.

Remembering the fifth floor, here: a sort of Californian market, Dean & Deluca lite, with a restaurant, a separate and weirdly modular robotic sushi operation humming oddly in its midst, and a bar where they served excellent coffee.

Caffeine she's held in reserve today, a silver bullet against serotonin-lack and big weird feelings. She can go there. There is a lift. Yes, a lift: a closet-sized elevator, small but perfectly formed. She will find it, and use it. Now.

She does. It arrives, miraculously empty, and she steps in, pressing 5. "I'm feeling rather excited," a woman says, breathily, as the door closes, though Cayce knows she's alone in this upright coffin of mirror and brushed steel. Fortunately she's been this way before, and knows that these disembodied voices are there for the amusement of the shopper. "Mmmmm," purrs the male of the species. The only equivalent audio environment she can recall was in the restroom of an upscale hamburger joint on Rodeo Drive, years ago: an inexplicable sound-track of buzzing insects. Flies, it had sounded like, though surely that couldn't have been the intent.

Whatever else these designer ghosts say, she blocks it out, the lift ascending miraculously, without intermediate stops, to the fifth floor.

Cayce pops out into a pale light slanting in through much glass. Fewer lunching shoppers than she remembers. But no clothing on this floor, save on people's backs and in their glossy carrier bags. The swelling can subside, here.

She pauses by a meat counter, eyeing roasts illuminated like newly minted media faces, and probably of a biologic purity she herself could never hope to attain: animals raised on a diet more stringent than the one propounded in interviews by Stonestreet's wife.

At the bar, a few Euromales of the dark-suited sort stand smoking their eternal cigarettes.

She bellies up, catching the barman's eye.

"*Time Out?*" he inquires, frowning slightly. Brutally cropped, he regards her from the depths of massive, mask-like Italian spectacles. The black-framed glasses remind her of emoticons, those snippets of playschool emotional code cobbled up from keyboard symbols to produce sideways cartoon faces. You could do his glasses with an eight, hyphen for his nose, the mouth a left slash.

"I'm sorry?"

"*Time Out*. The weekly. You were on a panel. ICA."

Institute for Contemporary Arts, last time she'd been here. With a woman from a provincial university, lecturer in the taxonomy of trade-marking. Rain falling thinly on the Mall. The audience smelling of damp wool and cigarettes. She'd accepted because she could stay a few days with Damien. He'd bought the house where he'd rented for several years, fruit of a series of Scandinavian car commercials. She'd forgotten the blurb in *Time Out*, one of those coolhunter things.

"You follow the footage." His eyes narrowing within their brackets of black Italian plastic.

Damien maintains, half-seriously, that followers of the footage comprise the first true freemasonry of the new century.

"Were you there?" Cayce asks, jostled out of herself by this abrupt violation of context. She is not by any means a celebrity; being recognized by strangers isn't part of her ordinary experience. But the footage has a way of cutting across boundaries, transgressing the accustomed order of things.

"My friend was there." He looks down and runs a spotless white cloth across the bar top. Gnawed cuticle and too large a ring. "He told me that he'd run into you later, on a site. You were arguing with someone about *The Chinese Envoy*." He looks back up. "You can't seriously believe it's him."

Him being Kim Hee Park, the young Korean auteur responsible for the film in question, an interminable art-house favorite some people compare with the footage, others going so far as to suggest that Kim Park is in fact the maker of the footage. Suggesting this to Cayce is akin to asking the Pope if he's soft on that Cathar heresy.

"No," she says, firmly. "Of course not."

"New segment." Quick, under his breath.

"When?"

"This morning. Forty-eight seconds. It's them."

It's as though they are in a bubble now, Cayce and the barman. No sound penetrates. "Do they speak?" she asks.

"No."

"You've seen it?"

"No. Someone messaged me, on my mobile."

"No spoilers," Cayce warns, getting a grip.

He refolds the white cloth. A waft of blue Gitane drifts past, from the Euromales. 'A drink?' The bubble bursts, admitting sound.

"Espresso, double." She opens her East German envelope, reaching for heavy mirror-world change.

He's drawing her espresso from a black machine down the bar. Sound of steam escaping under pressure. The forum will be going crazy, the first posts depending on time zones, history of proliferation, where the segment surfaced. It will prove impossible to trace, either uploaded via a temporary e-mail address, often from a borrowed IP, sometimes via a temporary cell phone number, or through some anonymizer. It will have been discovered by footageheads tirelessly scouring the Net, found somewhere where it's possible to upload a video file and simply leave it there.

He returns with her coffee in a white cup, on a white saucer, and places it before her on the glossy black counter. Positions a steel basket nearby, its sections containing a variety of colorful British sugars, at least three kinds. Another aspect of the mirror-world: sugar. There is more of it, and not only in things you expect to be sweet.

She's stacked six of the thick pound coins.

"On the house."

"Thank you."

The Euromales are indicating a need for fresh drink. He goes to tend to them. He looks like Michael Stipe on steroids. She takes back four of the coins and nudges the rest into the shadow of the sugar caddy. Smartly downs her double sans sugar and turns to go. Looks back as she's leaving and he is there, regarding her severely from the depths of black parentheses.

Black cab to Camden tube.

Her attack of Tommy-phobia has backed off nicely, but the trough of soul-delay has opened out into horizonless horse latitudes.

She fears she'll be becalmed before she can lay in supplies. On autonomic pilot in a supermarket in the High Street, filling a basket. Mirror-world fruit. Colombian coffee, ground for a press. Two-percent milk.

In a nearby stationer's, heavy on art supplies, she buys a roll of matte black gaffer's tape.

Heading up Parkway toward Damien's she notices a flyer adhering to a lamppost. In rain-faded monochrome a frame-grab from the footage.

He looks out, as from depths.

Works at Cantor Fitzgerald. Gold wedding band.

Parkaboy's e-mail is text-free. There is only the attachment.

Seated before Damien's Cube, with the two-cup

French press she bought on Parkway. Fragrant waft of powerful Colombian. She shouldn't drink this; it will not so much defer sleep as guarantee nightmares, and she knows she'll wake again in that dread hour, vibrating. But she must be present for the new segment. Sharp.

Always, now, the opening of an attachment containing unseen footage is profoundly liminal. A threshold state.

Parkaboy has labeled his attachment #135. One hundred and thirty four previously known fragments—of what? A work in progress? Something completed years ago, and meted out now, for some reason, in these snippets?

She hasn't gone to the forum. Spoilers. She wants each new fragment to impact as cleanly as possible.

Parkaboy says you should go to new footage as though you've seen no previous footage at all, thereby momentarily escaping the film or films that you've been assembling, consciously or unconsciously, since first exposure.

Homo sapiens is about pattern recognition, he says. Both a gift and a trap.

She slowly depresses the plunger.

Pours coffee into a mug.

She's draped her jacket cape-style round the smooth shoulders of one robotic nymph. Balanced on its stainless pubis, the white torso reclines against the gray wall. Neutral regard. Eyeless serenity.

Five in the evening and she can barely keep her eyes open.

Lifts her cup of black unsweetened coffee. Mouse-clicks.

How many times has she done this?

How long since she gave herself to the dream? Maurice's expression for the essence of being a footagehead.

Damien's Studio Display fills with darkness absolute. It is as if she participates in the very birth of cinema, that Lumière moment, the steam locomotive about to emerge from the screen, sending the audience fleeing, out into the Parisian night.

Light and shadow. Lovers' cheekbones in the prelude to embrace.

Cayce shivers.

So long now, and they have not been seen to touch.

Around them the absolute blackness is alleviated by texture. Concrete?

They are dressed as they have always been dressed, in clothing Cayce has posted on extensively, fascinated by its timelessness, something she knows and understands. The difficulty of that. Hairstyles, too.

He might be a sailor, stepping onto a submarine in 1914, or a jazz musician entering a club in 1957. There is a lack of evidence, an absence of stylistic cues, that Cayce understands to be utterly masterful. His black coat is usually read as leather, though it might be dull vinyl, or rubber. He has a way of wearing its collar up.

The girl wears a longer coat, equally dark but seemingly of fabric, its shoulder-padding the subject of hundreds of posts. The architecture of padding in a woman's coat should yield possible periods, particular decades, but there has been no agreement, only controversy.

She is hatless, which has been taken either as the clearest of signs that this is not a period piece, or simply as an indication that she is a free spirit, untrammeled by even the most basic conventions of her day. Her hair has been the subject of similar scrutiny, but nothing has ever been definitively agreed upon.

The one hundred and thirty-four previously discovered fragments, having been endlessly collated, broken down, reassembled, by whole armies of the most fanatical investigators, have yielded no period and no particular narrative direction.

Zaprudered into surreal dimensions of purest speculation, ghost-narratives have emerged and taken on shadowy but determined lives of their own, but Cayce is familiar with them all, and steers clear.

And here in Damien's flat, watching their lips meet, she knows that she knows nothing, but wants nothing more than to see the film of which this must be a part. Must be.

Above them, somewhere, something flares,

white, casting a claw of Caligarian shadow, and then the screen is black.

She clicks on Replay. Watches it again.

She opens the site and scrolls a full page of posts. Several pages have accumulated in the course of the day, in the wake of the surfacing of #135, but she has no appetite for them now.

It seems beside the point.

A wave comes crashing, sheer exhaustion, against which the Colombian is no defense.

She takes off her clothes, brushes her teeth, limbs wooden with exhaustion and vibrating with caffeine, turns off the lights, and crawls, literally, beneath the stiff silver spread on Damien's bed.

To curl fetal there, and briefly marvel, as a final wave crashes over her, at the perfect and now perfectly revealed extent of her present loneliness.

CHAPTER 4

MATH GRENADES

S omehow she sleeps, or approximates it, through the famously bad hour and into another mirror-world morning.

Waking to an inner flash of metallic migraine light, as if reflected off wings of receding dream.

Extrudes her head turtle-wise from beneath the giant pot-holder and squints at the windows. Daylight. More of her soul has been reeled in, it seems, in the meantime. Apprehending self and mirror-world now in a different modality, accompanied by an unexpected surge of energy that has her out of bed, into the shower, and levering the Italian chromed head to stinging new foci of needle jets. Damien's reno has involved hot water, lots of it, and for that she is grateful.

It is as though she is inhabited now by something single-minded, purposeful, yet has no idea what it plans, or wants. But she is content, for the moment, to go along for the ride.

Blow-dry. CPUs include the black jeans.

Mirror-world milk (which is different, though

she couldn't say how) on the Weetabix, with a sliced banana. That other part of her, that other self, moving right along.

Watching as that part seals over the cigarette burn with black gaffer's tape, the ends tooth-torn, a sort of archaic punk flourish. Pulls on the Rickson's, checks for keys and money, and descends Damien's still-unrenovated stairwell, past a tenant's mountain bike and hip-high bundles of last year's magazines.

In the sunlit street, all is still; nothing moves save the cinnamon blur of a cat, just there, and gone. She listens. The hum of London, building somewhere.

Feeling inexplicably happy, she sets off down Parkway toward Camden High Street, and finds a Russian in a mini-cab. Not a cab at all, really, just a dusty blue mirror-world Jetta, but he will drive her to Notting Hill, and he looks too old, too scholarly, too disgusted by the very sight of her, to be much trouble.

Once they are out of Camden Town she has little idea of where they are. She has no internalized surface map of this city, only of the underground and of assorted personal footpaths spreading out from its stations.

The stomach-clenching roundabouts are pivots in a maze to be negotiated only by locals and cabdrivers. Restaurants and antique shops rotate past, punctuated regularly by pubs.

Marveling at the luminous shanks of a black-haired man in a very expensive-looking dressing gown, bending toward the morning's milk and paper in his doorway.

A military vehicle, its silhouette unfamiliar, bulk-browed, tautly laced beneath its tarpaulin. The driver's beret.

Mirror-world street furniture: bits of urban infrastructure she can't identify by function. Local equivalents of the mysterious Water Testing Station on her block uptown, which a friend had claimed to contain nothing more than a tap and a cup, for the judging of potability—this having been for Cayce a favorite fantasy of alternative employment, to stroll Manhattan like an itinerant sommelier, addressing one's palate with the various tap waters of the city. Not that she would have wanted to, particularly, but simply to believe that someone could do this for a living had been somehow comforting.

By the time they arrive at Notting Hill, whatever rogue aspect of personality has been driving this morning's expedition seems to have decamped, leaving her feeling purposeless and confused. She pays the Russian, gets out on the side opposite Portobello, and descends the stairs to a pedestrian tunnel that smells of Friday-night urine. Overly tall mirror-world lager cans are crushed there like roaches.

Corridor metaphysics. She wants coffee.

But the Starbucks on the other side, up the stairs and around a corner, is not yet open. A boy, inside, wrestles huge plastic trays of cellophaned pastries.

Uncertain what she should do next, she walks

on, in the direction of the Saturday market. Seven-thirty, now. She can't remember when the antiques arcades open, but she knows the road will be jammed by nine. Why has she come here? She never buys antiques.

She's in a street of what she thinks are called mews houses, little places, scarily cute, still headed toward Portobello and the market, when she sees them: three men, variously jacketed, their collars up, staring gravely into the open trunk of a small and uncharacteristically old mirror-world car. Not so much a mirror-world car as an English car, as no equivalent exists, on Cayce's side of the Atlantic, to mirror. Vauxhall Wyvern, she thinks, with her complusive memory for brand names, though she doubts that this is one of those, whatever those might have been. As to why she notices them now, these three, she later will be unable to say.

No one else in the street, and there is something in the gravity they bring to their study of whatever it is they are looking down at. Careful poker masks. The largest, though not the tallest, a black man with a shaven head, is zipped like a sausage into something shiny, black, and only approximately leatherlike. Beside him is a taller, gray-faced man, hunched within the greasy folds of an ancient Barbour waterproof, its waxed cotton gone the sheen and shade of day-old horse dung. The third, younger, is close-cropped and blond, in baggy black skater shorts and a frayed jean jacket. He wears something like a mailman's pouch, slung across his chest. Shorts, she thinks, drawing abreast of this trio, are somehow always wrong in London.

She can't resist glancing into the trunk.

Grenades.

Black, compact, cylindrical. Six of them, laid out on an old gray sweater amid a jumble of brown cardboard cartons.

"Miss?" The one in shorts.

"Hello?" The gray-faced man, sharply, impatient.

She tells herself to run, but can't.

"Yes?"

"The Curtas." The blond one, stepping closer.

"It isn't her, you idiot. She's not bloody coming." The gray one again, with mounting irritation.

The blond one blinks. "You haven't come about the Curtas?"

"The what?"

"The calculators."

She can't resist, then, and steps closer to the car, to see. "What are they?"

"Calculators." The tight plastic of the black man's jacket creaking as he bends to pick up one of the grenades. Turning to hand it to her. And then she is holding it: heavy, dense, knurled for gripping. Tabs or flanges that look as though meant to move in these slots. Small round windows showing white numbers. At the top something that looks like the crank on a pepper mill, as executed by a small-arms manufacturer.

"I don't understand," she says, and imagines

she'll wake, just then, in Damien's bed, because it's all gone that dreamlike now. Automatically seeking a trademark, she turns the thing over. And sees that it is made in Liechtenstein.

Liechtenstein?

"What is it?"

"It is a precision instrument," the black man says, "performing calculations mechanically, employing neither electricity nor electronic components. The sensation of its operation is best likened to that of winding a fine thirty-five-millimeter camera. It is the smallest mechanical calculating machine ever constructed." Voice deep and mellifluous. "It is the invention of Curt Herzstark, an Austrian, who developed it while a prisoner in Buchenwald. The camp authorities actually encouraged his work, you see. 'Intelligence slave,' his title there. They wished his calculator to be given to the Führer, at the end of the war. But Buchenwald was liberated in 1945 by the Americans. Herzstark had survived." He gently takes the thing from her. Enormous hands. "He had his drawings." Large fingers moving surely, gently, clicking the black tabs into a different configuration. He grasps the knurled cylinder in his left, gives the handle at the top a twirl. Smoothly ratcheting a sum from its interior. He raises it to see the resulting figure in a tiny window. "Eight hundred pounds. Excellent condition." Dropping an eyelid partially, to wait for her response.

"It's beautiful," his offer finally giving her a context for this baffling exchange: These men are dealers, come here to do business in these things. "But I wouldn't know what to do with it."

"You've had me out for nothing, you silly cunt," snarls the gray man, snatching the thing from the black one's hands, but Cayce knows that it's the black man this is meant for, not her. He looks, just then, like a scary portrait of Samuel Beckett on a book she owned in college. His nails are black-edged and there are deep orangey-brown stains of nicotine on his long fingers. He turns with the calculator and bends over the open trunk, to furiously repack the black, grenade-like machines.

"Hobbs," the black man says, and sighs, "you lack all patience. She will come. Please wait."

"Bugger," says Hobbs, if that's his name, closing a cardboard box and spreading the old sweater over it with a quick, practiced, weirdly maternal gesture, like a mother adjusting the blanket over a sleeping child. He bangs the lid down and tugs at it, checking to see that it's closed. "Waste my bloody time . . ." He hauls the driver-side door open with a startling creak.

She glimpses filthy mouse-colored upholstery and an overflowing ashtray that protrudes from the dash like a little drawer.

"She will come, Hobbs," the black man protests, but without much force.

The one called Hobbs folds himself into the driver's seat, yanks the door shut, and glares at them through the dirty side window. The car's engine starts with an antique, asthmatic shudder, and he puts it into gear, still glaring, and pulls away, toward Portobello. At the next corner, the gray car turns right, and is gone.

"He is a curse to know, that man," says the black man. "Now she will come, and what am I to tell her?" He turns to Cayce. "You disappointed him. He thought that you were her."

"Who?"

"The buyer. Agent for a Japanese collector," the blond boy says to Cayce. "Is not your fault." He has those straight-across cheekbones she thinks of as Slavic, the open look that comes with them, and the sort of accent that comes with learning English here but not yet too thoroughly. "Ngemi," indicating the black man, "is only upset."

"Well then," Cayce ventures, "goodbye." And starts toward Portobello. A middle-aged woman opens a green-painted door and steps out in black leather jeans, her large dog on a lead. The appearance of this Notting Hill matron feels to Cayce as though it frees her from a spell. She quickens her stride.

But hears footsteps behind her. And turns to see the blond boy with his flapping pouch, hurrying to catch up.

The black man is nowhere to be seen.

"I walk with you, please," he says, drawing even with her and smiling, as if delighted to offer her this favor. "My name is Voytek Biroshak."

"Call me Ishmael," she says, walking on.

40

"A girl's name?" Eager and doglike beside her. Some species of weird nerd innocence that somehow she accepts.

"No. It's Cayce."

"Case?"

"Actually," she finds herself explaining, "it should be pronounced 'Casey,' like the last name of the man my mother named me after. But I don't."

"Who is Casey?"

"Edgar Cayce, the Sleeping Prophet of Virginia Beach."

"Why does she, your mother?"

"Because she's a Virginian eccentric. Actually she's always refused to talk about it." Which is true.

"And you are doing here?"

"The market. You?" Still walking.

"Same."

"Who were those men?"

"Ngemi sells to me ZX 81."

"Which is?"

"Sinclair ZX 81. Personal computer, circa 1980. In America, was Timex 1000, same."

"Ngemi's the big one?"

"Dealing in archaic computer, historic calculator, since 1997. Has shop in Bermondsey."

"Your partner?"

"No. Arrange to meet." He lightly slaps the pouch at his side and plastic rattles. "ZX 81."

"But he was here to sell those calculators?"

"The Curta. Wonderful, yes? Ngemi and Hobbs hope for combined sale, Japanese collector. Difficult, Hobbs. Always."

"Another dealer?"

"Mathematician. Brilliant sad man. Crazy for Curta, but cannot afford. Buys and sells."

"Didn't seem very pleasant." Cayce puts her facility with entirely left-field conversations down to her career of actual on-the-street cool-hunting, such as it's been, and as much as she hates to call it that. She's done a bit, too. She's been dropped into neighborhoods like Dogtown, which birthed skateboarding, to explore roots in hope of finding whatever the next thing might be. And she's learned it's largely a matter of being willing to ask the next question. She's met the very Mexican who first wore his baseball cap backward, asking the next question. She's that good. "What does this ZX 81 look like?"

He stops, rummages in his pouch, and produces a rather tragic-looking rectangle of scuffed black plastic, about the size of a videocassette. It has one of those stick-on keypads that somehow actually work, something Cayce knows from the cable boxes in the sort of motel where guests might be expected to try to steal them.

"That's a computer?"

"One K of RAM!"

"One?"

They've come out into a street called Westbourne Grove now, with a sprinkling of trendy retail,

42

and she can see a crowd down at the inter-section with Portobello. "What do you do with them?"

"Is complicated."

"How many do you have?"

"Many."

"Why do you like them?"

"Of historical importance to personal comput-ing," he says seriously, "and to United Kingdom. Why there are so many programmers, here."

"Why is that?"

But he excuses himself, stepping into a narrow laneway where a battered van is being unloaded. Some quick exchange with a large woman in a turquoise raincoat and he is back, tucking two more of the things into his pouch.

Walking on, he explains to her that Sinclair, the British inventor, had a way of getting things right, but also exactly wrong. Foreseeing the market for affordable personal computers, Sinclair decided that what people would want to do with them was to learn programming. The ZX 81, marketed in the United States as the Timex 1000, cost less than the equivalent of a hundred dollars, but required the user to key in programs, tapping away on that little motel keyboard-sticker. This had resulted both in the short market-life of the product and, in Voytek's opinion, twenty years on, in the relative preponderance of skilled programmers in the United Kingdom. They had had their heads turned by these little boxes, he believes, and by the need to program them. "Like hackers in Bulgaria," he adds, obscurely.

"But if Timex sold it in the United States," she asks him, "why didn't we get the programmers?"

"You have programmers, but America is different. America wanted Nintendo. Nintendo gives you no programmers. Also, on launch of product in America, RAM-expansion unit did not ship for three months. People buy computer, take it home, discover it does almost nothing. A disaster."

Cayce is pretty certain that England wanted Nintendo too, and got it, and probably shouldn't be looking too eagerly forward to another bumper crop of programmers, if Voytek's theory holds true. "I need coffee," she says.

He leads her into a ramshackle arcade at the corner of Portobello and Westbourne Grove. Past small booths where Russians are laying out their stocks of spotty old watches, and down a flight of stairs, to buy her a cup of what turns out to be the "white" coffee of her childhood visits to England, a pre-Starbucks mirror-world beverage resembling weak instant bulked up with condensed milk and industrial-strength sugar. It makes her think of her father, leading her through the London Zoo when she was ten.

They sit on folding wooden chairs that look as though they date from the Blitz, taking tentative sips of their scalding white coffee.

But she sees that there is a Michelin Man within her field of vision, its white, bloated, maggot-like form perched on the edge of a dealer's counter, about thirty feet away. It is about two feet tall, and is probably meant to be illuminated from within.

The Michelin Man was the first trademark to which she exhibited a phobic reaction. She had been six.

"He took a duck in the face at two hundred and fifty knots," she recites, softly.

Voytek blinks. "You say?"

"I'm sorry," Cayce says.

It is a mantra.

A friend of her father's, an airline pilot, had told her, in her teens, of a colleague of his who had impacted a duck, on climbout from Sioux City. The windscreen shattered and the inside of the cockpit became a hurricane. The plane landed safely, and the pilot had survived, and returned to flying with shards of glass lodged permanently within his left eye. The story had fascinated Cayce, and eventually she had discovered that this phrase, repeated soon enough, would allay the onset of the panic she invariably felt upon seeing the worst of her triggers. "It's a verbal tic."

"Tick?"

"Hard to explain." She looks in another direction, discovering a stall selling what seem to be Victorian surgical instruments.

The keeper of this stock is a very old man with a high, mottled forehead and dirty-looking white eyebrows, his head sunken buzzard-like between his narrow shoulders. He stands behind a counter topped and fronted with glass, things glittering within it. Most of them seem to be displayed in fitted cases lined with faded velvet. Seeing him as offering a distraction, for both herself and Voytek, else she be asked to explain the duck, Cayce takes her coffee and crosses the aisle, which is floored with splintery planking.

"Could you tell me what this is, please?" she asks, pointing at something at random. He looks at her, at the object indicated, then back at her. "A trepanning set, by Evans of London, circa 1780, in original fishskin case."

"And this?"

"An early nineteenth-century French lithotomy set with bow drill, by Grangeret. Brass-bound mahogany case." He regards her steadily with his deep-set, red-rimmed, pinkish eyes, as if sizing her up for a bit of a go with the Grangeret, a spooky-looking contraption broken down to its component parts in their slots of moth-eaten velvet.

"Thank you," Cayce says, deciding this isn't really the distraction she needs, right now. She turns to Voytek. "Let's get some air." He gets cheerfully up from his seat, shouldering his now-bulging pouch of Sinclairs, and follows her up the stairs and into the street.

Tourists and antiques-fanciers and people-watchers have been steadily arriving from stations in either direction, many of them her countrymen, or Japanese. A crowd dense as a stadium concert is contriving to move in either direction along

Portobello, in the street itself, the sidewalks having been taken up by temporary sellers with trestles and card tables, and by the shoppers clustered around them. The sun has come fully and unexpectedly out, and between the sun and the crowd and the residual wonky affect of soul-delay, she feels suddenly dizzy.

"No good now, for finding," Voytek says, clutching his pouch protectively under his arm. He downs the last of his coffee. "I must be going. Have work."

"What do you do?" she asks, mainly to cover her dizziness.

But he only nods toward the pouch. "I must evaluate condition. Have pleasure in meeting you." He takes something from one of the top front pockets of his jean jacket and hands it to her. It is a scrap of white cardboard with a rubber-stamped e-mail address.

Cayce never has cards, and has always been reluctant to give out particulars. "I don't have a card," she says, but on impulse tells him her current hotmail address, sure he'll forget it. He smiles, goofy and somehow winningly open under his ruler-straight Slavic cheekbones, and turns away into the crowd.

Cayce burns her tongue on her still-scalding coffee. Gets rid of it in an already overflowing bin.

She decides to walk back to that Starbucks near the Notting Hill tube, have a latte made with mirror-world milk, and take the train to Camden.

She's starting to feel like she's really here.

"He took a duck in the face at two hundred and fifty knots," by way this time of an expression of gratitude, and starts back toward Notting Hill station.

CHAPTER 5

WHAT THEY DESERVE

She finds the Children's Crusade just as she remembers it.

Damien's expression for what descends on Camden Town on a Saturday, this shuffling lemming-jam of young people, clogging the High Street from below the station up to Camden Lock.

As she comes up out of the rattling, sighing depths of the station, ascending vertiginous escalators with step grids cut from some pale and grimy heartwood that must be virtually indestructible, the pack starts to thicken and make itself known.

On the sidewalk outside, she is abruptly in it, the crowd stretching away up the High Street like some Victorian engraving of a public hanging or race day.

The facades of the modest retail buildings on either side are encrusted with distorted, oversized representations of vintage airplanes, cowboy boots, a vast six-eyelet Dr. Martens. These all have a slightly queasy handmade quality, as though they've been modeled from carloads of Fimo by the children of giants.

Cayce has spent hours here, escorting the creative executives of the world's leading athletic-shoe companies through the ambulatory forest of the feet that have made their fortunes, and hours more alone, looking for little jolts of pure street fashion to e-mail home.

Nothing at all like the crowd in Portobello; this one is differently driven, flavored with pheromones and the smoke of clove cigarettes and hashish.

Striking a course for the convenient landmark of the Virgin Megastore, she wonders whether she shouldn't go with the flow and try to put herself on another sort of professional footing today. There is cool to be hunted, here, and she still has clients in New York willing to pay for a Cayce Pollard report on what the early adaptors in this crush are doing, wearing, or listening to. She decides against it. She's technically under contract to Blue Ant, and anyway she's feeling less than motivated. Damien's flat feels like a better idea, and she can reach it, with a minimum of jostling, via the fruit and vegetable stalls in Aberdeen Street, where she can lay in additional supplies.

This she does, finding fresher produce than the local supermarket offers, and walking home with a transparent pink bag of oranges from either Spain or Morocco.

Damien's flat has no security system, and she's glad of that, as setting off someone's alarm, be it silent or otherwise, is something she's done in the past and has no desire to do again. Damien's keys are as big and solid and nearly as nicely finished as the chunky pound coins: one for the street door, two for the door into the flat.

When she reenters the place, she has a moment's benchmark as to the extent of her ongoing improvement in affect. Most of her soul must already have arrived, she thinks, remembering her predawn horrors; now it's just Damien's place, or a recently redecorated version of Damien's place, and if anything it makes her miss him. If he weren't off scouting a documentary in Russia, they could ford through the Camden crowd and up Primrose Hill.

Her encounter with Voytek and his friends and their little black calculators from Buchenwald, whatever that might have been, seems like last night's dream.

She locks the door and crosses to the Cube, which sits there blank-screened, its illuminated static switches pulsing softly. Damien has cable, so his service is never really off, or not supposed to be. It's time to check in on Fetish:Footage:Forum and see what Parkaboy and Filmy and Mama Anarchia and her other co-obsessives have made of that kiss. There will be much to catch up on, taking it from the top, getting the drift of things.

Parkaboy is her favorite, on F:F:F. They e-mail when the forum really gets going, and sometimes when it's dead as well. She knows almost nothing about him, other than that he lives in Chicago and, she assumes, is gay. But they know one another's passion for the footage, their doubts and tentative theories, as well as anyone in the world does.

Rather than retype the unbookmarked forum URL, she goes to the browser history.

SEE ASIAN SLUTS GET WHAT THEY DESERVE! FETISH:FOOTAGE:FORUM

She freezes, hand on mouse, looking at this last logged site.

Then she starts to feel it, that literal folkloric prickle in the scalp.

And she can't, through sheer mental effort, make Asian Sluts and F:F:F reverse their order on the screen. She desperately wants Asian Sluts to be below F:F:F, but it stays where it is. She sits there, unmoving, peering at the browser history the way she once peered at a brown recluse spider in a rose garden in Portland, a drab little thing her host reliably informed her contained enough neurotoxin to kill them both, and horribly.

Damien's flat is suddenly not a friendly place, not familiar at all. It has become a sealed and airless territory in which very bad things might happen. And it has, she now remembers, a second floor, to which, this trip, she has not yet even ascended.

She looks up at the ceiling.

And finds herself remembering the experience of lying more or less happily, or at least pleasantly abstracted, beneath a boyfriend named Donny.

Donny had been more problematic than most

other Cayce Pollard boyfriends, and she has come to believe that this had all been signaled in the first place by the fact that he was called Donny. Donny was not something, a woman friend had pointed out, that the men they went out with were usually called. Donny was of Irish-Italian extraction, from East Lansing, and had both a drinking problem and no visible means of support. But Donny was also very beautiful, and sometimes very funny, though not always intentionally, and Cayce had gone through a period of finding herself, though she never really planned to, under Donny, and Donny's big grin, in the none-too-fresh bed in his apartment on Clinton Street, between Rivington and Delancey.

But this final and particular time, watching him phase-shift into what she'd learned to recognize as the run-up to one of his ever-reliable orgasms, she'd for some reason stretched her arms above her head, perhaps even luxuriously, her left hand sliding accidentally under the cockroach-colored veneer of the headboard. Where it encountered something cold and hard and very precisely made. Which she brailled, shortly, into the square butt of an automatic pistol—held there, probably, with tape very similar to the tape she'd used here, this morning, to conceal the hole in her Buzz Rickson's.

Donny, she knew, was left-handed, and had so positioned this so that he could reach it conveniently as he lay in bed.

Some very basic computational module instantly had completed the simplest of equations: if boyfriend sleeps with gun, Cayce does not share bed, or bod, with (now abruptly former) boyfriend.

And so she'd lain there, her fingertip against what she assumed was the checkered hardwood of the gun's grip, and watched Donny take his last ride on that particular pony.

But here, in Camden Town, in Damien's flat, up a narrow flight of stairs, there is a room. It is the room where she's slept on previous visits, and she knows that Damien has now converted it to a home studio, where he indulges his passion for mixing.

Up there, she wonders, now, mightn't there be someone?

The someone who somehow got in here in her absence and idly took a look at those Asian sluts? It seems bizarre, and impossible, and yet horribly, if barely, possible. Or is it all too very possible?

She makes herself look around the room again, and notices the roll of black tape on the carpet. It is upright, as though it had rolled there. And remembers, very clearly, placing it, when she'd finished with it, on its side, so that it wouldn't roll off, on the edge of the trestle table.

Something takes her into the kitchen, then, and she finds herself looking into a drawer containing Damien's kitchen knives. Which are new, and not much used, and probably quite sharp. And, while she is not uncertain that she could defend herself with one of these if required, the idea of introducing sharp edges into the equation seems not entirely a good one. She tries another drawer and finds a square cardboard box of machine parts, heavy-looking and precise and slightly oily, which she assumes are leftovers from the robot girls. One of these, thick and cylindrical, fits neatly and solidly into her hand, squared-off edges just showing at either end of her closed fist. What you can do with a roll of quarters, she remembers, Donny coming in handy after all.

She takes this with her as she mounts the stairs to Damien's home recording studio. Which proves to be just that, and unoccupied, with no hiding places whatever. A futon, narrow and new, that would be her bed if Damien were here.

Back down the stairs.

She goes through the space carefully, holding her breath as she opens both of the two closets. Where there is very little at all, Damien being not a clothes person.

She looks into each of the lower cabinets in the renovated kitchen, and in the space beneath the sink. Where no prowler crouches, but the reno crew have left a big yellow metric measuring tape.

She puts the chain on the locked door to the hallway. It is not much of a chain, by New York standards, and she's lived in New York long enough to put very little trust in chains, regardless. But still.

She examines the windows, all of which are

closed, and all but one of which are so thoroughly painted shut that she estimates it would take a carpenter three very expensive hours and a fair number of tools to open one. The one that has been opened, no doubt by that same expensive carpenter, is presently secured by a pair of mirror-world sash bolts, their hidden tongues to be extended and retracted by a sort of key-like wrench or driver, with an oddly shaped head. She has seen these used in London before, and has no idea where Damien keeps his. Since this can only be done from within, and the glass is intact, she rules out the windows as points of entry.

She looks back at the door.

Someone has a key. Two keys, she remembers, for this door, and possibly a third for the street door.

Damien must have a new girlfriend, someone he hasn't mentioned. Or else an old one, someone who's retained the keys. Or a cleaner perhaps, someone who forgot something and returned for it while Cayce was out.

Then she remembers that the keys are new, the locks having been changed after completion of the renovation, causing hers to have had to be FedExed to New York on the eve of her departure. This by Damien's assistant, the one who'd come in to put the place back together. And she remembers this woman on the phone with her in New York, concerned because the keys she'd just sent off were the only set she had, and apologizing that Damien currently had no housecleaner.

She goes into the bedroom and examines her things. Nothing seems to have been disturbed. She remembers an eerily young Sean Connery, in that first James Bond film, using fine clear Scottish spit to paste one of his gorgeous black hairs across the gap between the jamb and the door of his hotel room. Off to the casino, he will know, upon returning, whether or not his space has been violated.

Too late for that.

She goes into the other room and looks at the Cube, which has gone back to sleep, and at the roll of tape on the carpet. The room is clean and simple, semiotically neutral, Damien having charged his decorators, on threat of dismissal, with the absolute avoidance of shelter magazine chic of any kind.

What else is there, here, that might retain information?

The telephone.

On the table beside the computer.

It is an unusually simple mirror-world telephone, none of the usual bells or whistles. It doesn't even have call-display, Damien viewing such things as time-sinks and needless recomplications.

It does, however, have a redial button.

She picks up the handset and looks at it, as though expecting it to speak.

She presses the redial button. Listens to a

sequence of mirror-world rings. She is waiting for the voice mail at Blue Ant to pick up, or perhaps a weekend receptionist, because she hasn't used this phone since calling them, Friday morning, to confirm that her car was on the way.

"Lasciate un messaggio, risponderò appena possible."

A woman's voice, brisk and impatient.

Tone.

She almost screams. Hangs frantically up.

Leave a message. I will reply as soon as I can.

Dorotea.

CHAPTER 6

THE MATCH FACTORY

"First priority," Cayce tells Damien's flat, hearing her father's voice, "secure the perimeter."

Win Pollard, twenty-five years an evaluator and improver of physical security for American embassies worldwide, had retired to develop and patent humane crowd-control barriers for rock concerts. His idea of a bedtime story had been the quiet, systematic, and intricately detailed recitation of how he'd finally secured the sewer connections at the Moscow embassy.

She looks at the white-painted door and guesses it to be made of oak. Like so many things Victorian, far more solidly built than it ever needed to be. Hinges are on the inside, as they should be, and this means that it swings inward, toward a blank section of wall. She judges the distance between door and wall, then looks at the table.

She gets the yellow tape she'd noticed earlier from beneath the sink, using it to measure the length of the table, then the distance between the closed and chained door and the wall. Eight centimeters to spare, and with the table in position, lengthwise, between door and wall, it will require either a fire ax or explosives to get into the flat.

She transfers the telephone, cable modem, keyboard, speakers and Studio Display monitor to the carpet, without disconnecting them or shutting the Cube down. The screen wakes when she does this and she sees Asian Sluts still there, same position. When she moves the Cube itself, her hand accidentally covers its static switch. It powers off. She touches the spot to reboot and turns to the table, the top of which lifts easily off the two trestles. It's heavy and solid, but Cayce is one of those slight-looking women who combine considerable wiry strength with low body weight. This had made her, in college, a much better rock climber than her psychologist boyfriend, to his ongoing and increasing annoyance. She would invariably reach the top first, never intentionally, and always by a more challenging route.

She props the tabletop against the wall, beside the door, and goes back for the trestles. Returning with them, one in either hand, she positions them, then picks up the tabletop and lowers it, careful not to scuff Damien's freshly painted wall. Unchains and unlocks the door, opening it the eight centimeters the table now allows. This proves to be not even enough to produce a gap to peer through. Perimeter secured, she closes the door, relocking and chaining it.

She sees that the Cube is showing her that it wasn't properly shut down, so she kneels beside it and clicks that that's okay. When she gets to the desktop, she reopens the browser and looks at the memory again, seeing that Asian Sluts still hasn't moved itself.

Seeing it there, this time, causes her a residual hair-prickle, but she gets past that by forcing herself to open it. To her considerable and unexpected relief, it turns out not to be snuff or torture or even anything singularly nasty. What these women deserve, evidently, is active attention from erect penises. These being, in that way of visual porn for men, weirdly disembodied, as though one were to imagine they had arrived at the brink of a particular orifice through no individual human agency whatever. When she exits, she has to click her way past an opportunistic swarm of linked sites, and some of these, in split-second glances, look considerably worse than Asian Sluts.

Now, in browser memory, F:F:F is followed twice by Asian Sluts, as if to prove a point.

She's trying to remember what would have come after securing the perimeter, in Win's bedtime stories. Probably maintaining the routine of the station. Psychological prophylaxis, she thinks he called it. Get on with ordinary business. Maintain morale. How many times has she turned to that, in the past year or so?

Hard to know what that would consist of, here and now, but then she thinks of F:F:F and the frenzy of posts the new footage will have generated. She'll make a pot of tea-sub, cut up an orange, sit cross-legged on Damien's carpet, and see what's going on. Then she'll decide what she should do about Asian Sluts and Dorotea Benedetti.

Not the first time she's used F:F:F that way. She wonders, really, if she ever uses it any other way. It is the gift of "OT," Off Topic. Anything other than the footage is Off Topic. The world, really. News. Off Topic.

In the kitchen, boiling water, she drifts back to her father's bedtime descriptions of that perimeter-containment job in Moscow.

She'd always secretly wanted the KGB spy devices to make it through, because she'd only ever been able to envision them as tiny clock-work brass submarines, as intricate in their way as Fabergé eggs. She'd imagined them evading each of Win's snares, one by one, and surfacing in the bowls of staff toilets, tiny gears buzzing. But this had made her feel guilty, because it was Win's job, and his passion, to keep them from doing that. And she'd never been able to imagine exactly what it was they were there to do, or what they'd need to do next in order to get on with it.

Damien's kettle starts to whistle. She takes it off the burner and fills the pot.

Settled in picnic mode before the Cube, she opens F:F:F and sees that the posts have indeed been flying. But also, to a certain extent, that the shit has been hitting the fan.

Parkaboy and Mama Anarchia are flaming one another again.

Parkaboy is de facto spokesperson for the Progressives, those who assume that the footage consists of fragments of a work in progress, something unfinished and still being generated by its maker.

The Completists, on the other hand, a relative but articulate minority, are convinced that the footage is comprised of snippets from a finished work, one whose maker chooses to expose it piecemeal and in nonsequential order. Mama Anarchia is the consummate Completist.

The implications of this, for some F:F:F regulars, border on the theological, but it's fairly simple for Cayce: If the footage consists of clips from a finished film, of whatever length, every footagehead, for whatever reason, is being toyed with, unmercifully teased, in one of the most annoying fashions ever devised.

The Ur-footageheads who discovered and connected the earliest known fragments had of course to entertain the Completist possibility. When there were five fragments, or a dozen, it seemed more easily possible that these might be parts of some relatively short work, perhaps a student effort, however weirdly polished and strangely compelling. But as the number of downloads grew, and the mystery of their common origin deepened, many chose to believe that they were being shown these bits of a work in progress, and possibly in the order in which they were being completed. And, whether you held that the footage was mainly live action or largely computer-generated, the evident production values had come increasingly to argue against the idea of a student effort, or indeed of anything amateur in the usual sense. The footage was simply too remarkable.

It had been Parkaboy, shortly after Ivy had started the site from her Seoul apartment, who had first raised the possibility of what he called "the Garage Kubrick." This was not a concept that argued from either a Completist or Progressive position, necessarily, with Mama Anarchia herself quite contentedly using the term today, even though she knows that it originated with Parkaboy. It is simply a part of the discourse, and a central one: that it is possible that this footage is generated single-handedly by some technologically empowered solo auteur, some guerilla creator out there alone in the night of the Internet. That it might be being generated via some sort of CGI, actors, sets and all, and entirely at the virtual hand of some secretive and perhaps unknown genius, has become a widespread obsession with a large faction of Progressives, and with many Completists as well, though the Completists necessarily put that in past tense.

But here is Parkaboy railing on about Mama Anarchia's tendency to quote Baudrillard and the other Frenchmen who annoy him so deeply, and Cayce automatically hits Respond and gives him her boilerplate oil-upon-the-waters copy:

This always happens when we forget that this site is only here because Ivy is willing to expend the time and energy to keep it here, and neither Ivy nor most of the rest of us enjoy it when you or anyone else starts yelling. Ivy is our host, we should try to keep this a pleasant place for her, and we shouldn't take it too much for granted that F:F:F will always be here.

She clicks on Post and watches her name and message title appear under his:

CayceP and Keep your shirt on.

Because Parkaboy is her friend, she can get away with this where someone else couldn't. She has become a sort of ritual referee charged specifically with flagging down Parkaboy whenever he goes off on anyone, as he's definitely inclined to do. Ivy can whip him into shape pronto, but Ivy is a policewoman in Seoul, works long shifts, and can't always be on the site to moderate.

She automatically clicks Reload, and his response is already there:

Where are you? nt.
    London. Working. nt.

And all of this is hugely comforting. Psychological prophylaxis, evidently.

The phone rings, beside the Cube, mirror-world rings she finds unnerving at the best of times. She hesitates, then answers.

"Hello?"

"Cayce dear. It's Bernard." Stonestreet. "Helena and I were wondering if you'd be up for a little dinner."

"Thank you, Bernard." Looking at the trestle table blocking the door. "But I'm feeling unwell."

"Jet lag. You can try Helena's little pills."

"It's kind of you, Bernard, but—"

"Hubertus will be here. He'll be horribly disappointed if he doesn't have a chance to see you."

"Aren't we meeting Monday?"

"He's in New York tomorrow evening. Can't be here for our meeting. Say you'll come."

This is one of those conversations in which Cayce feels that the British have evolved passive-aggressive leverage in much the way they've evolved irony. She has no way of securing the perimeter, here, once she leaves the flat, but this Blue Ant contract represents a good quarter of her anticipated year's gross.

"PMS, Bernard. Not to put it too delicately."

"Then you absolutely have to come. Helena has something completely marvelous, for that."

"Have you tried it?"

"Tried what?"

She gives up. Company, of almost any kind, seems not entirely a bad idea. "Where are you?"

"Docklands. Seven. It's casual. I'll send a car.

Delighted you can come. Bye." Stonestreet rings off with an abruptness Cayce suspects has required some learning in New York. There is ordinarily a singsong, almost tender cadence to the mirror-world termination of telephone conversations, a call-and-response of farewell she's never mastered.

Psychological prophylaxis is shot to hell.

Three minutes later, having Googled "North London locksmith," she's on the phone with a man at something called Judge Advocate Locks.

"You don't work on Saturdays," she opens, hopefully.

"Seven days a week, twenty-four hours a day."

"But you wouldn't be able to get here before this evening, would you?"

"Where are you?"

She tells him.

"Fifteen minutes," he says.

"You don't take Visa."

"We do."

As she hangs up, she realizes that she's lost Dorotea's number by making this call. Not that she would necessarily have been able to extract it from the phone, but it was the closest thing she had to evidence of the entire episode, other than Asian Sluts on the browser memory. She presses Redial, just to check, and gets the man at Judge Advocate. "Sorry," she says, "hit Redial by mistake."

"Fourteen minutes," he says, defensive now, and the truck arrives in more like twelve.

An hour later, Damien's door has two entirely

new and very expensive German locks, with keys that look like something you might find if you took apart a very up-to-date automatic pistol. The Cube is back on the table in its accustomed place. She didn't change the lock on the street door because she doesn't know Damien's tenants, or even how many there are.

Dinner with Bigend. She groans, and goes to change.

The car and driver from Blue Ant are waiting when she exits the street door, the two new keys on a black shoestring around her neck. She's hidden the set of spares behind one of Damien's mixing consoles in the upstairs room.

Evening now, a light rain just beginning to fall.

She thinks of it thinning the Children's Crusade still further, under the giant Fimo boots and aeroplanes and the streetlamps mounted with surveillance cameras.

Settled in the car's rear seat, she asks the driver, a slender and immaculate African, for the name of the station nearest their destination.

"Bow Road," he says, but she doesn't know it.

She looks at the back of his meticulously shorn head, at the niobium stud in the upper curve of his right ear, then out at passing shop fronts and restaurants.

Stonestreet's "casual" will translate as relatively dressy, by her standards, so she's opted for the CPU Damien calls Skirt Thing, a long, narrow, anonymously made tube of black jersey, with only the most minimal hemming at either end. Tight but comfortable, rides the hips well, infinitely adjustable in terms of length. Under this, black hose; over it, a black DKNY cardigan un-Dikini-ed with a pair of nail scissors. New-old-stock pumps from a vintage place in Paris.

And finds herself thinking wistfully of racketing along in the Metro, and of the impossibly great way Parisian women have of wearing scarves. She decides that this is either another sign of serotonin normalization, daydreaming of another place, or a get-the-hell-out-of-Dodge reaction to Asian Sluts on the browser.

This increasingly massive and entirely unre-solved issue she now has with Dorotea, someone she'd scarcely known existed. She's searched her memory for any way in which she might previously have earned this woman's enmity, but has found nothing.

She is not much in the business of making enemies, although the quieter side of her profession, the sort of yea-or-nay evaluation Blue Ant is currently paying her for, can be problematic. A nay can cost a company a contract, or an employee (once, an entire department) a job. The rest of it, the actual running to earth of street fashion, the occasional lectures to intent platoons of executives, generates remarkably little ill will.

A red double-decker grinds past, registering less

as mirror-world than as some Disney prop for Londonland.

On a wall she spies freshly shingled copies of a still from the new fragment. It is the kiss. Already.

In New York, once, on an uptown train in rush hour, during the anthrax scares, as she'd mentally recited the duck mantra, she'd found herself looking at a still no bigger than a business card, frame-grabbed and safety-pinned, from a fragment she'd not yet seen, on the green polyester uniform blazer of a weary-looking black woman. Cayce had been using the mantra to ward off a recurring fantasy: that they would drop light bulbs full of the very purest stuff on the subway tracks, where, as she too well remembered Win once having told her, it would take only a few hours, as the Army had evidently proven in experiments in the 1960s, to drift from Fourteenth to Fifty-ninth Street.

The black woman, seeing her notice the little still, had nodded, recognizing a fellow follower, and Cayce had been rescued from inner darkness by this suggestion of just how many people might be following the footage, and just how oddly invisible a phenomenon that was.

There are many more, now, in spite of a general and in her opinion entirely welcome lack of attention from the major media. Whenever the media do try to pick it up, it slides like a lone noodle from their chopsticks. It comes in mothlike, under radar evolved to detect things with massive airframes: a species of ghost, or "black guest" perhaps (as

70

Damien had once explained hackers and their more autonomous creations are known in China).

Shows dealing with lifestyles and popular culture, or with minor mysteries made to seem major, have aired the story, along with dubiously assembled sequences of fragments, but these elicited no viewer response whatever (except on F:F:F, of course, where the assemblages are ripped to shreds amid lengthy and passionate protestations of just how clueless it is to put, say, #23 before #58). Footageheads seem to propagate primarily by word of mouth, or, as with Cayce, by virtue of random exposure, either to a fragment of video or to a single still frame.

Cayce's first footage had been waiting for her as she'd emerged from the flooded all-genders toilet at a NoLiTa gallery party, that previous November. Wondering what she could do to sterilize the soles of her shoes, and reminding herself never to touch them again, she'd noticed two people huddled on either side of a third, a turtlenecked man with a portable DVD player, held before him in the way that crèche figures of the Three Kings hold their gifts.

And passing these three she'd seen a face there, on the screen of his ciborium. She'd stopped without thinking and done that stupid duck dance, trying to better align retina to pixel.

"What is that?" she'd asked. A sideways look from a girl with hooded eyes, a sharp and avian nose, round steel labret stud gleaming from beneath her lower lip. "Footage," this one had said, and for Cayce it had started there.

She'd left the gallery with the URL for a site that offered all of the footage accumulated to that point.

Ahead, now, in the wet evening light, a twirling blue pulse, as of something meant to warn of whirlpools, vortices . . .

They are in some larger thoroughfare, multi-lane traffic verging on gridlock. The Blue Ant car slowing, halting, locked in from behind, then edging forward.

As they pass the scene of the accident Cayce sees a bright yellow motorcycle on its side, front forks twisted strangely. The whirling blue light is mounted on a slender mast, rising from a larger, obviously official motorcycle parked nearby, and she sees that this is an emergency medical response vehicle, an entirely mirror-world concept, able to edge through the densest traffic to an accident site.

The bike medic, in a Belstaff jacket with huge reflective stripes, is kneeling above the fallen rider, whose helmet is on the pavement beside him and whose neck is immobilized in a foam collar. The medic is giving the man oxygen with a mask and bottle, and now Cayce realizes she can hear the insistent hooting, from somewhere behind, of a mirror-world ambulance. And for an instant she sees that unconscious, unmarked face its lower half obscured by the transparent mask, the evening's rain falling on closed eyes. And knows that this stranger may now inhabit the most liminal place of all, poised perhaps on the brink of nonexistence, or about to enter some existence unimagined.

She cannot see what hit him, or what he might have hit. Or else the street itself had risen up, to smite him. It is not only those things we most fear that do that, she reminds herself.

"It was a match factory," Stonestreet says, having greeted her and ushered her into two stories of lofted open plan, dark gleaming hardwood stretching to a wall of glass that opens on a full-length balcony. Candlelight. "We're looking for something else." He's wearing a black cotton dress shirt, its French cuffs unlinked and flapping. The at home version of that new but slept-in look, she supposes. "It's not Tribeca."

No, it's not, she thinks, neither in square footage nor in volumes of space.

"Hub's on the deck. Just arrived. Drink?"

"'Hub'?"

"Been in Houston." Stonestreet winks.

"Bet it would be 'Hube' if they had their druthers." Hube Bigend. Lombard.

Cayce's dislike of Bigend is indeed personal, albeit secondhand, a friend having been involved with the man in New York, back in, as the kids had recently quit saying, the day. Margot, the friend, from Melbourne, had always referred to him as "a Lombard," which Cayce had at first thought might be a reference somehow to his Belgian-ness, until learning, upon finally asking, that it was Margot's

73

acronym for "Loads of money but a real dickhead." As things had progressed between them, mere Lombardhood had scarcely covered it.

Stonestreet, at the wet bar sculpted into a corner of the kitchen's granite island, passes her, at her request, a tall glass of ice and fizzy water, garnished with a twist of lemon.

On the wall to her left is a triptych by a Japanese artist whose name she forgets, three four-by-eight panels of plywood hung side by side. On these have been silk-screened, in layers, logos and big-eyed manga girls, but each successive layer of paint has been sanded to ghostly translucency, varnished, then overlaid with others, which have in turn been sanded, varnished . . . The result for Cayce being very soft, deep, almost soothing, but with the uneasy hallucinatory suggestion of panic about to break through.

She turns, and sees Bigend through glass leading to a balcony, hands on the rain-slick railing, his back to her, in some sort of raincoat and what seems to be a cowboy hat.

"How do you think we look," Bigend asks, "to the future?" He looks as though he's somehow, in spite of the evening's cunningly vegan cuisine, been infused with live extract of hot beef. He's florid, glossy, bright-eyed, very likely bushy-tailed as well. The dinner conversation has been mercifully uneventful, with no mention of Dorotea or Blue Ant, and for this Cayce is grateful.

Helena, Stonestreet's wife, has been lecturing them about the uses, even today, in cosmetics, of reprocessed bovine neurological material, having gotten there via a discussion, over her stuffed eggplant, of spongiform encephalopathy as the price of forcing herbivores into an apocalyptically unnatural cannibalism.

Bigend has a way of injecting these questions into conversations that he's grown tired of. Caltrops thrown down on the conversational highway; you can swerve or you can hit them, blow your tires, hope you'll keep going on the rims. He's been doing it through dinner and their pre-dinner drinks, and Cayce assumes he does it because he's the boss, and perhaps because he really does bore easily. It's like watching someone restlessly change channels, no more mercy to it than that.

"They won't think of us," Cayce says, choosing straight into it. "Any more than we think of the Victorians. I don't mean the icons, but the ordinary actual living souls."

"I think they'll hate us," says Helena, only her gorgeous eyes visible now above her nightmares of BSE and a spongiform future. She looks, for just that instant, as though she's still in character as the emotionally conflicted deprogrammer of abductees on *Ark/Hive* 7's lone season, Cayce having once watched a single episode in order to see a friend's actor boyfriend in a walk-on as a morgue attendant.

"Souls," repeats Bigend, evidently not having

75

heard Helena, his blue eyes widening for Cayce's benefit. He has less accent of any kind than she can recall having heard before in any speaker of English. It's unnerving. It makes him sound somehow directionless, like a loudspeaker in a departure lounge, though it has nothing to do with volume. "Souls?"

Cayce looks at him and carefully chews a mouthful of stuffed egg-plant.

"Of course," he says, "we have no idea, now, of who or what the inhabitants of our future might be. In that sense, we have no future. Not in the sense that our grandparents had a future, or thought they did. Fully imagined cultural futures were the luxury of another day, one in which 'now' was of some greater duration. For us, of course, things can change so abruptly, so violently, so profoundly, that futures like our grandparents' have insufficient 'now' to stand on. We have no future because our present is too volatile." He smiles, a version of Tom Cruise with too many teeth, and longer, but still very white. "We have only risk management. The spinning of the given moment's scenarios. Pattern recognition."

Cayce blinks.

"Do we have a past, then?" Stonestreet asks.

"History is a best-guess narrative about what happened and when," Bigend says, his eyes narrowing. "Who did what to whom. With what. Who won. Who lost. Who mutated. Who became extinct."

"The future is there," Cayce hears herself say, "looking back at us. Trying to make sense of the fiction we will have become. And from where they are, the past behind us will look nothing at all like the past we imagine behind us now."

"You sound oracular." White teeth.

"I only know that the one constant in history is change: The past changes. Our version of the past will interest the future to about the extent we're interested in whatever past the Victorians believed in. It simply won't seem very relevant." What she's actually doing here is channeling Parkaboy from memory, a thread with Filmy and Maurice, arguing over whether or not the footage is intended to convey any particular sense of period, or whether the apparently careful lack of period markers might suggest some attitude, on the maker's part, to time and history, and if so, what?

Now it's Bigend's turn to chew, silently, looking at her very seriously.

He drives a maroon Hummer with Belgian plates, wheel on the left. Not the full-on uber-vehicle like a Jeep with glandular problems, but some newer, smaller version that still manages to look no kinder, no gentler. It's almost as uncomfortable as the bigger ones, though the seats are upholstered with glove-soft skin. What she'd liked, all she'd liked, about the big ones had been the huge transmission hump, broad as a horse's back, separating driver from passenger, but of course their affect had changed entirely, once the actual original Humvee had become a fixture on the streets of New York.

Never her idea of a date vehicle, your old-school civvie Hummer, and this little one has her closer to Bigend, who's placed his chocolate-brown Stetson on the down-scaled hump between them. Mirror-world traffic has her foot foolishly working a phantom brake, as though she, seated on the British driver's side, should be doing the driving. She clutches her East German envelope, in her lap, and tries not to do that.

Bigend's made it plain that he won't think of her taking a cab (though neither, apparently, would he think of resummoning the Blue Ant car and its natty driver) nor will he countenance her suggestion of the tender mercies of the Bow Street tube. Trains do not arrive at Camden Town, this time on a Saturday, he explains; they only depart, the better to thin the ranks of the Children's Crusade. She remembers now that she knew this, vaguely, herself, though imagining the logistics of it, now, after a glass or two too many of Stonestreet's wine, defeats her. How can trains depart without first having arrived?

The rain is done, the air clear as glass.

She spots a cluster of signage denoting things Smithfield as they whip through a roundabout, and thinks that they are near the market.

"We'll have a drink," Hubertus Bigend says, "in Clerkenwell."

CHAPTER 7

THE PROPOSITION

H e parks the Hummer on a well-lit thoroughfare in what is apparently Clerkenwell, nothing much to distinguish any very individual 'hoodness to Cayce. Street level is routine London retail and services, but the buildings themselves have the look of retrofitted residency, possibly of a more Tribeca-like sort than Stonestreet's match factory.

He opens the glove compartment and removes a rectangular sheet of thick glossy plastic that unfolds to approximately the size of a mirror-world license plate. She sees "EU" there, a British lion, and what seems to be a license number, as he places this, open and face-up, on the dash.

"Permission to park," he explains, and when she gets out she sees that they are parked against a double-lined, yellow-painted curb. Exactly how well connected is Bigend, here? she wonders.

Putting on his dark brown Stetson, he clicks his key, and the Hummer's lights flash, go dark, flash again, and a brief, truncated lowing issues forth as the vehicle comes to full alert. She wonders if it gets touched a lot, looking like a giant's Matchbox toy. Whether it allows that.

Then walking with him toward what is obviously their destination, a bar-restaurant retrofitted to look as little as possible like a pub, and whose lighting reminds her, as they approach its windows and the thump of bass, of the color of spent flashbulbs, fried steel wool through smoked glass.

"Bernard has always said you were very good." His voice reminds her of touring a museum with those earphones on. Strangely compelling.

"Thank you." As they enter the place, her eye-blink take on the crowd is about white powder, the old-fashioned kind.

But yes, she remembers these too-bright smiles, eyes flashing flat as glass.

Bigend obtains a table instantly, something she assumes not everyone could do under the circumstances, and she recalls that her friend in New York had initially cited this as one of the counterbalances to his Lombardhood: no waiting. Cayce assumes this is not because he's known here, but because of some attitudinal tattoo, something people can read. He's wearing a cowboy hat, a fawn waterproof of archaic hunting cut, gray flannels, and a pair of Tony Lama boots—so they probably aren't reacting to a fashion message.

A waitress takes their orders, Cayce's a Holsten Pils, Bigend's a kir. Cayce looks at him across two feet of circular table and a tiny oil lamp with a floating wick. He removes his hat, looking in that instant quite suddenly and remarkably Belgian, as though the Stetson should be a fedora of some kind.

Their drinks arrive, and he pays with a crisp twenty-pound note extracted from a broad wallet stuffed mainly with unreal-looking high-denomination euros.

The waitress pours Cayce's beer and Bigend leaves the change on the table.

"Are you tired?" he asks.

"Jet lag." Automatically returning Bigend's toast, lager clinking kir.

"It shrinks the frontal lobes. Physically. Did you know that? Clearly visible on a scan."

Cayce swallows some beer, winces. "No," she says, "it's because the soul travels more slowly, and arrives late."

"You mentioned souls earlier."

"Did I?" She can't remember.

"Yes. Do you believe in them?"

"I don't know."

"Neither do I." He sips. "You don't get along with Dorotea?"

"Who told you that?"

"Bernard felt you didn't. She can be very difficult."

Cayce is suddenly aware of her East German plastic envelope, where it rests beneath the table, across her thighs; its weight unaccustomed, uneven, because she's tucked her solid little bit of

81

robot girl knuckleduster in there, against she knows not what possibility.

"Can she?"

"Of course. If she feels that you are about to have something she has long coveted." Bigend's teeth seem to have multiplied, or metastasized perhaps. His lips, wet with the kir, are very red in this light. He shakes his dark forelock away from his eyes. She is on full sexual alert now, Bigend's ambiguity having finally gotten to her. Is this all about that, then? Does Dorotea see her as a sexual competitor? Is she in the sights of Bigend's desire, which she knows, from her friend Margot's stories in New York, to be at once constant and ever-shifting?

"I don't think I follow you, Hubertus."

"The London office. She thinks I am going to hire you to run the London office."

"That's absurd." And it is, huge relief, as Cayce is not someone you hire to run an agency in London. Not someone you hire to run anything. She is hyper-specialized, a freelancer, someone contracted to do a very specific job. She has seldom had a salary. She is entirely a creature of fees, adamantly short-term, no managerial skills whatever. But mainly she's relieved if it isn't sexual. Or at least that he seems to have indicated that it isn't. She feels herself held by those eyes, against all conscious will. Progressively locked into something.

Bigend's hand comes up with his glass, and he finishes his kir. "She knows that I'm very interested in you. She wants to work for Blue Ant, and she coverts Bernard's position. She's been angling to leave H and P since well before they made her our liaison."

"I can't see it," Cayce says, meaning replacing Stonestreet with Dorotea. "She's not exactly a people person." An insane bitch, actually. Burner of jackets and burglar of apartments.

"No, of course not. She'd be a complete disaster. And I've been delighted with Bernard since the day I hired him. Dorotea may be one of those people who aren't going to make it through."

"Through what?"

"This business of ours is narrowing. Like many others. There will be fewer genuine players. It's no longer enough to simply look the part and cultivate an attitude."

Cayce has imagined something like this herself, and indeed has been wondering whether she's likely to make it through the narrowing, into whatever waits on the other side.

"You're smart enough," he says. "You can't doubt it."

She'll take a page from his book, then. Caltrop time. "Why are you rebranding the world's second-largest manufacturer of athletic shoes? Was it your idea or theirs?"

"I don't work that way. The client and I engage in a dialogue. A path emerges. It isn't about the imposition of creative will." He's looking at her very seriously now, and to her embarrassment she feels herself shiver. She hopes he didn't notice. If Bigend can convince himself that he doesn't impose his will on others, he must be capable of convincing himself of anything. "It's about contingency. I help the client go where things are already going. Do you want to know the most interesting thing about Dorotea?"

"What?"

"She once worked for a very specialized consultancy, in Paris. Founded by a retired and very senior French intelligence type who'd done a lot of that sort of work on his government's behalf, in Germany and the United States."

"She's . . . a spy?"

"'Industrial espionage,' though that's sounding increasingly archaic, isn't it? I suppose she may still know whom to call, to have certain things done, but I wouldn't call her a spy. What interested me, though, was how that business seemed in some ways to be the inverse of ours."

"Of advertising?"

"Yes. I want to make the public aware of something they don't quite yet know that they know—or have them feel that way. Because they'll move on that, do you understand? They'll think they've thought of it first. It's about transferring information, but at the same time about a certain lack of specificity."

Cayce tries to put this together with what she's seen of Blue Ant campaigns. It makes a degree of sense.

"I imagined," he continues, "that the sort of business Dorotea had been involved in would be about absolutely specific information."

"And was it?"

"Sometimes, yes, but just as often it was simply 'black PR.' Painting the competition with the ugly-brush. It wasn't really very interesting."

"But you were considering her for a position?"

"Yes, though not one she would have chosen for herself. But now we've made it clear we aren't interested. If she thinks that you may get the position she wanted, she could be very angry."

What's he trying to tell her? Should she tell him about the jacket, about Asian Sluts? No. She doesn't trust him, not at all.

Dorotea as corporate spook? Bigend as someone who'd be interested in someone like that? Or who claimed he'd been interested. Or claimed he wasn't still interested. None of it might be true.

"Well," Bigend says, leaning slightly forward, "let's hear it."

"Hear what?"

"The kiss. What you think about it."

Cayce instantly knows what kiss he's talking about, but the contextual shift required to reframe Bigend as a footagehead is so peculiar, so vast a rotation, that she can only sit there, feeling her diaphragm responding slightly to the bottom end of the music—which until an instant ago she'd ceased entirely to be aware of. Someone, a woman, laughs brightly at another table.

"What kiss?" Reflex.

Bigend responds by reaching inside the raincoat he hasn't taken off and pulling out a dapper-looking matte-silver cigarette case, which when he places it on the table becomes a titanium DVD player that opens as of its own accord, a touch of his fingertip calling up segment #135. She watches the kiss, looks up at Bigend. "That kiss," he says.

"What's your question, exactly?" Stalling for time.

"I want to know how significant you think it is, in terms of previous uploads."

"Since we can only speculate about its position in a hypothetical narrative, how can we judge its relative significance?"

He turns the player off, closes it.

"That's not my question. I'm not asking vis-à-vis segments of a narrative, but in terms of the actual sequential order of uploaded segments."

Cayce isn't used to thinking of the footage in those terms, although she recognizes them. She thinks she knows where Bigend is probably heading with this, but opts to play dumb. "But they clearly aren't in a logical narrative sequence. Either they're uploaded randomly—"

"Or very carefully, intending to provide the illusion of randomness. Regardless, and regardless of everything else, the footage has already been the single most effective piece of guerilla marketing ever. I've been tracking hits on enthusiast sites, and searching for mentions elsewhere. The numbers are amazing. Your friend in Korea—"

"How do you know about that?"

"I've had people look at all the sites. In fact we monitor them on a constant basis. Your contributions are some of the more useful material we've come across. 'CayceP,' when you start to know the players, is obviously you. Your interest in the footage is therefore a matter of public record, and to be interested, in this case, is to be involved to whatever extent in a subculture."

The idea that Bigend, or his employees, have been lurking on F:F:F will take some getting used to. The site had come to feel like a second home, but she'd always known that it was also a fishbowl; it felt like a friend's living room, but it was a sort of text-based broadcast, available in its entirety to anyone who cared to access it.

"Hubertus," carefully, "what exactly is the nature of your interest in this?"

Bigend smiles. He should learn not to do that, she thinks, otherwise he was undeniably good-looking. Or perhaps there were oral surgeons capable of artful downsizing? "Am I a true believer? That is your first question. Because you are one yourself. You care passionately about this thing. It's completely evident in your posts. That is what makes you so valuable. That and your talents, your allergies, your tame pathologies, the things that make you a secret legend in the world of marketing. But am I a believer? My passion is marketing, advertising, media strategy, and when I first discovered the footage, that is what responded in me. I saw attention focused daily on a product that may not even exist. You think that wouldn't get my attention? The most brilliant marketing ploy of this very young century. And new. Somehow entirely new."

She concentrates on bubbles rising through her almost untouched Pils. Trying to remember everything she's ever heard or Googled about Bigend's origins, the rise of Blue Ant: the industrialist father in Brussels, summers in the family's villa at Cannes, the archaic but well-connected British boarding school, Harvard, the foray into independent production in Hollywood, some sort of brief self-finding hiatus in Brazil, the emergence of Blue Ant, first in Europe, then in the UK and New York.

The stuff of lifestyle pieces, many of which she's read. And Margot's experience, which Cayce had shared, secondhand but real time, all this having to dovetail now with the knowledge that Bigend is himself some sort of follower of the footage, for what reason she can only guess. Though she finds that she is starting to guess, and doesn't like it.

She looks up. "You think it's worth a lot of money."

Bigend looks at her with absolute seriousness. "I don't count things in money. I count them in excellence."

And somehow she believes him, though it's no comfort.

"Hubertus, what are you getting at? I'm contracted to Blue Ant to evaluate a logo design. Not to discuss the footage."

"We're being social." And that's an order.

"No we're not. I'm not sure that you ever are."

Bigend smiles, then, a smile she hasn't seen before, less teeth and perhaps more genuine. It is a smile she suspects is meant to indicate that she has made it across at least the first moat of his persona, has become to some extent an insider. That she knows a realer Bigend: lateral-thinking imp of the perverse, thirty-something boy genius, seeker after truth (or at least functionality) in the markets of this young century. This is the Bigend that invariably emerges in the articles, no doubt after he's gotten to the journalist with this smile and his other tools. "I want you to find him."

"Him."

"The maker."

"'Her'? 'Them'?"

"The maker. Whatever you need will be put at your disposal. You will not be working for Blue Ant. We will be partners."

"Why?"

"Because I want to know. Don't you?"

Yes. "Have you considered that if we find 'him,' we might interrupt the process?"

"We don't have to tell her she's been found, do we?"

She starts to speak, then realizes she has no idea what she's about to say.

"Do you imagine that no one else is looking? Far more creativity, today, goes into the marketing of products than into the products themselves, athletic shoes or feature films. That is why I founded Blue Ant: that one simple recognition. In that regard alone, the footage is a work of proven genius."

Bigend drives her back to Camden Town, or rather in that direction, because at some point she realizes he's gone past Parkway and is switch-backing up the streets of what she recognizes as Primrose Hill, the closest thing London has to a mountain. Blue plaque territory, although the only name she remembers from walking here with Damien is Sylvia Plath's. A more upscale area than Camden. She'd had friends who'd lived here, once, and had sold their attic flat for enough to buy an Arts and Crafts in Santa Monica, a few blocks from Frank Geary.

She isn't feeling easy with any of this. She doesn't know quite what to do with Bigend's proposition, which has kicked her into one of those modes that her therapist, when last she had one, would lump under the rubric of "old behaviors." It consisted of saying no, but somehow not quite forcefully enough, and then continuing to listen. With the result that her "no" could be gradually chipped away at, and turned into a "yes" before she herself was consciously aware that this was happening. She had thought she had been getting much better around this, but now she feels it happening again.

Bigend, a formidable practitioner of the other side of this dance, seems genuinely incapable of imagining that others wouldn't want to do whatever it is that he wants them to. Margot had cited this as both the most problematic and, she admitted, most effective aspect of his sexuality: He approached every partner as though they already had slept together. Just as, Cayce was now finding, in business, every Bigend deal was treated as a done deal, signed and sealed. If you hadn't signed with Bigend, he made you feel as though you had, but somehow had forgotten that you had.

There was something amorphous, foglike, about his will: It spread out around you, tenuous, almost invisible; you found yourself moving, mysteriously, in directions other than your own.

"You've seen the guerilla re-edit of the most recent Lucas?" The Hummer rounds a corner set with a pub of such quintessential pub-ness that she assumes it is only a few weeks old, or else recently reconfigured to attract a clientele its original builders could scarcely have comprehended. A terrifyingly perfect simulacrum, its bull's-eye panes buffed to an optical clarity. Glimpsing, inside, a red-haired woman in a green sweater, open-mouthed, raising a glass in apparent joyous toast. Then gone, the Hummer galloping up a short and darker stretch of residential, then another corner. "They seem particularly to pick on him. One day we'll need archaeologists to help us guess the original storylines of even classic films." Another corner, tight. "Musicians, today, if they're clever, put new compositions out on the web, like pies set to cool on a window ledge, and wait for other people to anonymously rework them. Ten will be all wrong, but the eleventh may be genius. And free. It's as though the creative process is no longer contained within an individual skull, if indeed it ever was. Everything, today, is to some extent the reflection of something else."

"Is the footage?" She can't help herself.

"That's the question, isn't it? The maker has been positioned, via the strategy, outside of that. You can assemble the segments, but you can't reassemble them."

"Not at this point. But if he ever assembles them, then they can be reassembled."

"'He'?"

"The maker." She shrugged.

"You believe that the segments are parts of a whole?"

"Yes." Zero hesitation.

"Why?"

"It doesn't feel so much like a leap of faith as something I know in my heart." Strange to hear herself say this, but it's the truth.

"The heart is a muscle," Bigend corrects. "You 'know' in your limbic brain. The seat of instinct. The mammalian brain. Deeper, wider, beyond logic. That is where advertising works, not in the upstart cortex. What we think of as 'mind' is only a sort of jumped-up gland, piggybacking on the reptilian brainstem and the older, mammalian mind, but our culture tricks us into recognizing it as all of consciousness. The mammalian spreads continent-wide beneath it, mute and muscular, attending its ancient agenda. And makes us buy things."

Cayce takes him in, a sidewise glance. In that moment's silence seeing him unsmiling, and perhaps very much who he is.

"When I founded Blue Ant, that was my core tenet, that all truly viable advertising addresses that older, deeper mind, beyond language and logic. I hire talent on the basis of an ability to recognize that, whether consciously or not. It works."

She has to admit to herself that it evidently does, as he brings the Hummer to a halt at the verge of the steep park. Grass soft-looking under mirror-world lamps. The legend Damien told her, which she can't now recall: a sort of English Icarus, who flew from here, or crashed here, long before the Roman city. The hill a place of worship, of sacrifice, of executions: Greenberry, prior to Primrose. That Druid thing.

Bigend doesn't bother to unfold his parking permission, surely the truest modern equivalent of the freedom of the city, but climbs out, putting on his Stetson in that same fussy way, and marches toward the hill's unseen crest. Lost for a moment in darkness between lamps. Cayce follows him, hearing the Hummer's chopped-off security-groan as he thumbs the button on his key. No path for Bigend, but straight on, climbing. Cayce bringing up the rear, hurrying to catch up, mentally kicking herself for letting him play her this way. Fool: Walk away into the night, down to the canal and along it to the locks. Past homeless men drinking cider on benches. But she doesn't. The grass, longer than it looks, wets her ankles. Not a city feeling.

There's a bench there, at the very top, and Bigend is already seated, looking down and out, across the Thames valley, a fairylit London winking through a lens of climate in large part generated by the vast settlement itself.

"Tell me 'no,'" he says.

"What?"

"Tell me you won't do it. Get it out of the way."

"I won't do it."

"You need to sleep on it."

She tries to frown, but she suddenly finds him unexpectedly comic. He knows exactly how much of a pain he can be, and something in his delivery lets her in on that; a technique for disarming people, but one that works.

"What would you do with him, if I found him for you, Hubertus?"

"I don't know."

"Become the producer?"

"I don't think so. I don't think there's a title, yet, for doing whatever it is that would be required.

Advocate, perhaps? Facilitator?" He seems to be gazing out over London, hunched attentively in his fawn raincoat, but then she sees the DVD in his hand. The kiss starts to replay.

"You'll have to do it without me."

He doesn't look up. "Sleep on it. Things look different, in the morning. There's someone I'd like you to talk with."

"Here," she says, removing his cowboy hat. She takes it in her left hand, allowing the creases at the front of her hand to align her thumb and fingers, first and second fingers along the central depression, and tips it onto her own head. She leaves it there, but uses her forefinger to lower the brim with a single measured tap. "Like that." She looks at him from under the brim. "Remove it this way." Tipping it off. She replaces it on his head. "The way you do it, it looks like you'd need a stepladder to get on the horse."

He tilts his head back, to see her from beneath the brim. "Thank you," he says.

Cayce takes a last look, out toward the fairy city. "Now drive me home. I'm tired."

And in Damien's hallway, she stands on tiptoe to see that her single dark Cayce Pollard hair is still there, spit-pasted across the gap between door and frame, then removes her seldom-used compact from her envelope, fingers brushing the hard smooth cylinder from the robot girl. On her knees, then, to use the mirror to check that the powder she'd brushed across the underside of the doorknob is still there, undisturbed.

Thank you, Commander Bond.

CHAPTER 8

WATERMARK

After carefully checking that a number of other sub-miniature booby traps, follicular and otherwise, are intact and as she left them, she checks her e-mail.

One from Damien, one from Parkaboy.

She opens Damien's.

Hello and greetings from six feet down in the currently unfrozen swamps past Stalingrad. I am all bugbites and stubble but still do not fit in, as I am not drunk sufficiently constantly, tho am working at it. Most amazing scene here, hadn't time to tell you before I left. It's about the dig, which perhaps is my version of the footage now. The dig is a post-Soviet summer ritual involving feckless Russian youth, male, from all over, tho mostly Leningrad boys, who come out here to these infested pine forests to excavate the site of some of the largest, longest-running, and most bitterly contested firefights of WWII. Trench stuff, and the line moved back and forth forever, with unimaginable loss of life, so that when one finds a trench and digs, one digs through, well, strata of Germans, Russians, Germans. Who all of them are now bone of a peculiarly dark gray, everything having buried itself in this sticky-silty gray mud, which in winter is frozen solid. This mud is, I think the term is, anaerobic. Flesh is long gone, I'm glad to say, but bone remains, and also artifacts, in brilliant condition when you get the mud off, which is what brings the diggers. Weapons of all kinds, watches, one boy found an unopened bottle of vodka yesterday, but then it was thought that this might have been poisoned, left as a booby trap. Very strange. But visually, wow! All of it: drunken shaven-headed diggers, the things they bring up, and everywhere the rising pyramids of gray bone. And most of this we are getting on video, though the trick is that we have to drink enough to be felt a part of it, the party atmosphere you understand, but not enough to be too legless to shoot and remember to change batteries. Which is why you haven't heard from me, 24-7 on the dig. I had thought of course that this would be an exploratory foray toward a full shoot next summer, but (1) I can't imagine that this level of weirdness can repeat itself, even in Russia, and (2) I'm pretty sure I'll want never to see this place or these particular people again, once I get out of here. Mick the Irish camera has developed a persistent cough that he's convinced is drug-resistant tuberculosis, and Brian the Australian camera passed out drinking with the dig boys and woke up with a bloody, very ugly and authentically prison-style spiderweb motif etched into his left shoulder with something more like a knife than a tattooing instrument. Having survived this, tough bugger, Brian now enjoys the most status with the diggers (also he apparently broke someone's jaw in the aftermath) and he and I both think Mick's full of balls about the TB, whingeing little cunt, but we won't go near him anyway. And how are you??? Are you watering my plants and feeding the goldfish? Are those advertising wanks in Soho treating you in any way at all like a human being? I would kill someone to have a shower right now. I think I have scabies, and that's after shaving my bloody head so I won't get lice. Brian's been painting his balls every night with clear nail polish, says that it kills them (scabies) but I think it's really because he's a queen in the most massive denial and an outback masochist and he likes the way it looks.

XXX, Damien

PS In case it isn't clear from above, I am having an absolutely delightful time and couldn't be happier.

She opens Parkaboy's.

While everyone else is still trembling over The Kiss, as ever #135 will surely be known, Musashi and I have lit out for the territories. I don't know whether you are following F:F:F or earning what passes for your living, but everyone is mad for #135, no end in sight, and I suppose you know about CNN?

She doesn't.

In case you have been in a coma (lucky you) they showed a slightly compressed version yesterday and now every site on the planet is clogged with the clueless, newbies of the most hopeless sort, including ours.

Cayce pauses to do a recompute on her evening with Bigend. If #135 had been on CNN, Bigend knew it, and his not having mentioned it was deliberate, but to what end? Perhaps, she decides, he wants her to discover it after the fact, assuming that heightened global interest will tip her in the direction of his proposition. And she finds, to her annoyance, that it does. The idea of waking to find the identity of the maker revealed on the front page of a paper irks her direly.

In any case, et unpleasant cetera, I took the opportunity to exit F:F:F, made additionally unbearable by the pomo bellowings of fat cow A., and get together netwise with Darryl, to do further work on the result of some kanji-cruising we did while I was in California.

Darryl, AKA Musashi, is a California footage-head fluent in Japanese. The Japanese footage sites, resisting machine translation, are an area that fascinates Parkaboy. With Musashi as translator, Parkaboy has made several forays already, posting the results of his research on F:F:F. Cayce has looked at these sites, but, aside from being incomprehensible, the text, which comes up on non-kanji screens as a frantic-looking slaw of Romanic symbols, reminds her too much of the archaic cartoon convention for swearing; it looks like fizzing, apoplectic rage.

Darryl and I, burrowing deep into back posts on an Osaka-based board of quite singular tediousness, had happened across what seemed to be a reference to #78 having been discovered to be water-marked. (All of this I have archived for you, should you want to follow it step by thrilling step.)

Digital watermarking is something Cayce knows only a little about, but none of the footage she has seen has been watermarked. If it were watermarked, she wonders, what would it be watermarked as, or with?

This segment, I can now tell you in strictest confidence, probably is watermarked, invisibly. Does this mean that the other segments are? We don't know. It is watermarked steganographically, and there, God help us, is a word to conjure with. This is, let me say, in case you have suffered a stroke or blunt trauma in the meantime, the single greatest scoop since footage first found web. And you heard it here first. From me. And from Musashi as well, though before I let him take his bow we must do something about those T-shirts with the bits of dried food clinging to the front.

Cayce takes a deliberately slow sip of tea-sub, looking away from the screen as she does so. As long and flagrantly weird as her day has been, she senses that what she is about to read will probably be weirder still, and perhaps a lot more lastingly significant. Parkaboy does not joke about these things, and the mystery of the footage itself often feels closer to the core of her life than Bigend, Blue Ant, Dorotea, even her career. She doesn't understand that, but knows it. It is something she believes she has in common with Parkaboy, and Ivy, and many of the others. It is something about the footage. The feel of it. The mystery. You can't explain it to someone who isn't there. They'll just look at you. But it matters, matters in some unique way.

Steganography is about concealing information by spreading it throughout other information. At present I know little else about it. However, to get on with the narrative of Parkaboy and Musashi in deep kanji-space, we came back to the present, and our own language, with this one glancing and highly cryptic reference—which I at first was convinced might be nothing more than an artifact of Darryl's translation. I returned to Chicago, then, and Darryl and I, curiosity's cats, began to lovingly generate a Japanese persona, namely one Keiko, who began to post, in Japanese, on that same Osaka site. Putting her cuteness about a bit. Very friendly. Very pretty, our Keiko. You'd love her. Nothing like genderbait for the nerds, as I'm sure you well know. She posts from Musashi's ISP but that's because she's in San Francisco learning English. Very shortly, we had one Takayuchi eating out of our flowerlike palm. Taki, as he prefers we call him, claims to orbit a certain otaku-coven in Tokyo, a group that knows itself as "Mystic," though its members never refer to it that way in public, nor indeed refer to it at all. It is these Mystic wonks, according to Taki, who have cracked the watermark on #78. This segment, according to Taki, is marked with a number of some kind, which he claims to have seen, and know. No doubt motivated by lonely fantasies of getting up our deliciously short little plaid skirt, which we have described to him in passing, he now holds out the promise of showing this to us, upon our return to Tokyo. Of course I am delighted that my brilliant self (albeit with the help of my trusty takeout-encrusted kanjiman) has been the first to

103

bring this shattering new knowledge (if it isn't a tissue of sheerest otaku horseshit) to our virtual shores. La Anarchia will shit herself in lime-green envy, should my (or rather our, Darryl having had his part) discovery become public on F:F:F. But should it? And, indeed, what exactly are we to do next? Taki (who sends Keiko snapshots of himself: mouthbreather) is not about to offer up the Mystic number, should there prove to be one, else his little flower vanish from the screen. He's easy to fool, in one regard, but annoyingly bright in others. He wants Keiko facetime, and I remain, your frustrated Parkaboy

PS So what to do?

She sits there, thinking about this, and then gets up to double check the door and windows, touching the new keys around her neck.

Goes into the bathroom to brush her teeth and wash her face. Her face in the mirror, against the white tiles of the wall behind her. The tiles are square and she looks like something snipped from a magazine and placed on a sheet of graph paper. Not such good work with the scissors.

Images called up by Damien's e-mail. Heaps of bone. That initial seventeen stories of twisted, impacted girder. Funeral ash. That taste in the back of the throat.

And she is here, in this apartment, recently invaded by some shadowy figure, or figures. Dorotea as corporate spook? The woman in the mirror, lips foamed with toothpaste, shakes her head. Hydrophobia.

Bigend advising her to sleep on it. And she will, she's certain, though she doesn't want to.

She removes and folds the silver discomforter, stiff as a new tarpaulin, and replaces it with a duvet in a gray cotton cover, new and unused, that she finds in the closet.

"He took a duck in the face at two hundred and fifty knots." Her prayer in the dark.

Eyes closed, she finds herself imagining a symbol, something water-marking the lower right-hand corner of her existence. It is there, just beyond some periphery, beyond the physical, beyond vision, and it marks her as . . . what?

CHAPTER 9

TRANS

She wakes to sunshine through Damien's windows.

Squares of blue sky, decorative bits of cloud.

Stretches her toes beneath the duvet. Then remembers the complications of her current situation.

Determines to get up and out with as little thought as possible. Breakfast.

Avails herself of the surgical shower, jeans and a T-shirt, and goes out, locking up and doing the Bond thing with a fresh hair and mintflavored spit—sealing Damien's flat against whatever bad mojo there might be.

Down Parkway and over to little Aberdeen, the market street that runs its single block into Camden. She knows a café here, a French place. Remembering breakfast there with Damien.

Passing record and comics shops, windows papered with flyers (where she half looks for, but does not find, the kiss).

Here it is: faux-French with real French waiting tables. Chunnel kids, guest workers.

The first thing she sees, going in, is Voytek, seated at a table with silver-haired Billy Prion, the former lead singer of a band called BSE.

She's long kept track of certain obscure mirror-world pop figures, not because they interest her in themselves but because their careers can be so compressed, so eerily quantum-brief, like particles whose existence can only be proven, after the fact, by streaks detected on specially sensitized plates at the bottom of disused salt mines.

Billy Prion's streak is by reason of his having deliberately had the left side of his mouth paralyzed with Botox for the first BSE gigs, and because, when Margot was taking her NYU extension course in disease-as-metaphor, Cayce had suggested she do something with his mouth. Margot, struggling to outline a paper in which Bigend was the disease she needed to find a metaphor for, hadn't been interested.

Having automatically registered Prion media hits ever since, she knows that BSE had broken up, and that he'd been briefly rumored to be romantically involved with that Finnish girl, the one whose band had been called Velcro Kitty until the trademark lawyers arrived.

As she passes their table, she sees that Voytek has a scrawled tarot of spiral-bound notebooks spread out around the remains of his breakfast, everything executed in red ballpoint. Diagrams,

107

with lots of linked rectangles. From what she sees of Prion's mouth, the cosmetic toxin seems long since to have worn off. He isn't smiling, but if he were, it would probably be symmetrical. Voytek is quietly explaining something, his brow wrinkled with concentration.

An irritable-looking girl with red-rimmed eyes and very red lipstick fans a menu in her face, gesturing curtly toward a table farther in the rear. Seated, not bothering with the menu, Cayce orders coffee, eggs, and sausage, all in her best bad French.

The girl looks at her in amazed revulsion, as though Cayce were a cat bringing up a particularly repellant hairball.

"All right," says Cayce, under her breath, to the girl's receding back, "be French."

But her coffee does arrive, and is excellent, as do her eggs and sausage, very good as well, and when she's finished she looks up to see Voytek staring at her. Prion is gone.

"Casey," he says, remembering but getting it wrong.

"That was Billy Prion, wasn't it?"

"I join you?"

"Please."

He repacks his spiral-bound notebooks, closing each one and tucking it carefully away into his shoulder pouch, and crosses to her table.

"Is Billy Prion a friend of yours?"

"Owns gallery. I need space to show ZX 81 project."

"Is it finished?"

"I am still collecting ZX 81."

"How many do you need?"

"Many. Patronage also."

"Is Billy in the patronage business as well?"

"No. You work for large corporation? They wish to learn of my project?"

"I'm freelance."

"But you are here to work?"

"Yes. For an advertising agency."

He adjusts the pouch on his lap. "Saatchi?"

"No. Voytek, do you know anything about watermarking?"

He nods. "Yes?"

"Steganography?"

"Yes?"

"What might it mean if something, say a segment of digitized video, is watermarked with a number?"

"Is visible?"

"Not ordinarily, I don't think. Concealed?"

"That is the steganography, the concealment. Multi-digit number?"

"Maybe."

"Can be code supplied to client by watermarking firm. Firm sells client stego-encrypted watermark and means to conceal. Check web for that number. If client's image or video has been pirated, that is revealed by search."

"You mean you could use the watermark to follow the dissemination of a given image or video clip?"

He nods.

"Who does this, the actual watermarking?"

"There are companies."

"Could a watermark be traced to a particular company, its number?"

"Would not be so good for client security."

"Would it be possible for someone to detect, or extract, a secret watermark? Without knowing the code, or who placed it there, or even being sure it's there in the first place?"

Voytek considers. "Difficult, but might be done. Hobbs knows these things."

"Who's Hobbs?"

"You meet. Man with Curtas."

Cayce remembers the mean Beckett face, the filthy fingernails. "Really? Why?"

"Maths. Trinity, Cambridge, then works for United States. NSA. Very difficult."

"The work?"

"Hobbs."

The Children's Crusade is remounting in force, this sunny morning.

She stands in Aberdeen with Voytek, watching them troop past, looking dusty in this sunlight and medieval, slouching not toward Bethlehem but Camden Lock.

Voytek has put on a pair of shades with small round lenses. They remind Cayce of coins placed on the eyes of a corpse.

"I must meet Magda," he announces.

"Who is she?"

"Sister. She is selling hats, in Camden Lock. Come." Voytek pushes off into the current of bodies, clockwise, "Saturday sells in Portobello, the fashion market. Sunday, here." Cayce follows, thinking, framing questions about watermarking.

The sun on this shuffling press is soothing, and they soon arrive at the lock, carried along by a current of feet responsible for all those billions in athletic-shoe sales.

Voytek has implied that Magda, aside from designing and making hats, does something in advertising herself, although Cayce can't quite make out what it is.

The market is set back in a maze of Victorian brick.

Warehouses, she supposes, and subterranean stables for the horses that drew the barges down the canals. She isn't certain she's ever really gotten to the bottom of the labyrinth, though she's been here many times. Voytek leads the way, past sheet-hung stalls of dead men's clothes, film posters, recordings on vinyl, Russian alarm clocks, sundries for smokers of anything but tobacco.

Deeper into the brickwork vaults, away from the sun, illuminated by Lava lamps and fluorescents in nonstandard colors, they find Magda, who aside from those cheekbones looks nothing at all like her brother. Short, pretty, hennaed, laced into a projectile bodice that seems to have been retrofitted from some sort of pressurized flying gear, she is happily packing her goods and preparing to close her stall.

Voytek asks her something in whatever their native tongue is. She answers, laughing.

"She says men from France buy wholesale," Voytek explains.

"'She speak good English,'" Magda says to Cayce. "I'm Magda."

"Cayce Pollard." They shake hands.

"Casey is advertising too."

"Probably not the way I am, but don't remind me," says Magda, wrapping another hat in tissue and putting it into a cardboard carton with the rest.

Cayce starts to help. Magda's hats are hats that Cayce could wear, if she wore hats. Gray or black only, knit, crocheted, or yarn-stitched with a sailor's needle from thick industrial felt, they are without period or label. "These are nice."

"Thank you."

"You're in advertising? What do you do?"

"Look sorted, go to clubs and wine bars and chat people up. While I'm at it, I mention a client's product, of course favorably. I try to attract attention while I'm doing it, but attention of a favorable sort. I haven't been doing it long, and I don't think I like it."

Magda does indeed speak good English, and Cayce wonders at the difference in their fluencies. But says nothing.

Magda laughs. "I really am his sister," she says,

"but our mother brought me here when I was five, thank God." Putting away the last hat, she closes the carton and hands it to Voytek.

"You're paid to go to clubs and mention products?"

"Firm's called Trans. Doing very well, apparently. I'm a design student, need something to make ends meet, but it's getting to be a bit much." She's lowering a sheet of tattered transparent plastic to indicate that her makeshift stall is now closed. "But I've just sold twenty hats! Time for a drink!"

"You're in a bar, having a drink," Magda says, the three of them wedged into one darkly varnished corner of an already raucous Camden pub, drinking lager.

"I know," says Voytek, defensively.

"No! I mean you're in a bar, having a drink, and someone beside you starts a conversation. Someone you might fancy the look of. All very pleasant, and then you're chatting along, and she, or he, we have men as well, mentions this great new streetwear label, or this brilliant little film they've just seen. Nothing like a pitch, you understand, just a brief favorable mention. And do you know what you do? This is what I can't bloody stand about it: Do you know what you do?"

"No," Cayce says.

"You say you like it too! You lie! At first I thought

it was only men who'd do that, but women do it as well! They lie!"

Cayce has heard about this kind of advertising, in New York, but has never run across anyone who's actually been involved in it. "And then they take it away with them," she suggests, "this favorable mention, associated with an attractive member of the opposite sex. One who's shown some slight degree of interest in them, whom they've lied to in an attempt to favorably impress."

"But they buy jeans," Voytek demands, "see movie? No!"

"Exactly," Cayce says, "but that's why it works. They don't buy the product: They recycle the information. They use it to try to impress the next person they meet."

"Efficient way to disseminate information? I don't think."

"But it is," Cayce insists. "The model's viral. 'Deep niche.' The venues would be carefully selected—"

"Bloody brilliantly! That's the thing, I'm every night to these bleeding-edge places, cab fare, cash for drinks and food." She takes a long pull on her half pint. "But it's starting to do something to me. I'll be out on my own, with friends, say, not working, and I'll meet someone, and we'll be talking, and they'll mention something."

"And?"

"Something they like. A film. A designer. And

something in me stops." She looks at Cayce. "Do you see what I mean?"

"I think so."

"I'm devaluing something. In others. In myself. And I'm starting to distrust the most casual exchange." Magda looks glum. "What sort of advertising do you do?"

"I consult on design." Then, because this is not exactly the stuff of interesting conversation: "And I hunt 'cool,' although I don't like to describe it that way. Manufacturers use me to keep track of street fashion."

Magda's eyebrows go up. "And you like my hats?"

"I really like your hats, Magda. I'd wear them, if I wore hats."

Magda nods, excited now.

"But the 'cool' part—and I don't know why that archaic usage has stuck, by the way—isn't an inherent quality. It's like a tree falling, in the forest."

"It cannot hear," declares Voytek, solemnly.

"What I mean is, no customers, no cool. It's about a group behavior pattern around a particular class of object. What I do is pattern recognition. I try to recognize a pattern before anyone else does."

"And then?"

"I point a commodifier at it."

"And?"

"It gets productized. Turned into units. Marketed." She takes a sip of lager. Looks around the pub. The crew in here aren't from the Children's

Crusade. She guesses they are the folks who live nearby, probably back behind this side of the street, a neighborhood less gentrified than Damien's. The wood of the bar is worn the way old boats can be worn, virtually to splinters, held together by a thousand coats of coffin-colored varnish.

"So," Magda says, "I am being used to establish a pattern? To fake that? To bypass a part of the process."

"Yes," Cayce says.

"Then why are they trying to do it with bloody video clips from the Internet? This couple kissing in a doorway? Is it a product? They won't even tell us."

And Cayce can only stare.

"Helena. It's Cayce. Thank you for dinner. It was lovely."

"How was Hubertus? Bernard thought he might have the hots for you, to put it bluntly."

"Bluntness appreciated, Helena, but I don't think that's the case. We had a drink. I'd never really had a one-on-one with him before."

"He's brilliant, isn't he?" Something in her tone. A sort of resignation?

"Yes. Is Bernard there, Helena? Hate to disturb him, but I have a question about work."

"Sorry, but he's out. Take a message?"

"Do you know if there's a branch, a subsidiary of some kind, of Blue Ant, called Trans? As in—lation? Or—gressive?"

Silence. "Yes. There is. Laura Dawes-Trumbull has it. Lives with a cousin of Bernard's, oddly. In lawn care."

"Pardon?" A place name?

"The cousin. Lawn care. Lawn products. But Laura heads Trans, I do know that. One of Hubertus's pet projects."

"Thanks, Helena. Have to run."

"Bye, dear."

"Bye."

Cayce removes her card from the pay phone and hangs up, the receiver being immediately taken by a dreadlocked Crusader waiting on the sidewalk behind her.

The sunlight seems not so pleasant now. She's made her excuses, come out here, bought a phone card, waited in line. And now it seems that Magda is indeed employed, by a sub-unit of Blue Ant, to encourage interest in the footage. What is Bigend doing?

She fords the stream of the Crusade, making it to the opposite bank and heading back down toward Parkway. The street-wide flood of kids seems strangely removed, as though they themselves are footage.

A suggestion of autumn is in the light, now, and she wonders where she'll be this winter. Will she be here? In New York? She doesn't know. What is that, to be over thirty and not know where you'll be in a month or two?

She reaches a point where the Crusade flows

around a stationary, drinking knot of Camden's resident, revenant alcoholics. They are why Damien had been able to afford to rent here, years before he'd made any money or bought his house. Somewhere nearby is a Victorian doss house, a vast red brick pile of a hostel for the homeless, purpose-built and hideous, and its inhabitants, however individually transitory, have congregated in the High Street since the day it first opened. Damien had shown it to her one full-moon night, out walking. It stood as a bulwark against gentrification, he'd explained. The re-purposers, the creators of loft spaces, saw the inhabitants, these units dedicated to the steady-state consumption of fortified lagers and sugary ciders, and turned back. And these defenders stand now, drinking, amid the Children's Crusade, rocks in a river of youth.

A peaceful people for the most part, when their spells weren't on them, but now one, younger perhaps than the others, looks at her out of blue and burning eyes, acetylene and ageless, from the depths of his affliction, and she shivers, and hurries on, wondering what it was he'd seen.

In Aberdeen the market men are locking green-painted shutters across their stalls, closing early, and the place where she'd had breakfast is in full bistro swing, a spill of laughing, drinking children out across the pavement.

She walks on, feeling not foreign but alien, made so by this latest advent of something that seems to be infecting everything. Hubertus, and Trans . . .

118

You're not exactly bouncing them back to me, are you? What are you doing over there, anyway? Do you know that the Pope is a footage-head? Well, maybe not the Pope himself, but there's someone in the Vatican running the segments. Turns out that down Brazil way, where folks don't distinguish much between TV, the Net, and other stuff anyway, there is some kind of cult around the footage. Or not so much around it as desirous of burning it, since these illiterate but massively video-consumptive folk believe that it is none other than the Devil himself who is our auteur. Very strange, and there has apparently been a statement issued, to these Brazilians, from Rome, to the effect that it is the Vatican's business to say which works are the works of Satan, nobody else's, that the matter of the footage is being taken under consideration, and in the meantime don't mess with the franchise. I wish I'd thought of it myself, just to irritate la Anarchia.

She closes Parkaboy's latest, gets up now and goes into the yellow kitchen. Puts the kettle on. Coffee or tea? "I hate the domestication," Donny had confided, once, insofar as he was capable.

She wonders if an absent friend's flat in London is perhaps preferable to her own, back in New York, as carefully cleansed of extraneous objects as she can keep it, and why? Does she hate the domestication? She has fewer things in her

119

apartment than anyone, her friend Margot says.

She feels the things she herself owns as a sort of pressure. Other people's objects exert no pressure. Margot thinks that Cayce has weaned herself from materialism, is preternaturally adult, requiring no external tokens of self.

Waiting for the kettle to boil, she looks back, out into Damien's main room, and sees the robot girls, eyeless. No flies on Damien. He's kept his decorators from decorating, resulting in a semiotic neutrality that Cayce is starting to appreciate more, the longer she stays here. Her own place, in New York, is a whitewashed cave, scarcely more demonstrative of self, its uneven tenement floors painted a shade of blue she discovered in northern Spain. An ancient tint, arsenic-based. Peasants there had used it for centuries on interior walls, and it was said to keep flies away. Cayce had had it mixed in plastic enamel, sans arsenic, from a Polaroid she'd taken. Like the varnish on the bar in Camden High Street, it sealed the furry splinters of wear. Texture. She likes an acquired texture, evidence of long habitation, but nothing too personal.

The kettle whistles. She makes a single cup of Colombian and takes it back to the Cube. F:F:F is open there, and she flips back and forth between posts, getting a sense of what's been going on. Not much, aside from ongoing analysis of #135, which is normal, and discussion of this Vatican story from Brazil. Maurice, interestingly, posts to point out that both the story and the alleged papal interest seem to issue from Brazil, and that there has apparently been no independent confirmation from elsewhere. Is it true? he wonders. A hoax?

Cayce frowns. Magda's story. Shown #135 prior to an evening's assignment, then given a brief scripting: It is apparently a feature film, of unknown origin, very interesting somehow, intriguing, and has the one she addresses heard of it? And then debriefed, after, for responses, which she says is unique in her experience of the job so far. And where, Cayce had asked, had Magda been sent to spread this? A private club, Covent Garden: media people. She'd been taken in by a member, someone she'd been introduced to after the briefing, and left to work the room on her own.

Trans. Blue Ant. Bigend.

And tomorrow she meets with Stonestreet again. And Dorotea.

CHAPTER 10

JACK MOVES, JANE FACES

S he's down for a jack move.

Thinks this in the Pilates studio in Neal's Yard, doing the Short Spine Stretch, her bare feet in leather loops that haven't yet been softened up with use. That's how new this place is. They should get some mink oil. Her soles are chaffing.

She'd never really been sure what Donny had meant when he'd say that; he said it when he was angry, or frustrated, and she's both. Dorotea dicking with her and she doesn't do anything about it. She could tell Bernard or Bigend but she doesn't trust them. She has no idea what's going on with Bigend, what he's capable of. The sensible thing to do would be to finish the job, get her money, and write the whole thing off to experience.

But there'd still be Dorotea. Dorotea with the scary connections. Dorotea the mad bitch, just doing these things because she's decided to hate Cayce, or, maybe, Bigend's idea, because she thinks Cayce is being lined up to run Blue Ant's London office. Or maybe she's in the Bigend girlfriend pool. Anything seems equally possible, but some hard little knot in Cayce's core keeps heating up, trying for meltdown: the hole in the Buzz Rickson's, the Asian Sluts invasion, her period's coming, she'd like to get her hands around Dorotea's throat and shake her till her fucking brains rattle.

Jack moves. Context, with Donny, seemed to indicate that these were either deliberate but extremely lateral, thus taking the competition or opponent by surprise, or, more likely in Donny's case, simply crazy, same result. He'd never said what jack move, exactly, in a given situation, he was contemplating, and maybe that was because he didn't know. Maybe it had to be improvisational and completely of the moment. East Lansing Zen. Whatever it was supposed to be, she had an idea he'd never managed to do it. In memory now she associates the expression with his only-ever attempt at verbally communicating a sexual preference: "You think maybe you could make more, like, those jane faces?"

Jane faces being, she'd later learned, stripper-speak for, she guessed you'd call them, ritualized expressions conveying a certain ecstatic transport, or at least its potential.

Or was a jack move, she wonders now, simply a cash-related move? Jack in the sense of money? Donny's jack moves had tended to be invoked in situations of relative economic insecurity. Donny's ongoing situation being one of that, but to greater or lesser degrees. Resolved most often by asking Cayce for a loan, but only after invoking the jack move. If it meant a money move, she guesses she can't use the expression, because what she's tempted to do would just cost her.

What she's tempted to do, she knows, is crazy. She exhales, watching her straightened legs rise up in the straps to a ninety-degree angle, then inhales as she bends them, holding tension in the straps against the pull of the spring-loaded platform she's reclining on. Exhales, as they say, for nothing, then inhales as she straightens them horizontally, pulling the springs taut. Repeating this six more times for a total of ten.

She shouldn't be thinking about anything except getting this right, and that's partly why she does it. Stops her thinking, if she concentrates sufficiently. She is increasingly of the opinion that worrying about problems doesn't help solve them, but she hasn't really found an alternative yet. Surely you can't just leave them there. And this morning she has a big one, or several, because she's due soon for the meeting with Stonestreet and Dorotea, to see Heinzi's latest stab at the logo. To tell them whether it works or not. Per her contract.

She wants to go in there, the hot little knot of rage at her core is telling her, wearing the Buzz Rickson's with the tape on the shoulder (which is starting to curl at the edges) so that Dorotea will know that she hasn't simply neglected to notice the damage. But she won't say anything. Then, when Dorotea produces the logo-rethink (which Cayce imagines will almost certainly work for her, as Heinzi is nothing if not very good) she'll wait a beat or two and then shake her head. And Dorotea will know, then, that Cayce is lying, but she won't be able to do anything about it.

And then Cayce will leave, and go back to Damien's, and pack her things, go to Heathrow and get on the next business-class flight with her return ticket to New York.

And probably blow the contract, a big one, and have to hustle very hard indeed in New York, finding fresh work, but she'll be free of Bigend and Dorotea, and Stonestreet too, and all of the weird baggage that seems to come with them. Mirror-world will get put back into its box until the next time, hopefully a vacation, and when Damien is here, and she will never have to worry about Dorotea or Asian Sluts or any of it, ever again.

Except that that would mean that she'd lied to a client firm, and she really doesn't want to do that, aside from knowing that it's a ridiculous, infantile plan anyway. She'll lose the contract, probably do herself grave professional harm, and all for the sake of pissing Dorotea off. And what a pleasure that would be.

Makes no sense, except to the knot.

Now she's sitting cross-legged, doing Sphinx, springs lightened. Turns her hands palm-up for Beseech. No thinking. You do not get there by thinking about not thinking, but by concentrating on each repetition.

To the gentle twanging of the springs.

She's made certain the driver gets her to Blue Ant early.

She wants her own little bit of time in the street, her own paper cup of coffee. Soho on a Monday morning has its own peculiar energy. She wants to tap into that for a few minutes. Buys her coffee now and heads off, away from Blue Ant, trying to fit her pace to the pace of these people on their way to work, with most of whom she feels she has some passing affinity. They earn their living distinguishing degrees and directions of attractiveness, and she envies the youth and determination with which they all seem to be getting to it. Was she ever like that? Not exactly, she thinks. She got her start, out of college, working with the design team of a Seattle-based mountain-bike manufacturer, and had branched out into skatewear, then shoes. Her talents, which Bigend calls her tame pathologies, had carried her along, and gradually she'd let them define the nature of what it was that she did. She'd thought of that as going with the flow, but maybe, she thinks now, it had really been the path of least resistance. What if that flow naturally tended to the path of least resistance? Where does that take you?

"Down the tube," she says aloud, causing a very good-looking young Asian man, walking parallel with her, to start, and look at her with brief alarm. She smiles in reassurance, but he frowns and walks faster. She slows, to let him get ahead. He's wearing a black horsehide car coat, its seams scuffed gray, like a piece of vintage luggage, and he's actually carrying, she now sees, a piece of vintage luggage. A very small suitcase, brown cowhide, that someone has waxed to a russet glow, reminding her of the shoes of the old men in the home in which her grandfather, Win's dad, had died. She looks after him, feeling a wave of longing, loneliness. Not sexual particularly but to do with the nature of cities, the thousands of strangers you pass in a day, probably never to see again. It's an emotion she first experienced a very long time ago, and she guesses it's coming up now because she's on the brink of something, some turning point, and she feels lost.

Even her relationship to the footage is changing. Margot had called the footage Cayce's hobby, but Cayce has never been a person who had hobbies. Obsessions, yes. Worlds. Places to retreat to. "But it's no-name," Margot had said, of the footage, "that's why you like it. Isn't it? Like your trademark thing." Margot had discovered that most of the products in Cayce's kitchen were generic, unlabeled, and Cayce had admitted that it wasn't a matter of economics but of her sensitivity to trademarks. Now she glances ahead to see if the Asian man is still there, but she can't see him. She checks her Casio-clone.

Time for Blue Ant. Time for Dorotea.

The receptionist sends her up to the third floor again, where she finds Stonestreet in one of his exquisitely slept-in suits, this one gray, red hair sticking up in several new directions. He's smoking a cigarette and flipping through a document in a pink Blue Ant folder.

"Morning, dear. Lovely seeing you, Saturday. How was your ride home with Hubertus?"

"We went for a drink. In Clerkenwell."

"That's the real version of that place we're in now. Some lovely spaces there. What did he have to say?"

"No shop. We talked about the footage." Watching him carefully.

"What footage is that?" He looks up, as if concerned that he's somehow lost the plot.

"On the web. The anonymous film that's being released in bits and pieces. Do you know the one?"

"Oh. That." What does he know? "Helena said you called and asked about Trans."

"Yes."

"Word-of-mouth meme thing. We don't really know what it does, yet. Whether it does anything, really. Where did you hear about it?"

"Someone in a pub."

"Haven't had anything to do with it myself. Cousin of mine runs it, such as it is. I could arrange for you to meet her."

"I was just curious, Bernard. Where's Dorotea?"

"Due any minute, I'd imagine. She can be difficult, can't she?"

"Hardly know her." She checks her hair in a mirrored panel and takes a seat without removing her jacket. "Hubertus is in New York?"

"Yes. At the Mercer."

"I saw him there, once, in the lobby bar. He was talking to Kevin Bacon's dog."

"His dog?"

"Kevin Bacon was there with his dog. Hubertus was talking to it."

"Didn't know he liked pets."

"A celebrity dog. But he didn't seem to be talking to Kevin Bacon."

"What do you make of him?"

"Kevin Bacon?"

"Hubertus."

"Are you serious?"

Stonestreet looks up from the faxes. "Moderately."

"I'm glad I'm contract, Bernard, not salary."

"Erm," Stonestreet says, and seems relieved as Dorotea enters in serious Armani business drag, blackly deconstructed. This is, Cayce senses, for Dorotea, virtually an anti-fashion statement. A look that wouldn't be out of place at an upscale execution. "Good morning," she says. To Cayce: "You are feeling better, today?"

"Yes, thank you. And yourself?"

"I have been in Frankfurt with Heinzi, of course." And it's your fault. "But I think that

Heinzi has worked his magic. He has nothing but good things to say about Blue Ant, Bernard. 'A breath of fresh,' he calls it." She looks at Cayce. Blow me.

Cayce smiles back.

Dorotea takes her seat beside Stonestreet, producing another one of those expensive-looking envelopes. "I was in the studio with Heinzi when he did this. It's such a privilege, to see him work."

"Show it to me."

"Of course." Dorotea takes her time unfastening the envelope. She reaches inside. Pulls out a square of art board the size of the last one. On it is the Michelin Man, in one of his earliest, most stomach-churningly creepy manifestations, not the inflated-maggot de-shelled Ninja Turtle of the present day, but that weird, jaded, cigar-smoking elder creature suggesting a mummy with elephantiasis. "Bibendum," says Dorotea, softly.

"The restaurant?" asks Stonestreet, puzzled. "In the Fulham Road?" He's sitting beside Dorotea and can't see what's on the square of board.

Cayce is about to scream.

"Oh," says Dorotea, "how stupid of me. Another project."

Bibendum, for Cayce knows that that is his name, goes back into the envelope.

Dorotea produces Heinzi's revised design, which she shows to Cayce, and then, almost casually, to Stonestreet.

The sixties sperm Dorotea showed on Friday has

130

mutated into a sort of looping comet, a loosened-up, energized version of the manufacturer's logo of the past decade or so.

Cayce tries to open her mouth, to say something. How did Dorotea know? How does she know?

The silence lengthens.

She watches Stonestreet's red eyebrows go up, a millimeter at a time, wordlessly and incrementally interrogative. They reach a point of maximum ratchet. "Well?"

Bibendum. That's his name. And also the name of a restaurant in the retrofitted Michelin House, where of course Cayce has never gone.

"Cayce? Are you feeling well? A glass of water?"

The first time she'd seen Bibendum had been in a magazine, a French magazine. She'd been six. She'd thrown up. "He took a duck in the face at two hundred and fifty knots."

"What?" An edge of alarm in Stonestreet's voice. He's starting to rise.

"It's fine, Bernard." She's clutching the edge of the table.

"You don't want water?"

"No. I mean, the design is fine. It works."

"You looked as though you'd seen a ghost."

Dorotea smirks.

"I . . . It was Heinzi's design. It . . . affected me." She manages a mechanical grimace, something like a smile.

"Really? That's marvelous!"

"Yes," Cayce says, "but we're done now, aren't

we? Dorotea can go back to Frankfurt, and I can go back to New York." She gets up from her chair, feeling unsteady. "I'll need the car, please." She doesn't want to look at Dorotea. Dorotea's the one with the jack move, this morning. Dorotea's won. Cayce is spooked now, to the core, and this is nothing like the Asian Sluts flat-invasion feeling. This is way worse. Very few people have any idea of the extent of her most problematic trademark phobias, and fewer still of the specific triggers. Her parents, a number of doctors, therapists of various kinds, over the years a very few very close friends, no more than three of her former lovers.

But Dorotea knows.

Her legs feel wooden. She gets to the door, somehow. "Goodbye, Bernard. Goodbye, Dorotea."

Stonestreet looks puzzled.

Dorotea's beaming.

And now all those rushing eager people are gone from the streets of Soho, and thank God the car is waiting.

In Parkway she starts to pay the driver, then remembers it's the Blue Ant car. Unlocks the street door with Damien's big brass key, takes the steps two at a time, the two black German keys at the ready.

And finds a Michelin Man, its white rolls executed in felt, garroted to the doorknob with a thick black cord.

Starts to scream but catches herself.

Breathe.

"He took a duck in the face at two hundred and fifty knots."

She checks for the hair. It's still there. The powder dusted around the knob will be gone, but the perimeter is still secure.

She avoids looking at the thing lashed to the knob. It's just a doll. A doll. She uses the German keys.

Inside. Locking and chaining the door.

The phone rings.

She screams.

Answers on the third ring. "Hello?"

"It's Hubertus."

"Hubertus . . ."

"Yes. Of course. And?"

"And what?"

"You've slept on it."

She opens her mouth but nothing comes out.

"You've signed off on Heinzi's logo," he says. "That's a wrap, then. Congratulations."

She can hear a piano in the background. Lounge stuff. What time is it in New York?

"I'm packing, Hubertus. Car to Heathrow, first flight home." Exactly what she most wants to do, now she hears herself say it.

"That's very good. We can discuss it when you arrive."

"Actually I was thinking of Paris."

"I'll meet you there tomorrow, then. I've the use

of a client's Gulf-stream. Haven't taken them up on it yet."

"Really there's nothing to discuss. I told you that on Saturday night."

"You got over your difficulties with Dorotea?" He's changing the subject.

"You're changing the subject, Hubertus."

"Bernard said you looked ill, when she first showed you the design."

"You're changing it again. Will I work for you to determine the source of the footage, the identity of the maker or makers? No. I won't."

"Why not?"

That stops her. Because she has an acquired and highly generalized dislike for him? Because she absolutely doesn't trust him? Because she doesn't want to know what the footage is, is about, where it's going, who's behind it? This last is a stretch, because she really does want to know all these things, and has spent a huge amount of time discussing them with other footageheads. No, it's more that footage plus Bigend just seems such a bad idea on the face of it. Not Bigend the man, wearing his cowboy hat wrong, but Bigend the force behind Blue Ant. Bigend the genius at what he does, of these new ways of doing it. Any junction of the two seems dire, to her.

"There's someone I want you to meet," he says. "I had him come into the office, this morning, and Bernard was arranging lunch for the two of you, but you left so quickly."

"Who? What for?"

"He's American. His name is Boone Chu."

"Bunchoo?"

"Boone. As in Daniel. Chu. C-h-u. I think you could do something together. I want to facilitate that."

"Hubertus, please. This is pointless. I've told you I'm not interested."

"I have him on the other line. Boone? Where did you say you were?"

"Outside Camden tube," says a male voice, cheerful, American, "looking toward Virgin."

"You see," says Bigend, "he's right there."

Hang up, Cayce tells herself. She doesn't.

"Parkway, right?" The American voice. "Straight up from the station."

"Hubertus, this is really pointless—"

"Please," Bigend says, "meet with Boone. It can't hurt. If there's no chemistry, you can go to Paris."

Chemistry?

"A vacation. On Blue Ant. I'll have the office arrange the hotel. A bonus for vetting the H and P job. We knew we could rely on you. The client is going to the new logo for the spring line. We'll need you then, of course, to check each intended implementation."

He's doing it again. She realizes that it might actually be easier to meet this man, this Boone, and then go to the airport. She can always avoid Bigend in New York. She hopes.

"Is he still on the line, Hubertus?"

"Right here," says the American voice. "Heading up Parkway."

"Ring twice," she says, and gives him the street number and the number of the flat. Hangs up.

She goes into the kitchen and gets Damien's brand-new German paring knife and a black bin liner, as they call them here. Unlocks the door. It's still there, on the knob. She grits her teeth and bunches the black plastic around it, hiding it. Uses the knife to cut through the black cord. It falls into the bag. She puts the bag on the floor, just outside the door, closes the door, returns the knife to the kitchen. Back to the door. She takes a deep breath, steps outside. Takes the black keys from around her neck and carefully locks the door. Gingerly picks up the black bag, the thing deep within it now, like a dead rat but not as heavy, and descends to the landing, where she stuffs it down behind the stacked fashion magazines waiting to be carted away.

She sits down with her back to the wall and wraps her arms around her knees. The knot is back, and now she realizes, to her considerable annoyance, that her period has arrived.

Back upstairs to deal with that, and things barely under control when she hears the doorbell ring, twice. "Shit. Shit. Fuck . . ."

Forgetting to relock the door, she goes down.

This will take one minute, if that. She'll apologize for Bigend's having pushed their meeting, but she'll be firm: She isn't going to embark on any Bigend-financed search for the maker of the footage. It's that simple.

The street door is white-painted oak, but the enamel is yellowed, chipped and smudged, pre-reno. The spy-tube set into it hasn't been clean enough to see through since World War II.

She unlocks and opens it.

"Cayce? I'm Boone Chu. Glad to meet you." Extending his hand.

He's still wearing the leather car coat with the faded seams. Right hand extended, his left around the leather handle of the little suitcase, battered and buffed, that she'd noticed a few hours earlier, in Soho.

"Hello," she says, and shakes his hand.

CHAPTER 11

BOONE CHU

Boone Chu kicks back cowboy-style, legs crossed, on Damien's new brown couch. "You've worked for Blue Ant before?" He looks somewhat gimlet-eyed now, though maybe she's misreading some Chinese-American nerd thing, an unabashed intensity of focus.

"A few jobs in New York." From her perch on the workstation chair.

"Freelance?"

"That's right."

"Me too."

"What do you do?"

"Systems." He waits a beat. "University of Texas, Harvard, then I had a start-up. Which tanked."

He doesn't sound bitter, though people who say this seldom do, she's noticed, which she finds a little creepy. They generally know better. She hopes he isn't one of those. "I Google you, I get . . . ?"

"Sound of relatively high-profile start-up, tanking

138

loudly. Certain amount of 'white-hat hacker' coverage, before that, but that's media." He looks over at the robot girls propped against the wall, but doesn't ask.

"What was your start-up about?"

"Security."

"Where do you live?"

"Washington state. I've got a cliff on Orcas with a 'fifty-one Airstream propped up against it on railroad ties. It's held together with mold, and something that eats aluminum. I was going to build a house, but now I can't bring myself to spoil the view."

"You're based there?"

"I'm based in this." He toes the child-sized antique suitcase. "Where do you live, Cayce?"

"West One Hundred and Eleventh."

"Actually I knew you lived in New York."

"You did?"

"I Googled you."

She hears the kettle start to boil. She's left the whistle off. She gets up. He gets up too and follows her into the kitchen. "Nice yellow," he says.

"Damien Pease."

"Pardon?"

"Pease. Porridge hot. The video director. Know his work?"

"Not offhand."

"It's his flat. What did Bigend offer you, exactly, Boone?"

"Partnership, he said."

She watches him watching her expression as he speaks.

"With him," he continues. "Whatever that means. He wants me to work with you. To find the person or persons uploading the video clips. We'd have as much as we needed for expenses, but I'm not sure what the payoff might consist of." He has one of those tall, impossibly dense Chinese-guy brush cuts, and a long face that might seem feminine if it weren't tempered, she guesses, by having grown up in Tulsa having to deal with being a Chinese-American named Boone.

"Did he tell you why he wants us to work together? Or why he'd want me at all?" She tosses tea-sub into the pot and pours water over the bags. "Sorry. Forgot to ask if you wanted coffee."

"Tea's fine." He goes to the sink and starts rinsing out two mugs she's left there. Something about his movements reminding her of a chef she'd once dated. The way he briskly refolds the tea towel before using it to dry the mugs. "He said that you don't need to reinvent any wheels." He puts the mugs down, side by side. "He said that if anyone could figure out where this stuff comes from, it would be you."

"And you?"

"I'm supposed to facilitate. You have an idea, I make it happen."

She looks at him. "You can do that?"

"I'm not magic, but I'm handy. Hands-on generalist, you might say."

She pours. "Do you want to do it?"

He picks up his tea-sub. Sniffs. "What is it?"

"I don't know. It's Damien's. No caffeine, though."

He blows to cool it, then sips. Winces. "Hot."

"Well, do you? Want to do it?"

Looks at her, steam rising from the cup he still holds close to his mouth. "I'm of two minds." He lowers the cup. "It's an interesting problem, from a theoretical point of view, and as far as we know no one's solved it yet. I'm available, and Bigend has a lot of money to throw at it."

"That's your upside?"

He nods, sips more tea-sub. Winces again. "Downside is Bigend. Hard to quantify that, isn't it?" He goes to the kitchen window and seems to be looking out, but then he points to the round transparent ventilator fan set into a six-inch hole in one pane of glass. "We don't have those things. They're everywhere, here. Always have been. I'm not even sure what they're supposed to do."

"They're part of the mirror-world," Cayce says.

"Mirror-world?"

"The difference."

"My idea of a mirror-world is Bangkok. Asia somewhere. This is just more of our stuff."

"No," she tells him, "different stuff. That's why you noticed that vent. They invented that here, probably, and made it here. This was an industrial nation. Buy a pair of scissors, you got British scissors. They made all their own stuff. Kept imports expensive. Same thing in Japan. All their bits and pieces were different, from the ground up."

"I see what you mean, but I don't think it's going to be that way much longer. Not if the world's Bigends keep at it: no borders, pretty soon there's no mirror to be on the other side of. Not in terms of the bits and pieces, anyway." His eyes meet hers.

They each carry a cup of tea-sub back and take their seats again.

"How about you," he asks, "how do you feel about Bigend?"

And why, she wonders, is she even having this conversation? How much to do with their glancing encounter in the street this morning, which he shows no sign of remembering? Her sense of urban disconnect, then: seeing him as a passing stranger she'd never see again, and now having him turn up this way.

"Hubertus Bigend is a very smart man," she says, "and I don't like him very much."

"Why not?"

"I seem to have an attitude about how he operates as a human being. I don't feel strongly enough about it to refuse to work for his company, but the idea of working with him on a more personal basis makes me uncomfortable." Immediately thinking: Why have I told him this, I don't know him at all, what if he goes back to Bigend and tells him what I just said?

He sits there, his long fingers around his mug of tea-sub, looking at her over it. "He can afford to buy people," he says. "I don't want to wind up as a gadget on his key ring. I'm not exactly immune to the kind of money Bigend has to play with. When that start-up was on the fence, teetering back and forth, I found myself doing things I came to regret."

She looks at him. Is this the truth, or self-advertisment?

He frowns. "Why do you think he wants it?"

"He thinks he can productize it."

"Then monetize it." He puts the cup down on the carpet.

"He says it's about excellence, not money."

"Sure," Boone Chu says, "the money's just a sort of side effect. And that lets him keep it vague with us."

"But if he priced it, it would be less interesting, wouldn't it? If he put a fixed ticket on it for us, it would just be another job. He's appealing to something deeper."

"And treating it as though it's a done deal."

"I've noticed that." She watches his eyes. "But would you want to give him the satisfaction?"

"If I don't, I may never have the satisfaction of getting to the bottom of this," he says. "And I've tried already."

"You have?"

"Sometimes I can do it sitting around in a hotel room, playing with this." He nudges the suitcase with his foot. "I couldn't get anywhere, but that only has a way of getting me going."

"What do you have in there?"

He picks up the suitcase and clicks its latches. It's lined with cubes of gray foam, arranged to form a recess for a featureless rectangle of gray metal. He lifts this, a titanium laptop, out, and she sees more recesses, assorted coiled cables, three cell phones, and one of those big, specialist, multi-bit screwdrivers. One of the phones is cased in candy-apple mango.

"What's that?" she asks, pointing to the mango phone.

"Japan."

"And you can use a screwdriver too?"

"Never go anywhere without one."

And this, somehow, she believes completely.

They wind up eating noodles together in that pan-Asian place on Parkway, sanded wood and raku bowls, and now he's deep into the resolution thing. Old hat to the F:F:F veteran but he has a refreshingly clear take on it. "Each of the segments is of the same resolution, sufficient to allow theatrical projection. The visual information, the grain of that imagery, is all there. Footage of a lower resolution couldn't be enlarged and retain its clarity. If it's computer-generated, somebody had to put that there." He raises his chopsticks toward his mouth. "Rendering farms. Ever see one?" He pops the noodles into his mouth and chews.

"No."

He swallows, puts his chopsticks down. "Big

room, lots of stations, renderers working through your footage a frame at a time. Labor intensive. Shakespeare's monkeys, but working to a plan. Rendering is expensive, human-intensive, involves a lot of people, and would probably be impossible to keep a secret, for very long, in a situation like this. Someone would tell, unless there were unusual constraints in place. These people sit there and massage your imagery a pixel at a time. Sharpen it up. Add detail. Do hair. Hair is a nightmare. And they don't get paid much."

"So the Garage Kubrick hypothesis is just a dream?"

"Unless the maker has access to levels of technology that don't, as far as we know, exist yet. Assuming the footage is entirely computer-generated means that your maker either has de-engineered Roswell CGI capacities or a completely secure rendering operation. If you rule out the alien tech, where can you find that?"

"Hollywood."

"Yes, but possibly in the more globally distributed sense. You're doing CGI in Hollywood, your rendering might be being done in New Zealand, say. Or Northern Ireland. Or, maybe, in Hollywood. Point is, that's still the industry. People talk. Given the interest this stuff has been generating, you'd need a culture of pathological secrecy to keep it from getting out."

"You're not in 'Garage Kubrick,' then," she says, "you're in 'Spielberg's Closet': the supposition that the footage is being produced by someone who already has godlike production resources. Someone who, for some reason, is opting to produce and release very unconventional material in a very unconventional way. Someone with the clout to keep it quiet."

"You buy it?"

"No."

"Why not?"

"How much time have you spent with the actual footage?"

"Not much."

"How do you feel when you watch it?"

He looks down at his noodles, then up at her. "Lonely?"

"Most people find that that deepens. Becomes sort of polyphonic. Then there's a sense that it's going somewhere, that something will happen. Will change." She shrugs. "It's impossible to describe, but if you live with it for a while, it starts to get to you. It's just such a powerful effect, induced by so little actual screen time. I've never felt convinced that there's a recognized filmmaker around who can do that, although if you read the footage boards you'll see different directors constantly nominated."

"Or maybe it's the repetition. Maybe you've been looking at this stuff for so long that you've read all this into it. And talking with other people who've been doing the same thing."

"I've tried to convince myself of that. I've wanted

to believe it, simply in order to let the thing go. But then I go back and look at it again, and there's that sense of . . . I don't know. Of an opening into something. Universe? Narrative?"

"Eat your noodles. Then we can talk."

And they do, walking. Up to Camden Lock along the High Street, the weekend's Crusaders all gone home, passing the window of the designers of Damien's kitchen cabinets, Boone touching on his childhood in Oklahoma, the highs and lows of his start-up experience, vicissitudes of industry and the broader economy since the previous September. He seems to be making an effort to tell her who he is. Cayce in turn telling him a little about her work and nothing at all about its basis in her peculiar sensitivities.

Until they find themselves on the canal's shabby towpath, under a sky like a gray-scale Cibachrome of a Turner print, too powerfully backlit. This spot reminding her now of a visit to Disneyland with Win and her mother, when she was twelve. Pirates of the Caribbean had broken down and they'd been rescued by staff wearing hip-waders over their pirate costumes, to be led through a doorway into a worn, concrete-walled, oil-stained subterranean realm of machinery and cables, inhabited by glum mechanics, these backstage workers reminding Cayce of the Morlocks in *The Time Machine*.

It had been a difficult trip for her because she couldn't tell her parents that she'd started trying

147

to avoid having Mickey in her field of vision, and by the fourth and final day she'd developed a rash. Mickey hadn't subsequently become a problem, but she still avoided him anyway, out of a sense of having had a close shave.

Now Boone apologizes for having to check his e-mail; says he may have incoming he'd like her to see. Sits on a bench and gets out his laptop. She goes to the canal's edge and looks down. A gray condom, drifting like a jellyfish, a lager can half-afloat, and deeper down swirls something she can't identify, swathed in a pale and billowing caul of ragged builder's plastic. She shudders and turns away.

"Have a look at this," he says, looking up from his screen, the open laptop across his knees. She crosses the towpath and sits beside him. He passes her the laptop. Washed out in the afternoon light, she sees an opened message:

There's something encrypted in each of these but that's all I can tell you. Whatever it is, it's not much data, and that's uniform from segment to segment. If it were bigger, maybe—but as it is this is the best I can do: definitely a needle in your haystack.

"Who's it from?"
"Friend of mine at Rice. I had him look at all hundred and thirty-five segments."
"What's he do?"
"Math. I've never even remotely understood it.

148

Interviews angels for positions on pinheads. We had him onboard for the start-up. Encryption issues, but that's only a by-product of whatever it is he does theoretically. Seems to find it intensely comical that there's any practical application whatever."

And she hears herself say: "It's a watermark."

Then he's looking at her. She can't read the look at all. "How do you know?"

"There's someone in Tokyo who claims to have a number that someone else extracted from segment seventy-eight."

"Who extracted it?"

"Footageheads. Otaku types."

"Do you have the number?"

"No. I'm not even positive that it's true. He might be making it up."

"Why?"

"To impress a girl. But she doesn't exist either."

He stares at her. "What would it take to find out if it's true?"

"An airport," she says, having to admit to herself now that she's already worked it out, already gone there, "a ticket. And a lie."

He takes the laptop back, shuts it down, closes it, leaving his hands resting on the featureless gray metal. Looking down at it, he might be praying. Then he looks up at her. "Your call. If it's real, and you can get it, it might take us somewhere."

"I know," she says, and that's really all she can say, so she just sits there, wondering what she might have set in motion, where it might go, and why.

CHAPTER 12

APOPHENIA

Climbing the stairs, she realizes she's forgotten to do the Bond thing, but she finds that recent events have apparently broken the spell of Asian Sluts.

It doesn't even bother her that she knows what's stuffed down behind the pile of magazines on the landing. As long she doesn't dwell on it.

More worried about what she may just now have gotten into. Walking him to the station she's affirmed that she's up for it: They'll work for Bigend, she'll go to Tokyo and find Taki. Try, with the help of Parkaboy and Musashi, to get the number. Then they'll see.

There's no reason, he says, to regard it as a Faustian bargain with Bigend. They'll be free to end the partnership at any time, and can keep each other honest.

But this argument is somehow familiar from past contexts, past bargains, where things haven't really worked out that well.

But she knows she's going now, and she has the

two very black, very odd-looking keys around her neck, and right this minute she isn't worrying about the perimeter.

Fuck Dorotea.

Right now she believes implicitly in German technology.

Which is about to create a problem, she realizes, as she works those fine locks in turn.

She doesn't know where she can leave the new keys, or who to trust with them. Damien will want to be able to unlock his apartment, should he return, and she won't be here. He doesn't have an office, no agency affiliation that she knows of, and she doesn't know any of their mutual acquaintances here well enough to trust them with the valuable and highly portable music-production gear in the room upstairs. She doesn't know how constant Damien's e-mail connection is, at the dig, in Russia. If she e-mails him for advice, will he get it in time, and respond, telling her where to leave the keys?

Then she thinks of Voytek and Magda, who have no idea where this place is. She can leave one set with them, telling Damien how to contact them, and take the other set with her.

And, yes, letting herself in, everything looks fine here, even the knap on the couch, reversed where Boone had sat on it.

The phone rings.

"Hello?"

"Pamela Mainwaring, Cayce. I'm travel for

Hubertus. I have you British Airways, Heathrow-Narita, ten fifty-five hours, first class, tomorrow. Works?"

Cayce stares at the robot girls. "Yes. Thanks."

"Brilliant. I'll come round now and drop off the ticket. I also have a laptop for you, and a phone."

She's always managed not to acquire either, at least in terms of traveling with them. She has a laptop at home, but uses it, with a full-size keyboard and a monitor, only as her desk machine. And the mirror-world has always been a deliberate cellular vacation. But now she remembers Tokyo's lack of English signage, and her lack of spoken Japanese.

"I'll be there in ten. I'm calling from the car. Bye." Click.

She locates the piece of cardboard with Voytek's address and e-mails him, giving him the number here and asking him to call as soon as he can, that she has a favor to ask and that it's worth a few ZX 81s. Then she e-mails Parkaboy and tells him she'll be in Tokyo the day after tomorrow, and to start thinking about what she'll need to do to deal with Taki.

She pauses, about to open the latest from her mother, and remembering that she still hasn't replied to the previous two.

Her mother is cynthia@roseoftheworld.com, Rose of the World being an intentional community of sorts, back up in the red-dirt country of Maui.

Cayce has never been there but Cynthia has sent pictures. A sprawling, oddly prosaic sixties rancher set back against a red hillside in long sparse grass, that red showing through like some kind of scalp disease. Up there they scrutinize miles of audiotape, some of it fresh from its factory wrap, unused, listening for voices of the dead: EVP freaks, of which Cayce's mother is one from way back. Used to put Win's Uher reel-to-reel in their very first microwave. She said that blocked out broadcast interference.

Cayce has long managed to have as little to do with her mother's penchant for Electronic Voice Phenomena as she possibly can, and this had been her father's strategy as well. Apophenia, Win had declared it, after due consideration and in his careful way: the spontaneous perception of connections and meaningfulness in unrelated things. And had never, as far as Cayce knows, said another word about it.

Cayce hesitates, a mouse-click away from opening her mother's message, which is titled HELLO???.

No, she isn't ready.

She goes to the fridge and wonders what she'll eat before her departure, and what she'll throw out.

Apophenia. She stares blankly into the cold, beautifully illuminated interior of Damien's German fridge. What if the sense of nascent meaning they all perceive in the footage is simply that: an illusion of meaningfulness, faulty pattern recognition? She's been over this with Parkaboy and

153

he's taken it places (the neuromechanics of hallucination, August Strindberg's personal account of his psychotic break, and a peak drug experience during his teens in which he, Parkaboy, had felt himself to be "channeling some kind of Linear B angelic machine language"), none of which have really helped.

She sighs and closes the fridge.

The street door buzzes. She goes down to let Pamela Mainwaring in, a twenty-something blonde in a black mini and tartan-print tights, a black ballistic nylon briefcase in either hand. Cayce sees a Blue Ant car waiting in the street. Its driver stands beside it, smoking a cigarette, his ear plugged with plastic, conversing with thin air.

Everything about Pamela Mainwaring is fast, efficient, and intimidatingly clear. Not a woman who'd often have to repeat herself. They aren't even in the apartment yet before she's gotten Cayce to sign off on a suite in the Park Hyatt, Shinjuku, with a view of the Imperial Palace. "Part of one rooftop, at least," Pamela says, putting the briefcases down, side by side, on the trestle table.

"That's a nice yellow," glancing into the kitchen.

She unzips one case, exposing a laptop and printer.

"I'll just check this again," she says, booting up. "You can use the return whenever you like, and on any carrier. But you can also go anywhere you want, anytime. My e-mail and number's in your laptop here. I do all of Hubertus's travel, so I'm seven twenty-four." The screen fills with a dense frieze of flight schedules. "Yes. You're on." She takes blank airline tickets from an envelope and feeds them into the rectangular printer. It makes small, energetic buzzing sounds as the tickets emerge from the opposite end. "Minimum two hours check-in." Adroitly assembling the fresh-minted tickets in a British Airways folder. "We have an iBook for you, loaded, cellular modern. And a phone. It's good here, anywhere in Europe, Japan, and the States. You'll be met at Narita by someone from Blue Ant Tokyo. The Tokyo office is at your complete disposal. The best translators, drivers, anything you feel you need. Literally anything."

"I don't want to be met."

"Then you won't."

"Is Hubertus still in New York, Pamela?"

Pamela consults an Oakley Timebomb, slightly wider than her left wrist. "Hubertus is on his way to Houston, but he'll be back in the Mercer tonight. His e-mail and all of his numbers are on your iBook." She opens the second case, exposing a flat Mac, a gray cell phone large enough to look either passé or unusually powerful, various cables and small gizmos still sealed in the manufacturer's plastic, and a sheaf of the usual glossy how-to. There's a Blue Ant envelope on top of the computer. Pamela closes her own computer, zips up the case. Picks up the envelope, tears it open, shakes out a loose credit card. "Sign this, please."

Cayce takes it. CAYCE POLLARD EXP. Platinum Visa customized with the hieratic Blue Ant, which of course is a Heinzi creation, robotic and Egyptianate. Pamela Mainwaring hands her an expensive German roller-point. Cayce puts the card facedown on the trestle table and signs its virgin back. Something seems to clunk heavily, at the rear of her ethical universe.

"It's been a pleasure meeting you," Pamela says. "Have a brilliant trip, best of luck, and call or e-mail me if you need anything. Absolutely anything." She shakes Cayce's hand firmly. "I can show myself out, thanks."

And then she's gone, Cayce closing and locking the door behind her. She goes back to the table and picks up the cell phone. She sees that it's on. After a few tries she manages to turn it off. She puts it back in the case, which she closes and pushes to the rear of the table.

Takes a deep breath, another, then does a Pilates spine curl, rolling down vertebra by vertebra into a sort of upright fetal crouch. Comes up out of it as smoothly and slowly as she can.

Damien's phone rings.

"Hello?"

"Is Voytek."

"I need your help with something, Voytek. I'd like you to keep a set of keys, and give them to a friend of mine if he turns up. I'll give you twenty pounds."

"Is not needed to pay, Casey."

"It's a donation to your ZX 81 project. I have a new job and I'm on an expense account," she says, thinking she's lying but then realizing she isn't, necessarily. "Can you meet me in two hours, where we had breakfast?"

"Yes?"

"Good. See you." Hangs up.

And wonders, for the first time, and indeed for the first time in her life, whether the phone is tapped. Could that be what got the Asian Sluts invader in here in the first place? Dorotea's an industrial espionage bitch, or has been, so it probably isn't entirely unlikely. They do things like that. Bugs. Spy Shop stuff. She mentally reviews her calls since Asian Sluts. The only one of any substance, asking Helena about Trans, she'd made from a phone in Camden High Street. Now this one to Voytek, but unless a listener knew where she'd run into him at breakfast . . . But then couldn't they trace his number, wherever that is?

She goes into the room where she keeps her luggage and begins the pretravel yoga of folding and packing CPUs, which somehow tells her body that she will soon be free of reliance on this particular perimeter.

Completing these tasks, she lies down on the gray duvet and falls asleep, willing herself to wake in an hour, in time to meet Voytek at the bistro in Aberdeen Street. And knows that she will.

And dreams, though she seldom dreams, or seldom recalls them, that she is alone in the

157

back of a black cab, in London, the transience of late summer leaves accentuating the age of the city, the depth of its history, the simple stubborn vastness of it. Facades of tall houses, pokerfaced and unyielding. She shivers, though the night is warm, the air in the cab close, and the image from Damien's e-mail comes to her, wet gray pyramids of bone rising beside excavations in a Russian swamp. What was that, to do that to the dead, to history? She hears picks ringing, drunken laughter, and she is in the cab, feeling ill, and in the pine forest, the summer swamp, witness she knows to some cannibalization beyond expression, some eating of the dead, and she remembers telling Bigend that the past is mutable too, as mutable as the future, but now she must tell him that it shouldn't be dug up, ravaged, thrown away. She must tell him, but cannot speak, even though she now sees that it is Bigend who is driving this cab, wearing his cowboy hat, and even if she speaks, if she manages to break this thing that so painfully shackles speech, he is separated from her voice by a partition of glass or plastic, entirely bent on driving, driving she knows not where.

And wakes to the rapid beating of her heart.

Gets up, to splash cold water on her face and ascend the steep narrow stairwell to where she's hidden the second set of keys.

And she will be careful, in the street, on her way to meet Voytek. She has never before determined to try to discover whether or not she might be being followed, but now she does, and will.

Somewhere, deep within her, surfaces a tiny clockwork submarine.

There are times when you can only take the next step. And then another.

CHAPTER 13

LITTLE BOAT

Her seat on the upper deck of this British Airways 747 subsides into a bed that makes her think of a little boat, a coracle of Hexcel and teak-finish laminate. She's nearest the nose, no other seating units in her line of sight.

The cabin is like some optimally comfy cube-farm, a cluster of automated, supremely ergonomic workstation enclosures. It feels as though, with just a little more engineering, they could simultaneously tube-feed you and tidily exhaust the resulting wastes.

However many hours in the air now, her watch tucked ritually out of sight, dinner served, lights dimmed, she imagines her soul bobbing stupidly, somewhere back over the concrete of Heathrow, its invisible tether spooling steadily out of her. As does a certain degree of fear, she notes, now that she knows they must be far out over an ocean, where no human agents threaten. For most of her life, flying, she'd felt most vulnerable right here, suspended in a void, above trackless water, but now her conscious flying-fears are about things that might be arranged to happen over populous human settlements, fears of ground-to-air, of scripted CNN moments.

But commercial aircraft have also been problematic for Cayce in another way, with their endless claustrophobic repetition of the carrier's logo. BA has never been particularly difficult, but Virgin, with its multipronged product-associations, is completely impossible.

Her biggest problem with BA now, she reminds herself, is a more ordinary one: no movies she'd even consider watching in the armrest DVD, she's under a personally enforced video news ban in effect now for some time, she's neglected to bring anything to read, and sleep refuses to come. With London receding and Tokyo still largely unimagined, unremembered, she sits up cross-legged in the center of her narrow little bed and knuckles her eyes, feeling like a bedridden child, just well enough to be utterly restless.

Then she remembers Bigend's iBook, with its bright new Heathrow security sticker.

She hauls the nylon case up from the floor and opens it. She'd spent twenty minutes, the night before, poking around on the desktop, but now for the first time she notices an ummarked CD-ROM that proves, on insertion, to be a searchable database of all of F:F:F. Whoever does these things for Bigend has also provided, on the hard drive, a complete collection of the footage and her three favorite edits, one of them by Filmy and Maurice.

Still sitting cross-legged, she makes a Stickie: COPY CD FOR IVY.

Ivy's wanted a searchable database of the forum almost since the forum began, because the free software that allows her to keep the site up isn't searchable, and she hasn't had anyone willing or able to do the compiling. Posters have bookmarked their favorite threads, and swap them, but there's been no way to trace a particular topic or theme through the site's evolution.

Or, rather, now there is.

Cayce has no idea how many pages of posts have accumulated since the site's first day. She's never gone back and looked at that, at the Ursite, the early days, but now she enters and searches CayceP.

On the contrary, as I was saying yesterday . . .

Ah. Not her first post. At first she hadn't even been CayceP. Reenters Cayce.

Hi, How many segments, in all? Just downloaded the one where he's on the rooftop. Has anyone been able to do anything with those chimney-pots (is that what you call them?)?

She'd added the P later, because there had briefly been another Cayce, surname, a Marvin, in Wichita, who'd also pronounced it Case, not Casey.

162

She feels somewhat the way she might if she had uncovered her high-school yearbook.

Here's Parkaboy's first post:

Well suck me raw with a breast-pump! Thought I was the only one out here obsessing about the peculiar beauties of this particularly spotty stretch of anomalous cinematic prairie. Anybody into cowboy poetry as well? Because, let me assure you, I'm not.

This had been prior to La Anarchia's arrival, after three days of which Parkaboy had made the first of his many noisy departures from the site.

She fiddles with the matte alloy buttons on her armrest, converting her bed into a lounger. It feels good when it moves: powerful motors devoted to her comfort. She settles back in her black sweats (having declined the offer of a BA romper suit) and pulls the tartan blanket across her legs, iBook on her stomach. Adjusts the snaky fiber-optic reading lamp, with its head like a policeman's flashlight.

Exits the CD-ROM and clicks on Filmy and Maurice's edit.

It opens on that rooftop, against the oddly shaped chimneys. He is there. Walks to the low parapet. Looks out toward a city that never resolves. A framegrab on what he sees would reveal only a faint arrangement of vertical and horizontal lines. No focus. Definitely a skyline but not enough information to provide any sort of identification.

Rule out Manhattan, others; there are lists arguing the places it cannot, might not be.

Maurice cuts to that segment that consists entirely of long shots, the girl in the formal park.

Sometimes, when she watches a good edit, and this is one of the best, it's as though it's all new; she sinks into it with joy and anticipation, and when the edit ends, she's shocked. That's it. All there is. How can that be?

This is one of those times. It ends.

She falls asleep, iBook on her lap.

When she wakes, the cabin is darker, and she needs to pee.

Grateful that she isn't wearing a BA romper, she shuts the iBook down, stows it away, unbuckles her seat belt, puts on BA slippers, and makes her way back toward the toilets.

Passing, as she does, what can only be the sleeping form of Billy Prion, snoring lightly, his still-unparalyzed mouth slightly open. He has his tartan blanket arranged around his shoulders like an old man in a bath chair, his face slack and inert. She blinks, trying to convince herself that this cannot be the former lead singer of BSE, but it quite clearly is, all in what looks to be last season's Agnes B Homme.

In the coracle nearest Prion sleeps a blindfolded blonde, a pair of modest nipple rings clearly visible in outline through the taut black fabric of her top.

This, Cayce decides, further confirming her identification of Prion, is the singer from the

164

former Velcro Kitty, the one the music press had supposed he was no longer with.

She forces herself to shuffle on, in her navy vinyl slippers, to the almost-spacious safety of a first-class toilet, with its fresh flowers and Molton Brown face stuff, where she locks the door and sits, unable to put this together: Prion, at whose gallery Voytek hopes to show his ZX81 project, is on her flight to Tokyo. Why? If it's that small a world, it starts to smell funny.

Watching that intensely blue fluid pressure-swirl down as she flushes.

Returning to her seat, she sees the nipple-ringed singer awake, seated upright, blindfold discarded, studying a glossy fashion magazine under a tightly focused fiber-optic beam. Prion is still snoring.

Back in her own little boat, she accepts a lukewarm white washcloth from the flight attendant's tongs.

Why are they here, on this flight, Prion and the Velcro Kitty girl?

She remembers her father's views on paranoia.

Win, the Cold War security expert, ever watchful, had treated paranoia as though it were something to be domesticated and trained. Like someone who'd learned how best to cope with chronic illness, he never allowed himself to think of his paranoia as an aspect of self. It was there, constantly and intimately, and he relied on it professionally, but he wouldn't allow it to spread, become jungle. He cultivated it on its own special plot, and checked it daily for news it might bring: hunches, lateralisms, frank anomalies.

Is Prion's presence on this plane a frank anomaly?

Only, she decides, if she thinks of herself as the center, the focal point of something she doesn't, can't, understand. That had always been Win's first line of defense, within himself: to recognize that he was only a part of something larger. Paranoia, he said, was fundamentally egocentric, and every conspiracy theory served in some way to aggrandize the believer.

But he was also fond of saying, at other times, that even paranoid schizophrenics have enemies.

The danger, she supposes, is a species of apophenia.

The damp white cloth has grown cold in her hand.

She places it on the armrest and closes her eyes.

CHAPTER 14

THE GAIJIN FACE OF BIKKLE

Electric twilight now, and some different flavor of hydrocarbons to greet her as she exits Shinjuku Station, wheeling her black carry-on behind her.

She's taken the JR Express in from Narita, knowing that this avoids bumper-to-bumper rush-hour freeway-creep and one of the world's dullest bus rides. Pamela Mainwaring's car would have been equally slow, and would have meant contact with Blue Ant personnel, something she hopes to keep to a bare minimum.

Having lost sight of Prion and his girlfriend shortly after deplaning, she hopes they're now stuck in the traffic she's managed to miss, whatever their purpose in coming here might be.

Looking up now into the manically animated forest of signs, she sees the Coca-Cola logo pulsing on a huge screen, high up on a building, followed by the slogan "NO REASON!" This vanishes, replaced by a news clip, dark-skinned men in bright robes. She blinks, imagining the towers burning there, framed amid image-flash and whirl.

The air is warm and slightly dank.

She hails a taxi, its rear door popping open for her in that mysterious Japanese way. She swings her carry-on onto the backseat and climbs in after it, settling herself on the spotless white cotton seat cover and almost forgetting not to pull the door shut after her.

The white-gloved driver closes it with the lever under his seat, then turns.

"Park Hyatt Tokyo."

He nods.

They edge out into the dense, slow, remarkably quiet traffic.

She takes out her new phone and turns it on. The screen comes up in kanji. Almost immediately, it rings.

"Yes?"

"Cayce Pollard, please."

"Speaking."

"Welcome to Tokyo, Cayce. Jennifer Brossard, Blue Ant." American. "Where are you?"

"Shinjuku, on my way to the hotel."

"Do you need anything?"

"Sleep, I think." It's more complicated than that, of course, soul-delay coming in from some novel angle here. She can't remember how she'd dealt with jet lag when she was last here, but that was ten years ago. Dancing and quite a lot of drinking, possibly. She'd been that much younger, and that had been in the heyday of the Bubble.

"You have our number."

"Thank you."

"Good night."

"Good night."

Alone again, suddenly, in the crepuscular calm of a Tokyo taxi.

She looks out the window, reluctantly admitting more of the alien but half-familiar marketing culture, the countless cues and clues proving too much for her now. She closes her eyes.

More white gloves at the Park Hyatt, her carry-on lifted out and placed atop a luggage cart, then draped with a sort of bulky silken fishnet, its edges weighted, a ritual gesture that puzzles her: some survival from a grander age of European hotels?

White gloves in the vast Hitachi elevator, pressing the button for the lobby. Eerily smooth ascent, the speed of it pulling blood from her head, past floors unmarked and uncounted, then the door opens silently on a large grove of live bamboo, growing from a rectangular pool the size of a squash court.

Through registration, imprinting the Blue Ant card, signing, then up, that many more floors again, perhaps fifty in all.

To this room, very large, with its large black furniture, where the bellman briefly shows her various amenities, then bows and is gone, no tip expected.

She blinks. A James Bond set, Brosnan rather than Connery.

She uses the remote as demonstrated, drapes drawing quietly aside to reveal a remarkably virtual-looking skyline, a floating jumble of electric Lego, studded with odd shapes you somehow wouldn't see elsewhere, as if you'd need special Tokyo add-ons to build this at home. Logos of corporations she doesn't even recognize: a strange luxury, and in itself almost worth the trip. She remembers this now from previous visits, and also the way certain labels are mysteriously recontextualized here: Whole seas of Burberry plaid have no effect on her, nor Mont Blanc nor even Gucci. Maybe this time it will even have started to work for Prada.

She thumbs the drapes closed and sets about the unpacking and hanging up and putting away of CPUs. When she's finished, there is no sign that the room is occupied, save for her black East German envelope and the black iBook bag, both resting now on the ecru expanse of the enormous bed.

She examines the instructions for the room's Internet connection, gets out the iBook and goes to hotmail.

Parkaboy, with two attachments.

She'd e-mailed him from Damien's telling him she was on her way here, but not under whose auspices. Parkaboy is one of the few F:F:Fers who she's certain would know exactly who Bigend is and what Blue Ant is about.

She'd asked him for his and Musashi's best

advice on how to go about contacting Taki and obtaining the mystery number. This will almost certainly be that.

It's titled KEIKO. She opens it.

How'd you manage Tokyo? But never mind, because the 'Sash and I have been burning the midnight oil for you in the meantime. Well, mostly the 'Sash, cuz he's the one had to find us a Keiko. Cept she's not a Keiko but a Judy . . .

Cayce opens the first attachment.

"Parkaboy, you are outrageous."

A multilayered confection, message within message, and all of it targeting Taki, or Taki as Parkaboy and Mushashi imagine him.

Keiko/Judy is simultaneously pubescent and aggressively womanly, her shapely yet slender legs spilling out of a tiny tartan schoolgirl kilt, to vanish, mid-calf, into shoved-down, bunched-up cotton kneesocks of an unusually heavy knit. Cayce's cool-module, wherever it resides, has always proven remarkably good at registering the salient parameters of sexual fetishes she's never encountered before, and doesn't in the least respond to. She just knows now that these Big Sox are one of those, and probably culture-specific. There will be a magazine for Japanese guys into big socks, she's sure of it. The big socks go into retro faux-Converse canvas, but with platform soles to balance the very sizable bulk of sock-scrunch around the ankles, giving Keiko/Judy a knees-down look recalling a baby Clydesdale.

Keiko/Judy has pigtails, huge dark eyes, free-sized sweatshirt making her breasts a mystery, and something so determinedly carnal in her expression that Cayce finds it unnerving. Bigend would recognize the image-toggle instantly, child-like innocence and hardboiled come-on alternating at some frequency beyond perception.

She goes back to Parkaboy's e-mail.

Judy Tsuzuki, five-foot-eleven and about as Japanese as you are, aside from the DNA. Texas. Twenty-seven. Bartender in this place down the street from Musashi's. What we did to up the wattage for Taki, aiming to maximize libidinal disturbance, we shot this long tall Judy then reduced her by at least a third, in Photoshop. Cut'n'pasted her into Musashi's kid sister's dorm room at Cal. Darryl did the costuming himself, and then we decided to try enlarging her eyes a few clicks. That made all the difference. Judy's epicanthic folds are long gone, the way of the modest bust nature intended for her (actually we've got her wrapped up in an Ace bandage for the shot, but nothing too tight) and the resulting big round eyes are pure Anime Magic. This is the girl Taki's been looking for all his life, even though nature's never made one, and he'll know that as soon as he lays eyes on this image. The other attachment . . .

She opens it. Something in felt-penned kanji, with multiple exclamation marks.

That's Keiko's inscription. You'll need to get someone Japanese, preferably young and female, to write this on the printout for you. I'll spare you the translation. As to hooking you up with Taki, I have been working on that while Musashi did the glamour photograph. It's coming along but I haven't wanted to move too quickly as our boy seems a little erratic. Keiko has just sent him word that a friend of hers will be arriving in Tokyo and has a surprise for him. Will get back to you when I have his response. Are you there on business? I hear they actually eat raw fish.

She stands up, walks backward until her thighs bump the edge of the bed, throws up her arms, and falls back in snow-angel fashion, staring up at the white ceiling.

Why has she come here? Is there now some new and permanently non-undoable snarl in her trailing soul-tether?

She closes her eyes but it has nothing to do with sleep. It only makes her aware that they currently seem to be a size too large for their sockets.

The doormen are carefully neutral as she leaves the Hyatt in 501's and the Buzz Rickson's, declining their offer of a car.

A few blocks on, she buys a black knit cap and

a pair of Chinese sunglasses from an Israeli street vendor, shaking her head at his suggestion of a Rolex Daytona to complete the look. With the cap tugged low, hair tucked up into it, and the Rickson's to zip up and slouch down in, she feels relatively gender-neutral.

Not that it doesn't feel as safe here as she remembers it having felt before, but that in itself takes a little getting used to. Actually she's heard that violent crime is up, but she'll treat it as though it isn't. Because she can't stay up in her white box overhanging the city. Not now. She feels as though something more than her soul has been left behind, this time, and she needs to walk it off.

Win. She'd started to project Win on those white walls, and that won't do. The image still ungrieved.

No. Putting her feet down firmly as she walks on. Walk like a man. I fought the law. Hands in pockets, the right clutching the sunglasses.

And the law won.

She passes one of those spookily efficient midnight road crews, who've set up self-illuminated traffic cones prettier than any lamp she's ever owned, and are slicing into asphalt with a water-cooled steel disk. Tokyo doesn't so much sleep as pause to allow crucial repairs to its infrastructure. She's never actually seen soil emerge from any incision they might make in the street, here; it's as though there is nothing beneath the pavement but a clean, uniformly dense substrate of pipes and wiring.

She walks on, more or less at random, responding to some half-forgotten sense of direction, until she finds herself nearing Kabukicho, the all-night zone they call Sleepless Castle, its streets bright as day, very few surfaces lacking at least one highly active source of illumination.

She's been here before, though never alone, and knows it to be the land of mahjong parlors, tiny bars with highly specialized clienteles, sex shops, video porn, and probably much else, but all of it managed with a Vegas-like sobriety of intent that makes her wonder how much fun any of it could really be, even for the committed enthusiast.

Nothing more serious is liable to happen to her here, she trusts, than being accosted by the proverbial drunken salaryman, none of whom have ever proven insistent, or indeed even seriously mobile.

The noise level, as she keeps walking, is becoming phenomenal, industrial: music, songs, Godzilla-volume sexual midway-pitches in Japanese.

Pretend it is the sea.

The individual buildings are remarkably narrow, their restless street-level facades seeming to form a single unbroken surface of neon carnival excess, but overhead are small neat signs, identically rectangular, arranged up the fronts of each one, naming the services or products to be had on each small upper floor.

BEAUTY BRAIN'S FABULOUS FANNY

That one stops her, midway up, in red italics

175

on yellow. She's staring up at it when some-one blunders into her, says something harsh in Japanese, and staggers on. Suddenly she real-izes she's standing in the middle of the street outside a bellowing porno palace, a pair of bored-looking touts or security on either side of the open entrance. She gets an unwelcome glimpse of some decidedly foreign fucking, at once clinical and violent, on a big hi-def screen, and quickly moves on.

She keeps turning corners until it's dark enough to take the glasses off. The sea-roar somewhat diminished.

Here comes the wave. Her knees wobble.

They've got some serious jet lag here. Makes the London kind look like the morning after a restless night.

"Beauty brain," she says to the narrow, perfectly deserted street, "better get her fabulous fanny home."

But which way, exactly, is that?

She looks back, the way she came, down this narrow street, no distinction between sidewalk and roadway.

And hears the approaching whirr of a small engine.

A rider on a scooter appears at the junction with the previous street, a helmeted figure backlit by residual glare, and halts. The helmet turns, seeming to regard her, its visor is blank, mirrored.

Then the rider guns the little engine, wheels

around, and is gone, with the finality of hallucination.

She stands staring at the empty intersection, lit, it now seems, like a stage.

Several turnings on, she finds her way again, steering by distant views of a Gap sign.

Television resolves the mystery of Billy Prion.

Trying to open the curtains for another look at the electric Lego, having showered and wrapped herself in a white terry robe, the universal remote activates the room's huge set instead. And there he is, in full BSE neo-punk drag, half his mouth dead and the other twisted in demented glee, proffering a small bottle of Bikkle, a yogurt-based Suntory soft drink that Cayce herself is somewhat partial to. A favorite of hers in the land of Pocari Sweat and Calpis Water.

It tastes as though ice cubes have melted in it, she remembers, and instantly wants some.

Billy Prion, then, she thinks as the ad ends, is currently the gaijin face of Bikkle, his complete lack of recent exposure in the occident evidently posing no problem here at all.

When she figures out how to turn the television off, she leaves the curtains closed, and turns the room's lights off, one after another, manually.

Still wearing the robe, she curls up between the sheets of the big white bed and prays for the wave to come, and take her for as long as it can.

It comes, but somewhere in it is her father. And the figure on the scooter. Blank expanse of that chromed visor.

CHAPTER 15

SINGULARITY

Win Pollard went missing in New York City on the morning of September 11, 2001. The doorman at the Mayflower flagged an early cab for him, but couldn't remember a destination. A one-dollar tip from the man in the gray overcoat.

She can think about this now because the Japanese sunlight, with the robotic drapes fully open, seems to come from some different direction entirely.

Curled in a body-warm cave of cotton broadcloth and terry, the remote in her hand, she unforgets her father's absence.

Neither she nor her mother had known that Win was in town, and his reason or reasons for being there remain a mystery. He lived in Tennessee, on a disused farm purchased a decade earlier. He had been working on humane crowd-control barricades for stadium concerts. He was in the process, at the time of his disappearance, of obtaining a number of patents related to this work, and these, should

179

they be granted, would now become part of his estate. The company he'd been working with was on Fifth Avenue, but his contacts there had been unaware of his presence in the city.

He had never been known to stay at the Mayflower, but had arrived there the night before, having made reservations via the web. He had gone immediately to his room, and as far as could be known had remained there. He had ordered a tuna sandwich and a Tuborg from room service. He had made no calls.

Since there was no known reason for his having been in New York, that particular morning, there was no reason to assume that he would have been in the vicinity of the World Trade Center. But Cynthia, Cayce's mother, guided by voices, had been certain from the start that he had been a victim. Later, when it was revealed that the CIA had maintained some sort of branch office in one of the smaller, adjacent buildings, she had become convinced that Win had gone there to visit an old friend or former associate.

Cayce herself had been in SoHo that morning, at the time of the impact of the first plane, and had witnessed a micro-event that seemed in retrospect to have announced, however privately and secretly, that the world itself had at that very instant taken a duck in the face.

She had watched a single petal fall, from a dead rose, in the tiny display window of an eccentric Spring Street dealer in antiques.

She was loitering here, prior to a nine-o'clock breakfast meeting at the SoHo Grand, fifteen minutes yet to kill and the weather excellent. Staring blankly and probably rather contentedly at three rusted cast-iron toy banks, each a different height but all representing the Empire State Building. She had just heard a plane, incredibly loud and, she'd assumed, low. She thought she'd glimpsed something, over West Broadway, but then it had been gone. They must be making a film.

The dead roses, arranged in an off-white Fiestaware vase, appeared to have been there for several months. They would have been white, when fresh, but now looked like parchment. This was a mysterious window, with a black-painted plywood backdrop revealing nothing of the establishment behind it. She had never been in to see what else was there, but the objects in the window seemed to change in accordance with some peculiar poetry of their own, and she was in the habit, usually, of pausing to look, when she passed this way.

The fall of the petal, and somewhere a crash, taken perhaps as some impact of large trucks, one of those unexplained events in the sonic backdrop of lower Manhattan. Leaving her sole witness to this minute fall.

Perhaps there is a siren then, or sirens, but there are always sirens, in New York.

As she walks toward West Broadway and the hotel, she hears more sirens.

Crossing West Broadway she sees that a crowd

is forming. People are stopping, turning to look south. Pointing. Toward smoke, against blue sky.

There is a fire, high up in the World Trade Center.

Walking more quickly now, in the direction of Canal, she passes people kneeling beside a woman who seems to have fainted.

The towers in her line of sight. Anomaly of smoke. Sirens.

Still focused on her meeting with a German outerwear manufacturer's star designer, she enters the SoHo Grand and quickly climbs stairs made from something like faux bridge girder. Nine o'clock exactly. There is an odd, sub-aquatic quality to the light in the lobby. She feels as though she is dreaming.

There is a fire in the World Trade Center.

She finds a house phone and asks for her designer. He answers in German, hoarse, excited. He doesn't seem to remember that they are having breakfast.

"Come please up," in English. Then: "There has been a plane." Then something urgent, strangled, in German. He hangs up.

A plan? Change of? He is on the eighth floor. Does he want to have breakfast in his room?

As the elevator doors close behind her, she closes her eyes and sees the dry petal, falling. The loneliness of objects. Their secret lives. Like seeing something move in a Cornell box.

The designer's door opens as she raises her

182

hand to knock. He is pale, young, unshaven. Glasses with heavy black frames. She sees that he is in his stocking feet, his freshly laundered shirt buttoned in the wrong holes. His fly is open and he is staring at her as though at something he has never seen before. The television is on, CNN, volume up, and as she steps past him, uninvited but feeling the need to do something, she sees, on the screen beneath the unused leatherette ice bucket, the impact of the second plane.

And looks up, to the window that frames the towers. And what she will retain is that the exploding fuel burns with a tinge of green that she will never hear or see described.

Cayce and the German designer will watch the towers burn, and eventually fall, and though she will know she must have seen people jumping, falling, there will be no memory of it.

It will be like watching one of her own dreams on television. Some vast and deeply personal insult to any ordinary notion of interiority.

An experience outside of culture.

She finds the right button on the remote and the drapes track open. She crawls out of her white cave, the terry robe hanging wrinkled around her, and goes to the window.

Blue sky. A clearer blue than she remembers in Tokyo. They use unleaded fuel, now.

She looks down into the woods surrounding the

Imperial Palace and sees the few visible sections of rooftop that Bigend's travel girl promised.

There must be paths through those woods, paths of a quite unimaginable charm, which she will never see.

She tries to judge her degree of soul-delay but feels nothing at all.

She is alone here, with only the background hum of air-conditioning.

She reaches for the phone and orders breakfast.

CHAPTER 16

GOING MOBILE

There had been a smell, in the weeks after, like hot oven cleaner, catching at the back of the throat. Had it ever gone entirely away?

She concentrates on her breakfast, eggs poached to perfection and toast sliced from a loaf of slightly alien dimensions. The two slices of bacon are crisp and very flat, as though they've been ironed. High-end Japanese hotels interpret Western breakfasts the way the Rickson's makers interpret the MA-1.

She pauses, fork halfway from plate, looking toward the closet where she'd hung her jacket the night before.

Blue Ant Tokyo has been charged with helping her in any way it can.

When she's finished eating, cleaning her plate with the final corner of the last slice of toast, she pours a second cup of coffee and looks up the local Blue Ant number on her laptop. She dials it on her cell and hears someone say, "Mushi mushi," which makes her smile. She asks

185

for Jennifer Brossard, and tells her, no preface other than hello, that she needs a black MA-1 flying jacket reproduction by Buzz Rickson's, in the Japanese equivalent of an American men's size 38.

"Anything else?"

"They're impossible to find. People order them a year in advance."

"Is that all you need?"

"Yes, thanks."

"Shall we send it to the hotel?"

"Yes. Thank you."

"Bye, then." Jennifer Brossard clicks off.

Cayce hits End and stares briefly out at blue sky and oddly shaped towers.

Her requests don't have to make any sense, she gathers, which is interesting.

When the psychosomatic oven cleaner starts to stage a comeback, it's time to do more things, preferably purposeful things, to unremember. She showers, dresses, e-mails Parkaboy.

Mushi mushi. I hope you've gotten Judy out of that elastic bandage. She makes a great Keiko. I'll have that printed out and personally inscribed, and after that it's up to you. Got a laptop that goes cellular, though I haven't figured how to do that yet. But I'm taking it with me today and I will. I'll be checking my mail, and here's the number of my cell here, if you need to go to voice.

She checks the number of her phone and types it in.

All I can do now is wait for you to hook me up with Taki.

She's spoken with Parkaboy twice before, and both times it's been odd, in the way that initial telephone conversations with people you've gotten to know well on the Net, yet have never met, are odd.

She considers opening the latest from her mother, but decides it might be too much, after that waking reverie. It often is.

Downstairs, in the business center, an exquisite girl in something like the Miyake version of an office lady uniform inkjets the Keiko image on a stiff sheet of superglossy eight-and-a-half by eleven.

The image embarrasses Cayce, but the pretty OL exhibits no reaction at all. Emboldened, Cayce has her print out Darryl's kanji as well, requests a thick black marker, and asks the girl to copy it, inscribing the photograph for her.

"We need it for a shoot," she lies by way of explanation. Unnecessarily, because the girl considers whatever it says there, calmly judges the available space on the photo, and executes a very lively looking version, complete with exclamation marks. Then she pauses, the marker still poised.

"Yes?" Cayce asks.

"Pardon me, but would be good with Happy Face?"

"Please."

The girl quickly adds a Happy Face, caps the marker, hands the photograph to Cayce with both hands, and bows.

"Thank you very much."

"You are welcome." Bowing again.

Walking past the bamboo grove in the sky-high lobby she catches a glimpse of her hair in a mirrored wall.

Speed-dials Jennifer Brossard.

"It's Cayce. I need my hair cut."

"When?"

"Now."

"Got a pen?"

Twenty minutes later, in Shibuya, she's settling in to a hot-rocks massage that she hasn't asked for, in a twilit room on the fifteenth floor of a cylindrical building that vaguely resembles part of a Wurlitzer jukebox. None of these women speak English but she's decided just to go with the program, whatever it is, and count on getting her hair cut at some point in the process.

Which she does, in great and alien luxury, for the better part of four hours, though it proves to involve a kelp wrap, a deep facial, manifold tweezings and pluckings, a manicure, a pedicure, lower-leg wax, and close-call avoidance of a bikini job.

When she tries to pay with the Blue Ant card, they giggle and wave it away. She tries again and one of them points to the card's Blue Ant logo. Either Blue Ant has an account, she decides, or they do Blue Ant's models and this is a freebie.

Walking back out into Shibuya sunlight, she feels simultaneously lighter and less intelligent, as though she's left more than a few brain cells back there with the other scruff. She's wearing more makeup than she'd usually apply in a month, but it's been brushed on by Zen-calm professionals, swaying to some kind of Japanese Enya-equivalent.

The first mirror she sees herself in stops her. Her hair, she has to admit, is really something, some paradoxical state between sleek and tousled. Anime hair, rendered hi-rez.

The rest of the image isn't working, though. The standard CPUs can't stand up to this sushi-chef level of cosmetic presentation.

She opens and closes her mouth, afraid to lick her lips. She has their repair kit in with the laptop, probably hundreds of dollars' worth of that other kind of Mac product, but she knows she'll never get it on again like this.

But there, just down the block, is one or another branch of Parco, any of which houses enough micro-boutiques to make Fred Segal on Melrose look like an outlet store in Montana.

Less than an hour later she emerges from Parco wearing the tape-patched Rickson's, a black knit skirt, black cotton sweater, black Fogal tights that she suspects cost half a month's rent on her place in New York, and a black pair of obscurely retro French suede boots that definitely did. She has the CPUs she was wearing folded into a big Parco carrier bag, and the laptop in a graphite-colored, hip-hugging piece of ergonomic body luggage, with a single wide strap that passes diagonally between her breasts and lends the sweater a little help, that way.

Conversion to CPU status has been conferred with the aid of a seam ripper from the notions section of a branch of Muji, located on the eighth floor, leaving all the labels behind. All but the very small label on the hip bag, which simply says LUGGAGE LABEL. She might even be able to live with that. She'll have to see.

All of this on Bigend's card. She's not sure how she feels about that, but she supposes she'll find out.

There's a coffee place directly across the street, a two-story Starbucks clone in which everyone seems to be chain-smoking. She buys a glass of iced tea, blinks at tiny individual containers of liquid sugar and lemon juice (why didn't we think of that?), and makes her way to the second floor, where fewer people are smoking.

She settles at a Scandinavian-looking counter of pale wood that runs the length of a window overlooking the street and the entrance to Parco, and unpacks the laptop, phone, and manuals. She's not one of those people who won't ever read the manual, although she'll skip it if she can.

Ten minutes of concerted attention has F:F:F on the screen, wireless fully effected, so she sweetens her lemon tea and checks out the action. She knows this stage, after a new segment turns up: Everyone's had a chance to view it repeatedly, and brainstorm, and now the more personal, more deeply felt interpretations are emerging.

She looks down into the street, where odd-sized vehicles break the flow of spotless but otherwise non-foreign-looking cars (so many cars everywhere being Japanese) and sees a silver scooter go past, its driver wearing a matching silver helmet with a mirrored visor and what she recognizes as an M-1951 U.S. Army fishtail parka, an embroidered red-white-and-blue RAF roundel on its back, like a target. Flashing back to that morning in Soho, the window of the mod shop, before her Blue Ant meeting.

It's somehow her nature, she thinks, to pick out this one detail, this errant meme: a British military symbol re-purposed by postwar style-warriors, and recontextualized again, here, via cross-cultural echo. But the rider has it right: the '51 fishtail is the one.

She checks her mail. Parkaboy.

I hear, o Mistress Muji.

This startles her, just having been there, but then she remembers that Parkaboy knows she likes Muji because nothing there ever has a logo. She's told him about the logo problem.

Where are you exactly? Near as I can make out, Taki's day job is in Shinjuku. He proposes to meet you in Roppongi, early evening. I've told him you are going to convey Keiko's regards, and give him something she's sent specially for him. You are a teacher, though not one of hers, a recent friend, and have been helping her with her English. And, of course, a footagehead, which he knows, as Keiko is a footagehead too. Keiko has implied that your getting the number could, in some unspecified way, help her academically. He knows you don't speak Japanese, but claims to have enough English for an encounter of this sort. Whoo. I say whoo because we have been working very hard, Darryl and I, being Keiko. I think we have gotten it across that he really should give you that number, if he wants to encourage further interaction with her. Am assuming you will be up for that, even tho there on biz, but keep that cell on. I'll call you as soon as we have a time and place, and e-mail a map that Taki says he's going to e-mail Keiko.

She shuts down, closes the laptop, unhooks the phone, and repacks everything. The smoke is getting to her. She looks around. Every man there has obviously been staring, but immediately looks down or away.

She takes a last sip of sweet iced tea and swings down off the stool, Velcroing the Luggage Label back across her shoulder, picking up the Parco bag, and hitting the stairs to the street.

Soul-delay plays tricks with subjective time, expanding or telescoping it at seeming random. That big beauty brain session in Shibuya, all that making her fanny fabulous, and the shopping in Parco after it, had seemed to take the full five hours it had taken, but the rest, drifting from one personal landmark to the next, by cab and on foot, seem now, in the Hello Kitty section of Kiddyland, to have collapsed into a single moment of undifferentiated Japanese Stuff.

And why, she wonders, gazing blankly at more Hello Kitty regalia than seems possible, do Japanese franchises like Hello Kitty not trigger interior landslide, panic attack, the need to invoke the duck in the face?

She doesn't know. It just doesn't. No more than does Kogepan, the clueless-looking homunculus, whose name, she vaguely recalls, means "burnt toast." The Kogepan goods are arrayed beyond Hello Kitty, a franchise that has never quite found Hello Kitty's global legs. One can buy Kogepan purses, fridge magnets, pens, lighters, hair brushes, staplers, pencil boxes, knapsacks, watches, figurines. Beyond Kogepan lies the franchise of that depressive-looking boneless panda and her cubs. And none of this stuff, purest no-content marketing, triggers Cayce in the least.

But something is making a strange and annoying

sound, even above the low-level electronic uproar of Kiddyland, and eventually she realizes that it's her phone.

"Hello?"

"Cayce? Parkaboy." He sounds quite unlike he "sounds" on the screen, whatever that means. Older? Different.

"How are you?"

"Still awake," he says.

"What time is it there?"

"What day, you mean," he corrects her. "I'd rather not tell you. I might start to cry. But never mind. You're on. He wants to meet you in a bar in Roppongi. I think it's a bar. Says there's no name in English, just red lanterns."

"A nomiya."

"This guy's got me feeling like I live there, and I'm tired of it already. Darryl and I, we're like those Mars Rover jockeys: virtual jet lag. Tokyo time and we're trying to hold down paying jobs in two different time zones back here. So Taki's sent Keiko a map, right? And I've sent it to you, and he says six thirty."

"Will I recognize him?"

"What we've seen of him, he's not Ryuichi Sakamoto. Mind you, that's not what Keiko thinks. She's practically told him she'll fork over the booty as soon as she gets home."

She winces. This aspect of what she's up to here makes her extremely uncomfortable.

"But he'll give me the number?"

"I think so. If he doesn't, no pic of Keiko."

"You, I mean she, told him that?" She likes this part of it even less.

"No, of course not. That's a love-offering, something to hold him till she gets the booty back to Tokyo. But you've got to get that number. Make it clear."

"How?"

"Play it by ear."

"Thanks."

"You want to get to the bottom of this little footage thing, don't you?"

"You're implacable."

"So are you. It's why we get along. I'm going to eat this whole bag of chocolate-covered espresso beans now, and sit here grinding my teeth flat until I hear from you."

He hangs up.

She stares back at all those eyes: Hello Kitty and Kogepan and the boneless pandas.

CHAPTER 17

MAKING MAYHEM

W alking up Roppongi Dori from the ANA Hotel, where she's had the cab drop her, into the shadow of the multi-tiered expressway that looks like the oldest thing in town. Tarkovsky, someone had once told her, had filmed parts of *Solaris* here, using the expressway as found Future City.

Now it's been Blade Runnered by half a century of use and pollution, edges of concrete worn porous as coral. Dusk comes early, under here, and she spies signs of homeless encampment: plastic-wrapped blankets tucked back into an uncharacteristically littered scrim of struggling municipal shrubs. Vehicles blast past, overhead, a constant drumming of displaced air, particulates sifting invisibly.

Roppongi she remembers as not so nice a place, one of those interzones, a border town of sorts, epicenter of the Bubble's cross-cultural sex trade. She'd gone here with crowds, to bars that were hot then but now likely weren't, but always there'd been an edge of some meanness she hadn't noticed elsewhere in town.

She pauses, aware of the plastic handle of the Parco bag. It's been rubbing against her palm for hours. It feels wrong, for a meeting. Nothing in it but third-best skirt, tights, shrunken black Fruit. She slides it between two ragged bushes bonsai'd by the expressway's shadow, leaving it there, and walks on.

Out of the shadow and up the hill, into actual evening and Roppongi proper. Checking the napkin map copied earlier from laptop screen. Parkaboy had forwarded Taki's segment of a Tokyo map. X marks the spot. One of the little streets behind the main drag. She remembers these as being either glossy or shabby, depending on the business done there.

Shabby, it turns out, after a twenty-minute wander, orienting to the napkin, and at one point spotting Henry Africa's in the distance, that expat bar she remembers, though that's not where she's heading.

Where she's heading, she now sees, scoping it sidewise as she reconnoiters past, is one of those apparently nameless little red-lantern pub-analogs they have here, places where tourists generally don't drink. Set into ground-floor walls in back lanes like this one. Their bare-bones decor or lack of it reminding her of a certain kind of functionally alcoholic corner lounge in lower Manhattan, now nearing extinction as the city's ley lines shifted further still, initially in response to a decade's Disneyfication and now to a deeper whammy.

She glimpses, past a dingy noren in an open doorway, empty chrome stools of the soda-fountain spin-around kind, but very low, fronting an equally low bar. Their red upholstery split and bulging. Patched, like her jacket, with peeling tape.

She sighs, squares her shoulders, turns around, and ducks past the noren, into an ancient, complexly layered, and somehow not unpleasant odor of fried sardines, beer, and cigarettes.

No trouble recognizing Taki. He's the sole customer. Rising and bowing, tomato-faced with reflexive embarrassment, to greet her.

"You must be Taki. I'm Cayce Pollard. Keiko's friend from California."

He blinks earnestly, through dandruff-dusted lenses, and bobs there, uncertain whether he should resume his seat. She pulls out the chair opposite him, removes her bag and the Rickson's, hangs them across the back, and seats herself.

Taki sits down. He has an open bottle of beer in front of him. He blinks, saying nothing.

She'd gone back and looked at Parkaboy's initial explanation of Taki again, after she'd sketched the map on a napkin:

Taki, as he prefers we call him, claims to orbit a certain otaku-coven in Tokyo, a group that knows itself as "Mystic," though its members never refer to it that way in public, nor indeed refer to it at all. It is these Mystic wonks, according to Taki, who have cracked the watermark on #78. This segment, according to Taki, is marked with a number of some kind, which he claims to have seen, and know.

What she's confronted with here, she decides, is an extreme example of Japanese geek culture. Taki is probably the kind of guy who knows everything there is to know about one particular Soviet military vehicle, or whose apartment is lined with unopened plastic models.

He seems to be breathing through his mouth.

Catching the eye of the barman, she points to a poster advertising Asahi Lite and nods.

"Keiko's told me a lot about you," she says, trying to get into character, but this only seems to make him more uncomfortable. "But I don't think she's told me what it is that you do."

Taki says nothing.

Parkaboy's faith, that Taki has enough English to handle the transaction, may be unfounded.

And here she is, halfway around the world, trying to swap a piece of custom-made pornography for a number that might mean nothing at all.

He sits there, mouth-breathing, and Cayce is wishing she were anywhere else, anywhere at all.

He's in his mid-twenties, she guesses, and slightly overweight. He has a short, nondescript haircut that manages to stick up at several odd angles. Cheap-looking black-framed glasses. His blue button-down shirt and colorless checked sport coat look as though they've been laundered but never ironed.

He isn't, as Parkaboy has indicated, the best-looking guy she's recently had a drink with. Though that, come to think of it, would be Bigend. She winces.

"I do?" Responding perhaps to the wince.

"Your job?"

The barman places her beer on the table.

"Game," Taki manages. "I design game. For mobile phone."

She smiles, she hopes encouragingly, and sips her Asahi Lite. She's feeling more guilty by the minute. Taki—she hasn't gotten his last name and probably never will—has big dark semicircles of anxiety sweat under the arms of his button-down shirt. His lips are wet and probably tend to spray slightly when he speaks. If he were any more agonized to be here, he'd probably just curl up and die.

She wishes she hadn't had all this fabulous fanny stuff done, and bought these clothes. It hadn't been for him, but really she hadn't imagined she'd be dealing with anyone with this evident a social deficit. Maybe if she were looking plainer he wouldn't be as spooked. Or maybe he would.

"That's interesting," she lies. "Keiko told me you know a lot, about computers and things."

Now it's his turn to wince, as if struck, and knocks back the remainder of his beer. "Things? Keiko? Says?"

"Yes. Do you know 'the footage'?"

"Web movie." He looks even more desperate now. The heavy glasses, lubricated with perspiration, slide inexorably down his nose. She resists an urge to reach over and push them back up.

"You . . . know Keiko?" He winces again, getting it out.

She feels like applauding. "Yes! She's wonderful! She asked me to bring you something." She's suddenly experiencing full-on London-Tokyo soul-displacement, less a wave than the implosion of an entire universe. She imagines climbing over the bar, past the barman with his pockmarked, oddly convex face, and down behind it, where she might curl up behind a scrim of bottles and attain a state of absolute stasis, for weeks perhaps.

Taki fumbles in his sport coat's side pocket, coming up with a crumpled pack of Casters. Offers her one.

"No, thank you."

"Keiko sends?" He puts a Caster between his lips and leaves it there, unlit.

"A photograph." She's glad she can't see her own smile; it must be ghastly.

"Give me Keiko photo!" The Caster, having been plucked from his mouth for this, is returned. It trembles.

"Taki, Keiko tells me that you've discovered something. A number. Hidden in the footage. Is this true?"

His eyes narrow. Not a wince but suspicion, or so she reads it. "You are footage lady?"

"Yes."

"Keiko like footage?"

Now she's into improv, as she can't remember what Parkaboy and Musashi have been telling him.

"Keiko is very kind. Very kind to me. She likes to help me with my hobby."

"You like Keiko very much?"

"Yes!" Nodding and smiling.

"You like . . . Anne-of-Green-Gable?"

Cayce starts to open her mouth but nothing comes out.

"My sister like Anne-of-Green-Gable, but Keiko . . . does not know Anne-of-Green-Gable." The Caster is dead still now, and the eyes behind the dandruff-flecked lenses seem calculating. Have Parkaboy and Musashi blown it, somehow, in their attempt to generate a believable Japanese girl-persona? If Keiko were real, would she necessarily have to like Anne of Green Gables? And anything Cayce might ever have known about the Anne of Green Gables cult in Japan has just gone up in a puff of synaptic mist.

Then Taki smiles, for the first time, and removes the Caster. "Keiko modern girl." He nods. "Body-con!"

"Yes! Very! Very modern." Body-con, she knows, means body-conscious: Japanese for buff.

The Caster, its tan faux-cork filter glittering wetly, goes back between his lips. He roots through his pockets in turn, produces a Hello Kitty! lighter, and lights his cigarette. Not a plastic disposable but a chromed Zippo, or clone thereof. Cayce feels as though the lighter has followed her here from Kiddyland, a spy for the Hello Kitty! group mind. She smells benzene. He puts it away. "Number . . . very hard."

"Keiko told me that you were very clever, to find the number."

He nods. Seems pleased perhaps. Smokes. Taps ash into an Asahi ashtray. There's a small, cheap-looking television behind the bar, just at the periphery of Cayce's vision. It's made of transparent plastic and shaped something like a football helmet. On its six-inch screen she sees a screaming human face attempting to thrust itself through a sheet of very thin latex, then a quick clip of the South Tower collapsing, then four green melons, perfectly round, rolling along on a flat white surface.

"Keiko told me that you would give me the number." Forcing the smile again. "Keiko says you are very kind."

Taki's face darkens. She hopes it's a deeper level of embarrassment kicking in, or something to do with that specific alcohol-processing enzyme the Japanese lack, and not anger. He suddenly whips a Palm from his inside jacket pocket and pokes its infrared slit at her.

He wants to beam her the number.

"I don't have one," she tells him.

He frowns, fumbles out a fat, retro-looking pen. She's ready for this, slipping him the napkin she'd drawn her Roppongi map on. He frowns, scrolls on his Palm, then copies a number on the edge of the folded napkin.

She watches as he copies three groups of four numbers each, the pen's felt tip blurring in the coarse weave of the paper. Upside down: 8304 6805 2235. Like a FedEx waybill number.

She takes it as he closes his pen.

She quickly reaches down into the Luggage Label bag, which she's surreptitiously unzipped against just this eventuality, and comes up with the envelope containing the Judy image. "She wants you to have this," she tells him.

She's afraid he'll tear it, as he fumbles the envelope open. His hands are trembling. But then he gets it out, has a look, and she sees his eyes are wet with tears.

She can't handle this at all.

"Excuse me, Taki," gesturing in what she hopes will be the direction of the toilet, "I'll be right back." She leaves her Rickson's and the laptop bag hanging on her chair and gets up. She still has the napkin in her hand. Sign language with the barman gets her down a tiny hallway and into the least salubrious Japanese toilet she's seen in a while, one of those concrete hole-in-the-floor jobs from the old days. It reeks of disinfectant and, she supposes, urine, but it has a door she can get between herself and Taki.

She takes a deep breath, regrets it, and looks at the number on the napkin. The ink is spreading into the weave and there's a chance it will soon be illegible. But then she sees a blue plastic pen, left atop some kind of wall-mounted hand dryer. When she picks it up it leaves a shiny chrome print in a layer of gritty dust. She tests it on the yellowed, graffiti-free wall, getting a thin line of blue.

She copies the number on the palm of her left hand, puts the pen back on the dryer, wads the napkin up, and tosses it into the depression in the center of the floor. Then, since she's there, she decides to pee. It won't be the first time she's used one of these, but it could quite happily be the last.

He's gone, when she returns to the table, two crumpled pieces of paper money beside the empty beer bottle, her half-empty glass, the ashtray, and the torn envelope. She looks over at the barman, who scarcely seems to register her presence at all.

On the red television, insectoid superheroes on streamlined motorcycles buzz through a cartoon cityscape.

"He took a duck in the face," she says to the barman, shrugging into the Rickson's and slipping the Luggage Label over her head.

The barman, glumly, nods.

Outside, there is no sign of Taki, though she hasn't really expected any. She looks both ways, wondering where she might more easily hail a cab back to the Hyatt.

"Do you know this bar?"

Looking up into a smooth, tanned, evidently European face that she somehow doesn't like at all. She takes in the rest of him. A Prada clone: black leather and shiny nylon, shoes with those toes she hates.

Hands grab her, from behind, hard, just above the elbows, pinning her arms at her sides.

There's something that's supposed to happen now, she thinks. Something that's supposed to happen—

When she'd first moved to New York her father had insisted that she take lessons in self-defense from a small, fastidious, slightly portly Scotsman called Bunny. Cayce had argued that New York was no longer as dangerous as Win remembered it, which was true, but it had been easier to visit Bunny six times than to argue with Win.

Bunny, her father had told her, had been an SAS man, but when she'd asked Bunny about this he'd said that he had always been too fat for the SAS, and had in fact been a medic. Bunny favored cardigans and tattersall shirts, was very nearly her father's age, and told her that he would teach her how "hard men" fought in pubs. She'd nodded gravely, thinking that if she were ever set upon by literary types in the White Horse she would at least be able to hold her own. So, while some of her friends explored Thai kickboxing, she'd been schooled in no more than half a dozen moves most often practiced in the maximum-security wings of British prisons.

Bunny's preferred term for this was "making mayhem," which he always pronounced with a certain satisfaction, raising his pale sandy eyebrows. And, in the way of things, Cayce had never, that she knew of, come even remotely close to requiring Bunny's mayhem in Manhattan.

With the Prada clone's fingers scrabbling to undo the Velcro fastening between her breasts, trying to free her bag, it comes to her that what's supposed to happen now, in the Bunny plan of things, is this: She shoves her arms suddenly forward, just far enough to grab the glove-thin leather of both his lapels. And as the second assailant inadvertently cooperates, yanking her arms back, her hands buried in Prada's lapels, she pulls with all her might and smashes her forehead as hard as she can into Prada's nose.

Never having actually followed through on this move before, Bunny not having had a nose to spare, she's unprepared both for the pain it causes her and the extraordinarily intimate sound of cartilage being crushed against her forehead.

His dead weight, as he abruptly collapses, pulls his lapels from her hands, reminding her to step back, off-balancing whoever is behind her, look down between her legs (a man's shoe, black, with that same horrible squared-off toe), and stamp as hard as she can, with her heel, on the revealed instep, producing a remarkably shrill scream from very close behind her left ear.

Pull loose and run.

"And run" was invariably the footnote to any Bunny lesson. She tries to, the laptop banging painfully against her hip as she bolts for the end of this alley and the lights of a brighter Roppongi.

Which is instantly blocked, with a squeal of brakes, by a silver scooter and its silver-helmeted rider. Who flips up his mirrored visor.

It's Boone Chu.

She seems to inhabit some fluid, crystalline medium. Pure adrenal dream.

Boone Chu's mouth is open, moving, but she can't hear him. Hitching up her skirt, all in the logic of dream, she straddles the scooter behind him and sees his hand do something that throws them forward, yanking the two black-clad men suddenly out of frame and leaving her with a sculpturally confused image of the one trying to hop, one-legged, as he tries to pull the other, the one she'd head-butted, to his feet.

In front of her the RAF roundel on the back of Boone Chu's parka as she grabs him around the waist to keep from being thrown off, realizing simultaneously that it had been him she'd seen from the Starbucks clone earlier, and him in Kabukicho the night before, and now very fast, between two lines of cars waiting at the intersection, their polished doors gleaming like jellyfish in a neon sea.

Out into the crossing before the lights can change. A left that reminds her she has to lean with him when he turns, and that she's never liked motorcycles, and then he's bombing down a more upscale alley, past, she sees, something called Sugarheel Bondage Bar.

He passes her back a metallic blue helmet with flaming eyes painted on it. She manages to fumble this on, but can't fasten the strap, onehanded. It smells of cigarettes.

Her forehead throbs.

Slowing slightly, he turns left into another alley, this one too narrow to admit cars. It's one of those Tokyo residential corridors, lined with what she assumes are tiny houses, and punctuated with glowing clusters of vending machines. Billy Prion's paralyzed grin on one, proffering a bottle of Bikkle.

She's never seen a scooter driven this fast, down one of these, and wonders if it's illegal.

He stops where the alley intersects a wider, car-capable one, slams down the kickstand and swings off, removing his helmet. A pair of tough-eyed Japanese kids throw down cigarettes as he hands one of them his helmet and unzips his parka.

"What are you doing here?" Cayce asks him, sounding as if nothing very remarkable has happened, as she dismounts and tugs her skirt down. Boone removes her helmet and hands it to the second kid.

"Give him your jacket."

Cayce looks down at the Rickson's, sees the tape peeling where Dorotea burned it. She pulls the Rickson's off and hands it to the boy now fastening the strap of the blue helmet. Noticing a missing finger joint there against a flaming-eye decal. The boy puts the Rickson's on, zips it up, and hops on the scooter behind his partner, who's wearing Boone's helmet and parka. This one snaps the mirrored visor down, returns Boone's thumbs-up, and then they are gone.

"You've got blood on your forehead," Boone tells her.

"It's not mine," she says, touching it, feeling stickiness smear beneath her fingertips. Then: "I think I'm concussed. I might throw up. Or faint."

"It's okay. I'm here."

"Where did they go, with the bike?" The metal column of a traffic light, across the alley, furred with weird municipal techno-kipple, twins itself, dances, then comes together again.

"Back to see where those two are."

"They look like us."

"That's the idea."

"What if those men catch them?"

"The idea was that they might wish they hadn't. But after what you did to them, they might not be up to much."

"Boone?"

"Yes?"

"What are you doing here?"

"Watching them watch you."

"Who are they?"

"I don't know yet. I think they're Italian. Did you get the number? Is it in the laptop?"

She doesn't answer.

CHAPTER 18

HONGO

She holds a chilled can of vending-machine tonic water against the bump. Most of a pack of Kleenex-analog, splashed with tonic, has been used to sponge her forehead.

The cab negotiates a narrow lane. The back of a concrete apartment building, bristling unevenly with dozens of air conditioners. Motorcycles shrouded under gray fabric.

Boone Chu saying something in Japanese, but not to the driver. Speaking to his cellular headset. He looks back, through the cab's rear window. More Japanese.

"Have they found them?" she asks.

"No."

"Where did Taki go?"

"Up the street, walking fast. Hung a left. He was the guy with the number?"

She resists the urge to check the palm of the hand holding the sweating can. What if the ink is running? "When did you get here?" Meaning Japan.

"Right behind you. I was in coach."

"Why?"

"We were followed, when we left the restaurant in Camden Town."

She looks at him.

"Young guy, brown hair, black jacket. Followed us to the canal. Watched us from up on the locks. With either a camera or a small pair of binoculars. Then he walked us back to the tube and stuck with me. Lost him in Covent Garden. He didn't make the lift."

This makes her think of the first time she'd read Sherlock Holmes. A one-legged Lascar seaman.

"Then you followed me?"

He says something in Japanese, into his headset. "I thought it would be a good idea to establish some kind of baseline in terms of what we've got here. Start from scratch. We're working for Bigend. Are the people following us working for Bigend? If not . . . ?"

"And?"

"No idea, so far. I coasted past our two here, last night, and they were speaking Italian. That was when you were on your way to the pink zone."

"What were they saying?"

"I don't speak Italian."

She lowers the tonic water. "Where are we going now?"

"The bike is following us, to make sure nobody else is. When we're positive of that, we'll go to a friend's apartment."

"They didn't find those men?"

"No. The one you head-butted is probably in a clinic now, getting his nose taped back into shape." He creases his forehead. "You didn't learn that studying marketing, did you?"

"No."

"They might be Blue Ant, for all we know. You might have just broken the nose of a junior creative director."

"The next junior creative director who tries to mug you, you might break his nose too. But Italians who work in Tokyo ad agencies don't wear Albanian Prada knockoffs."

The cab is on some kind of metropolitan freeway now, curving past woods and ancient walls: the Palace. She remembers the paths she'd imagined, that morning, looking down from her room. She turns and looks back, trying to see the scooter, and discovers that her neck is painfully stiff. The walls and trees are beautiful but blank, concealing a mystery.

"They were trying to get your bag? The laptop from Blue Ant?"

"My purse is in there, my phone."

As if on cue, the Blue Ant phone starts to ring. She digs it out. "Hello?"

"Parkaboy. Remember me?"

"Things got complicated."

She hears him sigh, in Chicago. "It's okay. I live for fatigue poisons."

"We did meet," she tells him, wondering if Boone Chu can hear his side of the conversation.

She's left the volume cranked, against Tokyo street noise, and regrets it.

"No doubt about that. He hasn't even waited to get back home. Straight into an Internet café and pouring out his heart to Keiko."

"I want to talk, but it has to be later. I'm sorry."

"He told Keiko he'd given it to you, so I wasn't too worried. E-mail me." Click.

"Friend?" Boone Chu takes the tonic water and helps himself to a sip.

"Footagehead. Chicago. He and his friend found Taki."

"You did get the number?"

No getting around it, now. Either she lies to him because she doesn't trust him, or tells him, because, relatively speaking, she does.

She shows him her palm, the numerals in blue fiber tip.

"And you didn't enter it in the laptop? E-mail it to anyone?"

"No."

"That's good."

"Why?"

"Because I need to have a look at that laptop."

He has the driver stop in what he tells her is Hongo, near Tokyo University. He pays, they get out, and as the cab pulls away, the silver scooter arrives.

"I'd like my jacket back, please."

Boone says something in Japanese to the passenger, who unzips and removes Cayce's Rickson's without getting off the scooter. He tosses it to her and grins, unreassuringly, beneath the lowered visor of the flaming-eye helmet. Boone takes a white envelope from the waistband of his black jeans and passes it to the driver, who nods and stuffs it into the pocket of the fishtail parka. The scooter whines and they're gone.

The Rickson's smells faintly of Tiger Balm. She slides the tonic can into a convenient recyc canister and follows Boone, her forehead aching.

A minute later she's staring up at a three-story clapboard structure that seems to float above the narrow street, dilapidated and impossibly flimsy-looking. Clapboard doesn't quite describe it; the silvered wooden planks look as though they might be the blades of a giant venetian blind. She's almost never seen anything genuinely old, in Tokyo, let alone in this state of casual disrepair.

Ragged, browning palms lean on either side of an entrance ornately roofed with Japanese tiles, echoed by a pair of decaying stucco columns supporting nothing at all. One of these seems to have had its top gnawed off by something enormous. Turning to him. "What is it?"

"A prewar apartment building. Most of them went in the firebombing. Seventy units in this one. Communal toilets. Public bathhouse a block away."

The balconies, she guesses, following him, are

racks for airing bedding. They pass a dense low shrubbery of bicycles, climb three broad concrete steps, and enter a tiny foyer floored with shiny turquoise vinyl. Cooking smells she can't identify.

Up a poorly lit flight of bare wooden stairs and along a corridor so narrow that she has to walk behind him. A single fluorescent tube flickers, somewhere ahead. He stops and she hears the rattle of keys. He opens a door, reaches for a light switch, and steps aside. Cayce steps in and finds herself trying to remember Win's clever neurological explanation of déjà vu.

Strange but somehow familiar, the lighting consists of a few clear glass bulbs with dim, faintly orange filaments: reproduction Edison bulbs. Their light is inefficient, magical. Furniture low and somehow like the building itself: worn, strangely comforting, still in use.

He comes in behind her and closes the door, which is featureless and modern and white. She sees his little reddish-brown suitcase open on a low central table, his phones set out beside it and the laptop's screen up but dark. "Who lives here?"

"Marisa. A friend of mine. She designs fabrics. She's in Madrid now." He crosses to a crowded kitchen alcove and flicks on a much brighter, whiter sort of light. She sees a pink Sanyo rice cooker on a small counter, and a narrow white plastic freestanding appliance connected to transparent tubing. A dishwasher? "I'll make tea." Filling a kettle from a bottle of water.

She walks to one of two sliding paper windows inset with central panes of partially frosted glass. Through the clear sections she looks out at gently sloping rooftops that seem, impossibly, to be partially covered in knee-deep moss, but then she sees that this is something like the kudzu on Win's farm in Tennessee. No, she corrects herself, it probably is kudzu. Kudzu where it comes from. Kudzu at home.

The rooftops, in the light from surrounding windows, are corrugated iron, rusted a rich and uneven brown. A large tan insect strobes through the communal patch of light, vanishes. "This is an amazing place," she says.

"There aren't many left." Rattling canisters in a search for tea.

She slides the window open. She hears the kettle coming to a boil.

"Do you know Dorotea Benedetti?"

"No," he says.

"She works for Heinzi and Pfaff, the graphics people. She deals with Blue Ant for them. I think she had someone get into Damien's apartment for her. They used his computer."

"How do you know?"

She walks over to what she guesses was originally a storage alcove for bedding. This one has been converted into something closer to a Western closet. A woman's clothes are hung there, along a wooden pole, and they make her feel somehow self-conscious. If there were a door, she'd close it.

"Whoever did it called her from Damien's phone. I redialed and heard her voice-mail message." And she tells him the story then: Dorotea, the Rickson's, Asian Sluts.

By the time she's finished, they're sitting cross-legged on cushions on the tatami, the kitchen light off, drinking green tea he pours from an earthenware pot. "So it might be that our Italians here aren't about the fact that you're working for Bigend, or about the footage," he says. "The break-in predated that."

"I don't know if I'd call it a break-in," she says. "Nothing broken. I don't know how they got in."

"A key-gun, if they were pros. Nothing you'd notice. You wouldn't have noticed anyway, if they hadn't used your browser and your phone. Neither of which is entirely professional, but we'll let that pass. And Bigend told you she'd worked for someone in Paris who'd done industrial espionage?"

"Yes. But he thought she had it in for me because she assumed he was going to offer me a job she wants, at Blue Ant London."

"And you didn't tell him about the jacket, or your apartment?"

"No."

"And our boys speak Italian. But we don't know whether they were here to begin with, or whether they were sent here. They weren't on our flight, I'm sure of that. I watched them watch you, today. Hard to say if they know the city or not. They had a car and a Japanese driver."

She studies his face in the glow of the bamboo filaments, the Edison bulbs. "Dorotea knows something about me," she says. "Something very personal. A phobia. Something that only my parents, my therapist, a few close friends would know. That worries me."

"Could you tell me what it is?"

"I'm allergic. To certain trademarks."

"Trademarks?"

"Since I was a kid. It's the downside of my ability to judge the market's response to new logo designs." She feels herself blushing, and hates that.

"Can you give me an example?"

"The Michelin Man, for one. There are others. Some are more contemporary. It's not something I'm very comfortable talking about, actually."

"Thank you," he says, very seriously. "You don't need to. Do you think Dorotea knows about this?"

"I know she does." She tells him about the second meeting, Bibendum, the doll hung from Damien's doorknob.

He frowns, says nothing, pours more tea. Looks at her. "I think you're right."

"Why?"

"Because she knows something about you, something she couldn't easily have found out. But she has. That means someone's gone to a lot of trouble. And she was the one who pulled that image out of the envelope and showed it to you. Then she left the doll, or had someone leave it. But I think the doll was supposed to help make you go away, back to New York. But you didn't, and then I turned up, and now we're both here, and my guess is that the men who were watching you are working for her."

"Why?"

"Unless we can find them, which isn't very likely now, and convince them to tell what they know, which very likely isn't much, I have no idea. And less idea who she might be working for. Will you let me have a look at your computer now?"

She gets the iBook out of the bag, where it lies on the matting beside her, and passes it to him. He puts it on the low table beside his own and takes a neatly coiled cable from his suitcase. "Don't mind me. I can do this and talk."

"Do what?"

"I want to make sure this isn't sending your every keystroke to a third party."

"Can you do that?"

"These days? Not absolutely." Now both computers are cabled together, and on, and she watches as he turns to his and inserts a CD-ROM. "Things have been different in computer security, since last September. If the FBI were doing what they admit they can do, to your laptop, I might be able to spot it. If they were doing what they don't tell you they can do, that would be another story. And that's just the FBI."

"The FBI?"

"Just an example. Lots of people are doing lots of different things, now, and not all of them are American, or government agencies. The ante's been upped right across the board." He does things to her keyboard, watching his screen.

"Whose apartment is this?"

"Marisa's. I told you."

"And Marisa is?"

He looks up. "My ex."

She'd known that, somehow, and hadn't liked it, and doesn't like it that she doesn't like it.

"Just friends now," he says, and looks back to the screen.

She raises her hand and opens it, palm out, exposing Taki's number. "So what can you do with this?"

He looks up. Seems to brighten. "Find the company that did the watermarking, if it was done by a company. Then see what we can find out from them. If they've marked each segment, there should be an account. The client would be that much closer to your maker."

"Would they tell you?"

"No. That's not the same as my finding out, though."

She lets him work, and sips her tea, and looks around at the eight-mat apartment in the amber glow of the Edison bulbs, and wonders, though she doesn't want to, about the woman who lives here.

She has a lump on her forehead, and the fabulous fanny stuff is probably a disaster now, and she wants to find a well-lit mirror and check the damage, but she doesn't.

She doesn't feel tired, though, or lagged, mirrored-out, or anything at all. Whatever else is going on, she seems to have graduated to a more serious league of soul-displacement. Wherever her serotonin levels are, right now, it's like she lives there.

CHAPTER 19

INTO THE MYSTIC

The night security man at her hotel looks like a younger, slightly less approachable version of Beat Takeshi, the Japanese actor whose existential gangster films have been the favorites of two former boyfriends. Ferociously upright and tightly buttoned into an immaculate black blazer, he leads her into the elevator and up to her room.

She's told them at the desk that she's left her key in the room, and so is accompanied there by this stern man, who produce his own key, a real metal one, sturdily chained to his belt, and unlocks her door. He opens it for her, turns on the lights, and gestures her in.

"Thank you. Just a moment, please, while I find my key." Actually it's in the pocket of her Rickson's, ready to be palmed when needed, but she checks the bathroom, the closet, glances behind the black furniture, then notices a large gray carrier bag, with the Blue Ant logo on the side, at the foot of her bed. She kneels to look under the bed, discovers that it isn't the kind you can look under, and comes up, still kneeling, with the key, a plastic mag-strip card, in her hand. "I've found it. Thank you very much."

He bows and goes, closing the door behind him. She locks and chains it. Just to be sure, she manages to scoot the large black armchair close enough that the door can be only partially opened. This hurts her neck. She resists the urge to curl up, there, and become unconscious. Instead she goes back to the bed and looks in the Blue Ant bag. It contains, carefully folded in black tissue, an unworn black Rickson's MA-1. The morning seems a very long time ago.

She becomes aware of the smell of Tiger Balm from her own Rickson's. She stuffs the new one back into its bag, removes the Luggage Label bag, and undresses.

In the bathroom mirror, clinically illuminated, her forehead looks only lightly bruised. The remains of the fabulous fanny job, she thinks, have come to resemble the first attempts of a trainee mortician. She unwraps a bar of soap, reminds herself not to use the hotel's shampoo, which will have the wrong pH for gaijin hair, remembers to carefully copy Taki's number from her palm onto a Park Hyatt notepad, and shuts herself in the glass-walled shower, which is approximately the size of Boone's girlfriend's kitchen in Hongo.

Feeling much cleaner, if no less exhausted, she wraps herself in a terry robe and checks the room-service menu, deciding on a small pizza and a side of mashed potatoes. Non-Japanese comfort food.

The pizza turns out to be very good, though very Japanese, but the potatoes are amazing, a Rickson's-like super-simulacrum of a Western classic. She's also ordered two bottles of Bikkle, opening her second as she finishes the potatoes.

She needs to check her e-mail. She needs to phone Pamela Mainwaring about getting out of here as soon as possible. And really she should phone Parkaboy.

She slugs back her Bikkle and plugs her iBook into the room's dataport.

One e-mail. As it pops up in her in-box she sees that it's from Parkaboy.

Wondrous Strange

She opens it. There is an attachment titled WS.jpg.

No rest for the wicked. After e-mailing us, or rather Keiko, from two separate cafes, as soon as Taki got home he sent the attached.

She clicks on the jpeg.

A map. A broken T scribed with city streets and strings of numbers. It reminds her of a steak's T-bone, the upright tapering raggedly, the left cross-arm truncated. Within its outline are avenues, squares, circles, a long rectangle suggesting a park. The background is pale blue, the T-bone gray, the lines black, the numbers red.

If Taki was in love before, he is now in lust. Or maybe the other way around. But in his new frenzy of adoration and desire to please, he has sent this, which he explains to Keiko is the latest from Mystic. Darryl, who has otaku DNA himself, is convinced that Taki is not a member of this Mystic, but a peripheral character of some kind—possibly, since he designs games for a Japanese phone system, one of their sources of information. Darryl says that the highest level of play, for techno-obsessives, is always and purely about information itself, and he thinks that Mystic may have battened on the footage not in a footagehead way but simply for the sake of solving a puzzle that no one else has solved. He posits a cell of professional info-theorists, of some kind, who are also, in this ultimate otaku sense, info-junkies. Perhaps employed in the R&D arm of one or more large corporations. Perhaps they need something that Taki knows. It doesn't matter, really, since Taki seems somehow to have reversed the flow of data, and the psychosexual cruise missile that is Judy, tweaked, has found its mark. To save you the trouble of counting them, there are one hundred and thirty-five numbers, here, each number consisting of three groups of four digits.

Her scalp prickles. She gets up, goes into the bathroom, returns with the notepad.

8304   6805   2235

She puts the pad beside her iBook and peers into the red cloud cover of numbers partially masking the T-city.

There it is. The streets directly beneath it are small and twisted, down toward the bottom of the peninsula that forms the T's upright. Although, she reminds herself, she has no reason to believe this the representation of any island, actual or imaginary. It might be a T-shaped segment extracted from some larger map. Though the streets, if they are streets, align with its borders . . .

Remember the whiteout, when they kiss? As though something explodes, overhead? If you've been following F:F:F you'll know that that set off major Blitz reverb in our British posters. Various proofs that our story is set in London in the 40s, none ultimately convincing. But that whiteout. Blank screen. Taki says that "Mystic" decrypted this graphic from that whiteness. As to how blankness can yield image, I do not pretend to know, though I suppose that is the question, ultimately, that underlies the entire history of art. Nonetheless, where are we, with this thing? If each segment is watermarked with one of these numbers, then the action in each segment seems to be mapped here, and we have, for the first time, a geography of sorts, and possibly, if we knew the numbers for each segment, a formal order. (I've entered them all in a database and don't see that they are sequential. Suspect random generation and/or random assignment.) Darryl is looking into a graphics bot that only searches maps. Meanwhile, exhausted, baffled, but unhealthily excited, I remain, Parkaboy.

She stares at the T-bone city.
She phones Pamela Mainwaring.

CHAPTER 20

UBER-BONES

Her watch wakes her, chirping mercilessly. She sits up in the huge bed, uncertain where she is.

Six in the morning. Pamela Mainwaring has her on a flight out of Narita just after noon.

She makes sure the red light is on, on the oversized kettle-analog, wraps herself in last night's white robe, goes to the window, powers open the drapes, and dimly discovers Tokyo at the bottom of an aquarium of rainy light. Gust-driven moisture shotguns the glass. The lavish lichen of the wooded palace grounds tosses darkly.

Her cell rings. She goes back to the bed, roots through the covers, finding it.

"Hello?"

"Boone. How's your head?"

"Tired. I called Pamela . . ."

"I know. So did I. I'll meet you in the lobby at eight-thirty. JR reservations for both of us."

Something about a lack of autonomy here that bothers her.

229

"See you," he says.

The water reaching boil as she's rummaging through the snacks atop the minibar, looking for a shrink-wrapped filter-coffee unit.

The hotel's fitness center, a room so large that it seems designed primarily to illustrate interior perspective, has its own Pilates reformer, a fauxclassical Japanese interpretation in black-lacquered wood, upholstered with something that looks like sharkskin. She's able to get in her workout, then shower and wash her hair, pack, and make the lobby by eight-thirty.

Boone arrives minutes later, in his black horsehide coat, carrying his small leather suitcase and one of those Filson outfitter bags that look like L.L. Bean on steroids.

She picks up her own black generic Korean nylon and they walk out, past the bamboo grove and into the elevator.

She wakes to the offer of a hot washcloth. For an instant believes she's still on her way to Tokyo, and that it's all been a dream.

This is terrifying, and she hurts her neck, so quickly does she crane around, to find that Boone Chu is in fact in the nearest seat-nest, in full recline and apparently asleep, looking as strangely canceled as anyone does when wearing a black blindfold.

They hadn't had much to say to each other, on

the train to Narita. She'd slept in the lounge, after security measures including a sort of CAT scan for their shoes and answering questions in front of an infrared device that registered minute changes in the temperature of the skin around the eyes, the theory being that lying about having packed one's own bag induced a sort of invisible and inevitable micro-blush. Though the Japanese also believe that personality is determined by blood type, or had when she was last here. Boone had been impressed, though, and had told her to expect the blush machines soon in America.

She'd told him, as they were boarding, that she'd gotten something more from Taki, via Parkaboy, but that she was too tired to explain it, that she'd show it to him when she'd had more sleep.

What is that about, she wonders, that holding back? Something to do with the newness of their working relationship, but also, she knows, something to do with something she'd felt in that apartment. She doesn't want to look at that too closely. But also she wants time to get her head around this idea of the T-bone city. And there's a way in which she simply finds him pushy.

But there's the T-bone to try to figure out, she thinks, powering her bed up into lounger mode and hauling the bag with her iBook up from the floor. She boots up, finds Parkaboy's jpeg, and opens it.

If anything, it's even more enigmatic than when she first saw it.

Taki. Is there any chance that he's just making

this all up to impress Keiko? But Parkaboy and Darryl had found him on a Japanese website, where he'd already made some mention of something encrypted in a segment of the footage. They hadn't invented Keiko yet. No, she knows that Taki is for real. Taki is too sad not to be real. She imagines him going to someone, while Keiko emerged more clearly for him through her messages, and somehow, perhaps at some strange cost, obtaining this image, extracted from that white flare.

But in his shyness, his caution, he hadn't brought it to their meeting. He'd brought only the one number. Then the Photoshopped version of Judy Tsuzuki had impacted, and he'd gone home and sent this to Parkaboy, thinking he was sending it to his big-eyed, Clydesdale-ankled love.

She thinks of Ivy, in Seoul, F:F:F's founder. What would Ivy make of this?

She frowns, seeing for the first time how working for Bigend, with Boone Chu, has skewed her relationship to F:F:F and the footagehead community. Even Parkaboy, who's been instrumental in all of this, doesn't know what she's up to, who she's working for.

"What is it?" Boone, looming beside her in the twilit aisle, his black T-shirt and the blindfold slung beneath his chin offering the odd suggestion of a priest's collar. A single one-inch square of white paper and he'd have a costume: the young priest, eyes somewhat swollen with sleep.

She elevates to chair and he joins her, crouching

on the little visitor seat at the unit's foot. She passes him her iBook. "Taki really liked the photograph. He couldn't wait to get home. Had to keep stopping in cafés to e-mail her. When he did get home, he sent her this."

"Are there a hundred and thirty-five of these?" Indicating the numbers.

"I haven't counted them myself, but yes. The one that matches the number Taki gave me is near the bottom of the T."

"It looks as though each location corresponds to a segment of footage. Not the way you'd map a virtual world, though. Not if mapping virtual worlds was ordinarily your business."

"What if it weren't?"

"What do you mean?"

"What if you were just making something up as you went along? Why should we assume that the maker knows what he's doing?"

"Or we could assume that he does, but he's just doing it his own way. The people who designed all the early Nintendo games drew them on long rolls of paper. There was no better way to do it, and you could unroll the whole thing and see exactly how it would move. The geography of the game was two-D, scrolling past on the screen . . ." He falls silent, frowning.

"What?"

He shakes his head. "I need more sleep." He stands up, passing her the iBook, and returns to his seat.

She stares blankly at the jpeg, the iBook slightly warm atop her thighs, and wonders exactly what she should do when they get to Heathrow. She has the new keys to Damien's place in her Stasi envelope, in the Luggage Label bag. That's where she feels like going, really, though the residual ache in her forehead is causing her some doubt.

Would someone have been able to fiddle the locks in the meantime? She has only a very fuzzy idea of who might live in the other two flats, but whoever they are, they seem to go out to work on a regular basis. A burglar might be able to get in, then, during the day, and do whatever it took to open the apartment.

But her only other option is a London hotel, and, even with Blue Ant footing the bill, she's feeling hoteled out. She'll go to Camden, then. Heathrow Express to Paddington, then a cab. Decision out of the way, she closes Taki's jpeg, puts the iBook away, and returns to bed-mode.

When they exit immigration, Bigend is waiting, the only smiling face in a scrum of glum chauffeurs holding hand-lettered sheets of cardboard. Bigend's says "POLLARD & CHU" in coarse-tipped red felt pen.

He really does seem to have too many teeth. His Stetson is set too squarely on his head and he's wearing the raincoat she'd last seen him in.

"Right this way, please." He makes a point of taking over the luggage trolley from Boone, and they follow him out, throwing glances at each other, past the cab queue and the recent arrivals coughing gratefully over first cigarettes. She sees his Hummer parked where she's certain no one at all is allowed to park, ever, and watches as he and Boone open the square doors at the rear and load the bags.

Bigend holds the passenger-side door for her as she climbs in. Boone gets the seat behind her.

She watches Bigend fold his enormous plastic parking permission.

"You didn't need to pick us up, Hubertus," she says, because she feels the need to say something, and because it seems so abundantly the truth.

"Not at all," says Bigend, ambiguously, pulling away from the curb. "I want to hear all about it."

Which he does, mainly via Boone, but, Cayce gradually notes, with two serious omissions. Boone never mentions the head-butting or Taki's jpeg. He tells Bigend that they went to Tokyo to follow up a lead suggesting that at least one segment of the footage has an encrypted watermark.

"And does it?" Bigend asks, driving.

"It may," Boone says. "We have a twelve-digit code that may have been extracted from a specific segment of footage."

"And?"

"Cayce was followed, in Tokyo."

"By whom?"

"Two men, possibly Italian."

"Possibly?"

"I overheard them speaking Italian."

"Who were they?"

"We don't know."

Cayce sees Bigend purse his lips. "Do you have any idea," he asks her, briefly making eye contact, "why you would be followed? Unfinished business elsewhere? Something unrelated?"

"We were hoping you might be able to answer that one, Hubertus," Boone says.

"You think I had Cayce followed, Boone?"

"I might myself, Hubertus, if I were in your position."

"You might well," says Bigend, "but you aren't me. I don't work that way, not in a partnership." They're on the evening motorway now, and raindrops suddenly strike the vertical windshield, causing Cayce to imagine that the weather has followed them from Tokyo. Bigend turns on the wipers, spatular things that swing from the top of the glass rather than the bottom. She watches as he touches a button, fractionally reduces air pressure in the tires. "However," he says, "as I'm sure you understand, partnership with me makes you more likely to be followed. This is an aspect of the downside of a high profile."

"But who would know that we're your partners?" Cayce asks.

"Blue Ant is an advertising agency, not the CIA. People talk. Even the ones who've been hired not to. Secrecy, when we're planning a campaign, for instance, can be of the utmost importance. But still things leak. I'll look at that, at exactly who would have reason to believe the two of you are working for me, but now I'm more curious about these putative Italians."

"We lost them," Boone says. "Cayce had just received the code from her contact, and I thought it was the right time to get her out of there. When I had a look for them, later, they were gone."

"And this contact?"

"Someone I turned up through the footagehead network," Cayce says.

"Exactly the sort of thing I was hoping for."

"We doubt he has anything further to offer us," Boone says, causing Cayce to glance back at him, "but if this watermark is genuine, it may be a good start."

Cayce looks straight ahead, forcing herself to concentrate on the arcing of the wipers. Boone is lying to Bigend, or withholding information, and now she feels that she is too. She briefly considers bringing up Dorotea and Asian Sluts at this point, just to send things in a direction Boone isn't expecting, but she has no idea of his agenda in lying. He may be doing it for a reason she'd approve of. The next time they're alone together, she needs to have this out with him.

She blinks, as they abruptly leave the motorway, entering London's maze. Streetlights coming on.

After Tokyo, everything here feels so differently scaled. A different gauge of model railroad. Though if asked, she'd have to admit that the two do have something mysteriously in common. Perhaps if

London had been built, until the war, primarily of wood and paper, and then had burned, the way Tokyo had burned, and then been rebuilt, the mystery she's always sensed in these streets would remain somehow, coded in steel and concrete.

To her considerable embarrassment, and confusion, they have to wake her when the Hummer pulls up outside of Damien's.

Boone carries her bag to the door. "I'll go in with you."

"It isn't necessary," she says. "I'm tired. I'll be fine."

"Call me." On the plane, approaching Heathrow, he'd tapped his various cell numbers into her phone. "Let me know you're okay."

"I will," she says, feeling like an idiot. She unlocks the front door, manages a smile, and goes in.

On the landing, she sees that the bundles of magazines have been removed, and with them the black bin liner.

She's up the last flight and almost to Damien's door, the second German key in hand, before she realizes that light is showing, from the crack at the foot of his door.

She stands there, the key in one hand, her bag in the other, hearing voices. One is Damien's.

She knocks.

A young woman, taller than she is, opens the door. Enormous cornflower-blue eyes, tilted slightly above extraordinary cheekbones, regard her coldly. "Yes? What do you want?" the blonde asks, with what Cayce assumes is a stage accent, some aspect of a joke, but as this woman's mouth, with its perfectly outlined, extravagantly full underlip, sets itself in grim distaste, she realizes that it isn't.

Damien, stubble-headed after a recent shaving and for an instant quite unrecognizable, appears behind uber-bones and playfully squeezes her shoulders, grinning over one at Cayce.

"It's Cayce, Marina. My friend. Where on earth have you been then, Cayce?"

"Tokyo. I didn't know you were back. I'll go to a hotel."

But Damien will have none of that.

CHAPTER 21

THE DEAD REMEMBER

arina Chtcheglova, whom Cayce quickly gathers is Damien's Russian line producer, is not the first of his girlfriends to have taken an immediate dislike to her. Seeing the torsos of the robot girls again, she remembers that the one from whom those had been so fetchingly cast had been the most vicious of cows—till now, anyway.

Fortunately she and Marina are almost immediately separated, conversationally, by Voytek, whose presence here Cayce initially accepts as a function of the Great Whatever of multiply impacted jet lag, and by Fergal Collins, Damien's Irish accountant and tax advisor, someone Cayce knows from several previous occasions. Voytek re-engages la Chtcheglova in whatever rant he must have embarked on prior to Cayce's arrival, this conducted in what Cayce assumes is Russian, and with a tempo and apparent fluid assurance very unlike his delivery in English. Marina doesn't seem to like this, particularly, but seems compelled to listen.

Voytek wears his usual orphaned skateboard gear, but Marina is wearing what Cayce is trying not to admit to herself is probably this season's Prada exclusively, everything black. Her cheekbones actually make Voytek's look relatively non-Slavic. It's as though she somehow has an extra pair folded in, behind the first set; Caucasian in some primordial, almost geological sense.

She looks, Cayce decides, like a prop from one sequel or another of *The Matrix*; if her boobs were bigger she could get work on the covers of role-playing games for adolescent boys of any age whatever.

Fergal, some genially carnivorous species of businessman draped in the pelt of an art-nerd, works mainly in music but has been with Damien for as long as Cayce has known him. "What's it like in Tokyo, after the devaluations?" he asks, seated beside her on Damien's brown couch.

"It's more the way it is now than it's ever been," Cayce replies, a line of Dwight David Eisenhower's that she sometimes resorts to when she has nothing whatever to offer. Fergal frowns slightly. "Sorry, Fergal. I was hardly even there. Has Damien finished his film?"

"Would to God he had, but no. He's back to re-up financing, collect three more cameras and additional crew, and, I think," he lowers his voice slightly, "because herself fancied a visit to the capital."

"She's his line producer?"

"We call her that but really it's more post-Soviet. She's the blat girl."

"The what?"

"Blat. What the old boys in your country called juice, I think. She's connected, Marina is. Her father was the head of an aluminum plant, back in the dreamtime. When they privatized, somehow he wound up owning it outright. Still does, and a brewery and a merchant bank as well. The brewery's been a godsend, actually. They've been trucking beer to the site since the day we started shooting. Makes Damien a very popular fellow, and otherwise they'd be drinking vodka."

"Have you been there?"

"For an afternoon." He winces.

"What's it like?"

"Somewhere between a three-month 1968 rock concert, mass public grave-robbing, and *Apocalypse Now*. Hard to say, really, which is of course the big draw for our boy here. Do you know that Pole, there?"

"Voytek."

"Who is he?"

"An artist. I've been staying here, and when I went to Tokyo I left the keys with him."

"He can certainly occupy Marina in her native tongue, which keeps her out of ours, but do you think he's chatting her up?"

"No," Cayce says, seeing Voytek produce one of his notebooks from his pouch, "he's trying to get her to fund a project." Marina makes a dismissive gesture and goes into the bedroom, closing the door behind her. Voytek crosses to the couch, smiling, notebook in one hand, bottle of beer in the other. "Casey, where have you been?"

"Away. Have you met Fergal?"

"Yes!" He sits on the couch. "Damien calls me from airport, asks me to meet here with keys and tandoori and beer. This producer, Marina, she is very interesting. Has gallery connections in Moscow."

"You speak Russian?"

"Of course. Magda, she was born there. Myself, Poland. Our father was Moscow civil engineer. I do not remember Poland."

"Christ," cries Damien from the kitchen, "this khoorma is heaven!"

"Excuse me," Cayce says, standing. She goes into the yellow kitchen and finds Damien transfixed with joy, half a dozen foil dishes open on the counter in front of him.

"It's not fucking stew," Damien says. "At the dig we live on stew. No refrigeration. Stew's been simmering for the better part of two months. Just keep tossing things in. Lumps of mystery meat and boiled potato in what looks like gray Bisto. That and bread. Russian bread's brilliant, but this khoorma—"

She gives him a hug. "Damien, I can't stay here."

"Don't be silly."

"No. I'm pissing off your girlfriend, being here."

Damien grins. "No you aren't. It's her default setting. Nothing to do with you."

"You aren't making a lot of progress in your relationship choices, since I last saw you, are you?"

"I can't make this film without her."

"Don't you think it might be easier if you weren't in a relationship as well?"

"No. In fact, it wouldn't be at all. She's like that. When are you coming?"

"Where?"

"The dig. You have to see this. It's amazing."

The tower of gray bone. "I can't, Damien. I'm working."

"For Blue Ant again? I thought you said that that was over, when you e-mailed me about the keys."

"This is something else."

"But you've just gotten off the plane from Tokyo. You're here, there's a bed upstairs, and I'm back tomorrow. If you go to a hotel, we won't see one another at all. Go upstairs, sleep if you can, and I'll deal with Marina." He smiles. "I'm used to it."

Suddenly the idea of actually having to find a hotel room and go there seems far too difficult. "You've convinced me. I can't see straight. But if you go back to Russia without waking me, I'll kill you."

"Go up and lie down. Where did you find this Voytek, anyway?"

"Portobello Row."

"I like him."

Cayce's legs feel like they belong to someone else, now. She'll have to try to communicate with them more deliberately, to get them to carry her upstairs. "He's harmless," she says, wondering what that means, and heads for her bag and the stair to the room overhead.

She manages to get the futon unfolded, up there, and collapses on it. Then remembers Boone asking her to phone him. She gets out her cell and speed-dials the first of his numbers.

"Hello?"

"Cayce."

"Where are you?"

"Damien's. He's here."

A pause. "That's good. I was worried about you."

"I was worried about me too, when I heard you bullshitting Bigend on the way in from Heathrow. What was that about?"

"Playing it by ear. There's a chance he knows, you know."

"How?"

"How is academic. It's possible. Who gave you the cell you're using?"

He's right. "And you thought he might give something away?"

"I thought I'd take the chance."

"I don't like it. It makes me complicit, and you didn't give me the opportunity to decide whether or not I wanted to be."

"Sorry." She doesn't think he is. "I need that jpeg," he tells her. "E-mail it to me."

"Is that safe?" she asks.

"Taki's e-mailed it to your friend, and your friend e-mailed it to you. If anyone is keeping track of us that way, they already have it."

"What are you going to do with it?"

"Count angels on pinheads, with a friend of mine."

"Seriously."

"Improvise. Poke at it. Show it to a couple of people smarter than I am."

"Okay." She doesn't like the way she winds up doing what he tells her to do. "Your address in the iBook?"

"No. This one. Chu-dot-B, at . . ." She writes it down. "What's that domain?"

"My former company. All that's left of it."

"Okay. I'll send it. Good night."

"Good night."

Sending the jpeg to Boone requires getting out the iBook and cabling it to the phone. She does this on automatic pilot, apparently remembering how to do it correctly, because her message to chu.b sends immediately.

Automatically, she checks her mail. Another from her mother, this one with unfamiliar-looking attachments.

Without really thinking about it, she opens Cynthia's latest.

These four ambient segments were accidentally recorded by a CCNY anthropology student making a verbal survey of missing-person posters and other signs near the Houston and Varrick barricade on September 25th. We've found this particular tape to be remarkably rich in EVP, and have recovered several dozen messages by a variety of methods.

"He took a duck in the face," Cayce says, closing her eyes. Eventually she has to open them.

Four of them, I believe, are from your father. I know that you aren't a believer, but it seems to me that Win is addressing you, dear, and not me (he quite clearly, twice, says "Cayce") and that there's some urgency to whatever it might be that he's trying to tell you.

Messages of this sort do not yield very easily to conventional studio techniques; those on the other side are best able to modulate those aspects of a recording that we ordinarily think of as "noise," so improvement of the signal to noise ratio amounts to the erasure of the message. However, if you use headphones, and concentrate, you will be able to hear your father say the following:

File #1: Grocery store . . . [??] The tower of light . . . [life?]

File #2: Cayce . . . One hundred and . . . [start of your address?]

File #3 Cold here . . . Korea . . . [core error?] Ignored . . .

File #4 Cayce, the bone . . . In the head, Cayce . . . [headcase, someone here suggested, but frankly it isn't an expression your father would have used]

I know this isn't your reality but I've long since come to accept that. It doesn't matter. It's mine, though, and that's why I'm here at ROTW, doing what I can to help with this work. Your father is trying to tell you something. Frankly, at this point, I wish he would tell us exactly when, and how, and most importantly exactly where he crossed over, as we'd then have a shot at some DNA and proof that he is in fact gone. The legal aspects of his disappearance are not progressing, although I've changed lawyers and had them obtain a writ of . . .

Cayce looks at her hand, which has closed Cynthia's message as if of its own accord.

It isn't that her mother is mad (Cayce doesn't believe that) or that her mother believes in this stuff (though she does, utterly) or even the banal, inchoate, utterly baffling nature of the supposed messages (she's used to that, when EVP are quoted) but that it leaves Win somehow doubly undead.

248

To have someone disappear in Manhattan on the morning of September 11, with no proven destination in the vicinity of the WTC, not even a known reason why they might have gone there, is proving to be an ongoing nightmare of its own peculiar sort. They had only been alerted to the fact of Win's disappearance on the nineteenth, ordinary police procedures having been disrupted, and Win's credit card company having been slow to provide next-of-kin information. Cayce herself had dealt alone with all of the initial phases of the hunt for her father, Cynthia having stayed in Maui, afraid to fly, until well after commercial flights had resumed. On the nineteenth, Win's face had joined the others, so many of them, that Cayce had been living with daily in the aftermath, and very likely his had been among those the CCNY anthropology student had been surveying when (in Cynthia's universe) Win had whispered through the membrane from whatever Other Side it was that Cynthia and her cronies in Hawaii imagined for him. Cayce herself had put up several, carefully sheathed in plastic, near the barricade at Houston and Varrick, having run them off at the Kinko's nearest her apartment uptown. Win, deeply and perhaps professionally camera-shy, had left remarkably few full-face images, and the best she'd been able to do had been one that her friends had sometimes mistaken for the younger William S. Burroughs.

Still more missing strangers had become familiar,

then, as she'd made the stations of some unthinkable cross.

She had, while producing her own posters, watched the faces of other people's dead, emerging from adjacent copiers at Kinko's, to be mounted in the yearbook of the city's loss. She had never, while putting hers up, seen one face pasted over another, and that fact, finally, had allowed her to cry, hunched on a bench in Union Square, candles burning at the base of a statue of George Washington.

She remembered sitting there, prior to her tears, looking from the monument that was still taking shape at the base of Washington's statue to that odd sculpture across Fourteenth Street, in front of the Virgin Megastore, a huge stationary metronome, constantly issuing steam, and back again to the organic accretion of candles, flowers, photographs, and messages, as though the answer, if there was one, lay in somehow understanding the juxtaposition of the two.

And then she had walked home, all the way, to her silent cave with its blue-painted floors, and had trashed the software that had allowed her to watch CNN on her computer. She hadn't really watched television since, and never, if she could help it, the news.

But Cayce's missing person, it had developed, was missing in some additional and specially problematic way.

Where was her father? He had left the Mayflower

and hadn't returned, and that was all that anyone seemed to know. On the advice of her mother's lawyers, she had hired private investigators, who had interviewed cabdrivers, but the city seemed to have acquired a very specific amnesia with regard to Wingrove Pollard, a man gone so thoroughly and quietly missing that it might be impossible to prove him dead.

The dead, her mother had forever been fond of saying, remember. Remember what? Cayce had never wanted to ask.

"Are you awake?" Damien's stubbled head appearing at the top of the stairs. "We're going out to the Brasserie. You're welcome."

"No," she says. "I'm going to sleep." And desperately hopes it's true.

CHAPTER 22

TARN

Sleep takes her down fast, and very deep, whirls her through places too fragmentary to call dreams, then spits her abruptly back to the surface. To lie there in the dark, heart thumping, eyes wide.

By the light in her watch she sees that she's been asleep for no more than forty-five minutes.

The flat below is silent. She remembers they've gone to the Brasserie, a restaurant in Camden High Street, Damien's favorite.

She gets up, pulls on jeans and sweater, and hobbles barefoot down the narrow stair, moving as she imagines she might move if she lived to be eighty. This is beyond soul-delay metaphors, now; it's into physical collapse.

Glancing into Damien's bedroom, she sees that Marina's luggage is the Louis Vuitton stuff with the repeating monograms, the real and loathsome thing, to which she is intensely allergic. Two very new suitcases are open, spilling what she takes to be black Prada exclusively. On the twisted sheets, the silver oven-mitt comforter tossed aside on the floor, she sees a crumpled military garment in a camouflage pattern that she seems to recall is called tarn—information garnered during her time in the skateboard-clothing industry. She knows most of the patterns, and even that the most beautiful is South African, smoky mauve-toned Expressionist streaks suggesting a sunset landscape of great and alien beauty. Is tarn German camouflage, or Russian? English? She can't remember. It means something else as well. A Poe word. Dead lakes?

In the bathroom she avoids looking at herself altogether, fearing what might seem to be revealed at this level of serotonin-lack. Showers quickly, towels, puts her clothes back on, spreads the used towel neatly on the rack (Marina is clearly a pig) and wrinkles her nose at the number of expensive cosmetic products spread around Damien's sink. But here, she discovers, spotting a bit of non-beauty packaging, is a bottle of fine California melatonin, a prescription drug in the UK but not in America. She helps herself to half a dozen of the large beige gelatin capsules, washing them down with weirdly flavored London tap water, and creeps back upstairs, desperately pretending that she's someone very tired (which she supposes she is) who is about to fall deeply and soundly asleep (which she very much doubts she will).

But she does, to her subsequent amazement: a

shallow but mercifully uninhabited sleep, though with a certain sense of sound and fury walled off behind the neurological dryer lint of the melatonin.

She opens her eyes and sees Damien's head there again, at the top of the stairs. He's wearing that tarn jacket, buttoned to the neck. 'Sorry. Just checking. Didn't mean to wake you," he says, almost a whisper.

She looks at her watch. It's seven in the morning. "No," she says, "this is good. I'm awake."

"Marina's not. She'll sleep in. If we're quiet, we can go out without waking her, have coffee and a talk."

"Five minutes."

His head disappears.

Flecktarn. That's what it's called. Like chocolate chips sprinkled on confetti the color of last autumn's leaves.

You pay more, here, to sit with your coffee. Take-away is less expensive. They probably do that in Tokyo, too, but she hadn't noticed.

It's raining, and Damien's worn a black hooded sweatshirt under his flecktarn. He keeps the hood up, here, seated in the back of this Starbucks clone, and she's glad of that, as his stubbled scalp disorients her. She's always known him as someone with a shoulder-brushing, center-parted shoe-gazer anti-haircut.

It feels like old times, to sit here with him,

diagonally opposite Camden Town station, wearing damp clothing and nursing large multi-shot lattes.

"What about your father?" he asks, brown eyes peering from beneath the black cotton cowl.

"No sign. My mother's in Hawaii, picking up messages from him on dead-air sections of audiotape, so she's convinced he's gone." This sounds odd even to her, but how do you say these things?

"Fucking hell," he says, with such evident and simple sympathy that she feels like hugging him. "That must be horrible."

She nods. Sips from the tall paper cup. "Problems with the insurance, but that's probably just a matter of time."

"But you think he's dead?"

"I've never doubted it, really. I don't know why." She looks out from this brightly lit urban cave, past the queue of customers and the sounds of steam, to the strangers passing steadily in the rain.

"And you're over here working for Blue Ant?" He's shot several commercials for them. A Bigend favorite, she's heard. "And in Tokyo?"

She turns back to him. "They wanted me here to tell them whether or not a new logo worked." She names the company and he nods. "Then it all went sideways."

"Can't say you sound happy about the kind of sideways."

"No. You haven't asked me why I changed your locks."

"I wondered."

"Visitor. Uninvited. I wasn't there."

"Someone broke in?"

"Nothing broken, that I could see. But the door was locked when they got in. Any chance anyone else had a key?"

"No. I'd been careful with that. Had them changed just as the reno was completed."

"And there's a chance your computer's been compromised somehow." Thinking of Boone checking her iBook.

"A lot of good that will do anyone. Any idea who it was?" More curious than angry. In fact not angry at all. She'd known he wouldn't be. People fascinate him, in some peculiarly abstract way: the things they do, though not so much why they do them.

She tells him about Dorotea and the Rickson's and Asian Sluts. The changing of the locks. Then her second encounter with Dorotea. The Michelin man in the meeting, and then the doll on the doorknob.

"Wait a minute. You don't talk about that, really, do you?"

"No."

"Who knows, then?"

"Well—you, a very few other close friends, three or four ex-boyfriends I regret having told, a psychiatrist, and two psychologists."

"And why were you in Tokyo?"

"Bigend. He's after the maker of the footage."

She watches him take that one in. He's one of those people apparently immune to the lure of the footage; in his case, she knows, it has to do with his being his own maker, with his own obsessive need to generate his own footage. "Does he say why?"

"Not exactly, but he's convinced that it's big, in some entirely new way, and he wants to get in on the ground floor."

"So you're working for Blue Ant, on that?"

"No. Bigend describes it as a partnership. With him. And an American computer security consultant named Boone Chu."

"Boonchoo?"

"Boone as in Daniel. C-h-u."

"And you're getting somewhere with it?"

"Irritated, mainly, though if I weren't so jet-lagged I'd have room for serious paranoia." She quickly outlines her experience in Japan, not going into detail about Parkaboy or Taki, just a thumbnail of the supposed Italians, and Boone.

"You nutted him?"

"No, I smashed him in the face with my forehead."

"No, that's what we call that, here. Or used to, I think. Amazing. Never imagined you'd have it in you."

"Neither did I." Around them, people with damp, loosely furled umbrellas are chatting and sipping coffee. Over them, now, she hears an amazing Glaswegan accent order a quadruple-shot latte. Damien hears it too, and grins.

"What about you?" she asks. "You're obviously fully engaged in project, more than somewhat with producer."

"Sometimes I think it would be easier if I could sleep with her father instead. He's an old New Russian. Made it looting his own economy, basically, but there's no long-term future in that. Russia's had a GNP on par with Holland, but that's changing. The new New Russians are into transparency: companies that actually have books, pay taxes. They've figured out that you can make even more money, that way. It's no accident that Putin always describes himself as a lawyer. He is. But Marina's dad is old school, and that's what we need in this particular situation. Square it with the people who actually control the land we're digging on, keep the local militia away." He raises one hand, fingers crossed. Raises his cup with the other, to sip.

"Fergal said you were back for re-funding?"

"Done. We met with the moneymen at the Brasserie."

"You don't want old New Russian funding?"

"Very last thing I want. I think we've got another three weeks, shooting."

"You aren't worried, getting hooked up with the don's daughter?"

"He's not mafia," Damien says, very seriously, though she'd meant it only jokingly. "A lesser oligarch. We're okay, Boris and I. I think he's glad to have her out of his hair, actually."

"Then you don't want him to get too used to it, do you?"

"You're scaring me." He finishes the last of his latte. "But I'd be more worried if I were you. Working with Hubertus Bigend would be a scary proposition at the least complicated of times." He stands up, then, and so does she, taking her Luggage Label bag from the back of her chair.

"What's the rest of your day?"

"We're on Aeroflot to Saint Petersburg this afternoon. I have to get our freight on, plus the additional cameramen. Plus Marina. It's a TU 185. Getting Marina on a Russian plane can take some doing. Fergal's got a very tight rein on budget. I have to come out of this owning the film, and that's a stretch. What about you?"

"I'm going to a Pilates studio. When's your flight?"

"Two twenty-five."

"I'm going to stay out of your way, then. You don't mind me being there, with people breaking in?"

"Wouldn't have you anywhere else."

Outside, under the awning, he puts his hands on her shoulders. "Are you going to be all right? You have a lot going on, all of it very weird."

"I'll be okay. It's great to see you."

"I know," hailing a black cab. "I mean yes—it

is, both ways!" The cab pulls over, he opens the door for her, gives her a quick kiss on the cheek. She gets in and he closes the door.

"Neal's Yard," she says.

CHAPTER 23

DICKHEADS

Leaving Neal's Yard and the Pilates studio, she tries to become just another lost tourist, though she knows she'll never be one. Like Magda going out to spread whatever shabby micro-meme her Blue Ant subsidiary requires her to, Cayce knows that she is, and has long been, complicit. Though in what, exactly, is harder to say. Complicit in whatever it is that gradually makes London and New York feel more like each other, that dissolves the membranes between mirror-worlds.

She knows too much about the processes responsible for the way product is positioned, in the world, and sometimes she finds herself doubting that there is much else going on. But this is a mood, she tells herself, a bad one in its low-key way, dealt by soul-delay. Somewhere that lagging part of her is being wound in, and her job here is simply to walk, to be in London and let her body know that she is here.

The rain has stopped but drops still fall from

ledges and awnings, beading on the nylon of her new Rickson's. Absently she reaches to touch the place where the tape should be, but it isn't there. No hole. History erased via the substitution of an identical object.

Just now she wishes lives could be replaced as easily, but knows that that isn't right. However odd things seem, mustn't it be to exactly that extent of oddness that a life is one's own, and no one else's? Hers has never been without its share of oddness, but something in its recent texture seems to belong to someone else. She's never lived her life in such a way as to generate sliding doors and secret passages, the hallmarks, she believes, of some basis in bullshit, of an underlying lack of honesty that she doesn't believe has been hers. She hasn't ever, previously, been a person to be burgled, followed, assaulted with intent to rob. All the time she's spent in the world's various streets, scouting cool for the commodifiers, these things hadn't happened. Why now? What has she done wrong?

Or is it, she considers, simply that the world had gone in such a different direction, in the instant of having seen that petal drop, that nothing really is the same now, and that her expectations of the parameters of how life should feel are simply that, expectations, and increasingly out of line the further she gets from that window in the SoHo Grand.

Pausing now to stare through a sheet of glass at a Duffer of St. George anorak, weirdness of serotonin-lack coursing through her, she suddenly shivers, remembering the hard grip of the man in Roppongi, the one who'd come from behind. She hasn't really felt the fear in that, before now, and now it comes up from her core, a cold thing and hard.

"He took a duck in the face." Well, the other had, really. Took Cayce herself in the face, at however many sudden knots.

Food. In the prolonged absence of: craziness. She moves along until she finds a sandwich shop, small and preglobalized, but also rather smart, as she's in St. Martin's Lane by now. She gets egg salad on a narrow baguette, a cup of filter coffee, and carries them to a small table by the window, where she sits, looking out into the street and eating her sandwich.

She'd first seen Covent Garden after a heavy snow, walking with her hand in Win's, and she remembers the secret silence of London then, the amazing hush of it, slush crunching beneath her feet and the sound made by trapezoidal sections of melting snow falling from wires overhead. Win had told her that she was seeing London as it had looked long ago, the cars mostly put away and the modern bits shrouded in white, allowing the outlines of something older to emerge. And what she had seen, that childhood day, was that it was not a place that consisted of buildings, side by side, as she thought of cities in America, but a literal and continuous maze, a single living structure (because still it grew) of brick and stone.

The Blue Ant cell rings, from the Luggage Label bag. Annoyed that she's left it on to ring, interrupting her thoughts, she fumbles it out, expecting Boone.

"Hello?"

"Cayce. How are you? Have you slept?" Bigend.

"Yes, I did."

"Where are you?"

"Saint Martin's Lane."

"Very close then. Come to Blue Ant. We need to talk."

Basic business instinct suppresses the groan, but only barely. "When?"

"As soon as you can."

"I'm having my breakfast."

"When you're done, then. I'll send a car."

"No," wanting as much time as possible in which to get herself up to something like Bigend-speed. "I need to walk."

"As soon as you can." He clicks off.

It rings again, immediately.

"Hello?"

"Parkaboy. Where are you?"

"Saint Martin's Lane."

"London? I need to run something by you. We're having a problem. With Judy."

"Judy?"

"Judy Tsuzuki. Keiko."

"The girl in the picture?"

264

"All five-eleven of her. She likes to drink, after work, so she started going over to Darryl's place, and Darryl, he's challenged in the girl department. So he gives her drinks and tries to impress her with how big his computer is. That doesn't work, he demonstrates what a great linguist he is, and the effect her picture's having on this dork in Japan. He reads her parts of Taki's e-mails. She's fucking furious with him, all five-eleven in a leather mini-skirt from the bar. Because he's a dickhead to do this to this guy in Japan, this guy who's saying things to her that no man has ever said before—"

"But he thinks she's a schoolgirl—"

"I know, but she's had a few drinks, so Darryl is a dickhead—"

"You're a dickhead too. I'm a dickhead myself for going along with this." Two older British women look at her as they enter. Look away.

"Let's save the metaphysics for later. The problem is, Judy feels sorry for the guy, she's pissed at Darryl, and by extension with us, and she wants to write him back. She wants to send him more pictures, attachments this time, and make him happy. That's what she says she wants, and if Darryl doesn't want to go along with it, she says she'll go to this journalist from the *Chronicle* she was dating, before, and tell him about this pervy hacker in the Mission who's working this scam on this guy in Tokyo—because the guy in Tokyo knows something big about that footage in the Net."

"She knows it's about that?"

"It's evident from the translations of Taki's e-mails. She got them away from Darryl and read them herself."

"So what do you want from me?"

"How do we make her go away? Tell me."

"You don't. You can't. Let her write to Taki."

"You serious?"

"Of course I am. Try to keep her in character, if you want to keep it going. Remember, Taki's in love with who you've told him she is."

"I was afraid of that. Actually I'd pretty much come to the same conclusion. It's just I hate the loss of control, you know?"

"It was probably an illusion that you were ever in control in the first place."

"With a dickhead of Darryl's caliber around, no fucking kidding. What's happening on your end with that T-thing?"

"It's being looked at."

"Who by?"

"Friends of a friend. I don't really know."

"You okay, there? You sound tired."

"I am, but I'm okay."

"Keep in touch. Bye."

She looks at the phone and wonders who Parkaboy is. Other, that is, than Parkaboy, ascerbic obsessive theorist of the footage. What does he do when he's not doing this? She has no idea, and no idea what he looks like or, really, how he came to be as devoted as she knows he is to pursuing any further understanding of the footage. But now, in some way she can't quite grasp, the universe of F:F:F is everting. Manifesting physically in the world. Darryl Musashi's pissed-off Japanese-Texan barmaid seems to be an aspect of this.

But she's glad that someone else dislikes what they've done to Taki.

The phone rings again when she's nearing Blue Ant.

"Where are you?"

"Almost there. Two minutes."

He hangs up.

She walks on, past the window of a gallery where the central blue shape in a large abstract canvas reminds her of Taki's T-bone. What is that? Why bury it in that flare of light? What else might be hidden in other segments?

As she's reaching out to push the button on the Blue Ant intercom, the door is opened by a dark-haired man in sunglasses, his nose elaborately braced with flesh-colored fabric tape. He freezes for an instant, does an odd little duck-and-weave, then pushes suddenly past her outstretched arm and sprints off down the street, in the direction she's just come.

"Hey," Cayce says, catching the door before it can close, the back of her neck prickling.

She steps inside.

"They're waiting for you upstairs," says the young receptionist, smiling, a stud glinting on the side of her nose.

"Dickheads," Cayce says, and looks back at the door. "Who was that who just left?"

The girl looks puzzled.

"Tape on his nose."

The girl brightens. "Franco. He drives Dorotea, from Heinzi and Pfaff. Been in an accident."

"She's here?"

"Waiting for you." The girl smiles. "Third floor."

CHAPTER 24

CYPRUS

Bernard Stonestreet, uncharacteristically sour and distracted, is passing the head of the stairs as she reaches the third floor, his upthrust thatch and immaculately disheveled black suit reminding her all too clearly of her previous visit.

"Hullo," he says, with an instant's confusion. "I'd wondered where you were. Meeting Hubertus and Dorotea?"

"Looks like it."

"Is everything all right?" Seeming concerned at her tone.

"Dandy," she says, biting it off between her front teeth.

"It's a bit of a surprise, isn't it?" Lowering his voice slightly, though there's no one to hear. "Dorotea, I mean."

"What about her?"

"He's bringing her in as client liaison for graphics. Entirely counter to the way he structured it in the first place. Always insisted on the designers working

269

directly with the client." Bernard's mouth has gone a bit narrow, telling her this. "Though of course she's experienced." He shrugs, the beautiful black shoulders of his suit jacket moving expressively. "She gave Heinzi notice—this morning."

"When was she hired?"

Stonestreet looks surprised. "This morning. I've only just been told."

"Where are they?"

"The room where we met. There." Indicating a door.

She steps past him.

Opens that door.

"Good morning!" Bigend is seated where Stonestreet had sat, before, at the head of the long table. Dorotea is seated to his left, down the table's side, toward the door, closer to Cayce. Boone opposite her.

Neither Boone nor Dorotea say anything.

Cayce closes the door behind her, hard.

"Cayce—" Bigend begins.

"Shut up." It isn't a voice Cayce has often heard, but she knows when she hears it that it's her own.

"Cayce—" Boone, this time.

"What the fuck is going on here?"

Hubertus starts to open his mouth.

"Did you just hire her?" Pointing at Dorotea.

"It would be too much to expect you not to be angry," Dorotea says, with the utmost calm. She's wearing something soft-looking, in a very dark gray, but her hair is straining back as tightly as ever.

270

"The man," Cayce says, turning to Bigend in mid-sentence, "who tried to mug me in Tokyo—"

"Franco," Dorotea interrupts, quietly.

"Shut up!"

"Dorotea's driver," Bigend says, as though that explains everything. He looks, Cayce thinks, even more self-satisfied than usual.

"Mugger," Cayce says.

"And what did poor Franco do, when he encountered you?" Dorotea asks.

"He ran."

"Terrified," Dorotea says. "The doctors in Tokyo told him that if you had been an inch shorter, you might have killed him. The cartilage in his nose might have been driven into his forebrain, is that the word? He's concussed, has two black eyes, has to breathe through his mouth, and will probably require surgery."

The lightness of Dorotea's delivery stops Cayce, as much as the content.

"He isn't driving, now," Dorotea concludes, "certainly not for me."

"Is he mugging, then?" But it's not the same voice. Something is back in its accustomed box, now. She misses it.

"I'm sorry about that," Dorotea says. "If I had been there, it wouldn't have happened. Franco is not so heavy-handed, but someone was demanding results." She doesn't shrug, exactly, but somehow conveys the impression of having done so.

"Cayce," Hubertus says, "I know you're upset,

but would you sit down, please? We've just been having an extraordinarily fruitful meeting. Putting our cards on the table. Dorotea knows a great deal about what's going on, and all of it, it seems, concerns you directly. Very directly, as her business with you predates the Heinzi and Pfaff project—or, at least, our meetings here. Do. Sit."

Boone, Cayce notes, to her considerable resentment, looks attentive but absolutely neutral, sitting there in his old black coat; some kind of major Chinese-guy poker face going on. He looks as though he should be whistling, but isn't.

Cayce feels herself make a decision, though she couldn't say what exactly it is, pulls out the chair at the end of the table and sits, but without putting her legs under the table. If she needs to stand and walk out, it's one less movement.

"Boone," Bigend says, "decided that it was necessary to tell me about your interactions with Dorotea, what you knew had happened and what you supposed might have happened."

"'Supposed'?"

"Correctly supposed, in every case." Bigend leans back in his chair. He needs the Stetson now, she thinks; he's started to play to it. "She was very rude and unfriendly, she did burn your jacket, she did send Franco and his associate to burgle your friend's flat and install a keystroke recorder on the computer there. She did deliberately expose you to an image she knew would unsettle you, during your second meeting here, and she did leave a toy, again meant to frighten you, outside your friend's apartment. Your friend's phone is also bugged, incidentally, and Franco has followed you at various times, including your stroll with Boone, during your first meeting together. And of course in Tokyo."

Cayce gives Boone a look she hopes will be read as "I'll get to you when I have the time." Then she swings back to Bigend. "And? What, Hubertus? Knowing that, you hire her?"

"Yes," Bigend nods, patiently, "because we need her on our side. And now she is." He looks to Dorotea.

"Cayce," Dorotea says, "it's a career decision for me." She puts a particular stress on "career" that might once have been heard more often on "religious." "Blue Ant is where I need to be. Hubertus knows this."

"But, Hubertus," Cayce offers, "what if Dorotea is . . ."

"Yes?" He leans forward, palms flat on the table.

"A vicious lying cunt?"

Bigend giggles, a deeply alarming sound. "Well," he says, "we are in the business of advertising, after all." He smiles. "But you are talking about loyalty, not honesty. And I have a strong yet simple faith that Dorotea can be counted on to be absolutely loyal to . . ." He looks at Dorotea, his expression suddenly quite cold. "Her career."

Reluctantly, Cayce realizes he may be right.

He's buying Dorotea's allegiance with the one thing that literally no one else can offer her: a potentially fast-track position in Blue Ant. And as Cayce recognizes this, she's suddenly very curious as to what it is that Dorotea knows.

"Then tell me," she says, facing Dorotea, pointedly ignoring Boone, "what Hubertus imagines I'll find so very interesting."

"I like your jacket," Dorotea says. "Is it new?"

And Cayce will later think that Franco, just then, had come very close to not being the only one to risk having had nasal cartilage driven into his forebrain, but Dorotea is out of immediate reach and Cayce refuses to rise to the bait.

Dorotea smiles. "Three weeks ago," Dorotea begins, "I took a call in Frankfurt from someone in Cypress. Russian. A tax lawyer, he said. At first it seemed to be about a possible contract for Heinzi, but quickly it became obvious that he required services from my previous line of work." She raises one eyebrow at Cayce.

"I know about that."

"He wanted someone made sufficiently uncomfortable to not accept a position at a particular firm. This firm. And you, of course, are that person." Dorotea folds her hands in her lap. "He came from Cyprus immediately, if indeed he was from Cyprus, and we met. He told me, then, who you were, and of course I had some sense of that from my knowledge of the business, this business. He was clearly aware both of my background and of the way I was positioned vis-à-vis Blue Ant. I noted that, carefully."

"He was Russian?"

"Yes. Do you know Cyprus?"

"No."

"It is a tax-shelter domain, for the Russians. It caters to them. There are many Russians there. I was given information regarding you, and paid a retainer."

"Dorotea," Boone says, "I didn't want to interrupt, when you were telling us this earlier, but what form did payment take?"

"U.S. dollars."

"Thank you." Boone falls silent again.

"What information?" Cayce asks.

"When did you stop seeing Katherine McNally?" Dorotea asks in reply.

"In February," Cayce answers automatically, feeling her scalp creep.

"My Russian from Cyprus gave me typescripts of what seem to be her notes."

Katherine had taken notes, during the sessions, in shorthand.

"From this I learned about your sensitivity to—"

"You don't need to go into that." Cayce cuts her off. Could her therapist have betrayed her, this way? Katherine had had doubts about Cayce concluding, it was true, but they had come to an agreement, and had had a good closure. Katherine had wanted to work on her issues around Win, and his disappearance, but Cayce had been living them, and hadn't wanted to. "I can't believe that Katherine—"

"She probably didn't," Dorotea says, as if reading her thoughts. "This man from Cyprus, I doubt you know this sort of man. I do. It is at least equally likely that he sent someone, in New York, to enter this woman's office and photograph the documents. She would never know."

"Note," Bigend says, "that we cannot date that. If you quit seeing her in February, they might have gotten them at any point afterward, up until contact with Dorotea."

Cayce looks from Bigend to Boone, back to Dorotea. "And your . . ." She can't think of a term. "Mission statement?"

"To make you sufficiently uncomfortable that you would leave London. If possible, that you would then avoid Blue Ant, and particularly Hubertus. Also, I was to see that the software they gave me was installed on your friend's computer, and to monitor your movements in London."

"They insisted that Dorotea return the software they provided for that installation," Boone adds. "Unfortunately, she did."

"So Franco got into Damien's, put something in the computer. What about Asian Sluts?"

"Asian . . . ?" Dorotea's eyes widen slightly, as if in puzzlement.

"And he called you? To tell you he'd done it?"

"How do you know that?"

"He used Damien's phone."

Dorotea says something, evidently obscene, in Italian, under her breath.

A silence ensues. They look at one another in turn.

"When they learned you were going to Tokyo," Dorotea says, "they became, I think, excited. They insisted I cover you, there. With my responsibilities to Heinzi, I could not go. I sent Franco and Max."

"'They'? Who are they?"

"I don't know. I only communicate with this Russian. He obviously works for someone. He wanted whatever it was he thought you might get from whoever it was you were meeting with."

"But how did they know—?"

"That's down to me to sort out," Boone says.

"But Pamela Mainwaring is no longer with us," Hubertus says.

"She was easy," says Dorotea.

"And now," says Hubertus, standing, "if you and Boone will excuse us, I want to introduce Dorotea to the designers she'll be working with."

Leaving Cayce and Boone alone with each other.

CHAPTER 25

SIGIL

Starbucks, she thinks, seated in one near Blue Ant, beneath exactly the same faux-Murano pendulum lamps they have in the branch nearest her apartment in New York, is a strange place in which to feel this upset.

She and Boone have managed to get here via some highly uncomfortable and basically nonverbal form of decision-making, Cayce not having wanted to stay at Blue Ant for a second longer than she needed to, and now he's waiting for their order at that same round-topped drink-delivery counter they all have.

The decor somehow fosters emotional neutrality, a leveling of affect. She can feel it actually starting to calm her down (though perhaps that's simply a matter of its familiarity) but then he's there, placing their lattes on the table. "So why doesn't Starbucks drive you crazy," he asks, "if excessive branding's the trigger?"

She glares at him, struck dumb with the irritation she feels.

"You look angry." He takes the seat opposite her.

"I am. Aside from Hubertus having hooked up with Dorotea, and Dorotea having my therapist's notes, I'm questioning whether I can work with you."

"I think I understand."

"I didn't like it, in the car, when you took the lead with Bigend—"

"I'm sorry. I got ahead of myself, there, but I was pissed off that he'd turned up that way. I assumed you were too."

And she had been, actually.

"Now you've told him what I thought had been going on with Dorotea. Without consulting me. I'd shared that with you, not with him."

"I assumed you were sleeping—"

"You should have called me!"

"And I knew that Franco and Max were sitting in a car diagonally across the street from your friend's place."

"They were? When?"

"When I went round at one in the morning to have a look."

"You did? Why?"

"To see if you were okay."

She stares at him.

"That was when I called Bigend and told him what was going on, and that I thought these guys were working for Dorotea. He called her, then. He knew she was in London. I don't know what he said to her, initially, but inside of ten minutes, Franco was on his phone and then they were gone. I hung around for a while, decided you'd probably be okay, went to Bigend's hotel. We had a very early breakfast, then Dorotea joined us for coffee."

"Haven't you slept at all?"

"No."

"And you were there when he made his deal with Dorotea?"

"I was there when they negotiated the finer points of the deal they'd made on the phone. I was there to hear her story, though, so I know that Franco and Max were on their way back here almost as soon as you asked Mainwaring for a flight. They actually followed us in from the airport. Hubertus missed that, by the way. He doesn't really concern himself with that level of detail."

It's starting to sink in that if he did break her confidence, with Bigend, it was only in order to ensure her safety. Not that she's feeling any safer at the moment. "But what if she's still lying? Still working for whoever it is."

"She could be. Hubertus is a gambler. A very methodical one, in his way, but still a gambler. He's banking on understanding her better than they do. These Russians, Cypriots, whatever they are, probably all they can offer her is money. Or, as Bigend himself suggested, when he told me what he was doing, they might turn her again, more easily, with a threat."

"What do you mean?"

"She couldn't enjoy her career move very much if she were dead."

"Aren't you being overdramatic?"

"People who have Russians from Cyprus hire corporate espionage types for them can have a flare for drama. Particularly if they turn out to be Russian themselves."

"Is she still in contact with them? Are they Russian? Who are they?"

"She spoke with him last night. So far, today, she's dodging contact."

"Why did you use the plural, before? 'Them'?"

"She feels it's an organization of some kind. The Russian is the only one she's met, but she's spoken with several others by phone. They debrief her, basically. She thinks they're all either Russian or working for them."

She thinks about this, trying to get her head around at least the largest corners. It's not easy. "And do they know about you?"

"Only from the bug in your friend's phone, and then only that Hubertus wanted you to meet me. And they photographed us, by the canal. And they must know that that was me on the scooter, in Roppongi. Unless, that is, you've told someone else, particularly on that Camden phone."

"No. I haven't. What about my cell phone, if Pamela was working for Dorotea?"

"Dorotea says no. There wasn't time. Mainwaring took the phone from a batch Blue Ant has on hand. Dorotea would've tried to do something with that,

281

if she'd been given time. Your iBook was purchased about a block from here, by their tech-support kid, and I've talked to him. He unpacked it, made sure it worked, loaded whatever Hubertus wanted you to have, and gave it to Mainwaring as she was going out the door. And I couldn't see anything when I checked it in Tokyo. What else did she give you?"

"Nothing." Then she remembers. "Blue Ant expense card. Visa."

"Then you might want to assume they have that number. I'd ask for a fresh one."

"The guy who tried to take my bag, in Tokyo—"

"Franco. A potential weak link." He takes a phone from his pocket and checks the time on its screen. "But he's on his way to Heathrow now to catch a flight to Geneva. Bigend's ticket. He's going to recuperate and have a really expensive Swiss surgeon take a free look at his nose. Out of the way and handsomely remunerated for it. The other guy gets two weeks in Cannes plus a nice bonus. Less likely to talk to Cypriots, whoever. We hope. These hired-help situations always have the potential for problems."

"And what will Dorotea tell the man from Cyprus?"

"That Bigend has hired her. No way to hide it. The press release is going out now. They'll suspect he's buying her off, of course, but she's a player."

"What about her phone, the one Bigend got her on? How do you know that wasn't bugged?"

"He'd given it to her himself, at some point, and told her not to use it, just keep it charged and turned on, in case he needed her. Although the problem with cellular isn't that your phone's been bugged, usually, but that someone's got your frequency. Inherently insecure, unless you're encrypted."

"And you came to Damien's at one in the morning to see if I was safe?"

"I couldn't sleep."

She puts her coffee down. "Thank you."

"Are we even, now? Do you think you can work with me?"

She looks him in the eye. "Only if you keep me in the Boone loop. I have to know what you're actually doing. Can you do that?"

"Within practical limits."

"What's that mean?"

"I'm leaving for Columbus, Ohio. This evening. If I get lucky, I may not be able to risk telling you exactly what's happening. You may have to read between the lines, until we get face time."

"What's in Columbus?"

"Sigil Technologies. Watermarking for all forms of digital media. Website very pointedly doesn't say who their clients are, but friends of mine say they have a few big ones."

"You think they watermarked the footage?"

"Seems like it. I sent Taki's number to my friend at Rice. Once he knew what he was looking for, he could come at it from a different angle. That number is definitely encrypted in segment seventy-eight. But the way it's done, he says, is distinctive, and points to a certain school of thought. He says that a part of that school of thought is known to have found a home at Sigil Technologies."

"And what do you do when you get there?"

"Shoulder-surf. Social engineering."

"Are you good at that?"

"In certain contexts," he says, and sips his coffee.

"You sent your friend Taki's T-bone?"

"Yes. Using what he's learned about seventy-eight, he can try a number of different things. It might link each one to a point on the map. If it is a map."

"It looks like a map. I know someone," thinking of Darryl, "who's going to try giving it to a bot that only looks for maps. If it's been lifted from some actual city, we might get a match."

"That would be good, but what I'm after, now, is the nature of Sigil's involvement. Do they get each segment from somewhere, watermark it, and send it back? If they do, and we can find out where it comes from, or where they send it, we might have your maker."

"Would they have to actually view it, to water-mark it?"

"I don't think so, but I want to find out."

"How do you propose to do that?"

"I'm turning up on their doorstep as the repre-sentative of a small but very successful firm that's recently developed a need for nondetectable digital watermarking. That'll be a start. Why do you want to know whether they'd look at it?"

"There are footageheads everywhere. Or someone doing that work could become one, through exposure. There might be someone who already knows what you're looking for."

"There might be. But we'd have to advertise, wouldn't we?"

He's right.

He checks the time on his phone again. "I've got to go."

"Where?"

"Selfridge's. I need a suit, fast."

"I can't imagine you in a suit."

"You don't need to,' he says, standing, small leather suitcase already in his hand. "You're unlikely to ever see me in one." He smiles.

But I'll bet you'd look good in one, something in her says. It makes her blush. Now it's her turn to stand, feeling incredibly awkward. "Good luck in Ohio," she offers, reaching to shake hands.

He squeezes, rather than shakes, simultaneously leaning quickly forward to kiss her lightly on the cheek. "Take care of yourself. I'll be in touch."

And then she's watching him go out the door, past a girl with Maharishi parachute pants embroidered with tigers who, seeing the expression, whatever it is, on Cayce's face, smiles at her and winks.

CHAPTER 26

SIGINT

Cleaning Damien's flat becomes more of a project than she'd anticipated, but she keeps at it, trusting that manual labor, and the effort required to stay on task, somehow furthers soul-retrieval. Several video cameras have been unpacked, here, leaving the main room littered with abstract white foam shapes, innumerable foam peanuts, torn and crumpled shrink-wrap, empty Ziploc bags, warranties and instruction manuals. It looks as though a spoiled child has torn through a stack of very expensive presents, and she supposes that that might actually be seen to be the case, depending on how one looked at Damien.

Beer bottles, a saucer serving as an impromptu ashtray for lipsticked Marlboros, dirty dishes with remains of the tandoori take-away, a pair of very expensive-looking panties that she cheerfully bins, ditto various discarded makeup articles in the bathroom. She changes the sheets on the downstairs bed, straightens the giant oven mitt, dusts, and does a pass with a bright red upright German vacuum that's obviously never seen use before.

Goes upstairs to see what needs to be done, and a big cartoon hammer of sheer exhaustion comes down on her, slamming her into the waiting softness of the futon.

When she wakes, the phone is ringing, downstairs, and the light outside is different. She looks at her watch and sees that it's eight hours later.

She hears the phone stop ringing, then start again.

When she gets to it, it's Magda, asking if she'd like to have dinner.

Expecting only Magda, she sees Voytek and the large African as well, when she reaches the agreed meeting point near the station. They all seem wonderfully cheerful to her, but she supposes that that's because they aren't lagged and don't have lives as complicated as hers has recently become. Ngemi in particular, hugely zipped into his tight coat of black faux leather, is grinning enormously, and as they walk to a Greek restaurant somewhere behind the station, she hears why.

He has sold the calculators she'd seen near Portobello to the expected representative of that same Japanese collector, for what is evidently a very nice sum. He has the air of a man whose lost cause has most unexpectedly panned out, although at one point he does sigh, hugely. "Now I must go to Poole, and collect them from Hobbs."

She remembers the unpleasant man with the filthy little car.

"I don't like him," Magda says, bluntly, and seems to Cayce to be addressing mainly Voytek.

"He is a brilliant man," Voytek responds, shrugging.

"A horrid drunken old spy."

Attuned now to words like "spy," Cayce notes this but almost immediately forgets it.

The restaurant they've chosen is a homey, quiet little Greek place that shows every sign of predating the Children's Crusade. With its white-painted walls, bits of Aegean blue, and utterly characteristic Greek tourist tat, it somehow reminds Cayce of the experience of being in a Chinese restaurant in Roanoke, Virginia.

"I love your hair," Magda tells her, as retsina is being poured, and she quite evidently does. "Did you have it cut in Tokyo?"

"Thank you. I did."

"But you were only there for such a short time."

"Yes. Business." Cayce stifles a yawn that seems to come out of nowhere. "Excuse me."

"Are you still on their time? You must be exhausted."

"I think I'm all on my own time, now," Cayce says. "But I don't know what time that is."

Ngemi brings up yen devaluation, as this might affect his business, and that leads into a conversation about a classmate of Magda's who's recently been hired as part of a team designing clothing for the characters in a new Japanese video game. Ngemi and Voytek both find this slightly unbelievable, but Cayce assures them that it's utterly normal; that in fact it's a rapidly growing aspect of the design industry.

"But they don't wear hats, these anime characters," Magda laments, pouring herself another glass of the resinous yellow wine, then wincing at its bite. "They all have haircuts—exactly like yours!" She's laced into a leather bodice in a color called Turbo Blue, more traditionally used for painting large pieces of electrical equipment in factories. Her eye shadow matches.

"Life is more difficult for the serious artist," allows Voytek, who's seeming morose now. "Time is money, but also money is money."

"You'll get your scaffolding," Magda says. "It will work out." She explains to Cayce that her brother, having assembled close to three hundred ZX 81s, faces the daunting task of individually altering their cases to accept connections of some kind, each connection having to be painstakingly soldered into the actual Sinclair circuitry, such as it is. Voytek listens keenly, taking an evident pleasure in hearing his sister recount the tribulations of the serious artist.

He is creating, Cayce is starting to gather, some sort of lungfish-primitive connection machine. He draws it on a napkin for her: a representation of a three-dimensional grid, this to be made up from a batch of third-hand builder's scaffolding that Ngemi has located in Bermondsey. She watches the lines of ink spread into the paper, widening, and thinks of Taki, in the little bar in Roppongi.

It is very rusty, paint-spattered scaffolding, Ngemi has assured him, exactly what he wants for the texture of the piece. But if he's to do each Sinclair modification himself, he faces weeks if not months of work. The scaffolding is not expensive, but neither is it free, and must be transported, measured, sawed, assembled, probably re-sawed, then assembled again, then stored somewhere until a gallery can be secured. "A patron must be found," he says.

Cayce thinks of Billy Prion but restrains herself from saying that she'd seen him in Tokyo and knows he's currently busy.

"When you met us," Ngemi says to Cayce, "it seemed that Voytek's funding problems were about to be alleviated. But alas, no. Not as it worked out."

"How was that?" Cayce asks, with the intimation that she herself is being set up for a potential role as patron.

"Neither Hobbs nor I had anything sufficiently special to interest our Japanese collector on its own, but by combining available stock, we could employ the psychology of 'the lot.' Collectors behave differently then. 'Konvolut,' the German word for auction lot. I like this word; collectors approach it differently, become tangled in it. They want to believe there is hidden treasure, there." He smiles, his dark and shaven head glinting with reflected candlelight. "If the sale had gone through, it was my intention to advance Voytek what he needs for the scaffolding."

"But didn't you say that it had all worked out," Cayce asks, "in the meantime?"

"Yes," says Ngemi, with quiet pride, "but now I am negotiating to buy Stephen King's Wang."

Cayce stares at him.

"The provenance," Ngemi assures her, "is immaculate, the price high, but, I believe, reasonable. A huge thing, one of the early dedicated word processors. Shipping alone will require the funds I had earmarked for the scaffolding, and more."

Cayce nods.

"And now I must deal with Hobbs Baranov," Ngemi continues, less happily, "and he is in one of his moods."

If he hadn't been, when I saw him, Cayce thinks, I wouldn't want to see him when he was.

"Hobbs wanted his share of the Curta sale in order to bid on a very rare piece that went up for auction in Den Haag this past Wednesday. A factory prototype of the earliest Curta, exhibiting a peculiar, possibly unique variation in the mechanism. It went to a Bond Street dealer instead, and for not a bad price. Hobbs will be difficult, when I see him."

"But you've sold his, as well, haven't you?"

"Yes, but once anything's in Bond Street, it's beyond the reach of mere mortals. Even Hobbs Baranov. Too dear."

Magda, who's been working her way through the retsina a little more determinedly than the rest of them, makes a bitter face. "This man is appalling. You should have nothing to do with him. If that is what American spies are like, they are worse even than the Russians they defeated!"

"He was never a spy," Ngemi says, somberly, lowering his glass. "A cryptographer. A mathematician. If the Americans were as heartless, or as efficient, as people imagine them, they would never leave poor Hobbs to drink himself to death in a leaking caravan."

Cayce, feeling neither particularly heartless nor very efficient, asks: "What would they do, then, if they were?"

Ngemi, about to put a forkful of the remaining calamari into his mouth, pauses. "I suppose," he says, "they would kill him."

Cayce, having been raised to some extent within the ghostly yet in her experience remarkably banal membrane of the American intelligence community, has her own set of likelihood-filters when it comes to these things. Win had never, as far as she knew, been an intelligence officer in his own right, but he had known and worked with them. He had shared a certain experiential core with them, partaking in his own way of the secret world and its wars. And very little Cayce ever hears of that world, as described by those with even less a sense of it than her own, sounds like anything but fantasy. "Actually," she tells them, "it's sort of traditional to let them drink themselves to death."

Something about her tone stops the conversation, which she hadn't intended. "What did you mean, in a caravan?" she asks Ngemi, to end the silence.

Win had lived long enough to bury a number of his colleagues, none of them, as far as she knew, felled by anything more sinister than stress and overwork, and perhaps by a species of depression engendered by too long and too closely observing the human soul from certain predictable but basically unnatural angles.

"He lives in a little trailer," Ngemi says. "Squats, really. Near Poole."

"But he has a bloody pension from the CIA," protests Magda. "I don't believe this caravan! And he buys those Curta things, they cost fortunes. He's hiding something. Secrets." Drinking deep of her retsina.

"NSA," Ngemi corrects her. "Disability pension, I imagine, though I'd certainly never ask him. He has perhaps ten thousand pounds in net worth, I believe. Most of it, at any given time, in calculators. No fortune. Not even enough to keep them, really. A collector, he must buy, but a poor man, he must sell." Ngemi sighs. "It is that way for many people, not least myself."

But Magda isn't having it. "He's a spy. He sells secrets. Voytek told me."

Flustered, her brother looks from Cayce to

Ngemi, back to Cayce. "Not a spy. Not government secrets. You should not say this, Magda."

"Then what does he sell?" Cayce asks.

"Sometimes," Voytek says, lowering his voice slightly, "I think he locates information for people."

"He's a spy!" declares Magda, gleefully.

Voytek winces.

"He perhaps has retained certain connections," Ngemi qualifies, "and can find certain things out. I imagine there are men in the City . . ." His wide black brow creases with seriousness. "Nothing illegal, one hopes. Old-boy networks are something one understands, here. One doesn't ask. We assume Hobbs has his own, still."

"Sig-int," Magda says, triumphantly. "Voytek says he sells sig-int."

Voytek stares gloomily at his glass.

SIGINT, Cayce knows. Signals intelligence.

She decides to change the subject. Whatever this is about, it's detracting from what pleasure she's able to take in the evening.

After leaving the restaurant, they stop at a crowded pub near the station. Cayce, remembering from college that retsina is not a good mix with any other species of alcohol, orders a half shandy and leaves most of it.

Sensing that the patronage-hustle is probably about to be more overtly launched in her direction, she opts for preemptive action. "I hope you find a backer soon, Voytek. I'm sure you will. It makes me wish I had that sort of money myself, but I don't."

As she'd somehow expected, they all glance at one another.

It's Ngemi who decides to have a shot. "Is your employer perhaps in a position to—"

"I couldn't ask. Haven't been there long enough." Thinking, however, not of Bigend but of his credit card, in her wallet. She could indeed buy Voytek's load of rusty scaffolding for him. She will, she decides, if it looks like nothing else is going to turn up. Let Dorotea's Russians, who she isn't quite sure she believes in, figure that one out.

CHAPTER 27

THE SHAPE OF
THE ENTHUSIAST

Climbing the stairs, she reflects on how she feels no interest now in doing the Bond thing.

No spit-secured hair waiting to be checked. Less a matter of faith in the German locks than a sort of fatalism. Anyone able to get into Katherine McNally's Fifth Avenue office and steal or copy her notes on Cayce's sessions would be able get past those locks, she seems to have decided. But could that really have happened? Had some figure entered, in the dead of night, and crept past the low table in the small reception area, with its three-year-old copies of *Time* and *Cosmopolitan*?

She unlocks the door, twice. Opens it, seeing she's forgotten to leave a light on. "Fuck you," she calls, to anyone who might be waiting.

Turning on the light. Locking the door behind her, she has a look upstairs.

Cayce Pollard Central Standard indicating that sleep is not yet worth attempting.

She powers up Damien's G4, opens Netscape, and goes to F:F:F, watching the keystrokes required to get there. If Dorotea is telling the truth, her Asian Sluts boy had installed software on this machine that records the user's every keystroke. The recorded sequences can be retrieved from elsewhere, via some sort of back door. Does it give them mouse-clicks as well? She wonders. But how would they know what you were clicking on? Perhaps all they see is keystrokes, or keystrokes and URLs?

F:F:F is starting to look unfamiliar, after her relatively long absence. She doesn't recognize most of the handles of the posters on the current page. She remembers something about a recent television special having generated a wave of newbies. Are these unfamiliar names then? She scans a few threads without opening any posts, judging them by titles alone. Segment 78 is still a hot topic, as is the Brazilian Satanic Footage thing.

She sits back and stares at the screen, hands in her lap (the keyboard spooks her, now) and imagines more shadowy figures, in another room, a sort of *Man from U.N.C.L.E.* room, seated, staring at a huge screen on which there is nothing but this page of F:F:F, waiting for Cayce to open a post.

She lets them wait, then closes Netscape and powers down.

She no longer has to devote any thought to cabling the iBook to the cell phone. If Boone was right, back in Tokyo, this one isn't passing

297

any keystrokes to the *Man from U.N.C.L.E.* room. Although, she thinks, entering hotmail, what if they came round while she was out for Greek food, and . . . ?

"Fuck it," aloud, to Damien's robot girls. She can't live that way. Refuses.

Hotmail has three, for her.

The first is from Boone.

Hi. Greetings from LGA, the land of Very Intense Security. Out of here shortly for Colombus and initial meeting with The Firm In Question. Will have to play that completely by ear, of course. How are you? Let me know.

You are not, she thinks, the most eloquent of correspondents. But what, she asks herself, is she expecting? Shakespeare, from a layover at LaGuardia?

Hi yourself. On my laptop, as per our discussion. Okay here. Nothing to report.

Parkaboy next, opening on:

Jesus. (My mother was very religious, in her dysfunctional way. Have I told you that? Hence all my fear-words are blasphemous, I suppose.) Darryl is letting Judy script the Keiko mail, as you

298

said we had no choice other than to do. She's virtually moved in with him now, and has phoned in sick two nights running. She's mesmerized by the extent (she says the heartbreaking purity) of Taki's passion for her. This in spite of the fact that she knows Taki thinks she's a petite Japanese college girl, and that Darryl is translating for her both ways. Actually he indicates to me he's trying as much as possible to tone Judy's script down, and has told her that he doesn't really have that thorough a command of Japanese sexual vernacular. (Not true.) Says she's starting to cry a lot, and to say that the love Taki has to offer her is the love she's waited for all her life. This is, frankly, some of the weirdest shit to wash up my alley in a while, and I suppose it would be darkly funny if only we weren't trying to . . . BTW, what ARE we trying to do here? By insisting we let Judy do this, we've lost our fulcrum for extracting more Mystic material. Aside from which, we could lose Taki altogether—terminal priapism. Yrs, PB

Next up, Ivy, F:F:F's founder and owner, whom she hasn't heard from since she left New York.

Hello Cayce. Long time no see on the forum. Are you in Japan? Am still here in Seoul, in big numbered building!

Ivy had once sent Cayce a jpeg of her high-rise, with a ten-story "4" painted up the side. Behind it, receding into the distance, you could make out buildings 5 and 6, identical.

> Mama Anarchia does not write to me often. That is fine with me. You know she has always gotten on my nerves.

Ivy and Cayce have sometimes had to coordinate diplomacy, to prevent the friction between Parkaboy and la Anarchia from polarizing the site, or simply taking up too much space . . .
She freezes.

> Are you in Japan?

Unless Parkaboy has told Ivy about Cayce's trip, which Cayce cannot imagine him doing, under the circumstances, something is very wrong here.

> Today I had a very strange e-mail from her. Very friendly. Thanking me for F:F:F etc. Then asking about you like she is your old friend. From this I think you are in Tokyo? But something about this makes me worry. Here is the only part of her message referring to you. I can send the rest if you want.
> > And how is CayceP? She is not posting,
> > recently. You know of course that I was an
> > avid lurker, before I began to post, and
> > CayceP's insights struck me, from the first
> > post of hers I read, as the very shape of

300

> the enthusiast. That was the one in which
> she suggested that the maker had the
> resources of the Russian mafia, or some
> similarly secretive organization. Do you
> remember it? One day I hope to meet her in
> person, perhaps when she returns from
> Tokyo.

Cayce scowls at the screen. Feels like hurling it at the nearest robot girl. No fair. No fucking fair. She doesn't need this.

But if Mama Anarchia is somehow involved in the recent weirdness, why would she tip her hand this way to Ivy? To send a message to Cayce? Or?

Because Mama made a mistake? Freudian slip: meant to type "London," not "Tokyo"? The restraint of pen and tongue that Win always advised is difficult to maintain in a medium that involves neither, Cayce knows, and mistakes happen.

She and Mama Anarchia are not friends by any means.

At best they have exchanged a few strained messages. Cayce is too obviously Parkaboy's friend, on the site, and Parkaboy's loathing for Mama Anarchia has been far too vocal, from his scathing assaults on the French philosophers she quotes to deliberately absurd personal attacks (considering he's never met her, and has no idea of what she might look like). This e-mail to Ivy is a fishing expedition of some kind, and a clumsy one. Although Mama Anarchia has no way, that

Cayce knows of, to know that she and Ivy are friends, and discuss the site and its more prominent participants in private, and fairly frequently.

Creepy. She takes a deep breath. "He took a duck in the face at two hundred and fifty knots."

Reflexively, like a slot player pulling the lever in hope of bringing down a better reality, she clicks hotmail in case another message has arrived in the meantime.

Margot. Her Australian friend in New York, former Bigend girlfriend, currently assigned to visit Cayce's apartment on a frequent basis, pick up mail, check that all is well. Margot lives two blocks closer to Harlem proper, but still within the psychological footprint of Columbia.

"Lo dear. Bit of worry here. Went to your place today, as usual. Saw your super sweeping steps and he wasn't visibly pissed, but that isn't the unusual I have to report. Actually I wish I could be more certain about this, but I think someone else had been in your flat since I was last there. Two things: the toilet was running, when I went in. I'd used it, last time I was there, and it kept running, so I took the lid off the cistern and jiggled the bit that stops it running, and it did. Running again, this time, when I came in, but I didn't notice that at first. Everything fine, neat as a pin (how do you do that?) then I noticed the toilet running again. Gave me a shiver. But of course your plumbing was old when the Boer War was news, so it might just start, the way plumbing does sometimes. But it spooked me, a bit. Then I'm walking around looking at everything, and of course I can't remember exactly how everything was, but you've got so little in there, and it's so tidy, and really it all looked the same. But it was a sunny day, lovely really, sun coming in through your white drapes in the living room, open just a bit, and I was trying to remember how I'd placed the mail, day before yesterday. When I put it down beside your computer. You hadn't had any, today. And in that sunlight I could see how dusty things were getting, and thinking I'd be a pal and dust for you, and then I saw that I could just make out a rectangle, in the dust, where your mail had been when I put it there, last time! Your mail was just to the side, now. I could see that a bit more dust had settled there since. Am I the only one with the keys? Your drunken super, come to fix the toilet? Let me know, and if you think I should do anything about it. Are you coming back soon? I thought it was only a short one. Have you seen The World's Biggest Shit? No, don't tell me. Margot

Cayce closes her eyes and sees her blue-floored cave, her $1,200-a-month rent-stabilized apartment on 111th, secured when her former roommate, the previous lease holder, had moved back to San Francisco. Home. Who's been there? Not the super, not without a bribe.

How she hates this. How faint and peripheral somehow, these little things, yet how serious. A weight on her life, like trying to sleep under Damien's silver oven mitt.

And suddenly she's dead tired, as if Cayce Pollard Standard Time had clicked forward five hours. Trembling with it, though at the same time she doesn't trust that she'll be able to sleep. Shuts down the iBook, disconnects the cell phone, checks the locks. Looks in the bathroom for more melatonin but of course that's gone to Russia.

She feels like crying, though for no particular reason. Just this invasive weirdness that seems increasingly a part of her world, and she doesn't know why.

She turns off lights, undresses, crawls into bed, grateful for her own foresight in having removed and put away the oven mitt earlier in the day.

And has utterly no memory, subsequently, of any transition to West Broadway, where she stands in the middle of empty, white-coated pavement, a thin inch of fresh snow, in some deep and deeply silent hour of the night, the hour of waking alone, and she is alone, neither pedestrians nor traffic, and no light in any window, nor streetlights, and yet she can see, as though the snow of this Frozen Zone is sufficient illumination. Neither footprints nor tire tracks mar it, and as she turns to look behind she sees no footprints there either, not even her own. To her right the brick face of the SoHo Grand. To her left a bistro where she remembers taking

Donny, once. And then, down at the corner, middle distance, she sees him. The black coat that may or may not be leather, its collar turned up. The body language she knows from uncounted viewings of seventy-eight segments of footage.

And she wants to call out, but something in her chest prevents her, and she struggles to take a first step, and then another, imprinting the virgin snow, and then she is running, the unzipped Rickson's flapping beneath her arms like wings, but as she runs toward him, he seems always to recede, and with the awareness of this she is in Chinatown, white streets equally deserted, and she has lost him. Beside a grocery, shuttered. Gasping.

She looks up, then, and sees, borealis-faint but sharp-edged and tall as heaven, twin towers of light. As her head goes back to find their tops a vertigo seizes her: They narrow up into nothing at all, a vanishing point, like railway tracks up into the desert of sky.

"Ask him," her father says, and she turns to find him, dressed as she's imagined him to have dressed on that morning, his good overcoat open over his business suit, right hand extended, and in it, the black cylinder of a Curta calculator. "The dead can't help you, and the boy's no good."

Gray eyes framed with thin wires of gold. Become the color of that sky.

"Father—"

And managing to speak, wakes, awash with grief and terror and some sense of a decision made, though she knows not what, nor yet by whom, nor if indeed she ever will.

She has to turn on the light, to be sure that this is Damien's. She wishes Damien were here. She wishes anyone were here.

CHAPTER 28

WITHIN THE MEANING

Hi, Voytek.

When is Negemi going to visit Baranov? I need to talk with Baranov.

Send.

She uncables the printer from Damien's Cube, cables it to her iBook, hoping she has the right driver. She does. She watches the T-shaped city emerge in inkjet on a sheet of glossy. She'll need this, she thinks, without wanting to know exactly why.

Checking her mail.

Timing out, empty.

Sleep no longer an issue.

She looks at the printout. The squares and avenues. The overlay of numbers.

Checking her mail. One.

Casey he is going this morning, train from Waterloo to Bournemouth 8:10. He is spelled Ngemi. His friend there loans him a car to

drive to Baranov. Why are you awake now!
Voytek

Time in the upper-right corner of her screen:
four thirty-three.

Why are you awake yourself? Can you get in
touch with Ngemi and ask if I can go with him?
I can't explain but it's very important.

His almost instant reply:

I am working on ZX 81 project. He wakes early.
I will call him, call you.

She sends him thanks and the number of the
Blue Ant cell.
Showers.
Does not think.

The train from Camden High Street reaches
Waterloo at seven-fifteen. Ancient escalators carry
her to the concourse, beneath a few pigeons
and a four-faced Victorian clock, above schedule
boards and travelers wheeling black ballistic nylon
toward the Chunnel trains. Off to Belgium perhaps:
Bigendland.
She has been told to meet Ngemi beneath this
clock, but is early, so she buys a tabloid, a bacon
sandwich locked in rigid plastic, and a Fanta.

Coffee contraindicated now, as she hopes to nap on the train.

Stands chewing her sandwich, beneath the clock, while the Sunday morning station moves around her. Vast incomprehensible voices chant and gargle above the crowd, as if trying to push crucial information through the dusty tin of hundred-year-old gramophone speakers.

The Fanta has a nasty, synthetic edge. She wonders why she bought it. The tabloid doesn't go down any better, seemingly composed in equal measure of shame and rage, as though some inflamed national subtext were being ritually, painfully massaged, for whatever temporary and paradoxical relief this might afford.

She bins both, as she sees Ngemi approaching, large and black, zipped into his tight black jacket and carrying a sort of carpetbag in some African-looking hand-weave.

"Good morning," he says, looking mildly puzzled. "Voytek tells me that you wish to visit Baranov."

"I do. May I go with you?"

"It is a peculiar request. He is not a man whose personality can be said to improve. All of his moods are unpleasant. Have you purchased a ticket?"

"Not yet."

"Come with me, then."

Two hours to Bournemouth, according to Ngemi, though previously, he explains, it had been a quicker journey, the "high-speed" train running now on aging, unreplaced rails.

She finds him a surprisingly comforting presence, with his creaking leather and professorial gravitas.

"Last night you said that Baranov had been bidding on an auction, and had lost, and wouldn't be happy," she opens, as a man in a polyester blazer pushes a cart of very mirror-world morning snacks past them down the aisle: crustless white egg-salad sandwiches in rigid triangular packaging, cans of lager, miniatures of whiskey and vodka.

"Indeed," says Ngemi. "He would be angry enough to have lost that calculator to anyone, but he has lost it to Lucian Greenaway, of Bond Street."

"Who is . . . ?"

"The dealer. Most recently, exclusively of clocks, and much resented by collectors in that field. Last year he began to go after Curtas. The market is not yet entirely rationalized, you see."

"Rationalized?"

"Not yet established as a global specialist environment. As has long been the case, for instance, with rare stamps, or coins. Or, to almost that degree, with the clocks Greenaway deals in. Values are only just being established, for Curta calculators. One still finds the odd example gathering dust on a shelf, perhaps for relatively little. All such markets are being rationalized by the Internet, of course."

"Are they?"

"Absolutely. Hobbs himself," and Cayce has to struggle for a second before remembering that this is Baranov's given name, "is responsible for that, to some degree."

"How?"

"eBay," says Ngemi. "He's very adroit there, and has sold many Curtas to Americans, always for more than they would fetch here. Global values are being established."

"Do you . . . like them? The way he does?"

Ngemi sighs, his jacket creaking sharply. "I appreciate them. I enjoy them. But not to the depth of Hobbs's passion. I love the history of computing, you see, and the Curta is simply a step, for me. A fascinating one, but I have Hewlett-Packards that I enjoy as much, or more." He glances out at featureless fields, the dark spire of a distant church. "Hobbs," he says, turning back to her, "suffers and enjoys as only the specialist can. I imagine it is not so much about the artifact, in his case, as about the ultimate provenance."

"How's that?"

"The camps. Herzstark in Buchenwald, surrounded by death, by methodical erasure, by an almost certain fate. He continued to work. In the end, the camp was liberated. He walked free, never having abandoned his vision of the calculator. Hobbs honors that triumph, that escape."

"He has something he needs to escape, himself?"

"Himself exactly." He nods. Then changes the subject. "What is it that you do? I didn't understand it, in the restaurant."

"I'm in marketing."

"You sell things?"

"No. I find things, or styles, for other people, companies, to market. And I evaluate logos— trademark emblems."

"You are American?"

"Yes."

"I think it must be a difficult time to be American," Ngemi says, settling his large head firmly back against the headrest of his non-reclining second-class seat. "If you don't mind, I will sleep now."

"I don't mind."

He closes his eyes.

She looks out at the patchwork fields, sunlight flashing from the occasional puddle. When had she last ridden on a train, not a subway, through open country? She can't remember.

Instead she remembers her first view of Ground Zero, in late February. The viewing platforms. The unnaturalness of so much sunlight, in that place. They had been pulling out a PATH train, buried there.

She closes her eyes.

In Bournemouth, Ngemi leads her several blocks from the station, through the oddness, for her, of any England not London, to a greengrocer's shop.

Here he is greeted by an older, very earnest-looking man, lighter-skinned, with neat gray hair and a fine-bladed Ethiopian nose. The greengrocer, evidently, from his spotless blue apron, who looks to Cayce like a Tory Rastafarian. Ngemi and this man exchange extended greetings, or perhaps news, in what might, for all she knows, be Aramaic, or some utterly impenetrable dialect of English. Ngemi does not introduce her. The man gives Ngemi a set of car keys and a plastic bag containing plums and two ripe bananas.

Ngemi nods gravely, she assumes in thanks, and she follows him along the street, to where he stops and unlocks the passenger door of a dark red mirror-world car. This one, she notes, is a Vauxhall, but nothing like the car she'd seen Hobbs drive in Portobello. It's scented, inside, with some alien air freshener, more African than mirror-world.

Ngemi sits behind the wheel for a moment, then inserts the key.

Very shortly, they're negotiating complex round-abouts at speeds that have Cayce closing her eyes. Finally she opts to keep them shut.

When she opens them, she sees rolling green hills. Ngemi drives on, silently, giving great concentration to the task.

She sees a ruined castle, on a hill.

"Norman," Ngemi says, glancing over at her, but doesn't choose to elaborate.

Without waiting for the fruit to be offered, she removes a banana from the greengrocer's bag and

313

peels and eats it. Cloudy now, and a light drizzle settles in. Ngemi turns on the wipers.

"I'd offer you lunch before we see Hobbs," Ngemi says, "but timing, when visiting him, can be crucial."

"We can phone him, to make sure he'll be in."

"He has no phone. I was able to reach him at his local, last night. He was drunk, of course. He should be awake, by the time we arrive, and I hope that he won't have started again."

Twenty minutes later he exits from the main road, following what Cayce thinks of as two-lane blacktop. They are in countryside of a vaguely agricultural sort. Sheep on a hillside. Soon they are climbing single-lane gravel around the side of a hill. As they round it, Cayce sees, below them, a curiously desolate-looking complex of buildings of various sizes, all of brick. No visible activity.

Descending, the Vauxhall's tires crunching gravel, she sees chain-link and barbed wire.

"It is a former training facility," he says. "M15 or M16. I think 5. Now they breed and train police dogs here, according to Hobbs."

"'They' who?"

"No idea. A most ill-favored place."

Cayce has no idea where they are. Bournemouth? Poole?

He turns off the gravel, onto actual dirt, no more than a rutted path. Splashing through brown puddles.

She sees small trailers parked between woods and

the fenced compound. Perhaps seven of them. As deserted-looking as the brick structures. Next to that, but clearly not a part of it.

"This is where he lives?"

"Yes."

"What is it?"

"Gypsy families. These are their caravans. Hobbs rents one."

"Have you seen them? Gypsies?"

"No," he says, bringing the car to a halt, "never."

She looks out at a large rectangular sign, peeling plywood up on two lengths of galvanized pipe, lettered black on white:

MINISTRY OF DEFENCE
THIS IS A PROHIBITED PLACE
WITHIN THE MEANING OF
THE OFFICIAL SECRETS ACT.
UNAUTHORIZED PERSONS
ENTERING THE AREA MAY BE
ARRESTED AND PROSECUTED.

CHAPTER 29

PROTOCOL

Ngemi gets out stiffly, stretching his legs, jacket creaking. Reaches into the backseat for his colorful carpetbag. Cayce gets out too.

There is a silence here. No birds sing.

"If there are dogs, shouldn't we hear them?" Looking toward the low brick structures beyond the fence. The wire, she sees, is strung between tall square columns of discolored concrete. It all feels old, and somehow dead. World War II?

"I've never heard them," Negemi says, darkly, and starts along a footpath, skirting small puddles. His shoes are black four-eyelet DMs, the ur-Martens of the first decade of punk, long since de-recontextualized into the inexpensive everyman's footwear they'd been designed to be.

Uncut grass. Wild shrubbery with small yellow flowers. She follows Ngemi toward the nearest mirror-world trailer. It is two-tone, the upper body beige, the lower burgundy, dented and dull. It has a shallow, centrally peaked roof that reminds her of drawings of Noah's ark in books for children, and on its back a square, faded mirror-world license plate, "LOB" and four numerals. It doesn't look as though it's been anywhere in a long while, grass grown up around it, hiding any wheels it may still possess. Its windows, she sees, have been sealed over with galvanized sheet metal.

"Hobbs," Ngemi calls, though not very loudly, "Hobbs, it is Ngemi." He pauses, advances. The caravan's door, beige and burgundy as well, doesn't look as though it could ever fully close. "Hobbs?" He raps twice, softly.

"Piss off," says someone, she assumes Hobbs, from within. It is a voice of utmost weariness, made peevish with pain.

"I've come for the calculators," Ngemi says. "To complete the Japanese transaction. I have your share of the money."

"Cunt." Baranov kicks open the door, it seems, without having to rise from where he must be seated, the opening presenting as a depthless rectangle of darkness. "Who the fuck is she?"

"You met near Portobello, briefly," Ngemi says. "A friend of Voytek's." Which, Cayce supposes, is true, though after the fact.

"And why," Baranov says, leaning slightly forward, so that sunlight glints flatly on his glasses, "would you bring her here?" All weariness gone, now, the voice taut and careful, menacing in its precision.

"I'll let her explain that," Ngemi says, glancing

at Cayce, "after you and I have sorted present business." He hefts the carpetbag in Baranov's direction, as if indicating the nature of that business. To Cayce: "Hobbs has room for only one visitor at a time. Excuse us, please." He climbs into the caravan, which sways on its springs, alarmingly, with a sound like the rattling of empty bottles. "I doubt we'll be long."

"Tedious cunt," Baranov says, though whether about her, Ngemi, or life, she can't tell.

Ngemi, hunched almost double beneath the low roof, settles himself on something unseen, casts Cayce an apologetic look, and closes the door.

Alone now, though aware of their muffled voices, she looks toward the other caravans. Some are more dilapidated than Baranov's, others newer and slightly larger. She doesn't like them. To escape their lines of sight, she walks around Baranov's. Finds herself facing the wire fence and the dead-looking brick buildings. Likes this no better.

Beneath her breath, recites the duck-in-the-face mantra.

There is a black cable between the toes of her suede boots from Parco. She looks back and sees where it snakes from a vent in the side of Baranov's caravan. She walks forward, following it, and finds the point where it's been inserted through the fence, close to the ground. It leads off through tussocks of yellowing grass, toward the brick compound. Electricity? From M15, or whatever other keepers?

"Hello!" Ngemi calls her, from the side of the caravan. "Come and have your talk with Hobbs. He won't bite you. He might actually be in a better mood, now."

She walks back, pretending not to notice the cable.

"Go on," says Ngemi. He glances at the old-fashioned calculatorwatch on his wrist, its chrome case flashing in the wan sunlight. In his other hand, the carpetbag, looking heavier. "I don't know how long he might give you. I'd like to catch the next train, if we can."

The caravan sways as she climbs in, blinking in the dark. A gloom that reeks of stale cigarette ash and unwashed clothing, horribly close.

"Sit down," Baranov orders. "Close the door."

She does, discovering that what she sits on consists of chair-high stacks of books, very old ones, large jacketless volumes with dull cloth covers.

He leans forward. "Journalist?"

"No."

"Name."

"Cayce Pollard."

"American."

"Yes."

As her eyes adjust to the gloom, she sees that he is partially reclining on a narrow berth that must be his bed, though it seems so steeply piled with what she takes to be wadded clothing that she doesn't see how he could sleep on it. A narrow folding table has been let down from the wall in front of him, one-legged.

He jacks a pale cigarette into the corner of his mouth and leans forward. In the flare of his plastic lighter she sees that the grimy, littered surface of the little table is Formica, printed in that boomerang pattern from the fifties. There is a mound of butts there that may conceal, in its base, an actual ashtray. And three thick sheaves of banknotes, bound with wide pink rubber bands.

The coal of his cigarette flares mightily, like a meteorite entering Earth's atmosphere, fully half the cigarette apparently consumed on that first draw. She braces herself for the exhalation, but it does not come. Instead, he stacks the sheaves of banknotes and pockets them, tucking them away into the tattered Barbour she remembers from Portobello.

At last he lets his breath out, and the caravan fills with smoke, though less of it than she would have expected. Sunlight, through a few small holes in the metal skin, shafts dramatically in, giving the space the look of a Ridley Scott set scaled for dolls. "You know that bloody Pole."

"Yes."

"Reason enough to avoid you. You're wasting my time, darling." The meteorite enters the atmosphere again, putting paid to the second half of the cigarette. He stubs it out, or partially out, atop the mound.

It occurs to her that she hasn't seen his left

hand. Everything so far, the cigarette, the lighter, the banknotes, has been done with his right. "I can't see your left hand."

In answer, the gun appears, perfectly captured in one of the subminiature Ridley Scott floodlights. "I can't see either of yours." She has never looked down the barrel of a gun before, and this one seems to have very little left to look down. A huge old top-opening revolver, its barrel and the front of the trigger guard sawed roughly away, the rusted metal showing the tooth marks of hasty filing. Baranov's hand, slender and filthy, is too small for the massive wooden grip. A lanyard ring swings from the pistol's butt, suggesting tall white helmets and the Raj.

She lifts her hands; a gesture familiar, long ago, from a children's game.

"Who sent you?"

"I sent myself."

"What do you want?"

"Ngemi and Voytek say you can get information."

"Do they?"

"I want to trade something for one specific piece of information."

"You're lying."

"No. I know exactly what I need. And I can give you something you want, in exchange for it."

"Too late, darling. I've no need for whores." And then the rough metal of the muzzle, impossibly cold and distinct, is pressed against the center of her forehead.

"Lucian Greenaway." She feels the ring of cold move, a fraction, in reaction. "The dealer. Bond Street. The calculator. I can buy it for you."

The cold ring, pressing.

"I can't give you money," she says then, knowing that this is the one lie she needs to tell now, and tell well, "but I can use someone else's credit card to buy the calculator for you."

"Ngemi's gob needs stopping."

And then it comes to her, why she mustn't offer money, though surely Bigend would provide: Once paid, Baranov would then feel that he was giving his own money to the dealer he hates.

"If I could offer you money, I would, but all I can offer is to buy the calculator. To give it to you. In exchange for what I need." Done, she closes her eyes. The circle of cold steel becomes the very horizon.

"Greenaway." Horizon withdrawn. "Do you know what he's asking?"

"No." Eyes tight shut.

"Four thousand five. Pounds."

She opens her eyes. Sees the pistol pointed not so directly at her. "If we're going to talk, would you mind not pointing that at me?"

Baranov seems to remember the gun in his hand. "Here," he says, letting it drop, everything on the Formica rattling under the impact, "you point it at me."

She looks from it to him.

"Bought it at a boot sale. Boy dug it up in the woods here. Two quid. The inside's rust and earth. Cylinder won't turn." He smiles at her.

She looks back at the gun on the table, imagining picking it up, smiling back at him, raising it, and bringing it down, as hard as she can, on his forehead. She lowers her hands. Then she looks up at him again. "My offer."

"You've someone's credit line, good for four five?"

"Visa."

"Tell me what you're after. That isn't to say I'll do it."

"I'm going to get something out of this bag. A printout."

"Go ahead."

He pushes the revolver and a chipped white cup aside, so that she can place the glossy of the T-city on the table. He moves to touch something, to his right, and a halogen beam falls on the table. She thinks of the cable, snaking through the wire fence. He looks at the image, saying nothing.

"Each of these numbers is a code," Cayce says, "identifying a particular sequence in a piece of information. Each sequence has one of these numbers encrypted, for purposes of identification, and to enable it to be tracked."

"Stego," says Baranov, putting a slender, brown-stained forefinger down on the printout. "This one. Why's it circled?"

"The encryption is done by a firm in America called Sigil. I want to learn who they do it for, but the specific piece of information I'm asking you for is the e-mail address to which they sent this particular piece, when it had been encrypted."

"Sigil?"

"In Ohio."

He sucks his teeth, making an odd, small, bird-like sound.

"Can you do that?"

"Protocol," he says. "Assuming I could, what then?"

"If you tell me you can, I'll go to your dealer and buy the calculator."

"And then?"

"You'll give me the e-mail address."

"And then?"

"I'll give Ngemi the calculator. But if you don't give me the address . . ."

"Yes?"

"It goes into the canal, at Camden Lock."

He leans forward, eyes narrowing behind round lenses, lost in an intricacy of wrinkles. "You'd do that, would you?"

"Yes. And I'll do it if I think you're cheating me."

He peers at her. "I believe you would," he says, at last, with something close to approval.

"Good. Then call Ngemi, when you have something. He knows how to reach me."

He says nothing.

"Thank you for considering my offer." She rises, crouching beneath the low ceiling, elbowing open the door, and climbs out, into bright pallor and rich, extraordinarily fresh air. "Goodbye." She closes the door behind her.

Ngemi creaks, beside her. "Was he in a better mood, then?" he asks.

"He showed me his gun."

"This is England, girl," Ngemi says. "People don't have guns."

CHAPTER 30

.R U

On the train to Waterloo, Ngemi buys beer and a packet of chicken-flavored crisps from the refreshment cart.

Cayce buys a bottle of still mineral water.

"How did Baranov wind up that way?" she asks.

"In that specific place?"

"In his general situation. Did he drink himself there?"

"I had a cousin, back home," says Ngemi, "who drank an entire electrical appliance business. He was otherwise an ordinary fellow, well liked. His problem seemed simply the drink. With Hobbs, I imagine the drink might be a symptom of something else, though so established now that it hardly matters. Hobbs is his mother's maiden name. Hobbs-Baranov, hyphenated at birth. His father, a Soviet diplomat, defected in the fifties to America, marrying an Englishwoman of considerable wealth. Hobbs managed to lose the hyphen, but when drunk he still rails against it. He once

326

told me that he'd lived his whole life within that hyphen, in spite of having buried it."

"He worked for American intelligence, as a mathematician?"

"Recruited from Harvard, I believe. But again, it's difficult to know. He only mentions those things when drunk." He pops the top on his can of beer, and sips. "I suppose I have no business asking, but was your visit a success?"

"It may have been. But I'll have to ask for more of your help, if it was."

"Can you tell me more?"

"I need something, and Baranov may be able to find it for me. In exchange, I've offered to buy that calculator for him, from the dealer in Bond Street."

"Greenaway? His asking price is obscene."

"It doesn't matter. If Baranov gets me what I want, it's a bargain."

"And you need my help?"

"I need you to go with me, to this dealer, and help me buy it. Make sure it's the right one, the one Baranov wants. And if Baranov gives me what I want, I'll need you to deliver it to him."

"I can do that, certainly."

"How do we start?"

"Greenaway has a website. He doesn't open, Sundays."

She opens the Luggage Label and removes her iMac and phone. "I hope it's still there, the calculator."

"It will be," Ngemi assures her, "at Greenaway's price."

The evening version of a Waterloo Sunday moves differently, and the pigeons Cayce had seen flying, that morning, now race fearlessly amid the feet of hurrying passengers, pecking up the day's bounty.

Under Ngemi's tutelage, she's e-mailed Greenaway, asking for the Curta prototype, which is indeed still on offer, to be placed on hold, prior to her viewing it tomorrow, with intent to buy. "The hold is no protection," Ngemi explains, as she walks with him toward the escalators, "should another tragic victim turn up in the meantime, but it will serve to get his attention, and establishes a certain tone. It will help that he knows you are American." He had insisted she mention that she was from New York, and only in London briefly. "Do you know when Hobbs might have your information for you?"

"No idea."

"But you wish to go ahead with Greenaway?"

"Yes."

"You are not a wealthy woman?"

"Not at all. I'm using someone else's money."

"If you had offered Hobbs the amount of Greenaway's price, in cash, he might well have refused you. He could no more pay Greenaway's price, with his own money, than I could. I've known him to refuse offers, for that sort of service, that I took to be much larger."

"But doesn't he need money anyway, or want it?"

"Yes, but perhaps he has only a finite number of favors left, to call in."

"Favors?"

"I don't imagine that he himself has any particular resources. It isn't his talent that might find you what you want, or any knowledge on his part. I believe he calls in a favor, asks someone, and sometimes is told the answer."

"Do you know who he asks?" Not really expecting an answer herself.

"Have you heard of 'Echelon'?"

"No." Although she thinks she has, but can't quite place it.

"American intelligence have a system that allows for the scanning of all Net traffic. If such a thing exists, then Hobbs might be its grandfather. He may well have been instrumental in its creation." He raises an eyebrow, as if to signal that is all he knows, or is willing to say, about so outré a subject.

"I see," she says, wondering if she does.

"Well," Ngemi pauses near the descending escalator, "you must know what you're doing."

"No, I don't. I don't at all. But thank you, for all your help."

"Good evening, then. I will phone you, in the morning."

She watches the shaven dome of his large dark head descend, on an angle, into the London underground.

She goes to find a cab.

Fuck me. Do you know that expression? 70s. Not that I want you to fuck me, but that I'm expressing a profound and baffled amazement.

She's ready for an early night, on CPST, and is checking her mail prior to brushing her teeth. Parkaboy first up.

Judy hasn't left Darryl's since my last message. More hot and heavy with Taki, who wants to get on a plane for California but he's got a day job designing games for a Japanese phone system. What I want to know is, is any of this worth it? Are you getting anywhere? Any closer at all?

Maybe, she decides. That's all she can tell him.

Maybe. I've got something in play here, but it may take a while to see whether it works. When I know more, you will.

Send.
Boone next.

Greetings from the Holiday Inn down the road from the technology park. An original, lots of beige. Have made contact on supposed business but have no idea when anything useful might turn up. Next stop, the lounge downstairs, where

330

some of the weaker sheep of the firm in question may congregate. You okay?

That really is the slow route, she thinks, though she doesn't know what else he should be trying, other than buddying up with Sigil employees.

I'm fine.

She pauses.

Nothing to report.

Which may well be the case.
Send.
Next is . . . spam? An all-numerical hotmail address.

Yes It ends in .ru Observe the protocol H-B

Baranov, e-mailing from the hyphen.
.ru
Russia.

CHAPTER 31

THE PROTOTYPE

Monday morning, in Neal's Yard, she keeps the Blue Ant phone on, and nearby, while she works through her program.

It rings while she's on the PediPole, a device that makes her think of Leonardo's drawing of the human body's proportions as they relate to the universe. Her palms, fingers spread, are pressing down into black foam stirrups.

The woman using the nearest reformer frowns.

"Sorry." Cayce lets up the springs, releases the stirrups, retrieves the phone from the pocket of the Rickson's. "Hello?"

"Good morning. It is Ngemi. Are you well?"

"Yes, thanks. And you?"

"Indeed well. Stephen King's Wang ships today. I am very excited."

"From Maine?"

"From Memphis." She hears him smack his lips. "Hobbs phoned. He says he has what you need, and now it is up to you. Shall we visit Mr Greenaway and pay his ugly price?"

"Yes. Please. Can we do it now?"

"He will not open until eleven. Shall I meet you there?"

"Please."

He gives her the number in Bond Street. "See you there."

"Thank you."

She places the phone at the blond wooden base of the PediPole and gets back into position.

If there's any one thing about England that Cayce finds fundamentally disturbing, it is how "class" works—a word with a very different mirror-world meaning, somehow. She's long since given up trying to explain this to English friends.

The closest she can come is that it's somewhat akin, for her, if only in its enormity, to how the British seem to feel about certain American attitudes to firearms ownership—which they generally find unthinkable, and bafflingly, self-evidently wrong, and so often leading to a terrible and profligate waste of human life. And she knows what they mean, but also knows how deeply it runs, the gun thing, and how unlikely it is to change. Except, perhaps, gradually, and over a very long time. Class in England is like that, for her.

Mostly she manages to ignore it, though there's a certain way they can have, on first meeting, of sniffing one another's caste out, that gives her the willies.

Katherine, her therapist, had suggested that it might in fact be because it was such a highly codified behavior, as were all of the areas of human activity around which Cayce suffered such remarkable sensitivity. And it is, highly codified; they look at one another's shoes first, she's convinced, and Lucian Greenaway has just done that to Ngemi.

And doesn't like them.

Slightly dusty black DMs, their fat-proof (as advertised) air-cushioned soles now planted firmly before this counter in Greenaway's shop, which is known simply as L. GREENAWAY. Quite large, Ngemi's DMs, Cayce thinks, estimating a British size eleven. She can't see Greenaway's shoes, behind the counter, but if he were American, she guesses, they might be toe-cleavage loafers with tassels. Though they wouldn't be that here. Something by a Savile Row maker, but, she guesses, not bespoke.

She's met people here who can distinguish workable button holes on a suit cuff at twenty feet.

"I have to ask you, Miss Pollard, if you're entirely serious about this?" L. GREENAWAY is the sort of shop you must be buzzed into, and Greenaway himself looks as though his toe might be hovering over a button that would summon large, helmeted men, with truncheons.

"Yes, Mr. Greenaway, I am."

He looks at her black nylon flight jacket. "You are a collector?"

"My father."

Greenaway considers this. "I don't recognize the name. Curtas are rather a small field."

"Mr. Pollard," says Ngemi, "a retired American government official with a background in the sciences, has a number of Type Ones, all dating from 1949 and of course numbered below three hundred. And several Type Twos as well, chosen primarily for condition and case variety." The thumbnail of Win, not inaccurate, is the result of his gentle questioning on the pavement outside.

Greenaway glares at him.

"May I ask you a question?" Ngemi inquires, inclining slightly forward, with an audible creak.

"A question?"

"A question of provenance. Herzstark was known to keep three prototypes in his home in Nendeln, Liechtenstein. Upon his death, in 1988, they are known to have been sold to a private collector."

"Yes?"

"Would the one on offer be one of those, Mr. Greenaway? I found the description on your website somewhat ambiguous, in that regard."

Cayce watches Greenaway redden slightly. "No, it would not. It is from the estate of a master machinist, and comes with extensive documentation, including photographs of it in the hands of both Herzstark and the machinist, its fabricator. The three from the house in Nendeln are numbered one, two, and three, in romans. The one on offer is numbered four." His expression perfectly neutral, he continues to stare at Ngemi with what Cayce takes to be absolute loathing. "In romans."

"May we see it, please?" Cayce asks.

"Master machinist," says Ngemi. "Fabricator."

"I beg you pardon?" says Greenaway, who clearly doesn't.

"When exactly was this prototype fabricated, then?" Ngemi smiles blandly.

"And what are you implying by that?"

"Nothing at all." Ngemi raises his eyebrows. "In nineteen forty-six? 'Forty-seven?"

"Nineteen forty-seven."

"Please show it to us, Mr. Greenaway," Cayce tries again.

"And how would you propose to pay, were you to decide to purchase? I'm sorry, but I can't accept a personal check unless I'm acquainted with the buyer."

The Blue Ant Visa, ready in her hand, is withdrawn from the Rickson's pocket and placed on the rectangular blotter-like suede pad atop Greenaway's counter. He peers at it, obviously puzzled by the Egyptianate ant, but then, she guesses, makes out the name of the issuing bank. "I see. And your credit is adequate, for the price of the piece, plus VAT?"

"That's a very insulting question," says Ngemi, levelly, but Greenaway ignores him, watching Cayce.

"Yes, Mr. Greenaway, but I suggest you check, now, with the issuer." Actually she isn't entirely sure, but vaguely remembers Bigend mentioning that she is authorized to buy automobiles but not aircraft. Whatever other faults Bigend has, she doubts he's prone to exaggeration.

Greenaway is looking at them, now, as though they were in the process of robbing him at gunpoint, assuming that that process would cause him neither fear nor anxiety, just a sort of irritated amazement at their effrontery. "That won't be necessary," he said. "We'll find out during the authorization process."

"May we see it now, please?" Ngemi places his fingtips on the counter, as if laying claim to something.

Greenaway reaches beneath it, coming up with a gray cardboard box. It is square, perhaps six inches on a side, and has two U-shaped wire fasteners that protrude through slots at the edges of the lid. It is probably much older than she is. Greenaway pauses, and she imagines him counting, silently. Then he lifts the lid away and puts it to the side.

The calculator is cushioned in funereal gray tissue paper. Greenaway reaches into the box, draws it carefully out, and places it on the suede pad.

It looks, to Cayce, very similar to the ones she'd seen in Baranov's trunk, though perhaps less finely finished.

Ngemi has produced a loupe, and screws it carefully into his left eye. He leans forward, creaking, and gives the Curta his full and cyclopean attention. She can hear his breath, now, and the ticking of the dozens of clocks all around her, which before she'd not been aware of.

"Um," says Ngemi, and more deeply, "Um." Sounds she imagines are quite unconscious. He seems in that moment to be very far away, and she feels alone.

He straightens, removing the loupe. Blinks. "I will need to handle it. I will need to perform an operation."

"You're entirely certain you're serious about this? You wouldn't simply be winding me up, you two, would you?"

"No, sir," says Ngemi, "we are serious."

"Then go ahead."

Ngemi picks up the calculator, first turning it over. On its round base Cayce glimpses "IV," stamped into metal. Righting it, his fingers slide over it, moving those studs or flanges in their slots or tracks. He pauses, closes his eyes as if listening, and works the little pepper-mill crank at the top. It makes a slithering sound, if a mechanism can be said to slither.

Ngemi opens his eyes, looks at the numbers that have appeared in small circular windows. He looks from them to Greenaway. "Yes," he says.

Cayce indicates the Blue Ant card. "We'll take it, Mr. Greenaway."

A block from L. GREENAWAY, Ngemi carrying the boxed calculator against his stomach as though it contained the ashes of a relative, Baranov is waiting, a half-inhaled cigarette screwed into the corner of his mouth.

"That's it?"

"Yes," says Ngemi.

"Authentic."

"Of course."

Baranov takes the box.

"These are interesting as well." Ngemi unzips his black coat and withdraws a brown envelope. "Documentation of provenance."

Baranov tucks the box beneath his arm and takes the envelope. He hands Cayce a business card.

The Light of India Curry House. Poole.

She turns it over. Rust-colored fountain pen. Neat italics.

stellanor@armaz.ru

The eyes behind the round lenses fix Cayce with contempt, dismissal. "Baltic oil, is it? Thought you might be a bit more interesting than that."

He flicks his cigarette down and walks on, in the direction they've just come, the Curta prototype beneath his arm and the brown envelope in his hand.

"Do you mind my asking," Ngemi says, "what he meant?"

"No," she says, looking from the dung-colored back of Baranov's retreating jacket to the rust-colored e-mail address, "but I don't know."

"This is what you wanted?"

"It must be," she says. "I suppose it must be."

CHAPTER 32

PARTICIPATION MYSTIQUE

N gemi departs by tube from Bond Street Station, leaving her, in suddenly bright sunlight, with no idea where she might be going, or why.

A cab takes her to Kensington High Street, the card from Baranov's curry house zipped into the pocket on the sleeve of the Rickson's, the one originally designed to hold a pack of American cigarettes.

Liminal, she thinks, getting out of the cab by what had been the musty, multileveled cave of Kensington Market, with its vanished mazes of punk and hippy tat. Liminal. Katherine McNally's word for certain states: thresholds, zones of transition. Does she feel liminal, now, or simply directionless? She pays the driver, through the window, and he drives away.

Oil, Baranov had said?

She walks in the direction of the park. Bright gilt of the Albert Memorial, never quite real to her since they cleaned it. When she'd first seen it, it had been a black thing, funereal, almost sinister. Win had told her that the London he'd first seen had been largely as black as that, a city of soot, more deeply textured perhaps for its lack of color.

She waits at a signal, crosses the High Street.

Her Parco boots crunch gravel as she turns into the Gardens. Cayce Pollard Central Standard might now be approaching its own hour of the wolf, she thinks. Soul too long in a holding pattern.

The park is scribed with reddish gravel, paths wide as rural highways in Tennessee. These bring her to the statue of Peter Pan, bronze rabbits at its base.

She takes off the Luggage Label bag, puts it down, and removes the Rickson's, spreading it on the short-cut grass. She sits on it. A jogger passes, on the gravel.

She unzips the cigarette pocket on the Rickson's sleeve and looks at Baranov's card.

stellanor@armaz.ru. Looking faded in this light, as though Baranov had written it years ago.

She puts it carefully away again, zips up the little pocket. Opens her bag and removes the iBook and phone.

Hotmail. Timing out. Empty.

She opens a blank message, outgoing.

My name is Cayce Pollard. I'm sitting on the grass in a park in London. It's sunny and warm. I'm 32 years old. My father disappeared on September 11, 2001, in New York, but we haven't been able to prove he was killed in the attack. I began to follow the footage you've been

That "you" stops her. Pecks at the delete key, losing "you've been."

Katherine McNally had had Cayce compose letters, letters which would never, it was understood, be sent, and which in some cases couldn't be, the addressee being dead.

Someone showed me one segment and I looked for more. I found a site where people discussed it, and I began to post there, asking questions. I can't tell you

This time, it doesn't stop her.

why, but it became very important to me, to all of us there. Parkaboy and Ivy and Maurice and Filmy, all the others too. We went there whenever we could, to be with other people who understood. We looked for more footage. Some people stayed out surfing, weeks at a time, never posting until someone discovered a new segment.

All through that winter, the mildest she'd known in Manhattan, though in memory the darkest, she'd gone to F:F:F—to give herself to the dream.

342

We don't know what you're doing, or why. Parkaboy thinks you're dreaming. Dreaming for us. Sometimes he sounds as though he thinks you're dreaming us. He has this whole edged-out participation mystique: how we have to allow ourselves so far into the investigation of whatever this is, whatever you're doing, that we become part of it. Hack into the system. Merge with it, deep enough that it, not you, begins to talk to us. He says it's like Coleridge, and De Quincey. He says it's shamanic. That we may all seem to just be sitting there, staring at the screen, but really, some of us anyway, we're adventurers. We're out there, seeking, taking risks. In hope, he says, of bringing back wonders. Trouble is, lately, I've been living that.

She looks up, everything made pale and washed-out by the light. She's forgotten to bring her sunglasses again.

I've been out there, out here, seeking. Taking risks. Not sure exactly why. Scared. Turns out there are some very not-nice people, out here. Though I guess that was never news.

She stops, and looks over at Peter Pan, noticing how the bronze ears of the rabbits at his base are kept polished by the hands of children.

Do you know we're all here, waiting for the next

segment? Wandering up and down the web all night, looking for where you've left it for us? We are. Well, not me personally, lately, but that's because I seem to have followed Parkaboy's advice and started trying to find another way to hack in. And I guess I have—we have—because we've found those codes embedded in the footage, that map of the island or city or whatever it is, and we know that you, or someone, could use those to track the spread of a given segment, to judge the extent of dissemination. And through finding those codes, the numbers woven into the fabric, I've been able to get to this e-mail address, and now I'm sitting in this park, beside the statue of Peter Pan, writing to you, and

And what?

What I want to ask you is
Who are you?
Where are you?
Are you dreaming?
Are you there? The way I'm here?

She reads what she's written. Like most of the letters Katherine had had her write—to her mother, to Win both before and after his disappearance, to various ex's and one former therapist—her letter to the maker ends with question marks.

344

Katherine had thought that the letters Cayce most needed to write wouldn't end in question marks. Periods were needed, if not exclamation points, in Katherine's view, and Cayce had never felt particularly successful with either.

Sincerely yours,
Cayce Pollard

Watching her hands continue briefly to type, in best typing-class mode, in privately sarcastic imitation of a woman imagining that she is actually accomplishing something.

(CayceP)

Aware in just that instant of how the park distances the sound of London, giving her the sensation of existing at some still point around which all else revolves. As though the broad gravel avenues are leys, terminating at Peter Pan.

The angry child's fingers, typing.

stellanor@armaz.ru

And that in the address window, as though she would actually send it.

Touchpadding down menu to Send.

And of course she doesn't.

And watches as it sends.

"I didn't," she protests to the iBook on the grass, the colors of its screen faint in the sunlight. "I didn't," she says to Peter Pan.

She couldn't have. She did.

Cross-legged on her jacket, hunched over the iBook.

She doesn't know what it is that she feels.

Automatically, she checks for mail.

Timing out, empty.

A woman jogs past, crunching gravel, breathing like a piston.

Mechanically consuming a bowl of Thai salad in an all-Asia's restaurant across the street. She hasn't had breakfast today, and maybe this will calm her down.

She doubts it, after what she's done.

Accept that it happened, she tells herself. Table all questions of intentionality.

She almost feels as though something in the park had made her do it. Genius loci, Parkaboy would say. Too much sun. Convergence of lines. (Convergence of something, certainly, she guesses, but in some part of herself she can't access.)

The iBook is open again, on the table in front of her. She's just looked up the name and address of the person responsible (whatever that might mean) for the domain armaz.ru: one A. N. Polakov, in what she takes to be an office building, in Cyprus.

If she smoked, she thinks, she'd be giving Baranov a run for his money. Right now she almost wishes she did.

She looks at her anti-Casio and tries to do time-zone math for Ohio. Remembers that little map that Macs have, but it's too much trouble to remember where to find it.

She'll call Boone. She has to tell him what's happened. She shuts down the iBook and uncables the phone. Something tells her that it means something, that she isn't calling Parkaboy first, but she chooses to ignore that.

Sends the first of the cell numbers he'd loaded for her on the flight from Tokyo.

"Boone?"

A woman giggles. "Who's calling, please?" In the background she hears Boone say, "Give me that."

Cayce looks at her mug of steaming green tea, remembering the last time she drank green tea, in Hongo, with Boone.

"Cayce Pollard."

"Boone Chu," he says, having taken the phone from the woman.

"It's Cayce, Boone." Remembering the kudzu on the iron roof. Thinking: You said she was in Madrid. "Just checking in."

Marisa.

Damien has a Marina. Someone will turn up with a Marika soon.

"Good," he says. "News on your end?"

She looks out at traffic passing on the High Street. "No."

"I may be getting somewhere, here. I'll let you know."

"Thanks." Stabbing the button. "I'm sure you are."

A server, apparently noticing Cayce's expression, looks alarmed. Cayce forces a smile, looks down at her bowl. Puts the phone down with exaggerated calm and picks up her chopsticks. "Fuck," she says, under her breath, willing herself to continue eating.

How is it that she still sets herself up for these things? she asks herself.

When the noodles and chicken are gone, and the server's brought more tea, feeling a need to do something for herself, and on her own, she phones Bigend's cell.

"Yes?"

"Cayce, Hubertus. Question."

"Yes?"

"The man from Cyprus. Did Dorotea have a name?"

"Yes. Hold on. Andreas Polakov."

"Hubertus?"

"Yes?"

"Did you just look that up?"

"Yes."

"In what?"

"The transcript of the conversation."

"Did she know you were recording it?"

"Where are you?"

"Don't change the subject."

"I just did. Do you have any news for me?"

"Not yet."

"Boone is in Ohio."

"Yes. I know that. Bye."

She reconnects the phone to the iBook and boots up again. She needs to tell Parkaboy what she's learned, what she's done.

She checks for incoming.

One.

stellanor@armaz.ru

She chokes on her tea, coughing. Almost upsets it across the keyboard.

Forces herself to open it, just open it, as if it were any other e-mail. As if—

Hello! This is very strange mail.

Cayce closes her eyes. When she opens them, the words are still there.

I am in Moscow. I also have lost my father in a bomb. My mother too. How do you have this address? Who are these people you are telling me? Segments, you mean the parts of the work?

And nothing more.

"Yes," she says to the iBook, "yes. The work."

The work.

"Cayce again, Hubertus. Who do I call for travel?"

"Sylvie Jeppson. At the office. Where are you going?"

"Paris, next Sunday." She's on her third green tea and they're starting to begrudge her the table.

"Why?"

"I'll expain tomorrow. Thanks. Bye."

She calls Blue Ant and is put through to Sylvie Jeppson.

"Do I need a visa for Russia?"

"Yes, you do."

"How long does that take?"

"It depends. If you pay more, they'll do it in an hour. But they tend to leave you sitting in an empty room for an hour beforehand. A sort of Soviet nostalgia thing. But we have an in with their Department of Foreign Affairs."

"We do?"

"We've done some work for them. Quietly. Where are you?"

"Kensington High Street."

"That's convenient. Do you have your passport?"

"Yes."

"Can you meet me in thirty minutes? Five, Kensington Palace Gardens. At Bayswater. Queensway tube's closest. You need three passport-sized photographs."

"Can you do that?"

"Hubertus wouldn't want you to wait. And I know who to speak to, there. But you'll have to hurry. They don't stay open in the afternoon."

Leaving the visa section of the Russian Consulate, the tall, pale, unflappable Sylvie asks, "When do you want to go?"

"Sunday. In the morning. To Paris."

"That'll be BA, unless you prefer Air France. You wouldn't rather take the train?"

"No, thanks."

"And when to Russia?"

"I don't know yet. It's really just an outside possibility, at this point, but I wanted to have the visa ready. Thank you for your help."

"Anything," says Sylvie, smiling. "I've been told to take extremely good care of you."

"You have."

"I'm taking a cab back to Soho. Like a lift?"

Cayce sees two approaching, both vacant.

"No, thanks. I'm going to Camden."

She lets Sylvie take the first one.

"Aeroflot," she says, when the driver of the second asks where she's going.

"Piccadilly," he says.

She phones Voytek.

"Hello?"

"It's Cayce, Voytek."

"Casey! Hello!"

"I'm going out of town again. I need to give you Damien's keys. Can you come by the flat? Say four-thirty? I'm sorry for the short notice." She promises herself she'll buy him his scaffolding.

"No problem, Casey!"

"Thanks. See you."

She'll buy the scaffolding with Bigend's card. But she'll use her own, at Aeroflot.

"I've got your participation mystique right here,"

she says, though whether to Parkaboy, London, or the general or specific mysteries of her life today, she doesn't know.

She sees the cabbie glance at her in his mirror.

CHAPTER 33

BOT

Aeroflot flight SU244, departing Heathrow at ten-thirty in the evening, proves to be a Boeing 737, not the Tupolev she'd been hoping for. She's never been to Russia before, and thinks of it primarily in the light of childhood stories of Win's; the world beyond the perimeters of the world he'd been dedicated to protecting; a world of toilet-navigating spy devices and ceaseless duplicity. In her childhood's Russia it's always snowing. Men wear dark furry hats.

She wonders, finding her aisle seat in coach, whether Aeroflot had had to compete to retain the hammer and sickle as its logo, and how exclusive that is. Massive recognition factor. It's a winged version, rendered with considerable delicacy, and she finds it curiously difficult to date: a sort of Victorian Futurist look. She has a neutral reaction to it, she finds, which is a great relief.

National icons are always neutral for her, with the exception of Nazi Germany's, and this not so much from a sense of historical evil (though she certainly

353

has that) as from an awareness of a scary excess of design talent. Hitler had had entirely too brilliant a graphics department, and had understood the power of branding all too well. Heinzi would have done just fine, back then, but she doubts that even he could have managed a better job of it.

Swastikas, and particularly the fact that there had been that custom type-slug for "SS," induce a violent reaction, akin to her Tommy-phobia but in an even worse direction. She'd once worked for a month in Austria, where these symbols are not suppressed by law, as they are in Germany, and had learned to cross the street if she realized she was approaching the window of an antique shop.

The national symbols of her homeland don't trigger her, or so far haven't. And over the past year, in New York, she's been deeply grateful for this. An allergy to flags or eagles would have reduced her to shut-in status: a species of semiotic agoraphobia.

She stows her Rickson's in the overhead bin, takes her seat, and slides the bag with the iBook beneath the seat in front of her. The legroom isn't bad, and thinking this she experiences a kind of pseudonostalgia for Win's version of Aeroflot: vicious flight attendants flinging stale sandwiches at you, and small plastic bags provided in which to place pens, a thoughtful precaution against frequent depressurizations. He'd told her that Poland, from the air, looked like Kansas as farmed by elves; the patchwork fields so much smaller, the land as flat and vast.

Soon they are taxiing toward takeoff, the seats beside her empty, and it strikes her that, through luck, and for little more than she'd paid earlier for express service on a visa, she'll have almost as much space and privacy as she'd had to and from Tokyo.

Magda, who'd turned up in Voytek's stead to get the keys, knows where she's going, and her mother, on whom she's finally taken mercy with an e-mail, and Parkaboy. These three know she's going, but someone else, she doesn't know who, knows she's coming.

The Boeing's turbines shift pitch.

Hi Mom,

I hope you'll forgive my silence, or anyway not take it personally. I've completed the job I came here for, and have been hired by the man who runs/owns the company to do something more directly on his behalf—cultural investigation, not to sound so mysterious about it, around some new ideas about film distribution and how films can be structured. Sounds dull but actually I've been completely fascinated by it, which is largely why you haven't heard from me. Also, I think it's been good for me to get out of New York and stop thinking so much about Dad, which may also be why I haven't been writing. I know we've agreed to disagree about the EVP thing, but those clips you sent really creep me out. Can't think of a more honest way to put it. But, for all of that, I dreamed

355

of him recently and he seemed to give me a very specific piece of advice, which I acted on, and which proved correct, so maybe there's a point where we don't entirely disagree on that stuff. I don't know. I just know that I'm finally coming to terms with the idea that he really is gone, and the insurance stuff and the pension and all of that just feels like red tape. I wish that was over but sometimes I wonder if it ever will be. Anyway, I'm also writing to say that I'm headed for Moscow tonight, on that same business I mentioned. It's strange to finally be going to the place that Dad was always going off to when I was a kid. It's never seemed like a real place, to me, more a fairy tale; wherever it was that he'd come back from with those painted wooden eggs and his stories. I remember him telling me that it was just a matter of keeping them more or less in check until the food riots started, and when it all just changed, no food riots, I remember I reminded him of that. He said they'd been done in by the Beatles, so the food riots hadn't had to happen. The Beatles and losing their own Vietnam. Have to go now, I'm in departure at Heathrow. I'm glad you're at Rose of the World because I know you like those people. Thanks for keeping in touch and I'll try to do a better job of that myself.
Love, Cayce

I never really imagined writing to tell you this, but I may have found him. Actually I may have had an e-mail from him, to which I am about to reply. I'm at Heathrow, waiting to get on the red-eye to Moscow, arr 5:30 a.m. tomorrow. That's where he says he is. I found somebody who was able to do something with that number of Taki's, don't ask me how (actually much better we don't know) and got me an email address. I did something weird. Sitting in a park and started writing him a letter, not one I was ever going to send. Kind of like writing a letter to God, except I had the address, and I put it in and then I guess I sent it. I didn't mean to, or even, actually, see myself do it, but it sent. Less than half an hour, reply came. Said he was in Moscow. Look, I know you want to know EVERYTHING but there's not much else, not much content in the reply, and I don't want to copy you on that, not this way. Actually the way I got that address has left me feeling that none of what we do here is ever really private, and the last thing I want, right now, is to attract any attention. So bear with me, Parkaboy; hang in; more will be revealed. Maybe even all. Whatever, there's a chance I'll know more tomorrow, and then I'll call you. Need to info-dump bigtime. Am I excited? I guess so; it's funny but I can't even tell. It's like I don't know whether to scream or shit.

Hello! Thank you for replying. I don't really know what to say, but I'm happy you answered, and excited. You're in Moscow? I am going to be in Moscow tomorrow, on business. My name is

Cayce Pollard. I will be at The President Hotel, if you'd like to call me there. But you can also e-mail me. I hope you will. Regards, CayceP

Reviewing these on the iBook, when they've reached cruising altitude, she doesn't want to think what she'll feel like, tomorrow, or the next day, or the day after that, if she receives no reply to this last one. Which she supposes is a real possibility.

Russia. Russia serves Pepsi. She sips some.

Dorotea's handler from Cyprus, who is also the registrant of armaz.ru. She wonders what other Russian elements may have come up on F:F:F, during consideration of the footage.

Slotting the F:F:F CD-ROM, which she still hasn't had copied for Ivy, she goes to its search function.

What comes up, to her surprise, is a very early post of her own, well down a thread that begins with someone entertaining the possibility that the maker is an established cineast working in anonymous secrecy.

This doesn't work for me. Not just because we can't seem to agree on who, if that's the case, it might be, but because it's too obvious, too right in front of our noses. Why couldn't it, say, be some Russian mafia kingpin, with a bent for self-expression, a previously undiscovered talent, and the wherewithal to generate and disseminate the footage? That's deliberately farfetched, but it's not utterly impossible. What I'm saying is that I don't think we're getting lateral enough, here.

She can barely remember posting this. She's never been able to go back and reread her own posts, before, and it probably wouldn't occur to her anyway. But now she reads on, following the thread to the end.

And sees that the next thread begins with what she now remembers had been Mama Anarchia's first post.

Really it is entirely about story, though not in any sense that any of you seem familiar with. Do you know nothing of narratology? Where is Derridean "play" and excessiveness? Foucauldian limit-attitude? Lyotardian language-games? Lacanian Imaginaries? Where is the commitment to praxis, positioning Jamesonian nostalgia, and despair— as well as Habermasian fears of irrationalism— as panic discourses signaling the defeat of Enlightenment hegemony over cultural theory? But no: discourses on this site are hopelessly retrograde. Mama Anarchia

Well, Cayce thinks, Mama had gotten right down to it. And she had, Cayce notes, used the word "hegemony," without which Parkaboy will not admit any Mama post as fully genuine. (For a full positive identification, though, he insists that they also contain the word "hermeneutics.")

But Cayce Pollard Central Standard is saying it's time to try to sleep, so she ejects the CD-ROM, shuts down and puts the iBook away, and closes her eyes.

And dreams of large men, strangers but somehow Donny-like, in her New York apartment. She is there too, but they can't seem to see her, or hear her, and she wants them to get out.

In Sheremetevo-2, once past the uniform, very seventies beige of customs and immigration, there seems to be advertising on virtually every surface. There are at least four advertisements on the luggage cart she's using, one Hertz and three others in Russian. As in Japan, she's realized, she's partially buffered by her inability to read the language. For which she's grateful, as the density of commercial language here, in this airport at least, rivals Tokyo.

One sign she can read is above an ATM, and says BANKOMAT, which she decides is what ATMs would have been called in America if they had been invented in the fifties. She uses her own card, rather than Blue Ant's, to obtain an initial supply of rubles, and pushes her cart out, finally, into her first breath of Russian air, heavily laden with yet another nationally specific flavor of petro-carbons. There's a disorderly looking scrum of taxis, and she knows that her job now is to find what Magda had called an "official" one.

Which she shortly does, leaving Sheremetevo-2

in a landlord-green diesel Mercedes of a certain age, its dashboard sanctified by some sort of small Orthodox shrine atop an intricate white doily.

This huge, slightly grim eight-lane highway, she decides, consulting the *Lonely Planet Moscow* she'd bought at Heathrow, is Leningradskii Prospect, traffic solid either way, but moving right along. Huge muddy trucks, luxury cars, many buses, all changing lanes in a way that gives her little confidence, aside from which her driver seems to be simultaneously having a phone conversation via the headset screwed into one ear and listening to music from the CD-player earphones covering both. She gets the idea that the concept of lanes is a fluid one, here, as perhaps is attention to the road. Tries to concentrate on the grassy median, where wildflowers grow.

She glimpses smokestacks in the distance, and tall orange buildings, but the smokestacks, pouring white smoke, seem to rise from among those buildings in some unfamiliar way, suggesting alien or perhaps non-existent concepts of zoning.

Billboards for computers, luxury goods, and electronics appear, increasing in number and variety as they approach the city. The sky, aside from the plumes of the smokestacks and a yellow-brown smudge of petro-carbons, is cloudless and blue.

Her first impression of Moscow itself is that everything is far larger than it could possibly have any need to be. Cyclopean Stalin-era buildings in burnt orange brick, their detailing vaguely maroonish. Built to humble, and terrify. But lampposts, fountains, plazas, all partake of this exaggerated scale.

As they cross the eight lanes of the traffic-packed Garden Ring, the high-urban factor goes up several notches, and the advertising thickens. Off to the right, she sees an enormous Art Nouveau train station, a survival from an earlier era still, but on a scale to dwarf London's grandest. Then a McDonald's, seemingly as large.

There are more trees than she'd expected, and as she begins to adjust to the scale of things, she notices smaller buildigns, all remarkably ugly, which probably date from the sixties. If so, these are easily the worst sixties buildings she's ever seen, and visibly crumbling at the edges. Quite a few are being torn down, and indeed there is scaffolding everywhere, much renovation under way, and in what she guesses is Tverskaya Street the crowds are thick as the Children's Crusade, but moving far more determinedly.

Huge advertising banners are slung across the street, and billboards top most buildings.

An incredible number of blue-and-white electric buses here, a vintage Dinky Toy blue that she's never seen on a real vehicle before. A lot of them don't seem to be going anywhere.

Her sole previous experience of the Soviet, or post-Soviet, had been a single evening in the former East Berlin, a few months after the Wall's fall.

Back in her hotel, safely in the West, she'd come

very close to weeping, appalled at the manifest cruelty, not to mention sheer boneheaded stupidity of what she'd seen, and had been moved to call Win in Tennessee.

"Those sons of bitches had been cooking their own books for so long, they didn't even know it themselves," he'd explained. The CIA, he'd said, had done an assessment of East German industry, just prior to the nation's collapse, and had declared it the most viable industrial base in the Communist bloc. "That was because we were looking at their figures. Say a tire factory looked pretty good. Not up to our standards but better than Third World. Wall comes down, we go in there, whole factory's clapped out. Half of it hasn't been used for ten years. Worth its weight in scrap, basically. They were lying to themselves."

"But they were so nasty to their own people," she'd protested, "so petty. They only allowed two colors of paint, one dead gray and a brown that looked as much like shit as it's possible for brown to look. A brown you can smell."

"Not a lot of advertising to bother you, though, is there?"

She'd had to laugh. "Was it like that when you were in Moscow?"

"Certainly not. Germans doing communism? That even put the wind up the Russians. Like they saw the East Germans really believed in it, all of it. You could see they thought that was crazy."

Her cab drives under a vast Prada logo. She resists the urge to cringe.

A few of the billboards, amazingly, are in that antique Socialist Realist style, flat reds and whites and grays overshot with the black of absolute authority.

And looking up at these, she sees, or thinks she sees, grinning unevenly down at her, the familiar and half-paralyzed face of Billy Prion.

The lobby of The President could easily accept a military review stand, with Lenin's tomb fitting handily in a corner. Four small groupings of couches are arranged in a space half the size of a football field, a carpeted expanse across which Cayce, waiting out extended check-in formalities requiring the surrender of her passport, watches a young woman pace angrily back and forth, in thigh-high, high-heeled, emerald-green boots, boots suggesting the collaboration of Florentine glove makers with Frederick's of Hollywood. This girl has the same improbable cheekbones as Damien's line producer, their elegant angularity echoed in hipbones accentuated by a very tight, very short skirt, a sort of Miami-period Versace homage with appliquéd snakeskin hotrod flames accentuating each ass cheek.

It's ten in the morning now, and Cayce knows that three girls in similar outfits are arguing, outside, in the hotel's security corridor, with the four large, Kevlar-jacketed young men stationed there. Lobbying to be allowed in, Cayce decides, in order to join their impatient coworker.

When she tires of watching the green boots, which have a sort of fairy-tale quality against the autumnal palette of the lobby, she glances instead through an English-language brochure on offer at the beige marble check-in counter. This explains the oranges and browns, as she sees the place had formerly been The Oktobryskaya. And is still, she gathers, reading between the lines, owned by the Kremlin.

Her room, on the twelfth floor, is larger than she had expected, with a deep bay window offering a sweeping view of the Moscow River and the city beyond. On the far shore, a vast cathedral, and on its own little island a statue of quite unthinkable awfulness. Her Lonely Planet tells her it's Peter the Great, and must be guarded, else local aesthetes blow it up. It looks like a champagne fountain rented from caterers for an old-fashioned working-class wedding.

She turns back to the room: more autumnal murkiness and a mud-dark bedspread. A nagging low-level dissonance, as though everything was designed by someone who'd been looking at a picture of a Western hotel room from the eighties, but without ever having seen even one example of the original. The bathroom is tiled in three shades of brown (though none, she's thankful, East German) with a shower, a bathtub, a bidet and toilet, each with its own paper banner declaring it DISINFEKTED.

There is a sign on the desk inviting her to use her laptop from her room, or, if she prefers, to visit the BISNIZ SENTR in the lobby.

She gets out the iBook and cables it to the socket beside the desk. If what she remembers Pamela Mainwaring having said about her phone is right, that'll probably work here, but she's not sure. It's already occurred to her that she hasn't given the cell number to her latest and most mysterious correspondent, and she wonders if there isn't something subconscious going on, there. The link is slow, but finally she gets to hotmail.

Two.

Parkaboy and stellanor.

She takes a deep breath, lets it out as slowly as she can.

You are in Zarnoskvareche, it means across Moskow river from Kremlin, district of old apartments, churches. Hotel is on Bolshaya Yakimanka street, it means little Yakimanka. If you will follow Bolshaya Yakimanka toward Kremlin, see map I have made, you will cross Bolshoy Kamennii Most, means Big Stone Bridge, seeing Kremlin. Following marking on map to Caffeine, sign in Russian. Go in at 1700 today and please be seated beside fish so I will see you.

"Fish," says Cayce.

366

Yeah well sure yes I do indeed want to know EVERYTHING and preferably yesterday but you are probably in the air and anyway that number you gave me has this really annoying English woman, who says the mobile customer is blah blah. But, anyway, I hear you. You know, I for one have never doubted that we would arrive at this day in history. Never. The maker lives. Maker is there. Has been. Waiting for us. But now I'm waiting for you, to tell me EVERYTHING. The only news I have is relatively pedestrian, though under the circumstances, what wouldn't be? Two items. Judy is gone. Into the arms of love. Yesterday, so she's already there. Got a cheap flight out of SeaTac. Gone to be with Taki. Darryl is ecstatic to be rid of her. I guess this is going to blow our cover with Taki, seeing as how she's twice his idea of actual size and doesn't speak Japanese, but on the other hand I think we were starting to lose Darryl. Now that there's nobody there but him and his bowls of instant yakisoba, he seems to be getting back on track, and that's where item two comes in. That T-thing Taki sent. Darryl got all hacker on that, with this buddy of his in Palo Alto who's on a project to build a new kind of visually based search engine. Buddy has these bots that are CAD-CAM-based, look for things on the basis of how they're shaped. Darryl got him to send two out, one to search for a section of map that would correspond to the streets on the T. That was the one they had high hopes for,

367

but it came up zero. The other one was kind of an afterthought: find something shaped like this T-shaped thing. Well, they got a 100% match-up on 75% of Taki's T. Except for the branch with the ragged edge, this looks exactly like one specific part in the manual arming mechanism of the US Army's M18A1 Claymore mine, which is basically a wad of C4 explosive packed behind 700 steel balls. When the C4 goes off, the balls come out in a 60° pattern that expands to six feet; anything closer than 170 feet (with trees or foliage in the way, mileage may vary) is thereby made hamburger. Used for ambushes, remotely detonated. Looks sort of like an overweight but very compact satellite video-dish, rectangular and slightly concave. Don't ask me: it's what the bot brought home. Will you call me, please, NOW, and tell me EVERYTHING?

CHAPTER 34

ZAMOSKVARECH

But she doesn't phone Parkaboy. She's too excited, too anxious.

But this is a dressy city, in some way she wouldn't care for if she were to be here very long, so she changes into her Parco outfit, and even tries her luck with the makeup the Tokyo spa issued her. The result, she suspects, would have the spa girls trying not to laugh, but at least it's evident she's wearing makeup. She could probably be mistaken, she decides, for the correspondent for some obscure sub-NPR cultural radio operation. Definitely not television.

Making sure she has the room's magnetic key, she puts on her Rickson's, shoulders the Luggage Label bag containing iBook and phone, and finds her way back to the mini-lobby fronting the elevator banks. A uniformed woman sits there, she assumes, twenty-four hours a day, beneath an enormous arrangement of flowers and dried leaves. Cayce nods to her, but she doesn't nod back.

369

There is a large window between the two elevators, draped ceiling to floor in nubby ocher fabric. Beside this is an upright glass cooler stocked with champagne, mineral water, what must be several exceptionally well-chilled bottles of burgundy, and much Pepsi. Waiting for the elevator, Cayce edges the ocher nubbiness aside and sees ancient-looking apartment buildings, white spires, and one amazing crenellated orange-and-turquoise bell tower. In the deeper distance, golden onion domes.

This, she decides, is the direction she's going now.

No one at all in the vast main lobby, not even a girl in green boots.

She finds her way out, past the security cave with its wide boys in Kevlar, and tries to walk around the block, so that she'll be headed in the direction of those onion domes.

And is lost, almost immediately. But doesn't mind, as she's only out here to walk off an excess of nerves. And at some point, she reminds herself, to phone Parkaboy.

But why is she hesitating to do that? The reason, she admits, is that she knows she'll have to tell him about Bigend, and Boone, and the rest of it, and she's afraid to, afraid of what he might say. But if she doesn't, their friendship, which she values deeply, will start to cease to feel genuine.

She stops, staring at the streetscape of this old residential neighborhood, and is acutely aware of her mind doing the but-really-it's-like thing it does when presented with serious cultural novelty: but really it's like Vienna, except it isn't, and really it's like Stockholm, but it's not, really . . .

She wanders on, feeling like a child anxiously playing hooky, occasionally glancing up in case she finds the golden onions, until her phone starts to ring.

Feeling guilty, she answers. "Yes?"

"Everything. Now."

"I was just going to call you."

"Have you met him?"

"No."

"Are you going to?"

"Yes."

"When?"

"This evening, five o'clock, in either a restaurant or a coffee bar, I'm not sure."

"You can't meet him in Starbucks."

"It's not a Starbucks. I'm not sure they even have Starbucks."

"They will."

"Parkaboy?" It feels strange, to say his name. His handle, really. Suddenly it feels stranger still to remember that she doesn't know his name.

"Yes?"

"I have to tell you something."

A pause, on his end. "You're carrying our child."

"This is serious—"

"I'll say. It's probably an Internet first."

"No. I'm working for somebody."

371

"I thought you were working for that lethally pomo ad agency."

"I'm working for someone who has an interest in finding the maker. Someone who's backing me. That was how I could afford to go to Tokyo, and meet with Taki."

"So? Who?"

"Do you know who Hubertus Bigend is?"

"Spelled 'big,' and 'end'?"

"Yes."

"Founder and owner of said agency?"

"Yes."

"'Bullshit baffles brains' taken to new levels in the celebrity interview?"

"That's the one. And I'm working for him. Or, he says, with him. But it's gotten me here. It gave me the money I needed to get the address that got me here."

Silence.

"I've been afraid you'd hate me," she tells him.

"Don't be ridiculous. You're still having our child, aren't you?"

"I feel like a shit for not having told you."

"If you're about to meet the maker, and you're still talking to me, I really don't care what manner or number of goats you've had to blow to get there. And anyone you've had to kill in the process, I'll help get rid of the bodies."

"You're not just saying that?"

"I'm saying it, aren't I? What else do you want? Should I be carving it into my arm with a broken acrylic nail?" He falls silent. Then: "But what does your Mr. Bigend want with our maker?"

"He says he doesn't know. He says that the footage is the cleverest example of marketing the century's seen so far. He says he wants to know more. I think he might even be telling the truth."

"Stranger things have happened, I suppose. Least of my worries, right now."

"What are your worries, then?"

"How I'm going to get there. Whether my passport, when I find it, if I can find it, is still valid. Whether I can swing a deal for a quick ticket that won't require a mortgage."

"Are you serious?"

"What do you think?"

A blond, entirely Californian-looking nanny passes Cayce, leading a small, dark-haired Russian boy with a red balloon. She glances at Cayce and hurries the child along.

Cayce remembers Sylvie Jeppson, the two of them leaving the Russian Consulate. "You'll need a visa," she tells Parkaboy, "and you can get one fast if you pay extra, but you won't need a ticket. There's a woman named Sylvie Jeppson, at Blue Ant in London. I'm going to call her and give her your number. She'll find the quickest flight and have your ticket waiting at O'Hare. And I know this seems completely insane, but I need your name. I don't actually know it."

"Thornton Vaseltarp."

"Sorry?"

"Gilbert."

"Gilbert?"

"Peter Gilbert. Parkaboy. You'll get used to it. What's the bottom line on this flight to Moscow?"

"There isn't any. I'm covered for expenses. You just became one. I need you here. That simple."

"Thank you."

"But don't let her find out I'm already here. She thinks I'm coming in a week."

"Were you always this complicated?"

"No, but I'm learning. Parkaboy—Peter—I'm going to call her now."

A silence. "Thank you. You know I have to be there."

"I know. I'll call you later. Bye."

She walks on, phone in hand, until she finds a sort of thick, truncated granite bollard thrust up from the pavement. She has no idea what it might once have been, but she sits on its edge, the stone warm through the fabric of her skirt, and phones Blue Ant in Soho. There's an extra level of hiss to Moscow cellular, but she gets through, if only to Sylvie's voice mail. "Cayce Pollard, Sylvie. I have someone in Chicago I need to send to Moscow, ASAP. Peter Gilbert." The name feels strange on her tongue. She recites Parkaboy's number, twice. "Book him a room at The President Hotel. Get him there as soon as you can, please. It's important. Thank you. Bye."

An unmarked police car goes roaring past, a very

new Mercedes, with a flashing blue light off to the side of the windshield. She watches it take a tight medieval corner, tires shrieking.

She puts away the phone, gets up, walks on.

She hasn't gone much farther when a great wave of exhaustion rolls in, seemingly from the direction of the river, Cayce Pollard Central Standard announcing from some deep organic level that it is time to be unconscious. She thinks she'd better go with that, so turns around and starts tracing her route back to The President.

Her phone wakes her, rather than the call she's requested from the desk or the alarm she's set on her watch as backup. She sits up naked under thick white sheets and the mud-colored President bedspread, trying to remember where she is. Sunlight through the crack in the drawn curtains, as if from some odd direction.

She gets out of bed, fumbles with the zip on her bag.

"Hello?"

"It's Boone. Where are you?"

"Just waking up. Where are you?"

"Still in Ohio. Getting somewhere, though."

"Where's that?" She sits on the edge of the bed. Checks her watch.

"A domain name. Armaz-dot-ru."

She can't think of anything to say.

"Nazran," he says.

"What's that?"

"Capital of the Republic of Ingushetia. It's an ofshornaya zona."

"A what?"

"An offshore tax haven. For Russia. They liked Cyprus so much, for that, they decided to grow their own. Set it up in Ingush. The guy the domain is registered to is in Cyprus, but he works for some ofshornaya outfit in Ingush. That's probably where Dorotea's Russian flavor is coming from."

"How do you know he's from . . . Ingush?"

"Google."

She hadn't thought of that.

"And this is . . ." She hesitates, on the brink of lying. Lies. "This domain is where the footage comes from?"

"You got it."

"But you just have a domain, no address?"

"Hey, it's better than nothing." He sounds disappointed. "I've got something else, too."

"What's that?"

"Oil."

"Meaning?"

"I'm not sure. But I ran this guy past my friend from Harvard, State Department. He says the outfit our boy is with has links to some of the players who're looking central to Russian oil."

"Russian oil?"

"Saudi oil has not been looking so good to the really big guys, globally, since nine-eleven. They're tired of worrying about the region. They want a stable source. Russian Union's got it.

Means huge changes in the flow of global capital. Means we're going to be running on Russian oil."

"But what's that got to do with the footage?"

"If I find out, I'll let you know. How about you? Any progress on your end?"

She takes a deep breath, then hopes he hasn't heard her take it. "No. Nothing. Boone?"

"Yes?"

"Who was that you were with, when I phoned?"

A pause. "Someone who works for Sigil."

"Did you . . . know her, before?" It's the wrong question and she knows it, but she's still thinking of Marisa and the apartment in Hongo and something in his voice then.

"I met her in the lounge they all go to after work." There's a flatness to his tone now that she somehow knows he isn't aware of. "I don't like doing that, but she's in accounting, and that turned out to be what we needed."

"Oh." And remembers her hand finding the pistol behind Donny's bedstead. "Another date, you might get the whole address?" Immediately wishing she hadn't said it.

"That makes me sound pretty shitty, Cayce."

"I'm sorry. I didn't mean for it to. But I've got to go. I'm meeting someone at five. We'll talk. Bye."

"Well . . . Bye." He doesn't sound happy.

Click.

She sits there in the dark, wondering what just happened.

Then her watch starts to beep, and the room phone rings, a strange foreign ring she's never heard before.

CHAPTER 35

КОФЕИН

Bolshoy Kamennii Most, Big Stone Bridge, is big indeed, though probably many incarnations on from the bridge that had originally acquired the name.

No trouble finding it, and no trouble finding Caffeine, either, with the map she'd copied from the attachment on that last e-mail. She'd drawn it on a sheet of President letterhead, folded in quarters.

Definitely the place here, though Caffeine is КОФЕИН.

"He took a duck in the face . . ." she whispers, as she does a walkby, checking it out.

It looks more like a bar filled with high-backed armchairs than a coffeehouse, but then she remembers coffeehouses in Seattle, when she'd started in board-wear. More like that, but without the Goodwill sofas.

It's crowded.

Yet another of those undercover police cars goes bombing past, blue light flashing, maybe the fifth she's seen, all of them shiny and new and expensive.

The duck mantra doesn't seem to be helping, tonight.

"Walk through the fear," she tells herself, something Margot had said a lot when she'd still been going to her codependency group. That doesn't seem to help either.

"Fuck it." An older, deeper invocation perhaps. That gets her turned around and headed back through the door.

A cozy, crowded room, highlights of copper and polished wood.

Where every table is occupied, it seems, except for one, flanked by two enormous, empty, wingback armchairs, and there, quite clearly, is the fish: a large, freestanding sculpture, its scales cut from one-pound Medaglia d'Oro coffee cans like the ones Wassily Kandinsky used, but assembled in a way that owes more to Frank Gehry.

She's moving too fast to get a read on the crowd here, but is aware of a number of glances as she beelines through and seats herself in one of the wingback chairs.

A waiter materializes instantly. Young and quite beautiful, white-jacketed, a white cloth folded across his arm, he looks none too happy to see her there. He brusquely says something, in Russian, that clearly isn't a question.

"I'm sorry," she says, "I only speak English. I'm meeting a friend. I'll have coffee, please."

As soon as she speaks, there's an instant change in his demeanor, and not, she senses, out of any love of the English language.

"Of course. Americano?"

Guessing that Italian is the default language of coffee here, and that she's not being queried as to her nationality. "Please."

When he's gone, she does a crowd-scan. If there were visible logos on the clothes these people are wearing, she'd be in trouble. Lots of Prada, Gucci, but in a Moneyed Bohemian modality too off-the-shelf for London or New York. LA, she realizes: except for two goth girls in black brocade, and a boy gotten up in impeccable High Grunge, it's Rodeo Drive with an extra helping of cheekbones.

But the young woman crossing from the entrance now wears nothing that isn't matte and the darkest of grays. Pale. Dark eyes. Centerparted hair, unfashionably long.

Her white face, angular yet somehow soft, eclipses everything.

Cayce realizes that she's gripping the arms of her chair so hard that her fingers hurt.

"You are the one who writes, yes?" Only lightly accented, a low voice but very clear, as though she were speaking with perfect enunciation from a distance.

Cayce starts to rise, but the stranger waves her back and takes the other chair. "Stella Volkova." She offers Cayce her hand.

"Cayce Pollard," taking it. Is this the maker?

Is the maker named Stella? Is Stella a Russian name?

Stella Volkova squeezes her hand and releases it. "You are the first."

"The first?" Cayce feels as though her eyes are about to pop out of her head.

The waiter arrives with coffee for two, pouring it into fine white china cups.

"The coffee is very good here. When I was a child, only the nomenklatura had good coffee, and that was not as good as this. You take the sugar? Cream?"

Unable to trust her hands, Cayce shakes her head.

"I too. Black." Stella raises her cup, inhales the fragrance, then sips. She says something appreciative, in Russian. "Do you like it, Moscow? You are here, before?"

"No," Cayce says. "It's new to me."

"I think it is new for us. Every day, now." Unsmiling, eyes wide.

"Why are there so many police cars?" It's all she can think to ask, this pathetic attempt to prevent a silence that she somehow fears might kill her. Ask the next question. "They're always speeding by, but no sirens."

"Police cars?"

"Unmarked. With blue lights."

"Police cars, no! Those are the cars of important people, of the rich, or those who work for them. They have purchased a permit allowing ignorance of traffic regulations. Blue lights are courtesy to others, a warning. It seems strange, to you?"

Everything does, Cayce thinks. Or nothing does.

"Stella? May I ask you something?"

"Yes?"

"Are you the maker?"

Stella tilts her head. "I am twins." If she demonstrates some literal power of physical bilocation, now, it won't surprise Cayce. "My sister, she is the artist. I, I am what? The distributor. The one who finds an audience. It is not so great a talent, I know."

"My God," says Cayce, who doesn't think she has one, "it's really true."

Stella's eyes, already large, widen. "Yes. It is true. Nora is the artist."

Cayce feels herself starting to lock up again. Next question. Anything. "Are Stella and Nora Russian names?"

"Our mother was great admirer of your literature. Particularly of Williams, and of Joyce."

"Williams?"

"Tennessee."

Stella. And Nora.

"My father lived in Tennessee," Cayce says, feeling she sounds like a talking doll whose string has been pulled.

"You write he died, in the fall of the towers."

"Went missing, yes."

"Our parents died. A bomb. In Leningrad. My sister and I, my mother as well, lived in Paris.

Nora studied film, of course. I, business. My father would not have us in Russia. The dangers. He worked for his brother, my uncle, who had become a powerful man. He told us in Paris we should be prepared never to return. But our grandmother died, his mother, and we returned, for the funeral. Three days only, it was to be." Her great sad eyes stare darkly into Cayce's. "The bomb is in a tree, as we leave our house, all of us in black, to the funeral. They detonate it with a radio. Our parents die instantly, a mercy. It hurt Nora badly. Very badly. I had only dislocations, my shoulders, my jaw, and many small wounds."

"I'm sorry . . ."

"Yes." Stella nods, though in affirmation of what Cayce isn't sure. "Since then, we live in Moscow. My uncle is often here, and Nora needs many things. Who are your friends?"

"Pardon me?"

"You write you look for Nora's art with your friends. Passionately." The smile, when it breaks through Stella's pale calm, is a miracle. Or not calm, Cayce thinks, but some hyper-vigilant stillness. Do not move and they will not see us. "Who is 'Maurice'? It is a beautiful name."

"He works in a bank, in Hong Kong. British. I haven't met him, but I like him a lot. You understand we do this through a website, and e-mail?"

"Yes. I have seen it, perhaps. I have software. I watch Nora's art move, through the Sigil numbers.

It is very good, this software. Sergei found it for us."

"Who is Sergei?"

"He is employed to facilitate. A star at the Polytechnic. I worry that he will miss his career, because my uncle pays him too well. But also he loves what Nora does. Like you."

"Is the footage . . . Is Nora's art computer-generated, Stella? Are there live actors?" In fear that this is too direct, too blunt.

"At the film school, in Paris, she made three short films. The longest, sixteen minutes. This was shown at Cannes to good acclaim. You have been? The Croisette?"

Cayce bookmarking like the shutter of a camera. "Only once."

"After the bomb we were taken to Switzerland. Nora required operations. The blood here is not good. We were fortunate, there has been nothing from the first transfusions, done in Russia. I stayed with her, of course. She could not talk, at first. She did not recognize me. When she did talk, it was only to me, and in a language that had been ours in childhood."

"'Twin talk'?"

"The language of Stella and Nora. Then other language returns. The doctors had asked me her interests and of course there was only film. Shortly, we were shown an editing suite which our uncle had caused to have assembled there, in the clinic. We showed Nora the film she had been working on, in

Paris, before. Nothing. As if she could not see it. Then she was shown her film from Cannes. That she saw, but it seemed to cause her great pain. Soon she began to use the equipment. To edit. Recut."

Cayce, hypnotized, is nearing the bottom of her cup. The waiter arrives, to silently refill it.

"Three months, she recut. Five operations in that time, and still she worked. I watched it grow shorter, her film. In the end, she had reduced it to a single frame."

In chilling apparent synchronicity, Caffeine falls momentarily silent. Cayce shivers. "What was the image?"

"A bird. In flight. Not even in focus. Its wings, against gray cloud." She covers her own empty cup, when the waiter moves to refill it. "She went inside, after that."

"Inside?"

"She ceased to speak, then to react. To eat. Again they fed her with tubes. I was crazy. There was talk of taking her to America, but American doctors came. In the end they said they could do nothing. It could not be removed."

"What could not be removed?"

"The last fragment. It rests between the lobes, in some terrible way. It cannot be moved. Risk is too great." The dark eyes bottomless now, filling Cayce's field of vision. "But then she notices the screen."

"The screen?"

"Monitor. Above, in hallway. Closed circuit,

showing only the reception at the front of that private ward. The Swiss nurse sitting, reading. Someone passing. They saw her watching that. The most clever of the doctors, he was from Stuttgart. He had them put a line from that camera into her editing suite. When she looked at those images, she focused. When the images were taken away, she began to die again. He taped two hours of this, and ran it on the editing deck. She began to cut it. To manipulate. Soon she had isolated a single figure. A man, one of the staff. They brought him to her, but she had no reaction. She ignored him. Continued to work. One day I found her working on his face, in Photoshop. That was the beginning."

Cayce presses her head against the high back of the chair. Forces herself to close her eyes. When she opens them, she will see her old Rickson's, draped across the shoulders of Damien's robot girl. Or the open bedding closet in the apartment in Hongo, stuffed with a stranger's clothing.

"You are tired? Unwell?"

She opens her eyes. Stella is still there. "No. Only listening to your story. Thank you for telling it to me."

"You are welcome."

"Stella?"

"Yes?"

"Why did you tell it to me? Everything you and your sister do seems to be surrounded by so much secrecy. And yet, when I find your address, finally, which was very hard to do, and e-mail you, you reply immediately. I come here, you meet me. I don't understand."

"You are the first. My sister, she has no interest in an audience. I do not think she understands what I do with her work, that I make it possible for the world to see. But I suppose I had been waiting, and when you wrote to me, I decided you were real."

"Real?"

"My uncle is a most important man, a very big businessman, bigger now even than when our parents died. We do not see him often, but his apparat protects us. They are afraid of him, you see, and so they are very careful. It is a sad way to live, I think, but that is what it is like to be very rich in this country. I wished the world to see my sister's work, but they insisted it be anonymous." The sad gentle smile surfacing, through the stillness of the long white face. "When you told me your father was lost, I did not think you would hurt us." A troubled look. "She was very upset, my sister. She hurt herself."

"Because I came?"

"Of course not. She doesn't know. When we saw the attack, in New York." But she is looking not at Cayce but toward the entrance now, where Cayce sees two young men waiting, in dark slacks and black leather coats. "I must go now. Those are my drivers. There is a car, to return you to your hotel." Stella stands. "It is not good, a woman at night to walk alone."

So Cayce stands, seeing that Stella is several inches taller than she is. "Will I see you again?"

"Of course."

"Will I be able to meet your sister?"

"Yes, of course."

"When?"

"Tomorrow. I will contact you. I will send a car. Come." And leads the way, without asking for the bill, or paying, but the beautiful waiter bows low as they pass, as does an older man in a white apron. Ignoring the two in their leather coats, Stella steers her out into the street. "Here is your car." A black Mercedes. She takes Cayce's hand, squeezes it. "A great pleasure."

"Yes," Cayce says, "thank you."

"Good night."

One of the young men opens the passenger door for her. She gets in. He closes it. Walks around the back, opens the driver-side, and gets in.

They pull away, and Cayce looks back, to see Stella wave goodbye.

When the black Mercedes reaches the big stone bridge, the driver touches something on the dashboard and the blue light goes on, flashing. He accelerates, working smoothly through the gears, up the great stone hump of it and down, into Zamoskvareche.

CHAPTER 36

THE DIG

She opens her eyes to a wedge of light, dividing the darkened ceiling like the cross-section of a blade whose edge rests between the shadows of the ocher curtains.

She remembers watching the Maurice and Filmy edit on the iBook, after she'd returned from meeting Stella, and experiencing it in some entirely new way that she's still completely unable to describe or characterize.

She struggles out of the heavy sheets and drags one of the curtains aside. Light assails her, and the enormous, atrocious statue, on its island in the river.

In the bathroom, amid too many browns, she adjusts the taps in the shower. Knockoffs of Kohler, she notes automatically, minus the trademark. Unwraps a bar of soap and steps in.

Twenty minutes later, dressed, hair blown dry, she's downstairs, uneasily eyeing the breakfast buffet. Heaping platters of smoked meats, pyramids of preserved fish, silver bowls of red caviar, tureens of sour cream. Blinis. Things that aren't blinis but are filled with sweet cheese. Finally, at the far end, just as she's despairing, she finds granola and cornflakes and fresh fruit. Big pitchers of juice. Coffee in huge old pump-top nickel-plate thermos jugs.

She finds a table to herself. Eats methodically, eyes on her plate. French from a nearby table, light as birdsong against the dark weight of Russian.

She feels as though something huge has happened, is happening, but she can't define it. She knows that it's about meeting Stella, and hearing her story, and her sister's, but somehow she no longer is able to fit it to her life. Or rather she lives now in that story, her life left somewhere behind, like a room she's stepped out of. Not far away at all but she is no longer in.

Back upstairs, she phones Parkaboy in Chicago. "I'm going to level with you," she hears him say, after the final, uneven ring. "I'm away for a while. But there's no cash on the premises, no drugs, and the pit bull's tested positive. Twice."

She doesn't leave a message.

Does this mean he's already on his way?

She could phone Sylvie Jeppson and find out, but the idea of contact with Blue Ant, right now, does not appeal.

Stella trusts her. Whatever weird, sad, scary, deeply Russian scenario Stella and her twin are socketed into, she desperately doesn't want to

391

betray whatever it is she's seen rise behind the stillness of that white face.

Parkaboy would get it. But who else would? Not, she's now certain, Boone. Bigend, probably, but in that way of his, in which he seems to somehow understand emotions without ever having partaken of them.

She opens a bottle of Russian mineral water.

Dorotea had been hired by a Russian from Cyprus, the one listed as the registrant of armaz.ru, a domain that Boone says has something to do with the Russian oil industry.

Were those Russians, she wonders, who somehow got their hands on Katherine McNally's notes from Cayce's sessions? Not necessarily, she decides, as the men Dorotea had used in Tokyo had been Italian. It's an equal-opportunity conspiracy, maybe.

But Baranov, come to think of it, is Russian too, or anyway Anglo-Russian. Though that doesn't seem to click with the linkage she's trying to braille, here. And neither does Damien, off in the boonies shooting his punk archaeology project, even though his girlfriend's father sounds like another candidate for mafia czar.

There must always be room for coincidence, Win had maintained. When there's not, you're probably well into apophenia, each thing then perceived as part of an overarching pattern of conspiracy. And while comforting yourself with the symmetry of it all, he'd believed, you stood all too real a chance of missing the genuine threat, which was invariably less symmetrical, less perfect. But which he always, she knew, took for granted was there.

Russia. Something else . . .

She remembers, in mid-swallow, and lapses into a fit of coughing.

That old post of hers, the one that had turned up when she'd searched Russia on the F:F:F CD-ROM.

She slots the CD-ROM. Repeats the search.

Why couldn't it, say, be some Russian mafia kingpin, with a bent for self-expression, a previously undiscovered talent, and the where-withal to generate and disseminate the footage?

January. She'd still been seeing Katherine. She'd had no idea she'd be working for Blue Ant, or coming to London, or getting involved with Bigend.

Mafia.

Wherewithal.

She wipes her mouth with the back of her hand.

Not a bent for self-expression: orphaned nieces.

If Baranov could still have even one favor-owing friend, somewhere in the bowels of Langley or Falls Church, willing and able to somehow pluck the stellanor address from traffic on the Net, or from wherever it was found, what might a very rich, very important Russian be afforded in his own country, or even, perhaps, in hers?

And what might "very rich, very important" not be a euphemism for, today, when it came to Russians?

She feels a knot of tension beginning to complicate, between her shoulders.

When the on-line Moscow Yellow Pages refuses to produce a Pilates studio, she puts on her workout clothes and goes up, one floor, to the hotel gym. Deserted save for an older, overweight Russian wearing an expression of near-religious sorrow as he plods heavily along on a treadmill.

The machines here look to Cayce like domestic product, though new, and Damien would definitely want to document them. She finds what might be a boxing mat in a far corner of the room and tries to remember the mat exercises she'd been taught at the very beginning.

She senses the Russian's sad gaze as she works through what she recalls of the mat program, but realizes, to her surprise, that she's actually glad he's here.

It's that kind of morning.

She desperately wants to go out, walk to the nearest Metro station, pay the famously tiny fare, and descend into a world of ornate mineral marvels. The only true palaces of the proletariat, those stations. And doing that, have some temporary release from waiting

But she can't, and doesn't.

She's waiting for a message from Stella.

Shortly after noon, her cell rings.

"Hello?"

"Where are you?" Bigend.

"Poole," she lies reflexively, not exactly thinking on her feet.

"Swimming?"

"Silent 'e.' The city. Where are you?"

"Paris. Sylvie tells me you will be here soon?"

"I'm not sure, now. I'm following something up. I hope you aren't there only for my sake. I might not come."

"Not at all. You won't share this something?"

"Not on a cell. When I see you." Enough like a Boone reason, she hopes.

"You spoke with Boone." Not a question.

"Yes."

"He seemed to feel you weren't impressed with what he's been able to learn in Ohio."

"He's too sensitive, that way."

"The chemistry, it isn't working?"

"We're not dating, Hubertus."

"You'll keep me informed, though, won't you?"

She's taking it for granted that there's no way he can know where he's reaching her phone, and she hopes that that's true, but there's really nothing she can do about it now. "Yes, of course. Have to go now, Hubertus. Bye."

She imagines him looking at his phone.

Hers rings again. "Yes?"

"Hello. It is Stella. You wish still to visit?"

"Yes. I do. Very much."

"Is not too early? You have slept?"

"Yes, thanks." Wondering what sort of hours Stella keeps.

"If you will wait beside the guard booth, a car will come. Thirty minutes, will be good?"

"Yes! Please!"

"Goodbye."

She stands up, in her underpants and a Fruit T-shirt, and starts dressing. She feels that this requires as formal an effort as she can muster, somehow, so it's the good hose from Japan, her French shoes, and Skirt Thing, rolled out to its full length and pulled up, creating a passable imitation of a dress. She goes into the bathroom and applies makeup, then returns to put on her thin black cardigan and quickly check her e-mail.

Damien.

Hard day. I must've told you, probably fifty times, how deeply I believe in documentary. I know people don't believe I do, because I'm the master of artifice and nothing's ever what it seems, blah fucking blah but it's true because they say it in those little boxes in The Face. Well I'm questioning it tonight because today we got that Stuka completely dug out. Did I tell you? It's a whole plane, and for some fucking reason it wound up four feet under the muck, but this Guru character knew where it was. He claims it's dreams and visions but I think he walks around in the winter with a metal detector. So he'd said here, this plane is here, dig, and before we came back to London they'd sunk a trench, and hit it. But bribery and threats prevailed, at least till we got back with the extra cameras and crew, because I wanted this plane emerging to be the climax of the film. No idea it would be a Stuka; blew me away; it's just this most Nazi-looking aircraft, amazing. Dive-bomber, they used them on the Spanish, *Guernica* and that. Absolutely iconic. So there it is, finally, today, and it's sitting there, all caked in the gray stuff, like an airplane done up as New Guinea Mud Man, at the bottom of this great fucking hole they'd dug. By far the biggest excavation yet attempted here, as far as we know, and quite the feat of social engineering, to get it done without them opening the canopy and getting into the cockpit. We'd had Brian and Mick stand guard over it, the past two nights, and the diggers hadn't touched it. But come the day, we knew they would, and we'd be set to shoot, what we're here for. So a couple of the big ones with the spiderweb tattoos get boosted up, onto the wings, which are slippery with muck, but where their boots slip in it, looking down from the edge of the dig, I can see the thing's in museum condition. Just eerie, how well it was preserved. And then Brian gets boosted up to shoot handheld, close, and they're squeegeeing the gray off the canopy with the edges of their hands. And the fucking pilot's there. You can see the outline of his head, goggles it looked

397

like. Never seen Brian pull his eye off the viewfinder when he's shooting but he did, just turned around with this WHAT THE FUCK???!!! look and I signal GO FOR IT, GET IT. So he did. All of it: them yanking the canopy open, and how they simply tore him apart, the pilot. Just came to pieces. They got a watch, a compass from the other wrist and a pistol, and they were fighting over them, falling off the wing, and he just came apart. And Brian got it all, plus Mick was second camera and he got a lot, plus the new guys. I mean coverage, lots. And at some point I look around at Marina and she's fucking laughing. Not your hysterics of horror, she's just fucking laughing at the humor of it. So I'm sitting here in the tent by myself, writing this, because with one thing and another I told her to just fuck off. And Mick and Brian are drunk, and I'm afraid to look at what they shot. I know I won't be, maybe even tomorrow, but now I think I will go and get well pissed. And how the fuck did he get under there with his airplane? So thank you, as they say, for listening, and don't forget to water the fucking goldfish. I hope you are okay with that shit you had happening. I love you.

She shakes her head, reads it again.

I love you too. Can't write more now. Later. I'm okay. And I'm in Russia too, Moscow, I'll tell you later.

She starts to put the iBook back in the bag, but stops. It doesn't seem right to take it, somehow, to meet the maker. She'll carry her East German envelope instead, and as she's transferring her basic stuff from the Luggage Label she remembers that the desk hasn't returned her passport yet. She'll get it on the way out. Her hand strikes something cold, at the bottom of the envelope. She pulls it out: the metal piece from Damien's robot girl: her makeshift knuckle-duster in Camden. Good thing she'd had the envelope in checked luggage. She tosses it back in, for luck, makes sure she has the room key, and leaves, head full of the images from his message.

The driver who turns up for her has dark glasses and a closely shaven, interestingly sculpted head. Streamlined.

As they're driving away, in the direction she'd gone the evening before, she remembers she's forgotten to ask for her passport.

CHAPTER 37

KINO

They turn onto a wide street, one that Cayce, from her morning's Moscow Yellow Pages map foray, tentatively identifies as Tverskaya. Her driver, with a phone plugged into his ear now, is wearing cologne.

They stick to Tverskaya, if it is Tverskaya, and stay with the traffic flow. He doesn't use the blue light.

They pass beneath a banner in English: WAXEN FIGURES EXHIBITION.

Street-level signage offers snippets of the non-Cyrillic: BUTIQUE, KODAK, a drugstore called PHARMACOM.

As they turn left, she asks "What street is this?"

"Georgievsky," the driver says, though it might as easily be his name. He turns again, into an alley, and stops.

She starts to tell him that she hadn't meant for him to stop, but he gets out, walks around, opens the door for her. "Come."

Gray, distempered concrete. Cyrillic skater's

tags, their letters bulging in clumsy homage to New York and Los Angeles.

"Please." He hauls open a large, anciently battered steel door, which reaches the limits of a restraining chain with a dull boom. Within is darkness. "Here."

"Stella is here?"

"Kino," he says. Film. Cinema.

Stepping past him, she finds herself in a dim, indeterminate space. When the door crashes shut behind them, the only light is from above. A bare bulb, visible up a forbiddingly steep flight of narrow concrete stairs that seems to have no railing.

"Please." He gestures toward the stairs.

She sees now that there is a railing, the spidery ghost of one: a single length of half-inch steel. Supported by only two uprights, it droops between them, seemingly lank as rope, and sways when she grips it.

"He took a duck in the face . . ."

"Up, please."

"Sorry." She starts to climb, aware of him behind her.

There is another steel door, narrower, beneath the forty-watt bulb. She opens it.

A kitchen, bathed in red light.

Like the kitchens in the oldest, still-unrenovated tenements of New York, but larger, the stove a squatting pre-Stalinist presence wider than the car that brought her here. Coal-burning, or wood.

Where the tenement kitchen would have offered

a central bathtub, there is a shower: a square of raised tile surrounding a slightly lower concrete space for drainage. The ancient galvanized showerhead, looking either agricultural or veterinary in intent, is suspended from a sixteen-foot ceiling gone sepia with decades of smoke and soot. The source of the red glow is a stolen Metro sign, propped against one wall, with a bulb inside.

"You are here," says Stella, opening a door, light behind her. She says something in Russian to the driver. He nods, stepping back through the door to the stairs and closing it behind him.

"Where's here?"

"Come." Stella leads her into another room, this one with tall, unwashed windows, looking as though they might originally have been internally shuttered. "The Kremlin," Stella says, pointing out a view between the nearer buildings, "and the Duma."

Cayce looks around. The walls, unpainted since Soviet days at least, remind her of the nomiya in Roppongi, decades of nicotine deposited over what may once have been cream. Cracked, uneven. The individual planks of the wooden floor are lost under layers of paint, most recently maroon. There are two very new, very white Ikea desks, with articulated swivel chairs, a pair of PCs, and baskets of papers. On the wall above, a long, complex chart is being maintained across three adjoining white-boards.

"Sergei says it is a production that never ends,"

Stella says, seeing Cayce looking not at the view but the chart. "Only the start of the work can be done here, of course."

"But does it end?" Cayce feels herself blushing, appalled that she's been unable to resist immediately asking so pointed a question.

"You mean, is linear narrative?"

"I had to ask." She feels as though Parkaboy, Ivy, Filmy, and Maurice, the whole F:F:F crew are in the wings, counting on her.

"I do not know. One day, perhaps, she will start to edit as she edited her student film: to a single frame. Or perhaps one day they speak, the characters. Who knows? Nora? She does not say."

A young man with bushy ginger hair enters, nods to them, and seats himself before one of the computers.

"Come," says Stella, moving in the direction he'd come from. "You know this idea, 'squat,' like Amsterdam, Berlin?"

"Yes."

"You have not, in America?"

"Not exactly."

"This was squat, these rooms. Famous, in eighties. A party here. Seven years. Not once did party end. People come, make the party, more come, some go, make the party, always. Talking of freedom, art, things of the spirit. Nora and I were schoolgirls, first coming here. Our father would be very angry, seeing us here. He did not know." This room is larger, but filled with a makeshift cube farm, workstations walled off with sheets of unpainted composite board. The screens are dark now, the chairs empty. There's a plastic Garfield atop one monitor, other signs of workplace personalization. She picks up a square of clear acrylic: laser-etched in its core are the Coca-Cola logo, a crude representation of the Twin Towers, and the words "WE REMEMBER." She quickly puts it down.

"You see it now, you cannot imagine. Once Victor Tsoi sang here, in this room. People had time, in those days. The system was collapsing under its own weight, but everyone had a job, often a pointless one, very badly paid, but one could eat. People valued friendships, talked end-lessly, ate and drank. For many people it was like the life of a student. A life of the spirit. Now we say that everything Lenin taught us of communism was false, and everything he taught us of capitalism, true."

"What do you do now, in this room?"

"My sister's work is transferred to production facility."

"Is she here, now?"

"She is working. Now you will see her."

"But I couldn't interrupt her—"

"No. She is here, when she is working. You must understand. When she is not working, she is not here."

The fourth room is at the end of a narrow hall-way, its ceiling as high as those in the other rooms, its plaster darkened with the dirt of years of hands, lightening above shoulder-level. The door at its end is smooth and white, insubstantial-looking against the scabrous plaster.

Stella opens it, steps back, softly gestures for Cayce to enter.

At first she thinks this room is windowless, its sole illumination the largest LCD display Cayce has ever seen, but as her eyes adjust she sees that three tall narrow windows, behind the screen, have been painted black. But the part of her that notes this is some basic mammalian module tracking whereabouts and potential exits: All higher attention is locked on the screen, on which is frozen an image from a segment of footage that she knows she has never seen.

He is reaching out, perhaps from the girl's POV, as if to touch her in parting.

A cursor like a bombsight whips across the image, locking on the corner of his mouth. Mouse-click. Zoom. Into image-grain. Some quick adjustment. Clicks. Out of zoom.

The meaning of his expression, and the feeling of the frame, have changed.

So much for Completism, Cayce thinks. The footage is a work in progress.

"This is Nora," Stella says, stepping softly past Cayce to lay her hands on the shawl-draped shoulders of the figure in the chair before the screen. Nora's right hand pauses. Still resting on the mouse, though Cayce senses this has nothing to do with her sister's touch, or the presence of a stranger.

Cayce still cannot see her face. Her hair, like her sister's, is long and dark, center-parted, its gloss reflecting the glow of the screen.

Now Stella speaks to her sister in Russian, and slowly Nora turns from the screen, the manipulated image illuminating her face in three-quarter profile.

It is Stella's face, but some fault bisects it vertically, not quite evenly. There are no scars, only this skewing of the bone beneath. Nora's skin is smooth as Stella's, and as white.

Cayce looks into the dark eyes. Nora sees her. Then doesn't. Turns back to the screen.

Stella rolls a workstation chair into position. "Sit. Watch her work." Cayce shakes her head, her eyes stinging with tears.

"Sit," says Stella, very gently. "You will not disturb her. You have come a long way. You must watch her work."

Her watch tells her that over three hours have passed, when she leaves Nora's room.

She wonders if she will ever be able to describe her experience there to anyone, even Parkaboy. How she has watched a segment, or the bones of one, being built up from almost nothing. Mere scraps of found video. How once a man had stood on a platform in a station, and turned, and raised his hand, the motion captured, the grainy image somehow finding its way, however much later, to one of Nora's subsidiary screens. To be chosen, today, by the roving, darting cursor. Elements of that man's gesture becoming aspects of the boy in the dark coat, his collar up. The boy whose life, it seems, is bounded by the T-shaped city, the city Nora is mapping through the footage she generates. Her consciousness, Cayce understands, somehow bounded by or bound to the T-shaped fragment in her brain: part of the arming mechanism of the Claymore mine that killed her parents, balanced too deeply, too precariously within her skull, to ever be removed. Something stamped out, once, in its thousands, by an automated press in some armory in America. Perhaps the workers who'd made that part, if they'd thought at all in terms of end-use, had imagined it being used to kill Russians. But that was over now, Win's war and Baranov's, old as the brick compound behind Baranov's caravan: concrete fence posts and the echoing absence of dogs. And somehow this one specific piece of ordance, adrift perhaps since the days of the Soviets' failed war with the new enemies, had found its way into the hands of Nora's uncle's enemies, and this one small part, only slightly damaged by the explosion of the ruthlessly simple device, had been flung into the very center of Nora's brain. And from it, and from her other wounds, there now emerged, accompanied by the patient and regular clicking of her mouse, the footage.

In the darkened room whose windows would

have offered a view of the Kremlin, had they been scraped clean of paint, Cayce had known herself to be in the presence of the splendid source, the headwaters of the digital Nile she and her friends had sought. It is here, in the languid yet precise moves of a woman's pale hand. In the faint click of image-capture. In the eyes only truly present when focused on this screen.

Only the wound, speaking wordlessly in the dark.

Stella finds her in the hallway, her face wet with tears, eyes closed, shoulders braced against plaster as uneven as the bone of Nora's forehead.

She places her hands on Cayce's shoulders. "Now you have seen her work."

Cayce opens her eyes, nods.

"Come," says Stella, "your eyes are melted," and leads her past the workstations, into the crepuscular glow of the kitchen. She soaks a thick pad of gray paper toweling in the stream from an old brass tap and passes it to Cayce, who presses it against her hot eyes. The paper is rough, the water cold. "There are few buildings like this one, now," Stella says. "The land is far too valuable. Even this, this place from our childhood, which we both loved, our uncle owns. He keeps it from the developers, for us, because Nora finds it comforting. Whatever cost is of no importance to him. He wishes us to be safe, and Nora as comfortable as possible."

"And you? What do you wish, Stella?"

"I wish the world to know her work. Something

you could not know: how it was, here, for artists. Whole universes of blood and imagination, built over lifetimes in rooms like these, never to be seen. To die with their creators, and be swept out. Now Nora, what she does, it joins the sea." She smiles. "It has brought you to us."

"Are they your parents, Stella? The couple?"

"Perhaps, when they are young. They resemble them, yes. But if what she is doing tells a story, it seems not to be our parents' story. Not their world. It is another world. It is always another world."

"Yes," Cayce agrees, putting down the cold wet mass of paper, "it is. Stella, the people who protect you, on your uncle's behalf, who do you suppose they protect you from?"

"From his enemies. From anyone who might wish to use us to hurt him. You must understand, these precautions are not unusual, for a man like my uncle. It is unusual that Nora is an artist, and her situation, her condition, is unusual, and that I wish her work to be seen, yes, but it is not unusual, here, that we should be protected."

"But do you understand that they also, perhaps without understanding it, protect you from something else?"

"I do not understand."

"Your sister's art has become very valuable. You've succeeded, you see. It's a genuine mystery, Nora's art, something hidden at the heart of the world, and more and more people follow it, all over the world."

"But what is the danger?"

"We have our own rich and powerful men. Any creation that attracts the attention of the world, on an ongoing basis, becomes valuable, if only in terms of potential."

"To be commercial? My uncle would not allow this degree of attention."

"It's already valuable. More valuable than you could imagine. The commercial part would simply be branding, franchising. And they're on to it, Stella. Or at least one of them is, and he's very clever. I know because I work for him."

"You do?"

"Yes, but I've decided that I won't tell him I found you. I won't tell him who you are or where you are, or who Nora is, or anything else I've learned here. I won't be working for him, now. But others will, and they'll find you, and you have to be ready."

"How, ready?"

"I don't know. I'll try to figure that out."

"Thank you," Stella says. "It gives me pleasure, that you have seen my sister work."

"Thank you."

They hug, Stella kissing her on the cheek.

"Your driver is waiting."

"Send him away, please. I need to walk. To feel the city. And I haven't seen the Metro."

Stella produces a phone from her gray skirt and pushes a key. Says something in Russian.

CHAPTER 38

PUPPENKOPF

She finds herself on crowded Arbat.

Leaving the squat behind Georgievsky, she'd drifted, unmoored by her experience of the creation. That segment with the beach pan, she now knows, is mapped on the one jagged edge of the T-arm, unthinkable intimacy.

Through one street and the next, until she'd come upon the red M of a Metro station.

Descending, she'd purchased, with too large a bill and some difficulty, tokens of what appeared to be luminous plastic, the color of glow-in-the-dark toy skeletons, each with its own iconic M.

One of these had been sufficient for her voyage, whose directions and stations she now would never know.

She'd given herself to the dream, in this case to the eerie Stalinist grandeurs of Moscow's underground, which had fascinated her father.

That sense she'd had, of some things here being grotesquely large, had doubled, underground, the lavishness of the stations exceeding even her

411

childhood fantasies. Gilt bronze, peach marble shot with aquamarine, engine-chased Cartier lusters applied to the supporting columns of what seemed more like subterranean ballrooms than subway platforms, their chandeliers blazing, as if the wealth of what Win had called the final empire of the nineteenth century had come pouring in, all through the deepest, darkest thirties, to line these basilicas of public transport.

So overwhelming, so exceedingly peculiar in its impact, that it actually succeeded in distracting her, knocking her at least partially out of whatever it was that she'd been feeling as she'd descended those steep stairs to the clanging steel door, and out into a brightness that both startled and hurt.

She has no idea where she'd gone, riding for at least two hours, changing trains on impulse, taking madly majestic stairs and escalators at random. Until, finally, she'd emerged, here, to find herself on Arbat, broad and crowded, which her but-it's-really-like module keeps trying to tell her is really like Oxford Street, though, really, it isn't at all.

Thirsty, she enters a vaguely Italian-looking (the match-up module, failing again) establishment offering soft drinks and Internet access, and buys a bottle of water and half an hour, to check her mail.

The keyboard is Cyrillic; she keeps accidentally hitting a key that toggles it back from English-emulation, and then being unable to find it again, but she manages to retrieve a message from Parkaboy.

I like to think I'm as blasé as the next pretentious asshole, but your travel agent in London is, I've gotta say, the business. As in: I'm in Charles de Gaulle, in some kind of Air France cocoon hand-stitched from Hermès bridle-leather, watching CNN in French and waiting to get on their next flight to Moscow. Trouble is, no fault of Sylvie's, something's upfucked the bomb-sniffers here and even we of the uber-class have to wait until planes can fly. So they've put all five of us in here with what I sort of hate to admit is the best cold buffet I've ever tasted, and they keep opening champagne. I may not have mentioned it before but since the recent unpleasantness I've been one of those people not too happy at the thought of flying; why I took that train to visit Darryl. However, with the rush of events and the sheer level of cosseting, I haven't until now been very aware of actually doing any. America sort of ended at check-in. And when they get the sniffers sorted here, I'm your way fast, though I may need to be taught to feed and wash myself again. You can help by arranging a supply of those little hot towels. Thanks again.

She tries to reply but hits that toggle again.

When the boy from the counter sorts it for her,

she writes: I went there. I met her. Well, saw her. Watched her work. Her. I'm in a Net café and I guess I'm still processing. Hard to write. No point, really: you're almost here. I'm glad! Maybe you are, I haven't been back to the hotel.

A distant crash, or explosion. She looks up. A siren starts to wail.

The counter boy has gone to the door and is looking out, up Arbat, and suddenly she's back in the car on her way to Stonestreet's, seeing the motorcycle rider on his back, neck probably broken, his face up to the rain. A rush of sheer mortality.

You should have this, because so far nobody else does: *stellanor@armaz.ru*. Stella. Not the maker, her sister.

Send.

She finishes the last of her water, logs out, slides off the stool. She can still hear the siren, but it seems to be moving away.

Now she has to find a cab. An official one.

Nodding to the Kevlar security boys, she remembers that she still hasn't retrieved her passport from registration.

The lobby of The President is still as wide, and even less populated, and her request seems to

414

trigger one of those deep and atavistic pockets of Soviet affect in the clerk. He becomes instantly expressionless, stares at her narrowly, turns, vanishes through a paneled door behind his counter, and remains absent for what her watch shows as the better part of ten minutes. But he returns with her passport, and hands it to her silently.

She checks to make certain that it is in fact her passport and, remembering Win's stories, that all of its pages are still there, and that she hasn't acquired any new travel history. All seems correct and unchanged. "Thank you." She puts it in her Stasi envelope.

Time for a long hot bath, in a long brown tub, and then she'll call down and ask whether a Mr. Gilbert has arrived.

When she turns, she finds herself facing Dorotea Benedetti.

"We must talk." She's in black, with more than a touch of actual gold at her throat, as perfectly groomed as ever but wearing more makeup.

"Dorotea?" It is, of course, but instinct says stall for time. A deeper instinct says: Flee.

"I know you've found them. Hubertus does not know, but they do."

"Who?"

"Volkov's apparat. The people who employed me. We must have a conversation now, you and I. Come with me, to the lounge."

"I thought you were working for Hubertus."

415

"I am taking care of myself, and of you as well. I will explain. There's little time." She turns, without waiting for an answer, and marches out across the brown-and-ocher parade ground, toward what Cayce takes to be the entrance to the lobby bar. Dorotea's hose, from behind, reveal stylized serpents woven where a seam line would be, from heel to mid-calf.

Cayce follows her, in deepest distrust, a knot of fear tightening between her shoulders. But whatever this is about, she decides, she has to hear it out.

The lounge has the October theme in spades, haystack-sized arrangements of dried flowers flanking leaf-strewn sideboards piled with pale simulacra of gourds, worryingly skull-like. Much brownish mirror, darkly veined with gold.

The girl with green boots is here, though not wearing them; Cayce recognizes the snakeskin flames, deployed to maximum advantage atop a barstool. At least a dozen of this one's colleagues seem to have negotiated security as well, this evening, and attend to a clientele consisting entirely of large, clean-shaven, short-haired, remarkably square-headed men in dark suits. Like some lost America, down to blue strata of cigarette smoke and the completely un-ironic deployment of the Frank Sinatra, through both of which the gestures of these men are carving out the shapes of triumph and empire, defeat and frustration.

Dorotea is already seated at a table for two, a

white-jacketed barman unloading drinks from his tray: a glass of white wine for Dorotea, a Perrier and a tumbler of ice for the place opposite her. "I ordered for you," Dorotea says, as Cayce takes the other seat. "You are going to have to move, very quickly, so a drink is perhaps not the best idea."

The barman pours the Perrier over the ice and departs.

"What do you mean?"

Dorotea looks at her. "I don't expect you to like me. I am motivated in this by self-interest, of course, but my interests now are best served by aiding yours. You do not believe me, but please, entertain the possibility. What do you know of Andrei Volkov?"

Volkova. Stella Volkova. Stalling, Cayce takes a sip of Perrier. It seems flat.

"He is their uncle," Dorotea says, impatiently. "I know where you have been today. I know that you have met with them. Soon Volkov will know as well."

"I've never heard of him." Throat dry, she takes another sip.

"The invisible oligarch. The ghost. Very probably the richest of them all. He rode out the Bankers' War in 'ninety-three, untouched, then emerged to take even more. His roots are in organized crime, of course; it is natural here. Like many, he has suffered personal losses. His brother. That had more to do with what you think of as politics, than crime, but to make that distinction here has always been naive." Dorotea takes a sip of wine.

"Dorotea, what are you doing here?" Cayce wonders what she would be feeling, now, if she were having this encounter on any other day. Against her recent experience of the actual creation of the footage, it's difficult to feel frightened, or angry, though she remembers having felt both those emotions toward Dorotea. The knot in her upper back, relaxing.

"You are in danger now. From Volkov's apparat. You threaten them because you have met his nieces. That is not supposed to happen."

"But they can't be that tightly guarded. I sent an e-mail. Stella answered."

"How did you get the address?"

Baranov's glasses flash in the caravan, in a beam of British sunlight through some tiny hole. The depths of cold and utter distrust in his eyes. "From Boone," Cayce lies.

"It's not important," Dorotea says, and Cayce is glad it isn't, though she wants to tell Dorotea that Boone is in Ohio, at Sigil.

"Tell me about your father," Dorotea says. "That is more important. What was his name?"

"Win," Cayce says. "Wingrove Pollard."

"And he vanished, the day of the towers, in New York?"

"He checked into a hotel, the night before, and in the morning he took a cab. But we've never found the driver, and we can't find him."

"Perhaps I can help you find him," Dorotea says. "Finish your water."

Cayce drinks the rest of the Perrier, the ice hurting her front teeth when it clicks against them, hard. "I hurt my teeth," she says, putting down the glass.

"You should be more careful," Dorotea says.

Cayce looks across the bar and sees the snakeskin panels on the girl's dress crawling, wet and glistening. The flame-shaped cutouts in the taut fabric revealing the living greenish-black serpent skin beneath. She wants to tell Dorotea but somehow it might be embarrassing. She feels awkward, and very shy.

Dorotea pours the rest of the Perrier into Cayce's glass. "Did you ever guess," Dorotea says, "that I might also be Mama Anarchia?"

"You couldn't be," Cayce says, "you never say anything's hegemonic."

"What do you mean?"

Cayce feels herself blushing. "You're fluent, but I don't think you could make all that up. The stuff that Parkaboy hates." But maybe she shouldn't be saying this? "Could you?"

"No. Drink your water." Cayce does, being careful of the ice. "But I have a little puppenkopf, to help me. I say what I need to say, and he translates it into the language of Anarchia, to so annoy your most annoying friend." Dorotea smiles.

"Puppen—?"

"Puppet-head. A graduate student, in America.

419

That is how I am able to be the Mama. And now I think you are my little puppenkopf as well." She reaches across the table to stroke Cayce's cheek. "And I think we will have no more trouble from you, none at all. You are my very good girl, now, and you will tell me where you got the e-mail address, won't you?"

But there are skulls atop the sideboard, and as she's opening her mouth to tell Dorotea about them, she sees Bibendum himself behind the bar, the rolls of his pallid, rubbery flesh like the folds of a partially deflated blimp, greasy and vile. Cayce's mouth freezes open, no sound at all emerging, as the terrible eyes of the Michelin Man fix her with a truly dire regard—and she experiences, perhaps, her sole and only brush with EVP—as from some deep and hidden eddy in the river of Sinatra's voice emerges a strange bright cartoon-like whirling snarl of sound, which executes the sonic equivalent of a back flip and becomes, as though compressed for transmission over unimaginable distances, her father's voice.

"She's drugged the water. Scream."

Which she does.

So that, when things go black, she's just curling her fingers around something smooth and cold, at the very bottom of the Stasi envelope.

CHAPTER 39

RED DUST

There must be, though she's never noticed it before, a band of steel, cunningly fashioned, that ordinarily follows the exact irregularities of the inner circumference of her skull.

It seems, now that she's aware of it, to be made from rod no thicker than the wire of a coat hanger, but much stronger, and of enormous rigidity. She knows that because she can feel it, now that someone has been turning a central key, also of metal, which is T-shaped, and engraved, very finely, on one side only, with the map of a city whose name she once knew, though it escapes her now in her wretchedness at the band's expansion. With each turn of the key, it widens, causing her excruciating pain.

Opening her eyes, she finds that they don't work, not as she expects them to.

I'll have to have glasses, she thinks, closing them again. Or contact lenses. Or that operation they do with lasers. That had come from Soviet medicine, she knew, and by accident, the first patient having suffered cuts to the retina in a car crash, in Russia—

Opening them again.

She's in Russia.

She tries to raise her hands to her aching head, but finds she can't.

Spatial inventory. She's on her back, probably on a bed, and can't move her arms. She carefully raises her head, as she'd do in Pilates in preparation for the Hundred, and sees that her arms at least are there, or seem to be, beneath a thin gray blanket and a folded edge of white sheet, but that there are two restraining bands of gray webbing, one just below her shoulders and the other just below her elbows.

This seems not a good thing.

She lowers her head and groans, because this has caused the key to be turned at least twice, and quickly.

The ceiling, which she finds she can focus on now, is blank and white. Rolling her head gingerly to the right, she sees an equally blank wall, also white. To the left, the ceiling's light fixture, which is rectangular and featureless, and then a row of beds, three at least, which are empty, and made of white-painted metal.

All of that seems a lot to do, because it makes her very tired.

A gray-haired woman, wearing a gray cardigan over a shapeless gray dress, is there with a tray.

The bed has been cranked up to partial sitting position and the restraints are gone. So, she finds, is the expanding interior skull ring.

"Where am I?"

The woman says something, no more than four syllables, and places the tray, on wire supports, across Cayce's stomach. There is a plastic bowl of something that looks like thick clam chowder, perhaps minus the clams, and a plastic tumbler of grayish-white fluid.

The woman hands Cayce a strangely blunt-looking spoon that proves to be made of some rubbery, flexible plastic, rigid enough to eat soup with but soft enough to bend until its two ends meet. Cayce uses it to eat the soup, which is warm, and thick, and very good, and more heavily spiced than anything she's eaten in a hospital before.

Cayce eyes the gray beverage suspiciously. The woman points to it and utters a single syllable.

It tastes, Cayce finds, not entirely unlike Bikkle. An organic Bikkle.

When she's finished, and has returned the tumbler to the tray, she's rewarded with another monosyllable, neutral in tone. The woman takes the tray, crosses the floor, opens the room's single door, which is cream-colored, and goes out closing the door behind her.

The position of her bed has prevented Cayce from seeing anything of what might be beyond that door, but the geography of hospitals suggests a corridor.

She sits up, discovering that she's wearing a backless hospital gown, though one made of some thin, extensively laundered flannel print that seems once to have been decorated with small pink-and-yellow clown figures on a pale blue background.

The ceiling fixture fades abruptly, but doesn't go entirely out.

She tugs blanket and sheet aside, discovering a remarkable assortment of bruises on the front of both thighs, and swings her legs off the bed. She suspects that actually standing will be an experiment, but finds she doesn't do too badly.

The room, or ward, is floored with something seamless and gray and rubbery, faintly gritty beneath her feet.

She places her feet together now and finds the "magnets" from the Pilates towel exercises, points of focus, pulling the muscles of her legs together, into internal isometric alignment. Makes her spine as long as possible. A wave of vertigo. She waits for it to pass. She tries a roll-down, rolling her head forward one vertebra at a time, while bending slowly at the knees until she's in a crouch, head dangling . . .

There's something under the bed. Black.

She freezes.

She goes down on her knees, peering.

Touches it. Her carry-on. She slides it out. Unzipped, her clothing wadded, bulging out. She runs her hands through them, touch telling her she finds jeans, sweater, the cold slick nylon shell of the Rickson's. But the Stasi envelope isn't there, and neither is the Luggage Label bag. No phone, no iBook, no wallet, no passport.

Her Parco boots have been squashed flat and jammed into one of the outer pockets.

She stands and finds the tie, at the back of her neck, that frees her from the bare-ass flannel clown gown. Stands naked in greenish fluorescent twilight, then bends and starts feeling for her clothes. She can't find socks, but underpants, jeans, a black T-shirt will have to do. She sits on the edge of the hospital bed to tie the Parco boots.

And then it occurs to her that of course the door will be locked. It has to be.

It isn't. The institutional thumb-push depresses smoothly. She feels the door shift slightly on its hinges. Opens it.

Corridor, yes; hospital, no. high school?

A wall of faded turquoise lockers with small, three-digit number plates. Strip lighting. Synthetic floor the color of cork.

Looks left: The corridor terminates in brown fire doors. Looks right: glass doors with push bars, sunlight.

Easy choice.

Torn between the desire to run and the desire to pass, if possible, for someone with a reason to be here, wherever and whatever here is, she tries to open the door and step out normally.

The sun blinds her. Non-Moscow air, smelling of summer vegetation. Shading her eyes with her wrist, she walks forward, toward a statue lost in dazzle. Lenin, aerodynamic to the point of feature-lessness, molded in white concrete, pointing the proletariat forward like some kind of giant Marxist lawn jockey.

She turns and looks back. She seems to have just walked out of an ugly sixties orange brick community college, topped with a crenellated structure of concrete resembling the crown the Statue of Liberty wears, windows between each upthrust peak.

But she's not sticking around to see any more of it. She sees a dry grassy incline, a beaten, unofficial path, and follows that, into a shallow ravine or gully, drainage of some kind, and out of the building's line of sight.

The crushed yellow grass of the path is dotted with flattened cigarette filters, bottle caps, bits of foil.

She keeps going, until she finds herself in a dusty grotto of bushes, a natural hiding place and evidently a popular one. Bottle and cans, crumpled papers, a desiccated condom slung from a twig like part of the life cycle of some large insect. A bower of love, then, as well.

She crouches, getting her breath, listening for indications of pursuit.

She hears the ordinary sound of a jet, somewhere overhead.

The path leads out the far side and loses itself in a tumble of glacier-rounded rocks, a seasonal streambed. She follows these through thicker, greener vegetation, to where the path appears again, climbing the side of the ravine.

At its top, she sees the fence.

Newer than the building, concrete white and unweathered at the foot of each galvanized pole. Ordinary chain-link, topped with wire. Though the wire, she sees, walking slowly up to it, is barbed, not razor, and two strands only.

She looks back and sees the very tips of the crenellations atop the red brick building.

She extends her finger. Takes a breath. Taps the chain-link as lightly, as quickly as she can. No shock, though she supposes Klaxons may have just been set off, high on the walls of barracks full of bored and waiting men, heavily armed.

She looks at the chain-link and at the toes of her Parco boots. Not a good match. Summers in Tennessee had taught her that nothing climbed chain-link better than cowboy boots. You just stuck the toes straight in and walked right up. The Parco boots have toes that aren't narrow enough, and only lightly cleated soles.

She sits in the dust, unties, tightens, and reties them, takes off the Rickson's and knots its sleeves as tightly around her waist as she can.

Stands, looking up.

Sun at the zenith. She hears an electric bell. Lunch?

She hooks her fingers in the chain-link and goes up, leaning back and using her body weight to help keep the soles of her boots flat against the fence. It's the hard way, but the only way in these shoes. It hurts, but then the fingers of both hands are around the two-inch crosspiece at the top, inches below the lower strand of barbed wire.

She lets go carefully, with her left hand, reaches down, unties the jacket sleeves, and whips the Rickson's up and over, draping it across the upper strand of wire.

She almost loses it, maneuvering to get one leg up and over, but then she has it, straddling the Rickson's, already feeling the tooth of one barb finding its way through layers of lovingly crafted otaku nylon and milspec interlining.

Getting the other leg over to this side, the outside, is harder. She makes it an exercise. Smoothness, please. Grace. There is no hurry. (There is, because her wrists are trembling.) Then she has to unhook the Rickson's. She could leave it there but she won't. She tells herself she won't because they'd see where she went over, but really she just won't.

She hears it rip, her feet slip on the chain-link, and she lands on her ass in the dust, the Rickson's in her right hand.

She gets up stiffly, looks at the jacket's shredded back, and puts it on.

She stops when the sun tells her she's probably three hours out from the fence.

There's been steadily less vegetation, just more of this dry, reddish soil, no sign of a road, and no water. Her supplies consist of a very nice, hand-turned toothpick from the hotel in Tokyo, and a cellophane-wrapped mint she guesses is from London.

She's starting to wonder whether this might not be Siberia, and to wish she knew more about Siberia, to allow for a more educated guess. The trouble is, it looks more like her idea of the Australian outback, but more barren. She hasn't seen a bird, or bug, or anything at all, aside from crossing a curve of faint tire tracks about an hour back, which she now thinks she probably should have followed.

She sits down in the dust, sucks on her toothpick, and tries not to think about her feet, which hurt like hell.

She's got blisters in there she's trying not to think about, and certainly doesn't want to look at. She decides she'll try tearing up whatever's inside the Rickson's, to wrap her feet with.

She becomes aware of the sound of a jet, like part of the landscape, and wonders what she might think of it if she didn't know what it was. Were there still people in the world who wouldn't recognize that sound for what it is? She doesn't know.

Wincing, she gets to her feet and starts walking, sucking on the toothpick. It makes her mouth less dry.

★   ★   ★

Sunset seems to take a very long time, here. Fantastic shades of red.

When she realizes she won't be able to keep walking in the dark, she gives up and sits down.

"Well fucked," she says, an expression of Damien's that seems to cover things.

She gets out her mint, unwraps it, and puts it in her mouth.

It's starting to get cold. She unties the sleeves of the Rickson's, puts it on, and zips it up. She can feel the chill on her back, still, because it's in tatters now, where she tore out strips of the interlining to use to bind her feet. They'd helped, a little, but she doubts she's going to be able to do much more walking, even when the sun comes up.

She's trying not to suck on the mint, because that'll make it go faster. Probably she should take it out and save it for later, but she has nowhere to put it. She unzips the cigarette pocket on the jacket's left sleeve, discovering the card from the curry house, the one Baranov had written Stella's address on. She looks at his precise brown italics, the color of dried blood, until it's too dark to read them.

The stars are coming out.

After a while, when her eyes have adjusted, she realizes she can see two towers of light, off in the distance, in the direction she thinks she's been walking in. They aren't like the memorial display from Ground Zero, but like the towers of her dream, in London, only fainter, farther away.

"You aren't supposed to be in Siberia," she says to them.

And then she knows he's there.

"I think I might die here," she says. "I mean, I think I could."

You might, he says.

"Will I?"

I wouldn't know.

"But aren't you dead?"

Hard to say.

"Was that you in the music, last night?"

Hallucination.

"I thought it was Mom's EVP, finally."

No comment.

She smiles. "That dream, in London?"

No comment.

"I love you."

I know you do. I have to go.

"Why?"

Listen.

And he's gone, and this time, she somehow knows, for good.

And then she hears the sound of a helicopter, from somewhere behind her and, turning, sees the long white beam of light sweeping the dead ground as it comes, like a lighthouse gone mad from loneliness, and searching that barren ground as foolishly, as randomly, as any grieving heart ever has.

CHAPTER 40

THE DREAM ACADEMY

The helicopter passes directly overhead, but the searchlight goes swooping far off, to the side, away from her. Close enough that she can see details of its oblong yellow undercarriage illuminated by a red running light.

Then the searchlight winks off, and she watches the red light dwindle.

The towers are gone.

She hears the helicopter, coming back.

It hovers, about fifty yards away, and the beam snaps out again, through the prop-blown dust, to find her.

She shields her eyes. Between her fingers she watches it settle to the ground, a clumsy-looking thing, its fuselage nearly rectangular. A figure jumps down from the door in its side and walks toward her, throwing a vast unsteady shadow into the light and dust.

She hears the rotors beginning to slow, thrumming down, counting their way to stasis.

He walks up to her out of the glare and stops,

about six feet away, his back to the glare.

"Cayce Pollard?"

"Who are you?"

"Parkaboy."

This doesn't seem to want to process at all. Finally she asks, "Who started the thread that gave Completism its first formal basis?"

"Maurice."

"In response to what?"

"A post by Dave-in-Arizona, theoretical limits to live action."

"Parkaboy? Is that you?"

He walks around to where it's his turn to face into the light, and she sees a man with reddish, receding hair, combed straight back. He wears OD surplus combat trousers, a heavy black shirt open over a white T-shirt, and a large pair of binoculars slung across his chest. These have huge, goggle-like eyepieces, but taper to a single tube the size and shape of a flashlight.

He reaches into a shirt pocket and pulls out a card. Stepping forward, he offers it to her. She takes it and squints, through the dust in her eyes and the hard white light, at

PETER GILBERT
MIDDLE-AGED WHITE GUY
"SINCE 1967"

She looks up at him.

"Music business," he says. "In Chicago, if you're

433

a certain type of musician, you need one."

"One what?"

"M-A-W-G. Mawg." He hunkers down, two yards away, careful to give her space. "Can you walk? There's a medic in the copter."

"What are you doing here?"

"I thought you might have changed your mind."

"About what?"

"You just broke out of the only prison in Russia that people actively try to break into."

"They do?"

"The Dream Academy, they call it. That's where one particular batch of Volkov's people took you, after Mama fed you too much roofie."

"What—?"

"Rohypnol. Date-rape stuff. Could've killed you, but that's our Mama. You had a paradoxical reaction, though. Supposed to make you anybody's kitten, but it looked like you'd gone medieval on her."

"Did I? Were you there?"

"No. I was just checking in when the ambulance and the police arrived. You know that scene in old movies, when the cowboy's dying of thirst in the desert, and the cavalry arrives, and they say, 'Drink this, but not too much'?"

She stares at him.

He unclips a plastic canteen from his belt and passes it to her.

She takes a mouthful, swishes it around, spits it out, then drinks.

"Mama was still trying to lobby for control of the situation, looked to me," he says, "but with a bloody nose and one eye swollen shut, it was hard for her to be convincing."

"You knew it was her?"

"No. Wouldn't have known it was you, either, if I hadn't heard 'Pollard,' or something like it, about five times. Actually I'd seen a couple of pictures, on Google, but you weren't exactly looking your best, on that gurney there. Seemed to me that the lady with the nosebleed, though, she was pushing so hard that she was on the verge of getting arrested. I think she was arguing they should just take you up to your room and she'd stay with you. Then three guys in black leather coats showed up, and everyone but Mama went instantly deferential. You just sort of evaporated, with your little gurney, no more muss, and Mama went with the coats, looking none too happy about it. Me, I was feeling left out. I checked my e-mail. One from you, with Stella's address. I e-mailed her. Told her I was your friend, and what I'd just seen. Thirty minutes later I was in a BMW with a blue flasher and a fresh set of black coats, running reds and doing downtown Moscow in the wrong lane. Next thing I knew, I was up in one of the Seven Sisters, with Volkov—"

"Sisters?"

"Little old Commie Gothic skyscrapers with wedding-cake frills. Very high-end real estate. Your Mr Bigend—"

"Bigend?"

"And Stella. Plus a bunch of Volkovites and this Chinese hacker from Oklahoma—"

"Boone?"

"The guy who's been hacking your hotmail for Bigend."

She remembers the room in Hongo, Boone cabling his laptop to hers.

"Excuse me," he said, then, "but that dust you've been rolling in has way too much titanium in it. You've probably already exceeded your MDR on that stuff. Why don't you let me get the medic over here to help get you to the helicopter?" He takes the canteen, drinks, caps it, puts it back on his belt.

"Titanium?"

"Soviet eco-disaster. Not as big as drying up the Aral Sea, but you've been hiking down the middle of a forty-mile strip of catastrophic industrial pollution, about two miles wide. I think you want to have a very indepth shower."

"Where are we?"

"About eight hundred miles north of Moscow."

"What day?"

"Friday night. You went under Wednesday, and you were out until whenever you woke up today. I think they probably sedated you."

She tries to get to her feet, but suddenly he's there, hands on her shoulders. "Don't. Stay put." The weird one-eyed binoculars are dangling a few inches from her face. He straightens up, turning

436

into the glare. He waves to the helicopter. "If they hadn't had these night-vision glasses," he says, over his shoulder, "we might not have found you."

"What do you know about the Russian prison system?" he asks her. They're both wearing big greasy beige plastic headsets with microphones and green curly cords. The ear cups have enough soundproofing to muffle the roar of the engine, but he sounds like he's down a fairly deep well.

"That it's not fun?"

"HIV and tuberculosis are endemic. It gets worse from there. Where we're going is basically a privatized prison."

"Privatized?"

"A bold New Russian entrepreneurial experiment. Their version of CCA, Cornell Corrections, Wackenhut. Regular prison system is a nightmare, real and present danger to the public health. If they wanted to set up an operation to breed new strains of drug-resistant TB, they probably couldn't do a better job than their prisons are already doing. Some people think AIDS, in this country, in a few more years, will look like the Black Death, and the prisons aren't helping that either. So when one of Volkov's corporations decides to set up a test operation, where healthy, motivated prisoners can lead healthy, motivated lives, plus receive training and career direction, who's going to stand in the way?"

"That's where the footage is rendered?"

"And what motivates these model prisoners? Self-interest. They're healthy to begin with, otherwise they wouldn't have been chosen for this. If they stay in the regular system, they aren't going to be. That's one. Two is that when they get here, they see it isn't a bad deal at all. It's coed, and the food is a lot better than what a lot of people in this country make do with. Three is that they get paid for their labor. Not a fortune, but they can bank it, or send it home to their families. There's thirty channels on satellite and a video library, and they can order books and CDs. No Net access, though. No web browsing. No phones. That's an instant ticket back to TB Land. And there's only one choice, though, in occupational training."

"They render the footage?"

"All of it." He offers her the canteen. "How are your feet?"

She waves it away. "Okay unless I move them."

"We're almost there," he says, pointing forward, through the plastic nose. "Final motivating factor that keeps the campers here: Volkov. Probably the name's never mentioned, but if you were an inmate, and Russian, which of course they all are, I think you'd get the drift."

The helmeted pilot, whose face she hasn't seen, says something in crackly Russian, and is answered by another voice, out of the night.

She sees a ring of lights come on, ahead of them.

"I don't understand how this could all have been

put together, just to facilitate Nora's art. Well, *how* isn't a problem, I guess, but *why?*"

"Massive organizational redundancy, in the service of absolute authority. We're talking post-Soviet, right? And enormous personal wealth. Nora's uncle isn't Bill Gates yet, but it wouldn't be entirely ridiculous to mention them in the same sentence. He was on top of a lot of changes, here, very early, and largely managed to keep his name out of the media. Which must have been a downright spooky accomplishment. Always has brilliant government connections, regardless of who's in power. He's ridden out a lot, that way."

"You've met him?"

"I was in the same room with him. Bigend was doing most of the talking. Translators. He doesn't speak English. You speak French?"

"Not really."

"Me neither. Never regretted it more than when he and Bigend were having a conversation."

"Why?"

He turns and looks at her. "It was like watching spiders mate."

"They got along?"

"A lot of information being exchanged, but it probably didn't have that much to do with what they were actually saying, either through the translator or in French."

The helicopter's four wheels touch down unexpectedly on concrete. It's like being dropped ten inches while seated on a golf cart. It hurts her feet.

"They're going to check you over, patch you up, then Volkov wants to see you."

"Why?"

"I don't know. When you went missing, he flew us all up here in a lot faster helicopter than this."

"'Us' who?"

But he's already removed his headset. Unlatching his harness, he can't hear her.

CHAPTER 41

A TOAST TO MR. POLLARD

With her bandaged feet in oversized black felt house slippers, Cayce tries not to shuffle as she and Parkaboy traverse the corridor of yellow lockers. On their way, he says, to dinner.

The past hour or so (she still hasn't found her watch) have been spent being examined by a doctor, showering thoroughly, and having her feet bandaged. Now she's back in Skirt Thing and the black cardigan, Parkaboy having suggested that dressing for dinner would be a good idea.

Skirt Thing, along with the rest of her clothing, and her makeup kit, had been waiting for her, washed and folded, on one of the beds in the infirmary where she'd regained consciousness.

The slippers, provided by the same woman who'd brought her soup, make her feel ridiculous, but the blisters and bandages rule out her French shoes, and the doctor had used a pair of shears on the Parco boots, to get them off without hurting her any more than he'd had to.

"What was that you said Dorotea gave me?"

"Rohypnol."

"The doctor here said it was something else. At least I think he did. 'Psychiatric medicine'?"

"They told us they'd taken you to a private clinic, from the hotel. Then they told us you were being moved to 'a secure location,' which must've meant here. I guessed Rohypnol from the sound of it; something she thought would make you easy to push around."

"Where is she? Do you know? Do they?"

"That doesn't seem to be considered a proper topic of conversation. They go sort of fish-eyed if you bring it up. Any idea what she was after?"

"She wanted to know how I'd gotten Stella's e-mail address."

"I'm curious about that myself." He's showered, shaved, and changed into new black jeans and a clean but travel-creased white shirt. "But what she slipped you, that's anybody's guess. The bar staff thought you were hallucinating."

"I was."

"Up here," he says, indicating a flight of stairs. "You okay?"

She climbs a few steps, then stops. "I'm wearing Minnie Mouse shoes, I'm so tired I'm not sure I know what it's like not to be, jet lag seems like a luxury of those who don't travel much, and I feel like I've been beaten with rubber hoses. Not to mention a general lack of skin on my feet."

They climb three flights of concrete stairs, Cayce

increasingly relying on the railing, and enter what must be the interior of the ugly concrete tiara she'd seen as she was running away.

An oval, its windows set between canted concrete uprights. The ceiling vaults determinedly toward the front of the building, to reach a mural depicting the world, Eurasia front and center, bracketed by heroic wheat sheaves erupting with nose cones and Sputniks, colors faded from their original brightness, like an old globe discovered in a hot dusty room above a high school gymnasium.

She sees Bigend raise a glass in greeting, from the center of a group of people.

"Time to meet the big guy," Parkaboy says quietly, smiling and offering her his arm. Which she takes, in an absurd flashback to prom night, and they walk forward together.

"Peter," Bigend says, "we've all heard you were the one who found her." He shakes Parkaboy's hand, then hugs and air-kisses Cayce. "We've been very worried about you." He's roseate with some dire new energy she hasn't seen in him before. His dark forelock falls across his eyes; he tosses his head to throw it back, entirely too coltish for anyone's good, then turns to the man beside him. "Andrei, this is Cayce Pollard, the woman who's brought us all together. You've already met Peter. Cayce, this is Andrei Volkov." Displaying his white and worryingly numerous teeth.

Cayce looks at Volkov and thinks immediately of Eichmann in the dock.

A nondescript, balding man in indeterminate middle age, gold glinting at the temples of his rimless glasses. He wears the sort of dark suit that rewards its expense primarily with a certain invisibility, a white shirt whose collar might be linen-finish porcelain, and a necktie of thick, lustrous, patternless silk, midnight blue.

Volkov takes her hand. His touch is ritual and brief.

"My English is poor," he says, "but I must tell you how sorry we are, that you were treated so badly. I am sorry also," and here he turns to a young man Cayce realizes she recognizes from the squat behind Georgievsky, and continues in Russian.

"He regrets that he is unable to join you now for dinner, but he has pressing engagements in Moscow," translates the young man, his bushy ginger hair a few shades lighter than Parkaboy's. He's wearing a suit as well, but one that looks as though he's rented it.

Volkov says something more, in Russian.

"He says that Stella Volkova also apologizes for the discomfort you have so unnecessarily suffered, and that she would be here, tonight, but, as you know, her sister requires her in Moscow. Both the Volkovas look forward to your next visit, upon your return to Moscow."

"Thank you," Cayce says, noticing the neat deep

wedge missing from the upper curve of Volkov's right ear, and hearing the doctor's shears cutting through the suede of the Parco boots.

"Goodbye, then," Volkov says. He turns to Bigend and says something in what she guesses is quick and probably idiomatic French.

"Goodbye," Cayce says, automatically, as he starts for the door, two young men in dark suits falling into step beside him. A third remains, standing nearby, until Volkov is out of sight, then follows.

"Systema," Bigend says.

"What?"

"Those three. The Russian martial art, formerly forbidden to all but Spetsnaz and KGB body-guards. It has its formal basis in Cossack dancing. Quite unlike anything Eastern." He looks like a very determined child, on Christmas morning, who's finally gotten his way and been allowed downstairs. "But you haven't been introduced to Sergei Magomedov," he says, indicating the young translator, who offers her his hand.

"I saw you at the studio," the young man says. Twenty-three at the oldest.

"I remember."

"And Wiktor Marchwinska-Wyrwal," Bigend says, introducing the fifth member of the remaining party, a tall man with very carefully barbered gray hair, dressed for a French preppie's idea of a British country weekend, the silky tweed of his jacket looking as though it were woven from the wool of unborn lambs. Cayce shakes his hand. He has Voytek's perfectly horizontal cheekbones, and a phone plugged discreetly into his right ear.

"A great pleasure," this one says. "I am, of course, hugely glad to see you here, safe and I hope relatively sound. I am, I should tell you, Andrei Volkov's security chief, new to the job, and I have you to thank for it."

"You do?" She sees three men in white jackets and dark trousers enter, pushing stainless-steel carts on hard rubber wheels.

"Perhaps I can explain over dinner," he says, gesturing to a round table she hasn't noticed, its white cloth set for six. Two of the three in white coats are positioning the carts, but the third is removing the sixth setting.

"Who was that for?" she asks.

"Boone," says Bigend. "But he's getting a lift back to Moscow with Volkov instead. Asked me to tell you he's sorry."

Cayce looks from Bigend to Parkaboy, then back to the sixth chair, and says nothing.

"Andrei Volkov," says Marchwinska-Wyrwal, with no preface, as the plates from the soup course are being removed, "is now the wealthiest man in Russia. That this is not more common knowledge is a remarkable reflection on the man himself."

They're dining by candlelight, the curved strip lighting overhead dimmed to a faint amber glow.

"His empire, if you will, has necessarily been

446

assembled piecemeal, owing to the recent, extra-ordinary, and very chaotic history of his country. A remarkable strategist, but until recently unable to devote much time or energy to the shaping of that which he's acquired. Corporations and properties of all sorts have simply stacked up, if you will, awaiting the creation of a more systematic structure. This is now being done, and I am happy to say that I am a part of that, and you should know that you have had a part in it as well."

"I don't see how."

"No," he says, "it certainly wouldn't have been obvious, least of all to you." He watches as one of the waiters pours more white wine into his glass. Cayce notices the black tips of a tattoo of some kind, showing above the collar of the waiter's white jacket, and thinks of Damien. "He loved his brother deeply, of course," the Polish security chief continues, "and after the assassination made certain that his nieces would receive constant pro-tection, as well as whatever they might require in order to be as comfortable as possible. Nora's plight particularly moves him, as indeed it must any of us, and it was at his suggestion that an editing room was assembled for her in the clinic in Switzerland. As that aspect of the efforts toward her recovery evolved, so evolved a certain division in methodologies—"

"It was inevitable," interjects Sergei Magomedov, who perhaps has been drinking a little too quickly, "as the system created to assure the security of the Volkovas was about a rigid secrecy, and the mechanism created to make the work public was not. The anonymity, the encryption, the strategies, as they evolved—"

"Take credit, Sergei," says Marchwinska-Wyrwal, lightly but, Cayce thinks, meaningfully. "You yourself invented much of that."

"—involved an inherent risk of exposure," Sergei finishes. "The work would not be viewed unless it were somehow able to attract the attention of an audience, and it was Stella Volkova's heartfelt wish that that audience be global in scope. To that end, we devised the method you are familiar with, and we ourselves 'found' the first few segments."

"You did?" Cayce and Parkaboy exchange glances.

"Yes. We sometimes, also, were able to point people in the right direction. But the result, almost from the beginning, far exceeded anything any of us had anticipated."

"You watched a subculture being born," says Bigend. "Evolving exponentially."

"We hadn't anticipated the numbers," Sergei agrees, "but neither had we anticipated the level of obsession engendered in the audience, or the depth of the desire to solve the mystery."

"When did you come into this, Sergei?" Parkaboy asks.

"In mid-2000, shortly after the Volkovas' return to Moscow."

"Where from?"

"Berkeley. A private scholarship." He smiles.

"Andrei Volkov has been particularly farseeing, in his recognition of the importance of computing," Marchwinska-Wyrwal says.

"And what did you do, exactly, Sergei?" asks Cayce.

"Sergei was instrumental in the creation of this production facility," says Marchwinska-Wyrwal, "as well as arranging the watermarking operation with Sigil. We are particularly interested in learning how you were able to obtain the address you used to contact Stella. Did that come through Sigil?"

"I can't tell you," Cayce says.

"Would that be because it came through some connection of your father's? Or perhaps from your father himself?"

"My father is dead."

"Wiktor," says Bigend, who Cayce suddenly realizes has just been silent for far longer than she's ever known him to be, "Cayce has had a very long, very trying day. Perhaps this isn't a good time."

Cayce lets her fork drop, ringing on the white china. "Why did you say that, about my father?" she asks, looking at Marchwinska-Wyrwal.

Who starts to reply, but is cut off by Bigend. "To dispense with being so charmingly old world about it, Wiktor and Sergei represent the two malcoordinated tips of the pincers of Volkov's security operation. Wiktor in particular seems to have forgotten that he's here to apologize to you for the clumsiness of its grasp."

"I don't understand," Cayce says, picking up her fork. "But you're right: I'm very tired."

"I think I can explain," says Sergei, "if Wiktor will allow me."

"Please do," says the Pole, his tone now lethally amiable.

"There have always been two security operations around Stella and Nora. One is a branch, or subsidiary, of the group that protects Volkov himself. The flavor is ex-KGB, but in the sense that Putin is ex-KGB: lawyers first, then spies. The other, largely the creation of colleagues of mine, is less conventional, largely web-based. Wiktor has been brought in very recently to attempt to sort out a serious lack of understanding, of communication, between the two. Your arrival on the scene, via your discovery of the stellanor address, is glaring proof of our difficulties."

"But what does any of it have to do with my father?"

"You first came to their attention," Bigend says, "when you suggested in a post that the maker might be a Russian mafia type. It was merely for example, but you struck a nerve."

"Not with us, directly," Sergei says, "but with a pair of American graduate students we'd hired, to search for, read, and collect commentary on the footage. Your site had quickly emerged as the liveliest, the most interesting forum. And potentially the most dangerous."

"You paid people to lurk on F:F:F?"

450

"Yes. Almost from the start. We made it a rule that they weren't allowed to post, but we later discovered that one had created a persona and had been posting quite frequently."

"Who?" asks Parkaboy. "No," he decides, "I'd rather not know."

"Cayce," Sergei says, "when you attracted our attention, a report was passed on to the more traditional arm, and that is where your father comes in. You were tracked, via your post's ISP, your name and address determined, and logged. Somewhere, then, it rang a very old bell. They went into the paper files, in Moscow, and found your father's dossier, and verified that you were his daughter. To further complicate things, being traditionalists," and here he stops, and grins, "probably, I should say, simply being Russian— they became more deeply, more baroquely suspicious: that the name of this brilliant man, an old opponent, supposedly long retired, should be again before them . . . But they cannot locate him. He is gone. Vanished. On nine-eleven. But is he dead? No? Where is the proof? They took certain steps." Sergei pauses. "Your apartment was entered and devices were installed to allow your phone and e-mail to be monitored."

"When was that?" Parkaboy asks.

"Within a week of the post that attracted the attention."

"Someone's been in my apartment within the past two weeks," Cayce says.

451

"They were checking," Marchwinska-Wyrwal says, "to see whether the devices had been compromised. It is routine."

"Your psychologist's records were copied," Sergei continues. "She had absolutely no knowledge of this. Burglary, not bribery. But all of that was the traditionalist response, not ours. Ours was to employ Dorotea Benedetti to keep track of you, both through the site and through her ongoing business contacts with firms you worked for in New York."

"Why her?" Parkaboy again. They all look at him. He shrugs.

"The traditionalists had had dealings with her previous employer," Sergei says. "They felt they understood her. We felt she understood us."

"She bridged the two cultures." Bigend smiles, sips wine.

"Exactly. And when it became apparent, recently, that you were coming to London to work for Blue Ant, another bell rang. Mr Bigend had come to our attention as well, through Blue Ant's very creative investigation of the web culture around the footage. It registered quickly on the Sigil software we use to observe the movement of the footage. The interest of Blue Ant, and of Hubertus Bigend, for reasons that must be obvious, we found cause for concern."

"Thank you," says Bigend.

"The idea of both of you together, we did not like at all. The traditionalists liked it even less.

452

We allowed them to take over our handling of Benedetti, and she was ordered to disrupt your relationship with Blue Ant. She used her own people to compromise the phone and e-mail in your London flat."

"The man from Cyprus?" Cayce asks.

"A traditionalist, yes. Her handler."

Cayce looks from Sergei to Marchwinska-Wyrwal to Bigend, then to Parkaboy, feeling much of the recent weirdness of her life shift beneath her, rearranging itself according to a new paradigm of history. Not a comfortable sensation, like Soho crawling on its own accord up Primrose Hill, because it has discovered that it belongs there, and has no other choice. But, as Win had taught her, the actual conspiracy is not so often about us; we are most often the merest of cogs in larger plans.

The waiters are clearing the main course now, and bringing smaller glasses, and pouring some sort of dessert wine.

It occurs to her then that the meal has been entirely free of toasts, and that she's always heard that a multitude of them are to be expected at a Russian meal. But perhaps, she thinks, this isn't a Russian meal. Perhaps it's a meal in that country without borders that Bigend strives to hail from, a meal in a world where there are no mirrors to find yourself on the other side of, all experience having been reduced, by the spectral hand of marketing, to price-point variations on the same thing. But as she's thinking this, Marchwinska-Wyrwal taps his glass with the edge of a spoon.

"I wish to offer a toast to Miss Pollard's father, the late Wingrove Pollard. It is an easy thing, for those of us who remember how it was, to lapse for a moment into old ways of thought, old rivalries. I did that myself, earlier, and now I must apologize for it. Had there not been men like her father, on the side of democracy and the free market, where would we be today? Not here, certainly. Nor would this establishment serve the purpose it does today, assisting the progress of art while bettering the lives and futures of those less fortunate." He pauses, looking around the table, and Cayce wonders exactly what it is he's doing, and why? Is it a way of covering his ass with Volkov, after having upset her? Can he actually mean this, any of it?

"Men like Wingrove Pollard, my friends, through their long and determined defense of freedom, enabled men like Andrei Volkov to come at last to the fore, in free competition with other free men. Without men like Wingrove Pollard, Andrei Volkov might languish today in some prison of the Soviet state. To Wingrove Pollard."

And they all, including Cayce, repeat these last three words, raise their glasses, and drink, beneath the shadowed ICBMs and Sputniks of the faded mural high above.

As they're leaving, Parkaboy and Bigend to accompany Cayce to the guest house, originally

454

for visiting academicians, where the three of them are to stay the night, Marchwinska-Wyrwal excuses himself to the others and takes her aside. From somewhere he has produced a large rectangular object, about three inches thick, enclosed in what appears to be a fitted envelope of fine beige wool.

"This is something Andrei Volkov wishes you to have," he says. "It is only a token." He hands it to her. "I apologize again for pressing you, earlier. If we were to know how you obtained the address, we could mend a gap in the security of the Volkovas. We are very concerned now, with Sigil. But Sigil has become essential to the Volkovas' project."

"You suggested my father might still be alive. I don't believe that."

"Neither do I, I'm sorry to say. Our people in New York have studied the matter, very closely, and have been unable to prove his death, but I myself believe that he is gone. Are you certain that you will not help us, in the matter of Sigil?"

"I can't tell you because I don't know. But it wasn't any weakness or betrayal at Sigil. Someone with intelligence connections did me a favor, but I don't know its exact nature. Whatever it was, it took almost no time at all."

His eyes narrow. "Echelon. Of course." Then he smiles. "A friend of your father's. I had guessed as much."

She says nothing.

He reaches into his jacket and extracts a plain white envelope. "This also is for you," he says.

"This gift is mine. Traditionalists have their uses. Our people in New York are talented, extremely thorough, and have many options at their disposal." He places the envelope on the rectangular woolen parcel, which she's still holding before her as though it were a tray.

"What is it?"

"All that is known of your father's last morning, after he left his hotel. Good night, Miss Pollard." And he turns away and walks back into the shadows of the oval room, where she sees Sergei has reseated himself at the candlelit table, and has removed his tie, and is lighting a cigarette.

CHAPTER 42

HIS MISSINGNESS

Aside from looking as though they all shop at The Gap and nowhere else, the inmates of Volkov's rendering farm don't seem to be required to wear a uniform. Cayce sees several, in the halls, as she's leaving with Bigend and Parkaboy, and several more as they make their way to the guest house.

The fence she'd climbed, Bigend says, has been only recently installed to prevent teenagers from the surrounding countryside from sneaking in to pilfer things.

There are usually sixty people here, he says, fulfilling their debt to Russian society by rendering, as they have been taught to do, the rough segments of footage that arrive from the Moscow studio. The physical plant, formerly a technical college, is intended to accommodate a hundred and fifty, which accounts, she supposes, for its dozy summer-session atmosphere.

"What sort of crimes did they commit?" she asks, scuffing along in her slippers, Parkaboy carrying Volkov's gift.

457

"Nothing violent," Bigend says. "That's a requirement. Generally, they simply made a mistake."

"What kind of mistake?"

"Miscalculated the extent of blat required, or who had it. Paid off the wrong official. Or made the wrong enemy. Sergei's recruiters keep track of court calendars, sentencing . . . It's essential to get them before they've been exposed, literally, to the standard prison system. Then they undergo testing elsewhere, medical and psychological, before coming here. I suppose some don't make it."

Moths are whirling around the light atop a steel pole, beside the concrete path, and the sense of being on the summer campus of some down-at-heels community college is eerie.

"What happens when they graduate?" she asks.

"I don't believe any have, so far. The facility's quite new, and their actual sentences are generally of three to five years' duration. It's all being made up as it goes along. As are many things in this country."

The path climbs to a sparsely planted grove of young pines, screening a one-story orange brick building that resembles a very small motel. It presents them with four identical entrances and four windows. Ornate white lace curtains are drawn across the darkened windows, but there are lights on above three of the doors.

"You look bagged," Parkaboy says, handing her the cloth-covered rectangle. "Get some sleep."

"I know you're exhausted," Bigend says to her, "but we need to talk, if only briefly."

"Don't let him keep you up," Parkaboy advises. He turns and enters one of the doors, without using a key. She sees the lights come on behind the lace curtains.

"They aren't locked," Bigend says, leading the way into the one to the left. An overhead fixture comes on as she shuffles in after him, bandaged feet smarting.

Cream walls, brown tile floor, hand-woven Armenian rug, ugly forties-looking furniture in dark veneer. She puts the woolen package down on a bureau with a mirror whose borders are decorated with frosted grooves carved into the glass.

She smells disinfectant, or insecticide.

She still has the envelope in her hand.

She turns and faces Bigend.

"Boone was reading my e-mail."

"I know," he says.

"But did you know it before?"

"Not until after he'd called from Ohio to tell me we needed to go immediately to Moscow. I had a friend's Gulfstream pick him up and bring him to Paris. He admitted it to me on our way here."

"Is that why he didn't stay?"

"No. He left because I no longer wanted to be in partnership with him."

"You didn't? I mean, you don't?"

"No."

"Why?"

"Because he pretends to be better at what he does than he is. I prefer people who are better at what they do than they think they are."

"Where's Dorotea?"

"I don't know."

"Have you asked?"

"Yes. Once. They say they don't know."

"Do you believe them?"

"I think it's better left unasked."

"What was she trying to do?"

"Change sides. Again. She really did want the position in London, and she'd told them she'd still be working for them as well. Which I had discussed with her, of course. But when your e-mail reached Stella Volkova, and Stella replied, it caused a number of things to happen very quickly. All of the armaz.ru traffic is monitored by Volkov's security, of course. They immediately contacted Dorotea, who, in the course of what must have been a very intense conversation, realized for the first time who she had ultimately been working for—and who she was in the process of betraying, by coming over to my side. She must also have understood that if she could get to you first, and discover how you had obtained that address, she would have something very important to offer them. She might even be rewarded, and perhaps retain her job at Blue Ant as well."

"But how did she know I'd gone to Moscow?"

"I imagine she'd instantly hired replacements for the last two, or perhaps there were more to begin with. I doubt if she ever called off your surveillance, even after Tokyo. She would have needed to continue reporting on you. She isn't a very imaginative woman in any case. If they saw you check in at Heathrow, they knew you were going to be landing in Moscow. There are no other destinations, for Aeroflot, at that time of the evening. She could easily have arranged to have you followed, on this end. Not by Volkov's people, though. She still had connections from her previous job." He shrugs. "She'd been posting on your website, as someone else. Do you know that?"

"Yes."

"Amazing. She had no more idea who the maker actually was than we did, until they revealed it to her in an effort to facilitate her stopping you. But you're dead on your feet, aren't you? I'll see you in the morning."

"Hubertus? Boone hadn't been able to get any-thing, in Ohio?"

"No. He got the domain name from your e-mail to Stella. He had the entire address, of course, but nothing he could do with it. By telling you he'd at least learned the domain, in Ohio, he thought he might be able to garner partial credit, with me, after the fact. But in order to move as quickly as he knew we needed to move, he had to tell me the truth, all of it." He shrugs. "You weren't telling me what you were up to either, but at least you weren't lying to me. How did you get that address, by the way?"

"Through someone with NSA connections. I have absolutely no idea how he got it, and no way to ever find out."

"I knew I'd picked a winner, as soon as I met you."

"Do you know where Boone's gone?"

"To Tokyo, I imagine. To that designer girl-friend, the one he stayed with when you were there. Did you meet her?"

"I saw her apartment," she says, after a pause.

"I think it's all actually about money, for him." He grimaces. "Ultimately I find that was the whole problem, with most of the dot-com people. Good night."

He's gone.

She sits down on the sixties-orange bedspread and opens Wiktor Marchwinska-Wyrwal's white envelope.

It contains, on three pieces of blue bond paper, something that seems to be the précis or closing summation of some longer document. She reads through it quickly, struggling with the translation's peculiarities of syntax, but somehow it won't register.

An account of her father's last morning in New York.

She reads it again.

The third time through, it begins to cohere for her.

Win had come to New York to meet with a rival crowd-safety firm. His patents would be secure, soon, and he'd become unsatisfied with the firm he'd been developing them with. There were potential legal complications inherent in a move, and he had arranged to meet with the president of the rival firm, in their offices at 90 West Street, on the morning of September 11, to discuss this.

He had, as the Mayflower bellman had always maintained, gotten a cab.

Cayce sits looking at the license number of that cab now, at the Cambodian driver's name, his registration, telephone.

The collision had occurred in the Village, the cab pulling south into Christopher.

Minor damage to the cab, more damage to the other vehicle, a caterer's van. The driver of the cab, whose English was minimal, had been at fault.

And she herself, headed downtown by train, to arrive early for her own meeting—how close might she have passed? And had he seen the towers, as he'd climbed from the cab, the morning beautiful and clear?

He'd handed the cabdriver five dollars and gotten into an off-duty limo, the Cambodian anxiously copying the limo's plate number. He knew that Win, his fare, would know that he had been at fault.

In court, the driver had lied, successfully, and gotten off, and then he'd lied again to the police, when they'd interviewed cabbies, looking for Win, and again to the detectives Cayce had hired. He'd picked up no fare at the Mayflower. He hadn't seen the man in the picture.

Cayce looks at the name of the Dominican driver of the limo. More numbers. The name, address, and telephone number of his widow, in the Bronx.

The limo had been excavated from rubble, three days later, the driver with it.

He had been alone.

There was still no evidence, the unknown and awkwardly translated writer concluded, that Win was dead, but there was abundant evidence placing him on or near the scene. Additional inquiries indicated that he had never arrived at 90 West.

The petal falling from the dried rose.

Someone raps lightly on the door.

She gets up stiffly, unthinking, and opens it, the blue papers in her hand.

"Party time," says Parkaboy, holding up a liter bottle of water. "Remembered I hadn't told you the tap's a bad bet." His smile fades. "What's up?"

"I'm reading about my father. I'd like some water, please."

"Did they find him?" He knows the story of Win's disappearance from their correspondence. He goes into the bathroom and she hears him pouring water into a tumbler. He comes back out and hands it to her.

"No." She drinks, splutters, starts to cry, stops herself. "Volkov's people tried to find him, and got a lot further than we ever did. But he's not here," she holds up the blue sheets, "he's not here either." And then she starts to cry again, and Parkaboy puts his arms around her and holds her.

"You're going to hate me," he says, when she stops crying.

She looks up at him. "Why?"

"Because I want to know what Volkov's Polish spin doctor gave you as a souvenir. Looks to me like it might be a set of steak knives."

"Asshole," she says. Sniffs.

"Aren't you going to open it?"

She puts the crumpled blue report down and explores the beige envelope's flap, which she finds is secured with two tiny gold-plated snaps. She lifts it, works the fabric back.

A Louis Vuitton slim-line attaché, its gold-plated clasps gleaming.

She stares at it.

"You'd better open it," says Parkaboy.

She does, exposing, in tightly packed rows, white-banded sheaves of crisp new bills.

"What's that?"

"Hundreds. Brand-new, sequentially numbered. Probably five thousand of them."

"Why?"

"They like round numbers."

"I mean why is it here?"

"It's for you."

"I don't like it."

"We can put it on eBay. Somebody in Miami might want it."

"What are you talking about?"

"The briefcase. It's not your style."

"I don't know what to do with it."

"Let's talk about it in the morning. You need to get some sleep."

"This is absurd."

"It's Russia." He grins at her. "Who gives a shit? We found the maker."

She looks at him. "We did, didn't we?"

He leaves her the water.

She uses one fingertip to gingerly close the case, then drapes it with its beige dustcover. Carries the water into the bathroom to rinse with after she's brushed her teeth.

Sitting on the bed, she removes the slippers, seeing that her left foot has bled slightly, through its bandages. Her ankles look swollen. She takes off the cardigan, rolls Skirt Thing over her head, and tosses them both over the attaché and its obscene tray of cash.

She turns down the bed, turns off the light, and limps back, crawling in and pulling the orange spread and the coarse sheets up to her chin. They smell the way sheets can smell at the start of cabin season, if they haven't been aired.

She lies there, staring up into the dark, hearing the distant drone of a plane.

"They never got you, did they? I know you're gone, though."

His very missingness becoming, somehow, him.

Her mother had once said that when the second

plane hit, Win's chagrin, his personal and professional mortification at this having happened, at the perimeter having been so easily, so terribly breached, would have been such that he might simply have ceased, in protest, to exist. She doesn't believe it, but now she finds it makes her smile.

"Good night," she says to the dark.

CHAPTER 43

MAIL

My brother, up to his knees in dirty old pipe in Prion's gallery, sends loud and most amazed thanks. I told him you said it had been given to you by Russian gangsters and you didn't want to keep it, and he just stared at me, mouth open. (Then he becomes worried that it is not real, but Ngemi often accepts cash from American collectors and helped him with that.) But really it's absurdly good of you, because it looked as if he would have to give up his "studio" (ugh) and move in with me, in order to pay for it, the scaffolding, and he is filthy, a pig, leaving hairs. Of course it is much more than cost of the scaffolding but he is using the rest to rent a huge plasma display for the show. We are locking down date of opening with Prion now and you absolutely must come. Prion now has some connection with a Russian yogurt drink that is about to launch here, purchased I think by the Japanese. I know because it is part of my briefing for work now, this drink. Also because he has it in a cooler at the gallery—revolting! I think he will try to serve it at the opening but absolutely NO! So mystery Internet movie is out, yogurt drink is in, also some Russian oil magnate: how surprisingly cultured he is, "alternative," a sort of Saatchi-like patron figure, nothing nouveau riche or mafia or otherwise foul. This is what they are paying me to spread now in the clubs. O well. In the day I still make hats. Enjoy Paris! Magda

Really, dear, I'm sure it's illegal to do that. It says so right on the side of the FedEx box, that you mustn't enclose cash. But it did come through, thank you very much. And very timely, too, as the lawyers say that we can now prove Win's presence there at the time of the attack, and the declaration of legal death will be automatic, which means no more problems over the insurance or the pension. But it may take a month, so I'm very glad to have this in the meantime. They said that every last thing you told them proved absolutely correct, and they were very curious about how you'd found all that out, after the police and the detective agency hadn't been able to. I explained our work here at Rose of the World to them. Obviously you must have had help from your father, in order to obtain such a detailed account of his final hour, but I will honor your need, whatever it may be, to not share that with me, though I would hope that you will, eventually. Your loving mother, Cynthia

*   *   *

Hello, Cayce Pollard! Sorry we never had a chance to meet when you were here, but I'm writing to thank you for bringing Judy Tsuzuki to our attention. She met with us today, at HB's suggestion after hearing from you, and of course we'll be able to find something for her. Her enthusiasm for the city (and her boyfriend!) is completely engaging, and I'm sure she'll bring a real freshness to whatever it is she'll be doing for us. Regards, Jennifer Brossard, Blue Ant Tokyo (cc to HB)

I remember him: You used to say how funny he was, on that website. And he's not gay? A music producer from Chicago? And not, I take it, a Lombard? (If he's not a Lombard, just to be nosy, how can you be affording Paris?) Have to tell you I saw the Lombard of Lombards himself on CNN yesterday. He was between some Russian zillionaire and your Secretary of the Interior, and looked as though he'd just devoured the entrails of something clean-limbed and innocent: entirely pleased with himself. When are you coming home, anyway? Never mind! Enjoy yourself! Margot

Dear Cayce, There definitely are, in the literature, instances of panic disorders being relieved through the incidence of critical event stress, although the mechanism is far from understood. As for "Soviet psychiatric drugs," I have no idea.

I did ask a friend in Germany who volunteered to work with Chernobyl radiation victims; he said that any substances thus described were probably best regarded as instruments of torture, and usually consisted of combinations of industrial chemicals that otherwise would never have been considered fit for use on human beings. Rather grim. Whatever it was, I hope you didn't have very much. As to the cessation of panic-reactions, my advice would simply be to see where it goes. If you should feel further need to talk about it, I have a few appointment times coming open in the fall. Sincerely, Katherine McNally

All done here, packing to go. It was brilliant to see you, and I really liked Peter, and you were both good to put up with Marina, whose pain-in-arse factor has never quite made it back down to baseline. You especially were good, as you knew I'd told her to piss off after the Stuka but you never rubbed my nose in it. As was probably more obvious once you were on site, there simply wouldn't have been any way I could have continued shooting, sans blat. I'm fairly certain we'd never have gotten the tape out of the country, had I stuck to my guns. I do feel a bit more of a sleaze than usual but on the other hand I know I owe something to history, as revealed here for us to record. I'll sort it out back in London, I imagine, when I get to work toward a first cut. You are coming back here, after Paris, aren't you? Your Pole is having an opening at a gallery owned by Billy Whatsit from BSE and he and his sister are mad to have you there. Have you met her, his sister? Henna and pop-out tops, good fun, sort of early post-Wall Berlin thing. I could fancy her, I think! XXX Damien

Hello! When are you coming to see us again? The segment you saw here will be soon complete. It goes to academy and returns many times. Nora never will say but I feel it will go out soon. We hope you will like it! Stella

She still has the iBook but never uses it for mail. She keeps it under the hotel bed, along with the Louis Vuitton attaché, which, though she'd never buy or carry one, now causes her no discomfort at all. Nor had a section full of Tommy in Galleries Lafayette the week before, and even the Michelin Man now registers as neutral. She wonders whether this change, whatever it is, will affect her ability to know whether or not a given trademark will work, but there's no way to test that, short of going back to work, which she's in no hurry to do.

Peter says they're on vacation, and he himself hasn't had one, he says, for years. Various recording labels and groups have tried to reach him here, but he simply ignores them. He loves Paris, and says he hasn't been here since he was someone else, and very stupid.

She doubts that he was ever very stupid.

She goes alone to an Internet café every other day and checks the new hotmail account she's acquired with her new e-mail address, a .uk one that Voytek arranged.

She wonders about Bigend, and Volkov, and whether Bigend could somehow have known from the start that the maker, makers really, were Volkov's nieces, but she always comes back to Win's dictum of there needing always to be room left for coincidence.

She'd gone with Peter to visit Stella and Nora in the squat in Moscow, and then on to the dig, where Damien's shoot had been winding down, and where she'd found herself, out of some need she hadn't understood, down in one of the trenches, furiously shoveling gray muck and bones, her face streaked with tears. Neither Peter nor Damien had asked her why, but she thinks now that if they had she might have told them she was weeping for her century, though whether the one past or the one present she doesn't know.

And now it's late, close to the wolfing hour of soul-lack. But she knows, lying curled here, behind him, in the darkness of this small room, with the somehow liquid background sounds of Paris, that hers has returned, at least for the meantime, reeled entirely in on its silver thread and warmly socketed.

She kisses his sleeping back and falls asleep.

My thanks to the many friends who encouraged and supported me during the more than usually eventful course of the manuscript. Jack Womack, its dedicatee, rescued it countless times, and with the utmost patience, from its author's habitual lack of faith. Susan Allison and Tony Lacey, Penguin Putnam and Penguin UK respectively, were once again marvelous throughout, as was Martha Millard, my literary agent. Thanks to Douglas Coupland for the coffee so high above Shinjuku, and for fresh insights into Tokyo generally, to Eileen Gunn for sharing in fractal detail her memories of Moscow, to James Dowling for introducing me to the Curta calculator, to OCD for the tale of a duck in the face, to Alan Nazerian for Baranov's caravan, and to John and Judith Clute, whose hospitality over many years has been by far my best key to London.

And to Deborah and Graeme and Claire, who continue to put up with the process, love always.

—Vancouver, August 17, 2002